T5-CVU-003

OUTCRY WITNESS

BOOKS BY THOMAS ZIGAL

NEW ORLEANS TRILOGY

The White League

Many Rivers to Cross

Outcry Witness

ASPEN TRILOGY

Into Thin Air

Hardrock Stiff

Pariah

OUTCRY
WITNESS

A NOVEL

THOMAS ZIGAL

FORT WORTH, TEXAS

Library of Congress Cataloging-in-Publication Data

Names: Zigal, Thomas, author.
Title: Outcry witness / a novel by Thomas Zigal.
Description: Fort Worth, Texas : [TCU Press], [2019]
Identifiers: LCCN 2018054111| ISBN 9780875657189 (alk. paper) | ISBN
  9780875657196 (ebook)
Subjects: LCSH: Child sexual abuse by clergy--Fiction. |
  Priests--Louisiana--New Orleans--Fiction. | Sex
  crimes--Investigation--Louisiana--New Orleans--Fiction. | Catholic
  Church--Clergy--Sexual behavior--Fiction. | LCGFT: Thrillers (Fiction) |
  Detective and mystery fiction.
Classification: LCC PS3576.I38 O88 2019 | DDC 813/.54--dc23
LC record available at https://urldefense.proofpoint.com/v2/url?u=https-
3A__lccn.loc.gov_2018054111&d=DwIFAg&c=7Q-
FWLBTAxn3T_E3HWrzGYJrC4RvUoWDrzTlitGRH_A&r=O2eiy819IcwTGuw-
vrBGiVdmhQxMh2yxeggw9qlTUDE&m=Kwjc0Z6Ivwy6RAM92S2cf4EIYWOf58VuaIJE0exH
vYs&s=-P9vr2NVG8ywc-297WrAwGFPUrcMYsohPsnJJUhm6mQ&e=

TCU Box 298300
Fort Worth, Texas 76129
817.257.7822
www.prs.tcu.edu
To order books: 1.800.826.8911

Cover and Text Design by Preston Thomas

FOR LYNDA AND OUR CHILDREN
DANNY, ESTEBAN, OLIVIA, AND ISAAC

NEW ORLEANS, 2001

INTROIBO

IT IS HIS FIRST VISIT TO THE CHANCERY IN NEARLY TWENTY YEARS. The old gothic edifice is as timeless and weatherworn as a medieval cathedral, with its foreboding spires and stained-glass windows and flying buttresses from another century. There is a somber chill in the vestibule, not from a haunted otherworldly draft but from a central cooling system overcompensating for the unusual heat in late April. Peter expects to see someone from the old days hurrying up the marble staircase, Sister Ellen from Archives with an armful of files or Father Bill from Dispensations and Permissions, but he knows they retired long ago. On the third floor, a uniformed security guard sits at a desk outside the heavy oak doors to the Bishop's offices, a station that didn't exist when Peter worked here. At first he doesn't recognize Isaiah, who is older now and heavier, his face sagging and creased around the eyes. His strange dark freckles have faded with age and lost their distinction.

"Mistah Moore," the guard says, rising to shake Peter's hand. "You remember me, sir? I used to make the rounds when you was employed here."

Peter remembers his voice. "How have you been, Isaiah?" he asks with a warm smile. "You still keep up with all the box scores?"

"Yes, sir, I do. Yes, I do," he repeats with a nervous laugh. "I saw you was scheduled to meet with the Bishop this morning."

"How long has this guard station been here?"

"Awhile back some crazy dude come looking for His Excellency and squeezed off a couple rounds into the ceiling before we could take him down," he says, pointing up at the blue scrollwork in the arched ceiling. "You look hard enough, you can still see the bullet holes."

Peter looks upward but can't decipher details with this pair of bifocals, only a beautiful field of Regina Coeli blue.

"What brings you around, Mistah Moore?"

"I've been *summoned*," Peter says.

But there was really no grandiose command in the phone call from the Bishop's executive assistant, a personable middle-aged woman named Margaret Dunn who walks out to greet him now with a felicitous smile and firm handshake. His old friend Sister Colleen has been dead for several years, and Miss Dunn, a lay person, is her replacement. She offers coffee, bottled water, a fruit plate. He declines, intent on making this a formal appointment and not a cordial visit. His relationship with the Bishop had always been professional. Employer and employee, a respectful distance. He can only speculate why the man would want to speak with him after all these years. When he inquired over the phone, Miss Dunn had simply replied, "His Excellency didn't specify, Mr. Moore. He gave me the impression you would know."

"I'm supposed to check your bag," Isaiah says, nodding at the old leather briefcase Peter is carrying, a gift from his wife when he'd been hired as communications director for the diocese. "But you're good folk, Mistah Moore. You go right on in."

The Bishop is sitting at his spacious teakwood desk, opening letters with something shaped like a small curved Saracen blade. He stands with a smile and ambles across the plush crimson carpet to offer his hand. He is wearing a jeweled ecclesiastical ring—as the spouse of God and His Holy Church—but Peter makes no effort to kiss the ring. Instead, he shakes the Bishop's hand. The man is eighty years old now, his short, neatly parted hair completely white, his pronounced jaw softened by a layer of loose flesh under his chin. He is no longer the looming physical presence he once was. Without his robe and vestments, he looks like an ordinary parish priest on a warm spring morning in the Deep South. He's wearing a black short-sleeve shirt with a Roman collar, his horn-rimmed glasses so out of fashion they're *in*. His white ASICS tennis shoes are loose-laced, which leads Peter to believe that the Bishop has just returned from a match at the country club courts. This may explain why his hand is slightly moist and there is a dash of color in his face. By any measure, he's still a man of substance whose bearing conveys executive authority.

4

"It's so good to see you, Peter. You haven't aged a day. Come, let's sit down," he says, indicating a seating area of armchairs intended for intimate discussion in an otherwise grand and intimidating space. Peter sets the briefcase beside his chair.

The office hasn't changed, as far as he can tell, and it may not have changed since the day it was first occupied by the old French mother superior a century ago. It is a resplendent chamber that resembles something in the Vatican, a Renaissance *sala regia* with wall-to-wall books and the occasional religious statue placed on a shelf, St. Francis of Assisi and Our Lady of Fatima. The high ornate ceiling is winged with angels in bas-relief and Latin inscriptions from the New Testament. There is a railed walkway fifteen feet above, spanning three sides of the room, with a spy's view of the entire office. He had often seen Monsignor Fulweiler skulking about up there, paging through the more obscure theological treatises reserved for remote shelves.

Peter had always felt humbled when he entered this room. The formal atmosphere inspired silence and awe. Whenever he'd attended a meeting or sat down with the Bishop at the long oak conference table to work on a press release, a quotation, a story for the diocesan newspaper, he'd always struggled to concentrate and focus. He can't remember ever saying an intelligent word at the long table. At times he'd wondered why the Bishop had kept him on his staff. Probably as a favor to Peter's uncle.

"How is your family?" the Bishop begins. He has brought a bottle of Evian water to sip on as they converse. "I hear Ann is doing quite well. We're all grateful for her good works. How are your boys? They must be grown men by now."

"One is an associate professor at Rice," Peter says. "The other one hasn't quite discovered his calling yet."

"He'll find himself," the Bishop says with more confidence than Peter has in his son. "This new generation of young men, they're struggling. Too many distractions, I'm afraid. Video games and the Internet. Ridiculous movies. The girls are doing much better because they're not caught up in those childish diversions."

Peter is inclined to agree with him, but he doesn't intend to discuss his family. He and Ann raised two sons in turbulent times and it fatigues him to dredge up all that anguish and uncertainty.

"Your Excellency, I don't think you asked me here to talk about today's youth." He has a strong suspicion why he received the phone call.

Without meeting Peter's eye, the Bishop rummages through a stack of periodicals on the small round coffee table between them. "I've read some of your articles, Peter," he says, finding a magazine and holding it up as evidence. "I thought they were fair, for the most part. Painful but fair. Frankly, I thought you'd be harder on the Church."

"I don't take pleasure in any of this," Peter says.

The Bishop drops the magazine on the stack and leans back in the regal chair, gazing thoughtfully at Peter with his hands folded as if in prayer, index fingers pressed to his lips. "And now you're publishing a book," he says.

Peter was right to suspect this was about the book. He wonders how the Bishop knows. There has been very little advance publicity. "It's coming out in the fall," he says.

"Congratulations," the Bishop says with a tight smile. He pauses in contemplation, then goes on. "I'm told it's about Father Martin Landry."

Peter strives to hide his surprise. Is there a leak at the publishing company? "It's time to tell the story," he says.

The Bishop ponders this for a moment. His smile fades. "Are you sure you know the whole story, Peter?" he asks. "You didn't interview *me*."

"I tried," Peter says calmly. He is resolute now, and irritated by this attempt to cast doubt on a book he's spent several years researching and writing. "Your public relations director isn't as cooperative as I used to be. He put up walls. Conditions I couldn't accept." He thinks about the guard station, the layers of isolation. "*You've* put up walls, Your Excellency."

The Bishop stares past him toward the French doors that open onto a terrace of meticulously maintained flowerbeds and boxwood hedges. Peter remembers a pair of tangerine trees imported from Rome. "Walk with me, Peter," the Bishop says, distracted by something outside in the sunlight.

They walk out through the glass doors into the gleaming light. The morning feels tropical and the air is fragrant from the hibiscus beds and honeysuckle vines the gardener watered earlier. New Orleans is a fecund place, abundant and blooming this time of year. "Your tangerine trees seem to be thriving in this climate," Peter says. They've grown tall since he last saw them.

"Worms are eating all the fruit," the Bishop says with a sour expression, as if there's a bad taste in his mouth. "I hate to use pesticides, but what else can you do? I worry about spreading poison to the other plants and birds."

Peter strolls over to the stone balustrade and gazes south toward the river. He had always loved this view. The land was once cotton plantations but is now a wealthy neighborhood of Mediterranean tiled roofs and gingerbread cupolas dwelling in the live oaks. The bell tower of a quaint parish church rises above the tree line.

"I suppose I should get to the point, Peter. I didn't ask you here to pick a fight," the Bishop says, walking up beside him to survey their wooded surroundings. "I've been nominated to serve as president of the US Conference of Catholic Bishops."

Peter is not surprised to hear this. They stand together in silence, the sun bearing down on them in the still morning air. Blue jays shriek in the vault of trees.

"It's quite an honor," the Bishop says, "but an awesome responsibility. If I'm elected, I'll become the spokesman for the entire congregation of American bishops. I haven't decided whether to keep my name in play. My confreres tell me the job is mine if I want it. I have the overwhelming majority of votes. There's even talk that Rome is considering me for the College of Cardinals."

Peter remembers the anger and bitterness he'd lived with for too long. It had taken him years to manage that anger, but he is older now, a mellowing grandfather who plays with toddlers, and he tries not to waste emotion on the past.

"I understand your concern, Your Excellency. The leader of the American bishops should be beyond reproach, especially in these times, with so many scandals."

He turns to measure the Bishop's reaction. His response is stoic, unreadable. Peter imagines that this aging prelate had mastered the art of self-possession as part of his training many years ago as a young seminarian. It was yet another skill Peter had failed to perfect when he himself was studying for the priesthood.

"Your Excellency, did you ask me here because you want to know if my book will harm your reputation?"

The Bishop nods slowly, pensively. "Yes, Peter, that is precisely what I need to know," he says with a rueful smile. "My fate seems to rest in your hands." His sigh is deep and weary. "And so I'm asking you with all due respect. Should I let them elect me or not?"

THE 1980S

ONE

IT BEGAN WITH A CALL IN THE MIDDLE OF THE NIGHT. Is there anything more startling than the first ring of a telephone when you're dead asleep? The news is never good. I thought something had happened to our oldest son. I jolted awake and groped for the receiver, mumbling "Luke?" He was spending the night with friends, and I was worried he'd gotten in trouble again.

"Is it Luke?" Ann asked, rolling over and clutching my shoulder.

Until that phone call, we had had a good life together. Two wonderful sons, a nice two-story home on a safe block in the Broadmoor neighborhood, a reasonably happy family. The usual teenage shenanigans, but nothing traumatic.

"Peter, I'm sorry to wake you. Something terrible has happened and I need your help." It was my uncle, Father Edward McMurray, calling from his rectory. I had never heard the man sound so alarmed. "Can you please come over right away?"

I forced open my eyes and studied the red numerals on the clock radio. "It's after midnight, Ted," I managed to say.

A heavy rain had been falling for several hours, battering the bedroom windows on that cold winter night in Carnival season.

"I know what an imposition this is, Peter. But you've got to come over. *Please.*"

I sat up in bed. My uncle was a rock-solid, reliable man not given to hyperbole. It was disturbing to hear him desperate and shaken. "Ted, are you in any danger?" I asked. "Should I call nine-one-one?"

"*No!* No, please don't do that. Just get here as soon as you can. I'll be waiting at the side door."

I dragged myself out of the warm bed and searched in the dark for the pair of cuffed dress pants I'd folded over a cherrywood valet. Was this official business or a private matter? As director of communications for the diocese, I had been called to duty at awkward times, but never in the middle of the night.

"What's going on, Peter?" Ann asked, stirring under the covers. "Has something happened to Father Ted?"

"He's pretty upset," I said, zipping my pants. "It may be his diabetes again, I'm not sure. I thought he was out of town for the weekend."

"My God, you're not going over there in this weather, are you? The streets must be flooded by now."

Rain lashed the bay window. Thick oak limbs were groaning like giant oars against the house. Leaving home in a torrential thunderstorm was the last thing I wanted to do.

"Go back to sleep, hon. I'll call you from the rectory if it's something serious. You don't suppose Luke and his buddies are out gallivanting around in this, do you?"

It was a Friday night and Luke was sleeping over at the Hinojosa house, which was sometimes unsupervised when Dr. Hinojosa was called away to emergency surgery.

"You be careful out there, dear. Take the station wagon."

The windshield wipers on the old monster wagon battled the downpour as I plowed through pools of water rising in the grand oak haven of St. Charles Avenue. Our Lady of Sorrows was no more than ten minutes away in normal weather, a neighborhood parish with its own elementary school, but that night I had to negotiate the swampy streets with caution, like an oil barge creeping through a dark bayou. It was a maddening drive, and the tendons in my neck and back were tight and burning from tension. In time I pulled under the covered breezeway that separated the church and rectory. Burglar lights were blazing down from the pitched rooftops of the two buildings. When I stepped out of the station wagon, I was shocked awake by a cold, ankle-deep current flowing across the driveway. I turned up the collar of my overcoat and splashed to the side door of the stately old home where my uncle and his assistant pastor resided. As I reached out to bang the brass knocker, the door opened quickly and a voice said, "Come in, Peter." My uncle was standing in darkness. He grabbed my arm and almost dragged me into the unlit foyer.

"What's going on, Ted?" I said, cold wet socks squishing inside my shoes. "I thought you were at a retreat in Grand Coteau."

"Too many alcoholic old cranks at those things. I bailed out early," he said with a dismissive wave of the hand.

When this incident occurred, my uncle was a tall angular man of seventy years, with thin graying hair he oiled and combed straight back with a perfect part on the side, a style he hadn't tampered with as long as I'd been alive. He was my mother's older brother and the lone intellectual standout in a colorful family of Irish bar owners and longshoremen. That night he was wearing his Roman collar and black suit and not the bulky jogger sweats he usually wore around the rectory.

"Come," he said in a hushed voice, tugging my coat sleeve and guiding me through the dim living room of ancient leather furniture and overstocked bookshelves. Without lighting, his expression was impossible to read, but there was a tremor in the hand that clenched my arm.

He stopped at the foot of the stairwell. "Prepare yourself, Peter," he said, making the sign of the cross. "A prayer before we go up."

He closed his eyes and bowed his head and I did the same. But I remember being too distracted by his odd behavior to pray.

We mounted the stairs and he grasped my arm again and led me across the dark upstairs hallway to a bathroom door. It wasn't clear if he was holding onto me for my benefit or his own. The door was open slightly and he gave it a cautious push. The first thing I noticed was a wide streak of blood on the tile floor. When I entered the chill room, I saw a body submerged in a bathtub overflowing with bloody water.

"My God," I said, frozen in horror. Father Ted held my arm firmly and wouldn't let go. He was breathing heavily through his nose. "It's Father Martin, isn't it?"

Father Martin Landry was the assistant pastor. He'd been an upperclassman when I entered the seminary at the age of eighteen. My first thought was that he'd committed suicide using a blade.

"Yes, I'm afraid so," Ted said in a reverent whisper. "I've already given him the Last Rites. May his soul rest in peace."

"Amen," I responded, making the sign of the cross.

My uncle and I stood side by side in stunned silence and stared at the body. It took me several rapid heartbeats to understand that Father Landry had been murdered. He was lying on his back underwater, clothed in jeans and a buttoned shirt, shoeless, with a heavy cinder block on his chest, weighing his torso down while his arms floated freely. The bloody water obscured his face, but it looked as though he'd been beaten. I could see what appeared to be a bicycle chain wrapped around the cinder block and garroted around his neck.

My stomach churned at the sight of Martin Landry in such a horrible state. "Who would do something like this to a priest?" I said. And then I realized that the killer might still be on the premises.

"Let's get out of here, Ted," I said, panic-stricken, glancing back at the dark hallway. "He might be hiding somewhere in the house. Have you called the police?"

He gave my arm an admonishing shake. "Calm down, Peter. I've searched every room in the rectory," he said. "Whoever did this is gone."

I couldn't take my eyes off the body in the tub. Martin Landry had been two years ahead of me at Immaculata seminary in the early 1960s. I disliked the guy, an unkindness that shamed me as I thought about the violent manner in which his life had ended. He'd been a vain and arrogant young seminarian, with what the old-guard spiritual advisers had labeled a *choleric personality*. Quick of temper, sharp of tongue, always testy and difficult. One of those brilliant young dogmatists who understood every nuance of canon law and browbeat you with his superior knowledge. I dropped out of the seminary in my second year—it wasn't the life for me—but Martin was ordained among the chosen and had served God in various assignments over the years, including a short stint as a missionary in Guatemala. I was surprised when I learned that the Bishop was transferring him to Our Lady of Sorrows, a mundane parish appointment that seemed unworthy of such a luminous talent.

"Why haven't you called the police, Ted?" I asked my uncle.

He released my arm and turned to gaze at me with a grave expression. "Because there's something I want you to take care of first," he said. "Wait here, please."

He walked through an open doorway into Martin's adjoining bedroom. I watched him look around the room as if searching for something, and then he stooped over a large cardboard box. I moved closer to the doorway and saw that the room showed signs of a struggle. A floor lamp had been knocked down near the writing desk. Cigarette butts from a toppled ashtray were scattered all over the carpet. A bookshelf made of glossy-stained boards and cinder blocks had collapsed and the books were strewn about. It was clear to me that the lethal cinder block had come from that bookshelf.

The room was smoky and smelled of human sweat, and I thought I detected a faint trace of marijuana. Two empty wine bottles were sitting on a bureau, and overturned glasses had left red stains on the carpet. Shattered glass from another wine bottle lay only a few steps from where a bloody drag-mark began.

"Ted," I said, noticing a video camera mounted on a tripod near Martin's bed. "Are we looking at a party scene gone terribly wrong?"

My uncle's face was ashen and drawn. "Here," he said, pressing the heavy cardboard box against my chest. "You've got to leave now and take this box with you. The camera and stand, too. I have to call the police."

"What's in the box?"

"Wait until you get home," he said, unscrewing the video camera from its tripod and setting the camera on top of the box. "Find a private place. Don't let Ann and the boys see any of this."

I didn't like what I was hearing. "What's going on here, Ted?"

"Come," he said, seizing my shoulder to issue me out of the bathroom. "You've got to leave. I'll handle the police myself."

I took one final look at the tub and the cinder block resting like an anchor on the dead priest's chest and his arms floating in the bloody bathwater.

"Tell me what we're doing, Ted. Are we removing evidence from the crime scene? I'll probably be the one who has to face the media about all this and I can't be implicated."

We heard a noise somewhere in the house. My uncle and I exchanged quick glances. We were standing in a bright rectangle of light cast from the open bathroom door. "Someone's here," I whispered, my heart still racing. I wasn't convinced that Ted had made a thorough search of every closet and cranny in the rectory.

He took a deep breath to gather himself, then gripped the folded tripod legs like a club and walked ahead of me to the landing at the top of the dark stairs. "Hello!" he called out. "Is anybody there?"

The rainstorm still drummed against the roof and windows. A cool draft was blowing through the house, as if someone had left a door open. A tall, lean figure was standing at the foot of the stairs. "Who are you?" Ted asked in a firm voice.

"Zat you, Father Marty?" It was a young black man.

"Father Martin isn't available right now," Ted responded. "How did you get in?"

The young man turned and looked behind him. "Do' was open," he said.

"Is there anything I can help you with?" my uncle asked. The sharp impatience in his tone was meant to intimidate the intruder and send him away.

"Got a call said Party Marty was ready to party. Thass all I know." He laughed harshly and drank from the bottle in his hand. I could hear the tick of rainwater on wood. He seemed to be in some altered state, either drunk or stoned, or possibly both.

"You'll have to leave now," Father Ted said. "The hour is too late for visitors."

The intruder took three menacing steps up the creaking stairs and stopped to drink again. "What about them other dudes?" he asked. "They not here, either?"

My uncle set his feet like a baseball batter ready to swing that tripod. "No one is here," he said with authority. "Please leave or I'll call the police."

My eyes had adapted to the weak light and I could make out the young man's features now. He couldn't have been much older than my son Luke, sixteen, but he had a hard face with a scraggly goatee and unkempt dreadlocks dripping from the rain. His wet clothes clung to a long, thin body. I wondered if he was homeless and lived on the street.

"Okay, thass cool," the intruder said. "Ever-thang cool, boss. No need to run five-oh on my ass. I'm gone."

As he turned and walked back down the stairs, he waved the bottle over his head in a parting gesture and something gold flashed on his dark wrist. "Tell Father Marty I catch up with him next time," he said, disappearing into the deeper shades of the living room.

My uncle and I waited until we heard the slam of the rectory door before we dared to breathe or look at each another. "There's too much to explain and too little time," he said as he urged me down the stairs. "I've got to get the police in here."

By then it was clear to both of us that Father Martin had thrown a party in Ted's absence and that someone had brutally murdered him.

How many people had been in his bedroom? I'd counted five wineglasses on the floor.

The party didn't surprise me. It was Father Martin's job to organize parties and picnics and dance socials. He'd become the center of his own cult of personality and was wildly popular among the school kids at Our Lady of Sorrows Elementary and the CYO teenagers in the parish. His weekend fishing trips to the Gulf coast were highly coveted by the altar boys, and my son Luke had badgered me to go with them on several occasions. News of Father Martin Landry's murder was going to devastate our parish.

"Take that box somewhere very private and examine the contents," my uncle said.

The video camera shifted with each quick step across the murky living room, and I worried it might slip off the cardboard box if I didn't slow down. "Is there a tape in this camera?" I asked.

"I checked. It's empty," he said. "Make an inventory of what's in the box, Peter. You'll see why I'm being so cautious."

I knew that removing the box was improper, at the very least, and probably a crime. "I don't like the sound of this, Ted," I said. "Are we hiding something from the police?"

He stopped me abruptly. "You've got to trust me, Peter. We'll turn everything over to the police when the time is right," he said. I had never seen him this demanding and overwrought. "Will you please give me your trust?"

My uncle was an honest man, without pretense or false piety, a paragon of integrity and goodness, and the sole reason I'd studied for the priesthood in the first place. When I was growing up, he'd been the closest thing to a real saint in my schoolboy imagination. I wanted to be more like him and less like my father, a gruff shipyard foreman who cared little for the life of the mind or the condition of the soul.

"Of course I trust you, Ted," I said, staring into those piercing eyes. "But I wish you would tell me why I'm doing this."

"We'll talk later," he said. "I promise to straighten this out before you face the media."

"Will you call the Bishop?"

"I've already called him," he said, giving my shoulder an avuncular squeeze. "He was relieved to hear you were coming over to help."

Wind had flung the side door open again, and a cold mist was whirling into the foyer. Father Ted turned on a porch light and stepped outside, peering in both directions as the rain hammered the breezeway's overhead cover. I knew who he was looking for. "See him anywhere?" I asked.

"He can't be too far away," he said. "Let me help you to your car."

We slogged a few yards to the station wagon and shoved the cardboard box and video camera and its tripod into the back seat. "Drive safely, Peter. You don't want to be in an accident with these things in your possession."

I slid behind the wheel and quickly locked the doors. My shoes and socks and the cuffs of my pants were soaking wet and I was shivering now, chilled to the bone. It was nearly two a.m. I cranked the engine and slowly pulled out into the deluge, looking for signs of that young man. I couldn't be sure, but I thought I saw someone sitting on the steps of the church in the driving rain.

As I maneuvered the wagon back through the flooded streets of that dark sleeping neighborhood, I prayed for the soul of Father Martin Landry. His body was a nauseating sight I haven't forgotten in the many years since. With my hands gripping the steering wheel, I asked God to bring the killer to swift justice. I asked Him to forgive me for my lack of charity, harboring ill feelings against one of His worthy servants. I had my reasons for disliking Martin Landry, of course, but at that moment they seemed juvenile in light of the man's dreadful death.

The downpour was relentless, floodwater was seeping onto the floorboard near the brake pedal, and I considered the possibility that I would have to abandon the car and wade home in the pitch dark. It wouldn't have been the first time. New Orleans was six feet below sea level, and we were accustomed to deserting our vehicles on neutral grounds—called *grassy medians* in upper America—and strangers' front lawns. When Luke was a toddler, a storm had dumped eighteen inches of rain on the city in two hours, and I braved the elements to pick him up at his daycare center. On the return trip, the water had risen swiftly in the streets and I joined the others driving on the elevated streetcar tracks. Luke and I were only a few blocks from home when a huge produce truck roared past us, sending a tidal surge over the top of my little Mazda. I had to ditch the swamped car in someone's front yard and set out carrying Luke in crotch-deep water, the power down all over the city. Wading through those dark undercurrents, using my shirt to shield his little face from the rain, I whispered soft sweet tones in his ear, assuring him it was a fine adventure we would laugh about when we were older. But I feared for our lives, trudging one cautious stride at a time, and I was the happiest father on earth when I ascended the steps to our warm, unflooded house with my son safely in my arms and Ann waiting for us at the door with a pile of dry blankets.

I adjusted the rearview mirror of the old station wagon and glanced into the back seat at the wet cardboard box. Did my uncle know what he was doing? *Will you please give me your trust?* I loved the man dearly and wanted to trust him. But I kept hearing a small insistent voice in the back of my head telling me I had just made the worst decision of my life.

TWO

WHEN I ARRIVED AT HOME, the house was dark and cold and merci-
fully silent. I dropped my overcoat on a kitchen chair, removed my
wet shoes and socks, and carried the box and empty video camera
to my study and locked the door. I wasn't prepared for what I found
when I lifted the cardboard lid. Although I couldn't identify every object, I knew each one had a sexual purpose. I used my pocket handkerchief to remove a vibrator, a nearly empty tube of K-Y Jelly, a studded
leather dog collar, three metal rings, and a string of sleek black beads
whose function I couldn't imagine, except perhaps as some kind of
perverse rosary. I was as shocked and disgusted as my uncle must've
been when he'd gathered up these things and placed them in the box. I
understood now why he was looking around Father Landry's bedroom
before he closed the lid. He wanted to eliminate any trace of these sex
toys before the police arrived. Martin Landry was a Catholic priest,
after all.

There was a reason why I'd held a low opinion of Martin ever
since my studies at Immaculata, the seminary for the Diocese of New
Orleans. I had not forgotten what he'd done to my classmate, a
skittish first-year seminarian named Donny Bertrand. Donny was
a strange young man from an unappealing little working-class community across the river. He had country ways, poor diction, and
even poorer personal hygiene, and I'd wondered at the time why
the superiors had accepted his application. It was hard to imagine
Donny as the shepherd of a flock. But he was from a devout Catholic family, and he wanted to be a priest—it was that simple—and
the vocation director would not deny him his calling. In spite of no

apparent talent for theological thinking, Donny worked very hard to maintain his studies and approached seminary life with the zeal and innocence of a medieval novice. What caused some concern was that during our silent meditation periods, as we ambled around the oak-shaded grounds of the seminary in prayer and contemplation, he often talked to himself and batted his arms in the air, as if warding off dark angels. Much of his erratic behavior was overlooked by the Father Director and the teachers, but they couldn't ignore the unsettling drama of his night terrors and sleepwalking, which woke the entire dorm almost every night. They were forced to put him in a private room in the infirmary and lock the door after lights-out. Donny didn't complain. He laughed when he told me it allowed him to read and reread his hidden stash of *Mad* magazines by flashlight after the rest of us were sound asleep.

Martin Landry was a charismatic upperclassman and a "big brother" to two or three first-year sems he'd singled out for special attention. I wasn't one of them and neither was Donny. Martin clearly looked down on the young man he called "the hick from the sticks" and treated him with disdain. It was a clash of cultures and a gaping difference in intellectual ability. Martin never missed an opportunity to poke fun at Donny's bumpkin expressions and awkward table manners. So I was surprised when Donny revealed to me what had taken place one afternoon in the old white dorm that sat on the far side of the seminary grounds near a persimmon orchard.

The dorm was an abandoned two-story wood structure that had served as seminary living quarters before the new red brick dormitory was built in the 1950s. In my day it was used solely for storage. The building was in disrepair and there was a creepy pallor to the place. Third-year men insisted they'd often heard the mournful cries of long-dead flagellants escaping from those dark upper windows in the late hours of night. The ghost of a tragic young suicide named Brendan McIlhenny was said to roam the silent halls during a full moon.

At work period on the day in question, Martin told Donny that the Father Director had assigned the two of them to pick up a wheelbarrow and garden tools stored in the white dorm. Donny followed Martin back to the old building and they entered the place through an unlocked door. To this day I remember the details that Donny eventually described to me. He said the interior was as eerie and foreboding as we imagined it to be. The floorboards groaned under their footsteps and the sealed air reeked of mildew and something earthy, like wet fertilizer. Sunlight couldn't penetrate the gloom of the long central corridor and small dark enclosures. Martin walked ahead of Donny and opened the door to one of the cell-like rooms. There was space for scarcely more than a chair and bed. A water-stained mattress lay on rusted box springs and a couple of wire hangers dangled in a narrow doorless closet. Donny told me that the chamber reminded him of the damp little bedroom he shared with two brothers at home. He gazed about the room and asked Martin where were the wheelbarrow and tools they were supposed to retrieve.

Martin confessed that he'd invented the scenario so he could have a private conversation with Donny about his character and behavior, which he believed were unbecoming of a seminarian. He said he was scandalized by Donny's lack of modesty and self-respect, which had manifested itself earlier that afternoon, when he'd observed Donny toweling off in one of the changing stalls at the swimming pool. Martin accused him of leaving the door halfway open so sems could watch him masturbating in the stall.

Donny was horrified by the allegation. He insisted to Martin Landry—and to me later that day—that he had no idea he'd left the door partially open and he'd certainly not been abusing himself.

"We all have our faults and secret weaknesses," Donald recalled him saying. "I want to help you overcome this sinful habit before the Father Director finds out and intervenes."

Donny Bertrand was a nature boy who'd spent his childhood piroguing through snake-infested swamps with his father and brothers, fishing bare-chested in the wetlands south of the city and in the Gulf of Mexico. He was a thin, rubber-limbed young man, athletic and swift of foot, with a relaxed sense of his own body. But he knew that the seminary required a higher standard of modesty and he was mortified that he might have exposed himself to Martin and perhaps others.

Despite Donny's denial, Martin persisted. "Satan whispers unclean thoughts in our ears, Donald. We fight the temptation to touch ourselves, but the Prince of Darkness makes it so sweet when we give in," he said. "There is a way to overcome these temptations. The old French priests call it *La Méthode d'abnégation*. The Method of Self-Denial. I'll walk you through it. The Method will teach you self-control."

Donny told me that the entire conversation had made him light-headed and sick to his stomach, and he felt trapped and claustrophobic in the old dorm, with its tight corners and creaking noises and the foul odor of rodents nesting in the walls. He was desperate for it to end, so he agreed to do whatever it would take to release him into the sunlight of a normal day.

The Method, as Martin explained it, required the novice to remove his clothes and stand naked in front of his instructor for ten minutes.

"If you don't get an erection, we can put this behind us and work on other personal developments," Martin had said, sitting down on the sagging mattress. "All you have to do is stand in front of me for ten minutes with your arms outstretched like Jesus on the cross—and we'll know if you have impure urges."

By that point, Donny believed that if he walked away, Martin would report the changing stall incident to the Father Director. What choice did the poor guy have? He wanted to be accepted by his fellow seminarians. He'd been trying frantically to fit in. He was determined to become a priest and make his family proud. So he removed his clothes in the shadowy confines of that rank little cell and stood naked before Martin Landry with his arms outstretched like Jesus at the crucifixion.

I didn't ask Donny how the ordeal had ended. I didn't want to know.

When he told me the story, Donny was upset and needed consolation and spiritual repair. I encouraged him to go immediately to the Father Director and explain what had taken place. And I felt strongly that Martin Landry should be confronted by someone in authority and held accountable for his behavior. I couldn't imagine that the superiors condoned the so-called *Méthode d'abnégation* or had given Martin permission to deploy it. I suspected then—and I suspect now, many years later—that the ritual was a clever fantasy Martin Landry had devised for his own pleasure and amusement.

I probed deeper into the cardboard box and found a stack of pornographic magazines. I was no expert in languages, but they seemed to be published in Holland or a Scandinavian country. The worn covers featured nude boys in various sexual poses. As I thumbed through the pages, I was shocked and sickened by what I saw. Grown men with underaged boys, some no older than eight or nine. Our son Matt was their age, sleeping soundly upstairs in his comfortable bed, protected from all evil, and I wondered how the parents of these exploited children had lost them to such wickedness. Where were their fathers when these boys were being drugged and raped and photographed on bare mattresses in squalid hotel rooms? Where were their caring mothers? Or the cruelest possibility of all—Did their parents sell them to these monsters? There was no life in those damaged young faces, only dead eyes and a dazed shyness to perform as they were instructed. How could these boys recover from such outrageous mistreatment? Were they doomed to re-live these nightmares for the rest of their lives?

I piled the magazines on the carpet beside the box and thought about the man who'd collected them. I'd always believed that the incident with Martin Landry in the old white dorm was the beginning of Donny Bertrand's decline. He withdrew from contact with our classmates, failed to show up for meals in the refectory, and began missing chapel. One day I pulled him aside after a lecture on the liturgy and asked what was wrong. "Talk to me, Donny," I said. "Are you having doubts?"

Having doubts was seminary code for questioning your vocation. In that peculiar hermetic environment, we constantly monitored one another to make sure our friends and classmates weren't going to drop out of the religious life without thinking it through. Religious formation was arduous and psychologically demanding, not unlike military boot camp, and we bonded with our buddies like soldiers in battle.

"I'm tired, Peter. Real tired. And I can't keep up," Donny said to me that day. "My head feels like it's gonna explode."

Over the next two months, Donny's mental health deteriorated. The night terrors grew louder and more physical, and our classmates feared that Donny would harm himself. Early one morning before Matins, Donny was rushed to the emergency room at Hôtel-Dieu downtown, and although the Father Director declined to disclose what had happened, a sem named Armand Broussard told me in confidence that Donny had cut himself and there was blood all over his infirmary room. The following day he was admitted to a psychiatric hospital across Lake Pontchartrain in Mandeville. I saw him only once after that, when I visited him shortly after I'd left the seminary myself. Donny had received electroshock treatments and he didn't know who I was.

Considering what he'd told me about Martin Landry, I never trusted Landry again. Which is why I wouldn't allow Luke to travel with the priest and the other altar boys on fishing trips to Vermilion Bay.

The rain had stopped, but wind still shook the magnolia tree outside my blind-drawn window. I thought I heard a noise upstairs, a footstep in the narrow hallway between bedrooms. If Ann or Matt was stirring, I needed to hide the box and its contents. I opened my study door and stepped into the darkness, listening for signs of domestic life, a voice or movement. The lone sound was the old refrigerator humming in the kitchen. Convinced it had been nothing more than the house settling after a thunderstorm, I closed the door softly and returned to my desk.

When I picked up the first VHS cassette and studied the ballpoint printing on the label, which looked like the hand of a schoolmarm, I had no idea that I was embarking on a journey that would color everything I'd held to be true and morally good since my first catechism class at age six.

Cypremort 3, the label said.

The only *Cypremort* I knew of was Cypremort Point, the barnacled old fishing village on Vermilion Bay where Martin Landry's family owned a fishing camp and private dock. I checked the other video boxes and found two more *Cypremort* tapes, three others labeled *Rectory*, and two labeled *Stella 1* and *Stella 2*. There was also a smaller box, yellowed by age, its worn edges sealed by Scotch tape that had turned brown. Inside was an 8mm reel-to-reel tape, the kind I hadn't seen since the days of family home movies back in the sixties.

My brother-in-law had received a JVC Camcorder from his wife for Christmas only two months earlier, and he and I had taught ourselves how to use the camera, taking videos of our families opening Christmas presents with Ann's parents. Father Martin's camera was the same model of JVC Camcorder, and I slipped the video called *Rectory 1* into the tape slot and began to view it on the camera's small preview screen. The images began *in medias res*, the appalling specter of a Catholic priest, clad in a tank top and swim trunks, wrestling a naked teenage boy on the floor of what appeared to be Landry's bedroom. I pushed the off button immediately and sat very still for a moment, trying to compose myself. I couldn't imagine how he justified this indecent behavior with someone's son in the parish rectory, that safe and sacred ground.

My uncle expected me to examine everything in the box, but I didn't want to see the rest. I contemplated packing it up and carrying it out to the brick barbeque pit in our back yard, dousing the box with lighter fluid, and setting it on fire. I knew that destroying evidence from a crime scene was a felony offense that would plunge me into the Orleans Parish Prison, a direction I had no intention of taking on Martin Landry's behalf, but Father Ted was depending on me—as his dutiful nephew and director of communications for the diocese—to take inventory and report the findings to him. He clearly didn't want the police to discover what he knew was scandalous and criminal.

Against my better judgment, I turned the tape back on. Landry's young victim was lean and pale and scourged with acne. His long dark greasy hair fell into his face as they skirmished on the carpet, playing some kind of rough sex game. A voice off-camera spoke, and I realized that he was holding the video camera. "You're too old for him now, T-Trey." It was an adult male voice, cynical and daring. Was that a slight stutter? "Your b-body disgusts him. He likes them younger," the voice said, goading the boy on. "He doesn't w-want you anymore, and you've g-got to punish him."

In the swift agile move of a Greco-Roman wrestler, the boy named Trey slipped free of Landry's grip and shot his heel into the priest's ribs. Landry groaned and rolled into a clatter of beer cans, huffing and grabbing his chest. He began to laugh. Trey was stronger and more aggressive, and he sat on Landry's fleshy chest and slapped the priest across the face with his penis. The video frame began to shake from the cameraman's laughter. But the boy was not laughing as he fingered the long hair out of his eyes and began to punch Martin Landry in the chest with his fists, one flat thud after another, raw knuckles against flesh.

My God, I thought. Was this boy the one who murdered him? I picked up the cassette box and studied its label, searching for a date. Could the murder have been captured on tape?

There was a knock on my study door, followed by Ann's hoarse voice: "Is everything all right, Peter?"

I quickly threw the tapes and magazines back into the cardboard box and closed the lid.

"Why is the door locked? Is Ted okay?"

I took the Camcorder to the closet and shoved it on a shelf next to our collection of family board games.

"No, everything is not all right," I said, opening the door. She was wearing her blue winter bathrobe, and her eyes were struggling to focus in the bright light of the room. "Martin Landry has been murdered." I couldn't bring myself to call him *Father* anymore.

"Oh Jesus," she said with a gasp, clutching the folds of her robe. "What happened?"

"Ted found him in the bathtub. He was beaten. A cinder block from his bookshelf was chained around his neck."

I pulled her to my chest, holding her close.

"Do they know who did it?" she asked, her arms locked around my ribcage and her face buried in my shirt.

"The police hadn't arrived yet."

I glanced over her shoulder and noticed the old 8mm home movie lying on the floor beside the box. "Let's go brew some coffee," I said, directing her out of my study. "This may be a very long morning."

As we made our way to the kitchen arm in arm, Ann said, "What a nightmare for the parish, especially for the kids at O-L-S. He was so popular. I'll have to meet with Sister Monica and figure out how to handle the grief counseling."

My wife was a trained therapist and family guidance counselor by profession. She'd volunteered her services for years at Our Lady of Sorrows, the school that Matt was still attending.

"How are the boys going to take the news?" I asked her, doling spoonfuls of fresh ground coffee into a filter.

Ann was slicing two bagels at the counter. "Matt adores the man," she said. "Luke, I don't know. He went through his Father Martin phase a few years ago, but seems to be over it. He hasn't talked about him in quite awhile."

When the murder took place, Ann and I had both recently turned forty years old, but she looked ten years younger. In those days she was a robust woman with thick auburn hair to her shoulders and a scatter of freckles on that lovely Irish face. She jogged seven miles almost every day, and in bad weather she swam or lifted weights at the Tulane gym, which explained why her biceps and shoulders were impressively muscled, her calves shaped like an Olympic sprinter's.

"The PR on this is going to be very rough terrain, Peter." She'd set aside the bread knife and was giving me a disheartened look, something akin to pity. "More difficult than you can imagine."

I stopped spooning out coffee. She was trying to tell me something.

The phone rang, startling us both. It was Father Ted calling from the rectory. "I need you," he said in a near whisper, as if he'd pulled the phone into a dark closet to make the call. "The police are here and the Bishop is on his way."

I glanced at the wall clock. It was a little past four a.m.

"Please don't tell anyone you were here earlier," my uncle said. "Did you go through the box?"

"Yes, I did, Ted," I said, smiling thinly at my wife.

"We'll discuss that at the appropriate time. Get over here as soon as you can. The police have arrested a suspect."

THREE

WHILE ANN WAS TAKING HER SHOWER, I loaded the box into the back of the station wagon and threw an old paint-stained tarp over it. I couldn't risk leaving those things in our house for someone to discover. The truth is, I didn't want my family to be anywhere near that collection, which I regarded as toxic waste, its close proximity to my wife and sons a moral health hazard that would harm them in some invisible way. I'd decided to store it in my office at the chancery.

When I parked across the street from the rectory, the neighborhood trees were swaying in the wind, and cold rain shone like strings of silver in the church's floodlights. Every window in the somber rectory was glowing amber, an unusual sight. Three police cars were stationed out front, a carnival of red, white, and blue flashing in the early morning darkness. An EMS vehicle and a van marked *Crime Unit* waited side by side in the breezeway between buildings.

I got out of the station wagon and approached the two officers standing near one of the cruisers. They were wearing yellow rain slickers and deep blue NOPD ball caps. "Good morning, gentlemen," I said, reaching into my overcoat to produce my ID. "My name is Peter Moore and I'm the communications director for the diocese. My uncle is Father Ted McMurray, the pastor who lives here. He called me about the situation and asked me to come over."

The policemen didn't bother to check my ID. "Go ahead inside, Mr. Moore," one of the officers said. "Father Ted told us you were coming."

I glanced into their police cruiser and saw a dark figure slumped down in the back seat. It was the black teenager that Ted and I had encountered on the stairway. He grinned at me through the wet glass and hitched his chin, a gesture of recognition. My sudden appearance seemed to animate him. He sat up and pressed his face against the window. I could hear his muffled voice through the locked door: *"Yo, man, git me outta here!"*

He was their suspect.

"We found him wandering around by the church," one of the officers said, chuckling. "Didn't have sense enough to get out of the rain. Crack heads ain't the brightest puppies in the litter."

"Yo, mistah," the young man was shouting into the glass, *"tell 'em I didn't do nothing!"*

"Fool was wearing the priest's wristwatch," another officer said, shaking his head. "Had the man's name engraved right there on the back."

As I walked away, I could hear him pounding his handcuffed fists against the window. A cop was tapping the glass with the butt of his nightstick, telling him to quiet down. I felt horrible. He couldn't have been the murderer. I wanted to say something to the policemen before they booked the poor kid, but that would've gone against my uncle's instructions and put me at the scene of the crime.

In the rectory living room, Father Ted was speaking in solemn tones with a uniformed officer who was removing his slicker. I requested a private moment with my uncle and took him aside near the grand bookshelves.

"We both know that boy didn't do it," I said in an excited whisper. "We've got to clear him before this gets out of hand."

My uncle's brow creased in a certain way I'd seen countless times since I was a child. It was always the prelude to intense seriousness. "We really don't know anything for certain, Peter," he said. "Let the police do their job."

"When that kid showed up, he had no clue what had happened upstairs. He was looking for the party that Martin had invited him to."

He looked over his shoulder. Two crime scene investigators wearing lab coats and latex gloves were descending the stairs, discussing their work with a casual indifference. I heard one of them say the words *subdural hematoma*.

"That was his story, Peter," my uncle said, lowering his voice even more. "He may've been lying to us. We don't know this boy. When they arrested him, he was wearing Martin's gold watch. It's engraved 'To Father Martin Landry from his loving parents' and the date he was ordained. How did the boy get that watch, Peter? I can't imagine Martin giving away an ordination gift from his parents."

An ordination watch from parents was a precious object beloved by every priest I'd ever met. You didn't give it away. But considering what I'd seen on that videotape, it wouldn't have surprised me to learn that Martin had traded gifts for sex.

"I agree we should let the police do their job," I said. "The box is in the back of my station wagon, Ted. Let's turn it over to them and get out of their business."

We were huddled together like two nuns whispering in chapel, restraining our voices, our emotions. I was close enough to smell tobacco on my uncle's breath. He'd been a pack-a-day man for as long as I could remember.

"Did you go through everything?" he asked with a pained expression, looking nervously over his shoulder at a couple of rain-spattered police officers who'd wandered into the rectory and had stopped to talk near a heavy antique buffet that stood in the formal dining area.

"Most of it," I said. "I didn't have time to watch the tapes. Just a few minutes of one."

His discomfort was physical now, as if he'd smelled something spoiled. "How bad is it?"

"As bad as it gets."

He beckoned me to follow him into his small study and closed the door. It was a room with a low ceiling and paper-strewn desk and more bookshelves packed with intimidating canonical tomes. Pastor Edward McMurray's inner sanctum. It reeked of tobacco, an ashtray full of butts. A pair of worn slippers sat at the foot of an old leather reclining chair.

"I'm sorry I had to involve you, Peter. Right now we can't trust anyone but family. And we're going to need God's help to get us through this."

I had always trusted my uncle, his integrity, his compassion, but I must admit that on that cold rainy morning nearly twenty years ago, I wasn't certain he was being totally honest with me. And I doubted that God would help us save Father Martin Landry's reputation, because Martin Landry may not have saved his own soul.

"Did you know about him, Ted?" My agitation was at a low boil. There were too many unanswered questions. "You lived under the same roof. How in God's name could you not have seen what was going on?"

When I was younger, I'd watched my uncle, the beloved teacher and scholar, struggle many times with theological precepts, Church doctrine, biblical exegesis. As he worked through the permutations in his analytical mind, he would scratch at the dry patch of scalp near the part in his hair, where the summer sun had always left him burned and peeling. He was thoroughly human and he didn't mind admitting, with an apologetic smile, that he was of two minds over a difficult interpretation of faith and morals. Divorce, celibacy, contraception. He believed in dialogue and discussed even the most sacrosanct matters as open questions. His students had always admired that about him, and so had I. But I needed clarity now. I needed the absolute truth. And I was unhappy about what I read in my uncle's face. He was laboring to formulate a response, and that in itself tore at my heart. I needed a definitive *No, I did not know.* But what I saw instead was a conflicted man searching his conscience for a way to explain himself and failing utterly to give me the assurance I was looking for.

"Father McMurray?" The policeman I'd met by the cruiser was standing just outside the door, his slicker dripping rainwater onto the carpet. "The Bishop is here, sir."

The Bishop was preceded into the rectory by his driver and chief aide, the Vicar-General, a small combative man named Monsignor Karl Fulweiler who swept into the living room with the cautious eyes of a Secret Service handler. I had heard him referred to more than once as the *Holy Rottweiler.* Shaking his wet umbrella like a bloody saber, he surveyed the surroundings ablaze with lamplight and nodded at Father Ted, then gave me a dismissive glance, the usual slight I'd come to expect from him whenever we encountered each other in the chancery. Monsignor Fulweiler was an imperious little cleric of the old school, pre-Vatican II, and he didn't trust anyone like me, a seminary dropout who liked women and maintained daily commerce with the corrupt outside world.

The Bishop was close behind him, a much taller man with thick shoulders and a sturdy build who looked more like a Hungarian freedom fighter than a scholar of canon law from a wealthy family in Cleveland. Underneath his long dark overcoat, the Bishop was wearing a black suit with a Roman collar and red shirt, immortal amaranth, the traditional color of his office. He made his way toward Father Ted and me with deep concern etched into his strong-chinned Magyar face. I was surprised when he spoke to me first.

"Peter, that reporter friend of yours is snooping around outside," he said. "She's talking to the police and trying to interview the young man in custody. She wanted to talk to me."

Monsignor Fulweiler was glaring at me, an ill-tempered man who took pleasure in other people's failure. "She is not welcome on church property. Please get rid of her," he said in a German accent that always sounded like a command to stand up straight and fasten your tunic.

I turned to the Bishop. "What's our lead, Your Excellency?" I asked him.

We'd worked together on public quotes many times and he knew what I meant. Poised in concentration, he brought prayer-folded fingers to his lips and closed his eyes. "A man of God who has given his life in service to so many others has now joined Our Heavenly Father," he said, as if listening to a celestial voice the rest of us could not hear. "Father Landry was a dedicated priest, much loved by the parish he served. This is a terrible tragedy for the family of Christ. We offer our prayers for him and for the consolation of his flock. And we ask for God's mercy on the young man who took Father Landry's life."

The Bishop opened his eyes and patted me gently on the arm. "Something along those lines, Peter," he said. "Tell the reporter I will issue an official statement to the media later this morning."

If you polled public relations directors anywhere in the country, whether in the corporate world or politics or the Girl Scouts of America, they would've admitted they lied routinely, as par for the course, and slept soundly every night with an unburdened conscience. *It's my job,* we told ourselves after the third bourbon of the evening. *It pays the bills.* But some of us survived longer than others.

I pulled up the collar of my overcoat and walked outside into the blustery rain. Sharon Simon was speaking quietly to a police officer posted at his cruiser. She was a tall, attractive woman I'd known since our journalism classes at Loyola, the Jesuit-run university next door to Tulane. I had dated her a couple of times, without much romantic interest by either party, before I met Ann. At this point in her career, Sharon was serving double duty as a news writer and the religion reporter for the *Times-Picayune*. This was the consummate story for her—a murdered priest. When she saw me approaching, she smiled as if she'd been expecting me. It was her professional smile and not the large, generous, toothy smile full of laughter and goodness that I'd enjoyed when we were younger.

"Nasty morning, Sharon," I said. "You should have stayed in bed."

She was wearing a stylish gray raincoat, a whaler's hat, and heavy hiking boots. Wet strands of her long dark hair had slipped loose from the hat and clung to her slender neck. "We've all got to earn our dental coverage," she said. "Why don't you tell me what happened, Peter?"

I looked through the window of the cruiser and saw the young man lying on his side, sobbing. When he noticed me standing there, he pulled himself up halfway, gave me a despairing look, then dropped his head again, rubbing his face and nose with handcuffed wrists. He was older than I'd first conjectured, maybe old enough to die in the chair.

"Sharon, I hate to steal you away from our city's finest," I said, smiling weakly at the police officer, "but let's go talk. Please step into my office." I gestured toward the station wagon parked across the muddy street.

"I hope you've got a pot of coffee brewing in that thing," she said.

We sat in the rear of the old Plymouth wagon, fogging the glass like a couple of teenaged love birds in a borrowed car. She took off her wet whaler's hat, shook out her hair, and unbuttoned the top buttons on her raincoat. "It's been a long time since I've done this kind of thing," she said, the police lights casting her face in strange strobing colors. "Meet a man in the back seat of his car."

Sleepless and in no mood for banter, I asked, "What do you know already?"

She retrieved a notepad and pen from her coat pocket and shifted her hips to face me. She was even more attractive at forty than she was in college, with flawless skin and only the faintest signs of aging around her dark brown eyes. In close quarters I could smell the herbal fragrance of shampoo in her damp hair.

"I know someone has died in the rectory," she said, glancing down at her notes. "Not much more than that, Peter. I hope it's not your uncle."

"My uncle is fine," I said. "The Bishop is calling a press conference later this morning. He'll give you all the details."

She looked past my shoulder toward the flashing lights. "There's a crime truck," she said. "It's a lot more than a priest dying in his sleep." She checked her notes again. "If your uncle's okay, that leaves only one other possibility—what's his name? That popular priest all the kids like."

"How do you know so much about this parish?"

"I get around," she said, smiling at me. "It's what I do." She swatted me on the knee with her pad. "You remember what investigative journalism is, don't you, Mr. Moore? It's what you were trained to do before you went over to the dark side."

I would've smiled as well, but her remark cut too close to the bone.

"So tell me his name," she said.

"Father Martin Landry."

"I thought you were under orders to zip your lips under the pain of mortal sin," she said, writing down his name.

"I may need you to return the favor someday, Sharon."

This only encouraged her. "How did he die?"

My arm was resting on the back of the seat. I could've reached behind us and yanked the tarp off the cardboard box. There was enough evidence in there to expose criminal behavior, destroy a man's good name, and irreparably harm Holy Mother Church. And possibly some small revelation that would point to who killed Martin Landry and why. Sharon Simon could've won a Pulitzer Prize for writing about what was in that box.

"I'll call you as soon as the Bishop announces a time for the press conference," I said, opening my door to a rush of cold wind. "You'll be the first to know."

She grabbed the sleeve of my overcoat. "That kid in the cop car," she said, nodding toward the rectory. "What are they holding him for? He involved in the death?"

"Time to go, Sharon," I said, stepping out into the dark drizzle. "I'll call you when I know something more."

"Is this the thanks I get for introducing you to your wife and the mother of your children?"

Her version of the story was more or less true. Ann and Sharon had lived in the same dorm on the Loyola campus during our sophomore year. I had first laid eyes on Ann when I was saying good night to Sharon back in the days when coeds were required to sign in and out of their dorms for the evening. We were returning from an uninspired date at the same time that Ann was being delivered home safely by an oafish frat boy named Earl Doucet. The next day, in Journalism 220D, I nonchalantly asked Sharon for the name of that cute young woman at the sign-in desk.

"The only way that good Catholic girl will put out," Sharon had said with a coy smile, "is if you marry her."

"Come on, get out of the car, Sharon," I said, extending my hand to her. "You've got to leave the premises."

"I'm not on the premises, Peter. I'm sitting in a car on a city street."

"Okay, fine. But don't trespass on church property. The Vicar-General is in the rectory right now and his role model is Torquemada. You remember what happened to Jews during the Spanish Inquisition, don't you?"

"That's not very funny, jackass."

I walked around to her side of the station wagon, sloshing through puddles of rain. "We're still friends, aren't we?" I said, opening the door for her. "I promise to keep you front and center on this thing."

"You'd better give me a newsprint exclusive," she said, "or I'm going to tell everyone where the Catholics have been hiding the Body."

I left her standing on a dark sidewalk under the dripping live oak trees and crossed the wet lawn to the cruiser. "That reporter has been warned not to come on church property," I said, taking the police officer aside. "If she does, we'll press charges for trespassing."

He stepped back, freeing himself from my hand on his shoulder, and grinned. "I thought we were supposed to forgive our trespassers, Mr. Moore."

I forced a smile. "That was before property rights and church lawyers," I said.

When I went back inside the rectory, a police detective was conferring with the three clerics near the stairwell, wagging his hands as he spoke. A badge was clipped to the pocket of his navy-blue blazer, and he was wearing a rumpled dress shirt and badly creased Dockers that looked as if he'd fetched them from a dirty laundry hamper in the dark. He was a stocky man in his fifties, almost as short as the Vicar-General, with brown hair thinning in front and not enough to comb into a wave anymore. He had what my mother always referred to as an *olive complexion*, meaning anything but pasty Irish.

"We don't know if the trauma to his head was fatal," the detective was explaining. "He was dragged into the bathroom. The trail of blood is very clear. The medical examiner will have to determine if he was still alive when . . ."

He stopped speaking as soon as he saw me approaching.

"Peter, this is Detective Ray Duhon," my uncle said, pronouncing it *Dew-yawn,* Cajun French style. He told the investigator who I was and I shook his hand.

"I go way back with His Excellency here," Duhon said with a cocky familiarity. "I was a Grand Knight of the Altar when he came down here to civilize us coonasses at St. Alphonsus in the Irish Channel. His first gig as an ordained priest. Long time ago, eh, Your Excellency?"

Ray Duhon spoke with the hint of a Cajun accent and laughed with great abandon, a booming sound that echoed through the sepulchral quiet of the rectory. "I can still recite the *Ad Deum qui laetificat* if it ever comes back, y'all."

The Bishop was in a serious mood. "May we see him now, Ray?" he asked. "I would like to offer my blessing."

Detective Duhon lowered his eyes and ran a hand through his hair, a nervous altar boy endeavoring to say no to his old confessor. He was visibly uncomfortable with the Bishop's request. "It's a gruesome scene, Your Excellency," he said apologetically. "I recommend against it, me."

"If the Bishop wishes to bless the body," Monsignor Fulweiler interjected, pompous and self-important, "he should be allowed to bless the body."

The detective looked at him with a bemused expression. "I'm sorry, but the Bishop will have to bless him from the doorway," he said with more resistance than anyone had anticipated. "That's the best I can do. We don't want to introduce other footprints and the like."

The clergymen mounted the stairs with Detective Duhon in the lead and Father Ted in the rear. My uncle turned and quietly asked me if I was joining them. I shook my head. I'd seen enough of that bloody scene.

Ted hurried back down the steps to address me in a low voice. "We're meeting in the Bishop's office at seven to discuss strategy, Peter. Please be there."

Strategy? I thought. "I hope our *strategy* includes what we're going to do about that poor kid handcuffed in the back of a police car."

He gave me an ominous look. "Seven a.m. sharp, Peter," he said. "There's much to discuss."

FOUR

THE CHANCERY BUILDING HAD BEEN CONSTRUCTED AS AN URSULINE convent by French architects shortly before the Louisiana Purchase, and it now stood like a Norman fortress on the edge of the quaint Uptown district. The surrounding silk-stocking mansions had all been renovated by industrious *nouveau riche*, and charming streetcars clamored down nearby Carrollton Avenue and its neutral ground of towering palm trees and oleander shrubs flowering pink and white for half the year. But on that bitter morning, in the aftermath of a winter rainstorm, the neighborhood's southern charm had dissolved into chill darkness.

I was grateful that the diocese kept the chancery well lighted, day and night, and that our private security service was on duty twenty-four-seven. As I rolled into my space in the parking circle out front, I was pleased to see the security cruiser parked only a few spaces away. A conscientious young man named Isaiah usually worked the graveyard shift, and I assumed he was making his rounds.

I tossed aside the tarp in the back of the station wagon and carried the box up the granite steps to the dry shelter of the alcove entryway. After keying myself inside the building, I called Isaiah's name, alerting him to my presence. When he didn't respond, I called again, my voice echoing in the dome of silence: "Isaiah, are you here? It's Peter Moore, okay? I'll be in my office."

The communications suite was located in the north wing next to the stewardship and development offices. I thought I heard something down at the end of the corridor, so I wasted no time hurrying into my office and locking the door behind me. I was all too aware that a priest had been murdered only ten minutes away by car and that the killer was still on the loose and may have held a grudge against the Church. And there I was, alone and unprotected in the official seat of power for the entire diocese.

I sat down at my cluttered desk, found a notepad under a stack of folders, and began taking stock of what was in the box. I removed the sex toys one at a time, handling them with a thick bundle of fast-food napkins I kept in my drawer. It was disgusting work, but I tried to think of myself as a diligent coroner weighing and describing damaged organs. I wrote down the titles and publication dates of each pornographic magazine—about two dozen in all—and noted verbatim what was printed on the labels of the six video boxes. I saved the small 8mm reel for last, opening the cover and holding a strip of dark brown film up to the light. To view it, I would need a home-movie projector, but I hadn't seen one of those things in years.

Stashed at the bottom of the box was an old photo album with a cracked leather cover. Its pages were filled with fading photographs dating back to a teenaged Martin Landry and his school friends sporting ducktails and crew cuts and stylish Ray-Bans and tight bathing suits showing off their bulges and oiled summer tans. One chunky kid had forced a garden hose into his trunks to make the others laugh. Another kid was mooning with his lily-white butt. Their silly posturing was what my mother would've shrugged off as *boys will be boys*.

I thumbed through the album and eventually came across familiar faces from our seminary days. Most of the images were standard fare—young sems wearing starched white shirts and black clip-on ties, going about daily routines, sitting at desks in study hall, kneeling in chapel, eating together in silence in the refectory. I hadn't stayed in touch with these guys over the past two decades and struggled to remember their names. But I did remember our class clown—a manic, hot-tempered lunatic nicknamed Fozo who loved practical jokes and sometimes popped us with a wet towel as we left the steamy shower room. I was surprised to find myself in one of the photos, running to escape the sting of Fozo's towel while protecting my decency with a loose bathrobe. I had no recollection of Martin creeping around the shower room with a camera, waiting for these moments, but how else could that photograph be explained? Even puerile roughhousing took on a sordid sheen with Martin Landry lurking in the shadows, hiding behind his lens.

Those photographs brought back memories of my sexual anxieties and pubescent fantasies as a teenager, which had caused me great guilt at the time. I worried that I might be gay. But as a freshman at the all-male Blessed Benildus High School, I was greatly relieved when the charismatic Brother Fidelis set aside the biology textbook and explained someone's theory—possibly Freud's, I can't recall—that we boys would go through three periods of sexuality as we matured— autosexual, homosexual, and heterosexual. Brother Fidelis maintained that we would first discover our own developing bodies and the pleasures of masturbation, then we would experiment with other boys, and ultimately we would encounter girls, get married with the Church's blessing, and practice the joys of procreation in accordance with God's plan. He was telling us not to worry about masturbation or sexual horseplay with our buddies. *Boys will be boys.* It was a natural phase we would all pass through.

Of course, the pope and the Holy See would've burned him at the stake in an earlier century for that lenient, heretical interpretation of sexual development. After all, masturbation (wasting of seed) killed Onan. Homosexuality was an abomination and turned people into pillars of salt. They were mortal sins that would cast you into the everlasting fires of hell, child.

Brother Fidelis was a man of many unorthodox views. He claimed that true homosexuals became fixated on the male body and got stuck in that phase of sexual experimentation with boys, for some unknown reason, possibly psychological damage, and they remained stuck there for the rest of their lives. And while we pity their immaturity, their inability to move on to women, we should not scorn them, insisted the tolerant Brother Fidelis, because Jesus would not have scorned them, any more than he scorned lepers and prostitutes. Thus spake Brother Fidelis, circa 1959, current whereabouts unknown.

One evening, over glasses of pinot noir, I explained the brother's antiquated theory of homosexuality to Ann, the trained and credentialed guidance counselor. She laughed and said, "That theory is ridiculous, condescending, and *completely* without scientific or psychiatric evidence. My God, you poor messed-up boys. What do you suppose happened to all those young Church freethinkers like him, who thought they were enlightened and enlightening, but were totally misguided?"

I recalled that Brother Fidelis had left the order a few years later, after falling in love with the woman who supervised cafeteria services at our school.

"Ahh, he'd reached the third and final stage of sexuality," said Ann with a mischievous smile. "The irresistible lure of Jezebels."

I'd been turning album pages in a slow foggy haze of rumination when I realized I was staring at an image of the sleeping Donny Bertrand. It was the beginning of a long photo sequence of him in a hospital bed. Although he was unusually gaunt, with dark bags under his eyes from chronic insomnia and those horrible night terrors, I saw something in that picture I hadn't acknowledged before—Donny's face had great character. Asleep, untroubled, at peace with himself, he looked like an ordinary young man without a worry in the world. But the white gown revealed where he was—the mental hospital across the lake. And it appeared as if Donny was blissfully unaware of the camera and the photographer's presence.

My first reaction was that the photos were more evidence of Martin Landry's secret nature, his sordid, invasive manipulations. What the hell was he doing at the hospital? I was convinced this was another cruel violation until I reached the final print in the sequence. Donny's eyes were open and clear, unlike the hollow glassy eyes of the young man I'd seen after electroshock treatments. In that final image he was lying in repose, smiling fondly at the photographer, a tributary of laugh lines coursing from his eyes. Donny was happy, euphoric. Perhaps his spirits were elevated by medication. Or perhaps he was grateful that someone familiar had come to visit him in his darkest hour, a prisoner of that grim place. He looked alive, the way he'd looked when he first entered the seminary. His eyes were dancing, as though elated to see an old friend.

I closed the photo album and dropped it back in the box, surveying that medley of incriminating evidence and wondering where to begin. My office had purchased a VCR and we kept it in the A-V room. That seemed like a good place to start. I put the video cassettes in a smaller box, grabbed the notepad, and unlocked my office door.

A tall dark figure was standing in the reception area only a few steps away, aiming something at me.

"Jesus Christ!" I said, breathless and clutching my chest. "You damn near scared me to death, Isaiah."

"Sorry, Mistah Moore," the security guard said. He was pointing a can of mace, his other hand resting firmly on the grip of his holstered pistol. "You shoulda called me, sir. Let me know you was gonna be here this early."

He was a lanky young black man in his twenties, well over six feet tall, with dark freckles and short-cropped hair that took on a red hue in natural light. He'd always been friendly to me. We usually talked about sports.

"My apologies," I said, still catching my breath. "A bad thing happened at one of the parish rectories a few hours ago and we've got an emergency on our hands. The Bishop will be here soon."

I stepped out into the corridor and gazed toward the far end of the wing, where the muted light vanished into a black square. "Can you walk with me to the A-V room?" I asked. "This place gives me the creeps when it's dark."

"They say a crazy old nun still roams these halls every night," he said, "looking for the baby they taken away from her."

"Do yourself a favor, Isaiah. Don't mention that story to Sister Colleen."

He grinned. "Don't worry about nothing, Mistah Moore," he said with a two-fingered salute. "I got your back till the sun come up. Then you on your own."

I'd seen an old sepia photograph of the A-V room when it functioned as the convent's linen room, a crew of dour young novices working at long tables, sorting and folding clean sheets and towels and women's underclothing. The laundry tables had been replaced by work stations that housed a slide projector, tape recorders, an audio cassette player, a turntable with speaker boxes, the new VCR attached to a television set, and an IBM word processor, one of the first in the city. We were proud of our very advanced technology.

I dragged over a plastic bucket chair and began the long ordeal of watching scene after scene of Father Martin Landry's sexual abuses on the TV screen. I could hardly contain my anger and revulsion.

Most of the boys were nine or ten years old, drinking beer and prancing around the Landry family's beach house with erections like tent poles underneath their bathing trunks. I didn't recognize any of my sons' friends from Our Lady of Sorrows and that gave me some relief. But it wasn't clear how long ago these things had taken place. Last summer? The summer before? Landry prowled in the background of the recordings like a tracking predator, encouraging the boys to flex their stringy muscles and show off their bodies, daring them to strip naked and wrestle one another. He rolled around with them on the floor, his own arousal visible through wet trunks. The rough play struck me as an audition, Landry determining which ones might be willing to go further.

The first time he performed oral sex on a boy, I stopped the tape. Even though I suspected something like this would turn up, I wasn't prepared to actually visualize it. My hands were trembling. I didn't know what to write on the notepad. I really didn't know how to begin. I thought about what I would do if someone had sexually assaulted one of my sons. I was not a violent man, but I would've hunted him down and beaten him senseless. And that's when it hit me. Somebody had already done that. An enraged father. Or an unforgiving young man who'd once been abused by him. I knelt down on the cold hard tile and folded my hands in prayer, asking for God's pardon. Because I was glad that the son of a bitch was dead.

I realized I was too angry and too close to the situation to summon the kind of clarity and dispassion the report required. I was the wrong person for the job. I'd never liked Martin Landry, and now I loathed him. So how would I be able to put aside my indignation and help the diocese defuse this public relations time bomb?

At times like that, when I was under stress and in need of advice, I relied on Father Ted for his wise counsel. But I was unhappy with him at the moment and I didn't feel comfortable talking to him about any of this. In truth, I was beginning to lose faith in a man who'd always been my role model.

I needed to hear a consoling voice, so I picked up the phone and called home. Ann answered after the first ring. "I'm at the chancery," I said. "We've got a horrible mess on our hands."

"I was beginning to worry about you, Peter. There's nothing on the morning news channels yet."

I told her that the police had arrested an innocent teenager.

"How do you know he's innocent?"

I recounted our confrontation in the rectory and explained that the young man couldn't have known what had taken place upstairs in Martin Landry's bedroom.

"Have you spoken to the police about that?"

I hesitated, then reluctantly admitted I hadn't.

"Good Lord, Peter. Why aren't you telling the police everything you know?"

I hadn't even told *her* everything I knew. But I needed to get that awful burden off my chest. I glanced at the locked door, then lowered my voice. "Martin Landry was a pederast, Ann." I used the old-fashioned word I thought might be the correct clinical term. "He liked to videotape himself having sex with boys."

There was a long pause on her end. Dead air. The revelation seemed to have shocked her into silence.

"We recovered his collection of tapes and I'm here watching them," I said. "But I don't think I can watch them anymore."

When she didn't respond, I said, "Ann, are you there? I know how hard this is to take, believe me. But it's true. Martin Landry was a child molester."

A skillful mediator, she had been prudently contemplating her words. "Peter, we've got to talk," she said in a calm, professional manner. "I may be treating one of his victims."

FIVE

SHORTLY BEFORE SEVEN A.M. I FOUND MYSELF SITTING ALONE and in a despondent mood in the marble-pillared foyer outside the Bishop's administrative offices. The tall double doors to his inner sanctum were closed and his executive assistant, an aging Ursuline nun named Sister Colleen, one of the last of her order in the city, had surfaced from her adjoining office to explain that the Bishop's earlier meeting was running late.

I didn't know if she'd been briefed on Martin Landry's murder. "What's going on in there?" I asked with my tired version of a conspiratorial smile. Sister Colleen and I were on cordial terms and occasionally exchanged sensitive information or a low-level confidence if we knew it would help each other do our jobs.

"He's seeing several gentlemen I'm not acquainted with," she said with a puzzled expression. "One of them is a police detective."

She was a bespectacled, gray-haired woman whose daily uniform was a navy blue jacket and skirt, with a small silver crucifix resting on her white blouse. Gone were the days of my parochial school, when nuns wore Bride of Christ full body armor and eccentric headgear.

"I'm sure you have his office wired, Sister. Let's listen in."

Her eyes smiled. "Don't think I haven't considered it," she said.

Ten minutes later, the doors opened and two men emerged, striding with purpose across the polished terrazzo. One was Ray Duhon, the detective I'd met in the rectory, even more disheveled in his blazer and poorly knotted tie around his thick neck. He was listening to the much taller gentleman with silver hair, who was wearing a tailored gray suit with an overcoat draped dapperly across his arm. Duhon acknowledged me with a nod, but the district attorney at his side was enchanted with his own pontifications and didn't look my way. I'd seen DA Roger Finney many times on television, and he'd always struck me as an ambitious, glad-handing professional politician, like all big-city district attorneys who were using their positions to seek higher office. Finney was a trained Irish tenor who performed with the New Orleans Symphony every St. Patrick's Day, and a notorious partygoer famous for breaking into a perfect Sinatra imitation after a few drinks.

"Peter." My uncle was standing at the double doors, looking solemn and intense in his black clerical suit and Roman collar. "Join us, please."

Three others were waiting at the long oakwood conference table in the Bishop's *sala regia*. Picked-over fruit and croissants were scattered in front of them on silver serving platters, the telltale remnants of an early-morning work session, with pitchers of coffee and orange juice here and there like giant chess pieces left in random moves. Garbed in a black robe dotted with fuchsia-colored buttons, Monsignor Fulweiler—the Vicar-General and second in command—was sitting at the head of the table in the Bishop's customary seat. I wondered why the Bishop was missing.

I recognized Eric Gautier and his father, the venerable Russell Gautier, one of the most prominent attorneys in the city, impeccably dressed in an expensive business suit with a matching vest and crisp pocket handkerchief. The son was more relaxed and modish in his tweed sports coat and bright yellow square-end knit tie. He smiled at me and said hello. Eric was in his mid-thirties, not long out of law school, and I knew him as Matt's soccer coach from the previous summer. We'd become acquainted in that superficial way when your kids are on the same team. Eric mentioned that he enjoyed tennis, and I'd made the mistake of playing him one sultry summer morning in a gesture of friendship. The wiry little jock had a killer serve and a wicked backhand, and he'd crushed me without mercy.

Vicar-General Fulweiler began his remarks by addressing me. "Father McMurray has informed us that he collected very disturbing materials from Father Landry's bedroom," he said in his strong German accent. "We understand you have possession of the materials, Mr. Moore."

I glanced at my uncle and he nodded, giving me permission to speak freely.

"Yes, Monsignor. The box is in my office downstairs."

"Father McMurray speaks very highly of you, Mr. Moore," said Russell Gautier, a Garden District patrician with silky white hair and perfectly manicured nails. "He assures us that you understand the severity of the situation. And the need for absolute confidentiality." His eyes were as blue and piercing as winter light. "You cannot discuss what you've seen with anyone, Mr. Moore, not even your wife. If you're summoned to a deposition or court of law, we will counsel you in private before your appearance. Do you understand what I'm saying?"

"Yes, of course," I said. I may have already told Ann too much.

Fulweiler jotted something down using his fuchsia-colored fountain pen and turned to me again. "We've met with the district attorney this morning," he said, "and discussed our options. He's a friend of the Church. A good Irish Catholic. He has agreed to give us time to manage this problem ourselves."

To manage this problem ourselves? It sounded to me like *privilegium fori*—Privilege of the Legal Forum—an outdated ecclesiastical practice I'd learned about in a canon law class when I was in the seminary. It had once granted clerics the right to be tried solely by other clerics and not in secular courts. The same concept employed by military courts-martial.

"The first thing we must do is to identify every child with whom Father Landry had inappropriate relations," Fulweiler said.

It was an open admission of Martin Landry's transgressions. I realized that Father Ted had disclosed to this group what I'd told him about the videotapes.

"The diocese will negotiate with their families and compensate them for their suffering," Fulweiler said. "Father Landry was one of our own. It is our obligation to make amends for his indiscretions."

Indiscretions? They were monstrous violations. First-degree felonies in the eyes of the law.

Russell Gautier's long elegant hands were resting one on top of the other. He spoke with the honey drawl of southern gentry. "This could be a catastrophe for the Church and the diocese," he said with a grave countenance. "We have to limit the damage. There's no need to ruin the reputations of these boys and their families, or to drag Father Landry through the mud on the six o'clock news. The poor man is dead. We've got to turn our attention to the living—to the victims of his conduct—and take care of this privately."

I thought about my telephone conversation with Ann before the meeting. She'd told me that for more than a year she'd been treating a young man in his mid-twenties who'd been molested by a priest. "It started when he was a young altar boy," she'd said. And he suspected he wasn't the only one. "Do you have any idea how many children the average pedophile abuses in a lifetime, Peter? Two hundred and sixty-five. It's impossible to imagine. I can't wrap my mind around that number."

Out of shame and fear of reprisals, her client had not divulged the offender's name. But guilt had eaten away at him for seventeen years. He was an alcoholic with chronic colitis, and he'd attempted suicide more than once.

"Doesn't he realize he can stop this guy from harming more children?"

"A whistleblower is called an outcry witness, Peter. A case like this will get very visible in the media. And the court proceedings can be humiliating. He's trying to hold onto a job and save his marriage. His wife doesn't know about the molestations. He isn't ready for public exposure."

Reflecting upon what Ann had said, I leaned forward in the rigid high-backed chair and stared at Russell Gautier across the tray of fruit. "I'm not a lawyer, Mr. Gautier," I said, "but I know we're dealing with two separate issues here—a criminal matter and a civil matter. We can compensate these families for what Father Landry did to their sons— and we should. But the police will be conducting their own criminal investigation, won't they? They've got a suspect in custody. What if he tells them what Martin Landry was doing?"

Monsignor Fulweiler was displeased. "You are not listening very carefully, Mr. Moore," he said, his small sharp teeth chewing his words. "We have just met with the district attorney and the detective in charge of the case, and they don't see the point of persecuting a dead priest."

I was fed up with the Rottweiler's insults, which I'd endured for the seven years I'd been working in the chancery. It was my job to raise the hard public relations questions, and at that moment I was determined to push back. "So it's been decided that the diocese is *not* going to tell the public that Martin Landry was a child sex offender?" I asked with far too much bluntness.

My uncle was sitting next to me and he pressed his hand firmly against my wrist. It was a warning to back off.

"We don't know all the facts yet, Mr. Moore," Fulweiler said, the blood rising in his chiseled face. "As Our Lord and Savior said, 'Judge not, lest ye also be judged.'"

Sister Colleen had once pointed out to me that the Vicar-General bore a frightening resemblance to the German actor Klaus Kinski. I was beginning to see what she meant.

"I will be happy to show you the videotapes, Monsignor. You can *judge* for yourself."

Father Ted lifted his hand, signaling for a truce. "My brothers," he said, "we have much work ahead of us. Let's stay on task."

Eric Gautier slid his handwritten notes in front of his father, and the older man eyed them through reading glasses. "Ah, yes, of course," he said. "To be clear, my son and I will take charge of the evidence downstairs in your office, Mr. Moore. However, what we need from you is a systematic identification of the victims on those videotapes. Father McMurray tells us you're familiar with the parish and its schoolchildren. Even so, it won't be an easy undertaking, or a pleasant one. Eric will manage the process overall. We need names and contact information. Once we have them, Monsignor Fulweiler will work with our law firm to get in touch with families and present financial offers."

Eric elucidated the plan. The diocese would settle with victims and their families in exchange for their silence. And for their sworn written agreement not to pursue criminal charges or further damages. Holy Mother Church was going to make Martin Landry's victims an offer they couldn't refuse.

Russell Gautier hastened to add, "I'm afraid there's a great deal of urgency here, Mr. Moore. We have to find these boys and get there first," he said. "Because if this scandal breaks wide open—if his victims start coming forward now that Father Landry is deceased—people will hire their own attorneys and this whole thing will spin out of our control."

I felt overwhelmed by the responsibility. "Mr. Gautier, I don't have any experience in this kind of investigative work," I admitted. "I'm not even sure where to start."

"You were a newspaper reporter before we hired you," Fulweiler said. It was an accusation, not a compliment. "Surely you must have certain basic skills in procuring information."

I'd been a poor investigative reporter, which was why I'd left the field and tried to start my own public relations agency. A brilliant idea that led to bankruptcy, foreclosure, and nearly the end of my marriage. After a year of unemployment and mounting debt, my uncle had rescued me by securing this position with the diocese.

"Monsignor," I said with as much patience as I could summon, "there are several boys on those tapes. It's not entirely clear to me how long ago some of them were filmed. Or exactly where these things took place. Father Landry served in a number of parishes over the years. It's going to take more skill than I have to track these boys down."

Russell Gautier intervened with a kind smile. "I will put you in touch with a trustworthy private investigator," he said. "I've used him two or three times and he's quite professional at what he does." He glanced at the Vicar-General. "He's a good Christian Brothers' boy and he'll respect our need for confidentiality."

How could I force myself to do this assignment? I gave serious consideration to tendering my resignation and walking out of the room. The only thing preventing me from doing that was my all-too-clear memory of the nausea and panic I'd felt every morning for an entire year, when I was out on the streets looking for work, desperate and depressed, being rejected in interview after interview. I needed this job. I couldn't let Ann and our sons down again.

"Gentlemen, do we have a statement?"

The Bishop had ascended from his private dressing chamber located at the bottom of a hidden stairway behind his desk. Sister Colleen had once shown me the chamber when the Bishop was out of town. It was a monk's cell with a closet full of robes and tennis whites, a narrow bed for afternoon naps, and personal toilet facilities. She said that the starkness and simplicity were intended to remind bishops they were humble Servants of God. "It also has an emergency escape chute that will slide His Excellency to the floor below," she'd said with a wicked smile, lifting the hatch of a small floor panel that opened into darkness. "You know, for when the barbarian hordes come battering down our doors."

Dressed in an amaranth red cassock and skullcap, the Bishop strode across the crimson carpet toward the conference table. Everyone stood out of respect. He waved off Eric Gautier's attempt to kiss his ring and took his place at the head of the table. "Let me see what we've got," he said.

Vicar-General Fulweiler handed him a copy of the public statement that he and Eric Gautier had written earlier, and then he passed a copy to me. I was offended that they'd done this behind my back, leaving me out of the process. As director of communications, it was my job to write a first draft of the Bishop's statements.

I was still smarting from that personal slight and not concentrating on the text itself when the Bishop asked, "How does it read, Peter?"

I focused quickly, hurrying to catch up. *Father Martin Landry's death is a great loss to everyone who loved and admired him. He served the Church with great distinction and will be profoundly missed. We offer prayers and consolation for his many friends, parishioners, and the schoolchildren who cherished him as their beloved teacher and spiritual guide.*

It was a shameful exercise in mendacity. And then I came to the passage about the young suspect in custody. *We pray that God will have mercy on him. May justice be served.*

"Your Excellency, we shouldn't say anything about the suspect," I advised. "There's no need to mention him."

"And why not, Peter?" the Bishop asked, raising an eyebrow. He was a serious man with an explosive laugh that often took people by surprise, but I suspected we wouldn't be hearing his laughter anytime soon. "Shouldn't we show compassion?"

"It's a police matter, Your Excellency. Let them deal with any suspects."

The Bishop sat back in his chair and looked thoughtfully at me. "Detective Duhon is certain they have their man, Peter," he said. "They caught him red-handed with Father Landry's watch. What's the downside of showing our concern and Christian love for that disturbed young man?"

"The downside is he didn't do it," I said, turning to my uncle for his reaction. He'd been uncharacteristically quiet throughout the meeting.

Monsignor Fulweiler couldn't contain himself. "And what makes you more qualified than the police to determine his innocence, Mr. Moore?"

I'd been thinking about what I'd seen in the bloody bathtub. I gave Fulweiler a digging little smile. "Holy Scripture," I said. "The Gospel According to St. Mark. I'm sure you're familiar with the passage, Monsignor."

"Get to the point, Mr. Moore," he said, his voice rising with the color in his face.

"You and His Excellency saw Father Landry's body in the bath water. You saw the cinder block chained around his neck. Have you forgotten what Jesus said? 'Whosoever shall offend one of these little ones that believe in me, it is better that a millstone were hanged around his neck and he were cast into the sea.'"

There was a collective inhalation, as if the air in that faux Renaissance chamber had grown thinner, more difficult to absorb. I was certain I hadn't been the only eyewitness to recall that passage when I saw the body. It was the unspoken secret that no one at the table wanted to confront.

"The killer was making a statement, Monsignor. Whoever murdered Father Landry knows Scripture." I almost felt sorry for the Holy Rottweiler. Suddenly he looked pale and stricken and out of his depth. "A stoned black kid from the projects didn't murder Martin Landry. And if we let that young man rot in jail, God will not forgive us, gentlemen. No matter how hard we pray for His mercy."

SIX

THE PRESS CONFERENCE took place in the high arching vestibule of the chancery. Wearing an amaranth-trimmed cape over his cassock and a cloth sash around his waist, the Bishop delivered his statement behind a cumbersome podium that bore the diocesan seal, a medieval shield engraved with cross, crown, and chalice. I would've counseled against all that pomp and feudalism, but no one had invited the director of communications to be involved in the planning. It had become clear to me that I was in the loop only on a need-to-know basis.

His Excellency read the statement like a seasoned professor who'd memorized his lecture notes, and the event went quickly and without a hitch. The three local network affiliates were present with their cameras and caffeinated reporters, and the only one with an incisive question was Sharon Simon, who asked, "Your Excellency, can you tell us the motive for Father Landry's murder?"

"I will leave that to the police," he responded wisely, with a doting smile. Perhaps my lone dissenting voice had made an impression on him after all.

I didn't have a chance to speak with my uncle after the earlier meeting, so I wanted to buttonhole him before he left the building. I sensed he was avoiding me. As the press conference was breaking up, I saw him slip away toward the main corridor and I went after him. But Sharon Simon appeared out of nowhere and intercepted me. "Peter, let's talk," she said, taking my arm and leading me away from the jabbering reporters.

"Can you call me later, Sharon?" I said, struggling to free myself from her grip. "I've got to speak with someone else right now."

"What's going on here?" she asked, unwilling to let me loose, veteran reporter that she was. She was trying to keep her voice down, and her face was so close I could smell the minty antacids she'd been chewing. "Why do I get the feeling that your people aren't entirely forthcoming about Father Landry's murder?"

"As His Excellency said—talk to the police. They're the ones who conduct murder investigations, Sharon."

She sighed impatiently. "How did he die?" The details of the bathtub and cinder block had not been released, and if the black robes had their way, they never would be. "The cops are pinning it on the black kid," she said. "Was it a break-and-enter gone bad?"

I was deeply troubled that an innocent young man was being detained in some dark holding cell, fearing for his manhood and waiting for the slow-churning wheels of justice to assign him a competent public defender. That familiar voice in the back of my head was urging me to tell Sharon everything I knew, but in spite of my doubts and misgivings, I remained foolishly loyal to *my people*, as she'd put it.

"Please excuse me, I'm late for a meeting," I said.

She was a tall, imposing presence, comfortable with her size, and she wasn't backing down.

"Sharon, I promise I'll call you when I find out something useful."

I nudged her shoulder with the back of my hand and she reluctantly stood aside. "The question you ought to be asking yourself, Peter," she said, following me with those dark inquisitive eyes, "is what are they hiding from *you*?"

That thought was eating its way through my ego when I got outside. Father Ted's old-lady Buick Skylark was still in the parking lot. My station wagon was parked next to it, and I waited for him behind the wheel, knowing he would eventually complete his duties in the chancery and leave the grounds.

The rain had stopped two hours earlier and the heavy gray sky was lifting when he emerged. A cold wind ruffled his long black overcoat and mussed his thinning hair. He looked tired and somber and preoccupied with his thoughts. He didn't see me sitting in the wagon until I rolled down the window and spoke his name.

"Get in, Ted." I could hear impatience gnawing at my voice. "I want to talk to you."

My uncle glanced over at a news crew loading equipment into one of the network vans and decided it was better to talk privately in a closed vehicle.

"You didn't have much to say in the meeting," I began.

I hadn't turned on the engine and there was a raw chill in the car. He sat quietly in the passenger seat with his hands in his overcoat pockets and his neck tucked into the wool collar.

"It looks like you padres are playing the *privilegium fori* card. 'We take care of our own.'"

He stared through the fogged windshield at the tall evergreen hedge running alongside the stone wall of the chancery. "Nobody has used that privilege in a hundred years, Peter," he said.

"When the district attorney and the police investigator agree to turn their heads and let the Bishop handle it," I said, "that sounds *privilegium* to me."

He seemed as disillusioned as I was. "It's now in the hands of lawyers," he said, speaking directly to the windshield. "There's not much you and I can do about it."

My uncle suffered from diabetes, and his listless demeanor concerned me. I wondered if, in all this turmoil, he'd forgotten to give himself an insulin injection.

"Ted, you didn't answer the question I asked you this morning."

You lived under the same roof. How in God's name could you not have seen what was going on?

"I don't condone child molestation, if that's what you want to hear, Peter. Father Landry's behavior was vile and criminal. May God have mercy on his soul."

"I don't understand how he could've been carrying on like that in your rectory for so long."

When my uncle became angry, his voice dropped to a near whisper, his method of controlling himself. "I've already gone over this with Detective Duhon. He understands that I travel a great deal, conducting retreats on weekends in other parts of the state. And that I'm not at home every night," he said. "The detective was very courteous and considerate. It upsets me, Peter, when a stranger is more respectful than my own nephew."

I loved my uncle and didn't want to hurt his feelings more than I already had. But I thought he was letting himself off too easy.

"Detective Duhon hasn't seen the videos, Ted. If he ever does, he may not be so courteous. There's footage of Landry in your rectory. God knows where else."

He opened the car door and planted one polished black shoe on the damp concrete, then decided against departing so abruptly. He swiveled in the seat to face me directly for the first time since he'd sat down. "The Vicar-General has given you an assignment, Peter. I suggest you devote your undivided attention." Message delivered with a healthy measure of admonition. "You do your job, I'll do mine. Let's leave the recriminations in the gutter, where they belong."

My uncle slid behind the wheel of his Skylark and started the engine. Waiting for it to warm, he was lighting a cigarette when I tapped on the glass. He looked up, startled.

"There's one more thing," I said as the window whirred, lowering halfway. "Martin had an accomplice. Somebody who worked the video camera while he played his sex games. I've heard the man's voice."

Ted stared at the dashboard, processing the information, taking a long pensive drag of the cigarette. His doctors had warned him to stop smoking. It had a negative effect on diabetes. He stubbed out the butt in the car ashtray, showing the discouragement that comes when you thought you'd already heard the worst. "My God," he said, "this is unbearable. Do you have any idea who it might be?"

"I was going to ask you the same question."

He shook his head, confused and speechless, a rare state for him. And then he shifted into reverse, backed out of the parking space, and drove away.

I hunkered down in the old wagon until the last news truck was gone and there was no chance of running into Sharon. Back inside the chancery, the building's mood had returned to silence and furtive shadows. In the small meditation garden outside my office window, the gray morning fog was spun like Christmas-tree angel hair around the gnarled, bare branches of the wild plum trees. I sat at my desk and stared at the cardboard box filled with the damning evidence of Martin Landry's crimes. My assignment, as Ted had called it, was a filthy business and there was a long day ahead of me. I was already exhausted and I didn't think I could muster the energy, so I called home to hear Ann's voice again.

"Have you told Matt?" I asked her after a warm exchange.

"He's pretty upset," she said. Landry was his religion teacher at Our Lady of Sorrows. "I've called some of the fifth-grade mothers. Everyone's in shock."

Matt was our gregarious, lighthearted ten-year-old, maker of many friends, the center of attention wherever he went. His older brother, Luke, was very different. Luke had always been a solitary child given to brooding, but now that he was sixteen and in the full clinch of adolescence, he'd become even more surly and difficult. His grades had begun to slip and he was in outright rebellion against schoolwork. For days on end he remained moody and nonverbal. Ann assured me this was typical behavior for his age, but we sometimes looked at each other and wondered who had kidnapped our son and replaced him with this tall, rangy, melancholy stranger living under our roof.

"Is Luke home yet?" I asked.

"I called Roberto and he said the boys are still asleep. There's no telling when they went to bed."

Dr. Roberto Hinojosa was a Honduran-born surgeon whose wife had lost her battle with breast cancer when their sons were only six and ten years old. Stephanie had been our favorite parent to hang out with at birthday parties, ball games, and back-to-school nights. In the six years since her death, we'd helped Roberto as much as possible, feeding his sons at our dining table, treating them to movies, driving them to school while their father was saving lives in emergency surgeries. The good doctor did his best to be involved, but he was pulled in a dozen different directions.

"When you have time this afternoon," I said to Ann, "I want you to explain something to me."

There was a pause on her end. "About Father Landry?" she asked.

"Help me understand how a pedophile operates."

She hesitated. "Most of what I know is confidential, Peter," she said.

"I don't want the details of your client's . . ." I stopped mid-sentence. "Ann, will you tell him I would like to speak to him?"

"You know I can't do that," she said.

"I'm not sure how far back this Martin Landry thing goes. Maybe fifteen or sixteen years. The older victims are going to be more helpful than the recent ones."

She paused again, reflecting. "Why are you involved in the investigation, Peter? This is police work. You're a PR guy, for Christ sake, not a detective."

My task was morally complicated and she would not have approved of the buyoffs, the lack of transparency, the absence of responsibility.

"I've been asked to give the police and the DA whatever help I can," I said, although that wasn't true. The diocese and our lawyers were intent on keeping everything to themselves.

I was beginning to understand why the Bishop hadn't attended our discussion about legal settlements and reparations. It was the first time the concept of *plausible deniability* had crept into my head. If something went wrong, the Rottweiler would take the bullet for His Excellency. He would swear before a judge and jury that the Bishop had not been present and had not sanctioned what his staff was doing.

"One thing you should understand about Father Landry's victims—the ones who are still children and the ones who are now grown men," Ann said. "His death may free them or it may make things worse. Some will cheer. Some will grieve. Some will regret they didn't get a chance to punch him in the face."

"Or crush his skull with a cinder block," I said.

I picked up a framed photograph from my desk, our sons when they were younger. I smiled at how beautiful they were. I couldn't imagine how we were going to tell loving parents what had happened to their boys.

"Confronting their abuser is what a whole lot of them have been preparing to do for years," Ann said, "and if their abuser dies before that can happen, it's unfinished business that may bother them for the rest of their lives."

After we hung up, I studied the name and phone number of the private investigator neatly penned on the back of Russell Gautier's business card. Vincent Scalco. I knew the man Mr. Gautier had recommended. New Orleans was a small town, really, when it came to schools and social circles. Vince was a grade ahead of me at Blessed Benildus and I knew some of his personal history. This was going to require more emotional investment than a simple phone call.

To delay the inevitable, I thumbed through my Rolodex for the phone numbers of my staff members. It was a Saturday morning, and

I found them all at home. Beth Sanders, the editor of publications, had already heard the news through the grapevine, and so had the irascible Father Norbert, our whisky-voiced radio commentator and self-proclaimed Christian broadcast expert who resided in the community of retired priests at the seminary. They were both upset by Martin Landry's murder, but fairly subdued compared to Barbara Lavergne, my executive assistant, who burst into tears when I told her.

"He was such a wonderful priest," she kept saying through breathless sobs. "Why would anyone want to harm him?"

Why, indeed. I stared at the name Vincent Scalco and the phone number on the back of the business card, took a deep breath, and lifted the receiver.

SEVEN

WHEN I DROVE INTO THE FRENCH QUARTER THAT AFTERNOON, the bars and narrow sidewalks were teeming with tourists, despite the raw air and heavy gray cloud cover. Vince Scalco leased an office on the second floor above a landmark corner café owned by the same Italian family for seventy years. In the early nineteenth century, the building was the private residence of a wealthy mercantile mayor of New Orleans, who'd hatched a plot to rescue the exiled Napoleon from St. Helena and instate him in opulent living quarters the mayor had prepared on an upper floor. An urban legend persisted that the suite of rooms remained exactly as Mayor Girod had readied them in 1820, the same drapery and antique furnishings and the same fading French flag mounted above a fireplace.

Two blocks from Jackson Square, the café was a local favorite beloved for its distinctive New Orleans cuisine and raffish, weather-stained stucco façade. In the dining area, the chipping, patinated plaster walls were covered with framed photographs, family portraits, and yellowed drawings, all of them hanging askew for decades. I entered an unassuming side door and found the stairwell and Scalco's small business card Scotch-taped to a metal plate next to the buzzer. I set the box of videotapes on the gritty floor, pushed the button, and waited. One of those three-wheel Amigo scooters was parked in the tight space, the kind that disabled people rode around in supermarkets. A Mardi Gras cup stained with bright red lipstick, a soggy roll of toilet paper, and other trash littered the floor. This didn't surprise me. I wasn't expecting Vince to office in a brass-and-mahogany corporate suite at the top of the Ritz Carlton. He wasn't Napoleon, after all.

I pushed the button a second time. I could hear a woman crying somewhere up the stairs. After another long silence, the intercom squawked: "Yeah, what can I do you for?"

"It's Peter Moore."

"I'm with a client, Pete," the intercom said. "Be a minute. Come on up to the crow's nest and grab some pine wherever you can."

I carried the box up a stairway covered in dingy carpet. The top landing was crammed with cardboard packing crates and a stack of discarded tables and broken chairs from the café below. The woman was weeping on the other side of a door whose smoked glass panel was stenciled in black lettering:

VINCENT SCALCO INVESTIGATIONS
PRIVATE, DO NOT ENTER

I sat on a wobbly throwaway bar stool and tried to overhear their conversation. It was a bleak, moody scene straight out of a pulp detective novel. A woman in anguish, the clatter of dishes in the café below, the rancid smell of a grease trap. I couldn't picture the well-heeled attorney Russell Gautier walking up those dingy stairs to hire Scalco's services.

When I called on him that day, Vince was meeting with a mother whose fourteen-year-old daughter had run away from home two weeks earlier and hadn't been heard from since. It was a long wait on the bar stool, but eventually he opened his office door and walked his client out with a consoling hand on her shoulder. She was a diminutive woman in her mid-thirties, dressed in jeans and a light jacket, with big shoulder-length blonde hair permed in curly spirals. All of my nieces wore that same hairstyle in the 1980s.

"It's gonna be all right, tee na na," Vince said, New Orleans slang for *little mama*. "I'll find Leah fuh ya and bring her on home." While giving his client an avuncular hug, he glanced over her shoulder and winked at me.

I hadn't seen Vince Scalco since his son's funeral four years earlier. Spending long hours above a café wasn't a good idea for him. He'd gained forty pounds from eating fried shrimp po boys every day at lunch with a couple of Brandy Alexanders. His head was almost as large as a medicine ball, with an oddly shaped mop of thick black hair that occupied his scalp like a dyed wig. He was cleanshaven and smelled of either cologne or scotch whisky, I couldn't decide. Rainbow suspenders held up an acre of pleated pants, and he shuffled around in soft canvas boat shoes that had long ago raised the distress flag.

"How's it hanging, Pete? Jeezum, man, you ain't aged a day since Jack Kennedy was banging Marilyn Monroe," he said, shaking my hand with a warped smile. He was watching his client descend the stairs in those tight jeans. "No sign of a Nwalins' tumor, either," he said, patting his corpulent belly. "You must be working out at a gym, you bastard."

Because of my job with the diocese, I had returned to short, well-combed hair, a straighter version of my Kookie Byrnes ducktails in high school, but without the Vitalis. I hadn't worn specs since the invention of contact lenses in my early college years, but at age forty, I was beginning to feel the need for reading glasses.

"Thanks for making time to meet with me on such short notice," I said, stooping to pick up the box. "I hope I didn't disrupt anything."

"It's all oaks and herbs, man. Come on into my penthouse."

With a mellow Ninth Ward accent that sounded more Brooklyn than south Louisiana, Vince spoke like the musician Dr. John. *Dis and Dat. Where y'at?* As long as I'd known him, he'd been clever at inventing words and phrases, usually a concoction of jazz scat, New Orleans street lingo, and his parents' Americanized Italian.

At his desk he showed me a stack of posters the mother had made at Kinko's with little Leah's photograph, a phone number, and the message *Leah, please call home.* She'd chosen a school picture of the girl, who looked like every innocent young brown-haired girl wearing a school uniform blouse and hiding her braces behind a tightlipped smile.

"This is my thing now, Pete. My spess-e-al-ity. I'm the great white hunter that brings 'em back alive," he said with his arms spread wide, gesturing at his shelves of manila file folders. I looked around his attic-like office and noticed a television set and VCR in one corner of the room. "As long as the family structure keeps going down the shitter, business is hunky dunky, my man. I'm getting so rich and fat, I just might buy myself a dancing monkey and a snowball machine."

He studied the girl's image on the poster. "Same old story," he said. "Single mother in denial about the creep boyfriend she's cribbing with. A boozer and probably a doper, too. Talks dirty to the kid, rubs on her when the mother ain't at home. What I really wanna do for Carrie Bordelon and her runaway daughter," he said, turning to me with a strange dark glee in his eyes, "is smack the boyfriend around, maybe grab his nuts and see how he likes being bullied by a cat that can hurt him. But I don't usually offer that service until you get to know me better. At least not on the first date," he said with a wheezy laugh. "I listen to everybody's soap opera, Pete, and hand them a Kleenex," he said, nodding at the box on his desk, "and I hold the mother's hand while she comes unglued telling me about her heartache. Sometimes I wonder if there's enough Kleenex in the whole damn world to cover the grief that walks through that door."

Before they kicked him off the police force, Vince Scalco had been a cop for nineteen years and knew the street. But he'd become an expert on teenage runaways the hard way. His son, Ned, started disappearing when he was Leah's age, and Vince managed to bring him back home every time except the last one.

Something had been pricking my conscience for too long, and I needed to address it. "I feel terrible about not calling when you and Martha were going through your divorce, Vince. I'm not doing a very good job of keeping up with old friends," I said. "I think I'm becoming my father. I go to work, come home and eat dinner, spend a few quality minutes with the family, and then it's bedtime. I never get a chance to sit down and call anyone. I'm sorry about that, Vince. I really am."

"Don't worry about it, bro'. It's done. Nobody's keeping score," he said, dropping his large body into a well-worn leather chair behind his desk. "How is my man Luke?"

Although Luke was four years younger than Ned, they had played on the same Little League baseball team, and I was the assistant manager that season. Between innings, Vince and I usually leaned against the cyclone fence near the dugout and shot the breeze like we did when we were bench warmers on the Benildus High football team, riding the pine and talking about girls and Wolfman Jack's radio show until the coach yelled at one of us to go in and spell a starter for a down or two.

"Luke is going through a tough time right now," I said, knowing Vince would understand. "Ann and I don't know what's bothering him and he won't talk about it."

"It's a hard call at his age. You don't want him to get away from ya too fast. And you don't want him to live on your couch till he's forty. But I wouldn't worry about Luke," he said. "He'll be all right. Nobody with that smile is ever gonna break his old man's heart."

Vince locked his hands behind his head and rocked back in the chair. "I never made a poster with Ned's picture on it, or checked out the missing teen networks and all that jive. I didn't do any of the sensible things I advise my clients to do now," he said, gazing up at the ceiling. "I went after Ned like a cop, pulling some shit I'll regret for the rest of my life."

Besides losing his son, he'd also lost his job and eventually his marriage.

"After he died and some things came out, the cops I'd cruised around with for years wouldn't look me in the eye anymore. I had *bad news* written all over me, like Job." He lowered his double chin and regarded me with a fond smile. "Remember reading the Book of Job in Brother Jerome's class? Tell ya the straight honest truth, Pete, for a solid year I was pretty much living on a dung heap. The diff being Job was a righteous standup guy and I was an asshole father and all-around son of a bitch. I got into this private snoop business to pay some bills and maybe do some good with what's left of my life. And the lesson I've learned is that misery damn sure *does* love company, my friend, and mothers like the Bordelon woman—who's got a deep hole in her soul right now—will walk on sharp splinters to get her kid back."

I was worried about Vince. Darkness and gloom had claimed his days, as the Bible said. Trouble had come to his heart and he had no peace.

"Do me a solid and don't tell Father Ted I stopped going to church," he said. "I used to light candles and pray for Ned to come home safe and sound. I did everything the Brothers taught us to do, man. Throw yourself at God's mercy, pray hard on your knees, and believe in miracles."

There was a catch in his throat. He tried to slow down and breathe. After a moment he pulled what looked like a small light-brown pebble from his pocket and placed it on the desk. "I'm still carrying around a fucking fava bean," he said, laughing at himself. The New Orleans Italian families considered fava beans to be good luck, their version of four-leaf clovers. They ladled cooked fava beans onto the food-filled St. Joseph's Day altars they created for their special feast day every year.

"I got so desperate, I axed a hoodoo lady to come by and scrub my front steps with red-brick powder," he said.

I knew the local superstition. Red brick was supposed to have magic powers and remove evil spells cast over a household. People used red bricks to scratch X marks on voodoo priestess Marie Laveau's grave.

"I did all the right hocus-pocus, Pete, but it didn't make a damn bit of difference. I still lost him."

His emotions were raw and he was still in mourning and too angry at himself to accept my words of solace. But I wanted him to hear them anyway. "You loved Ned and tried to save him, Vince," I said. "That matters."

He pressed his hands on the desk, lifted his huge body off the chair, and made his way to the tall green shutters that opened onto a wrought-iron balcony. "When I was a rookie walking patrol, I hated this shit-bag part of town," he said, stepping out into the gray mist. "Long days, nasty drunks, and always a fucking bottle aimed at your head. Now look at me." He raised his arms like the pope blessing crowds in St. Peter's Square. "*King of the dung heap!*" he bellowed.

I joined him on the small balcony. Packs of tourists were stumbling around in the damp streets below, shouting and singing, already loaded at two o'clock in the afternoon. The usual hustlers tagged along on their flanks, trying to con them out of a few bucks with their shuck-and-jive routines. *Mistah, I bet I know where you got dem shoes.* A band of loud frat boys wearing LSU football jerseys was roving underneath the balcony and they stopped to applaud Vince and bow to him like subjects before their monarch.

"Pete, I'm never gonna forget that tear rolling down your cheek at Ned's funeral," he said, waving to them. "It showed me the kinda guy you are. And what kinda father I shoulda been. I admire you for keeping the faith and believing in honor and decency . . . good and evil . . . things that don't change. But I've lost my faith, brother," he said, "and if the Bishop's people are looking for a good Catholic boy to do this gig, I'll need to borrow a cup of your faith till I get back on my feet."

The poor man thought I was some kind of plaster saint. "I'm not a Boy Scout, Vince," I said. "I don't believe half the stuff the nuns taught us from the Baltimore Catechism. I question my faith every day."

Outwardly, I was a devout Catholic who worked for the diocese and Our Lord's holy servants on earth. Inwardly, I'd always been skeptical of many tenets of Church dogma, even when I was an idealistic seminarian fresh out of high school. *Transubstantiation* troubled me. The doctrine that priests have the power to turn bread and wine into the actual body and blood of Jesus Christ. Bread to actual flesh, wine to actual blood. Cell for cell. Transubstantiation wasn't mere symbolism, the Church insisted, it was real. I remembered Sister Catherine of Siena telling us second graders that we shouldn't chew the consecrated host at communion but let it dissolve in our mouths. Chewing was sacrilegious because it would hurt Jesus. And she told us that a young Catholic girl once chewed the host to see if anything would happen, and her mouth filled with blood.

The Christian Brothers had counseled us that it was healthy to grapple with vexing spiritual dilemmas and to challenge our beliefs, but sometimes there was no rational explanation for what we were required to believe. Imperfect and fallible, the sons of Adam, we were duty bound to choose faith over reason, and to reconcile our doubts with the teachings of the Church.

To ingratiate myself with my employer, I made sure that Ann and our family attended Mass every Sunday and on holy days of obligation. We sent Luke and Matt to Catholic schools and encouraged them to become altar boys, as I had been. But we were what disapproving clerics called *Cafeteria Catholics*, because privately, Ann and I would pick and choose which doctrines we adhered to and which ones we didn't. We quietly ignored several papal decrees. We practiced birth control, as did most of our Catholic friends, contrary to the papal encyclical condemning contraception. And after years of soul-searching, Ann and I had come around to supporting a woman's right to terminate her pregnancy, even though we wouldn't have done that ourselves. Not after the miracles of Luke and Matt.

In reality, Ann was a far more pious Catholic than I was. She firmly believed that Jesus was the Son of God and had risen from the dead. It didn't matter to me if he was or wasn't, if he did or didn't—his teachings were virtuous and inspiring, and I followed them.

Ann embraced a loving God and trusted in the power of prayer. I doubted that God kept tabs on our every thought, word, and deed, but I prayed anyway.

Ann yearned to understand the deeper mysteries of the soul. She read the Church mystics, St. John of the Cross and St. Teresa of Ávila, and she puzzled through the convoluted theology of Father Teilhard de Chardin. I had had my fill of those explorations in the seminary, but I admired her relentless pursuit of the ineffable.

"So what the hell did you bring me, Pete?" Vince asked with a bewildered grin as he left the balcony and stepped back inside his office. "A box of holy cards?"

I told him what I knew at that moment. The phone call from my uncle, the body in the tub, Landry's collection of videotapes, sex toys, and magazines. I was surprised that he didn't have a more visceral reaction, but he was a veteran cop who'd witnessed his share of vice.

"You knew this priest?" he asked.

"We were in the seminary at the same time. And he taught religion class to Luke and Matt at Our Lady of Sorrows."

"You didn't make this guy for a pervert? He didn't give that vibe?"

His eyes narrowed and he seemed disappointed in my weak intuition. It was the same suspicious question I'd asked Father Ted.

"I had no clue he was capable of abusing nine-year-olds," I said. "I never liked the man, Vince, but he was a priest. You went to twelve years of Catholic school just like I did. Could you ever imagine? . . ."

New Orleans was a Catholic city, founded by French colonizers and their missionaries. Mardi Gras owed its existence to Lent. St. Patrick's Day celebrations were for the Irish, St. Joseph's Day for the Italians. Perhaps because of that dominance, the Protestant kids in my neighborhood often belittled the Church, its foreign rituals, its Latin gobbledygook. They were the same idiots who thought John F. Kennedy would take orders from the Vatican. They made jokes about priests buggering altar boys and sneaking through underground tunnels to have sex with nuns. We smug Catholics laughed at their ignorance. But after Father Martin Landry, I wondered if we had the moral authority to laugh anymore.

Vince lifted the lid off the box and chose a videotape, examining the label. "You want me to deep-six this crap for the team?" he asked.

I explained what the job entailed.

"So all we gotta do is find out who these kids are and give the info to Russell Gautier?"

"It's not going to be easy, Vince. Landry was stationed in four or five parishes. There's even an eight-millimeter home movie from way back. We'll have to scrounge up a projector."

"Can you get your hands on his jacket? You know, his work history?"

"Every priest in the diocese has a file in the diocesan archives down the hall from my office," I said, one of the few things I was confident I could access.

I watched him return to his seat in the leather chair behind his desk. Walking fatigued him. He was breathing hard, and I became concerned about the extra weight on his heart. That's when I realized that the Amigo scooter downstairs belonged to him. I would soon learn that he suffered from high blood pressure, cardiac arrhythmia, and asthma. His doctors had berated him for years to limit the alcohol, get some exercise, and improve his diet. Given the terrible shape he was in, I wondered if Vince Scalco would live to see fifty.

He retrieved an asthma inhaler from his desk drawer and sucked a quick dose into his lungs. "I know how to find runaways," he said, slumping back with his eyes closed, absorbing the inhalant. "A little dirty work on the street. Some inside juice with old buddies on the force. Plus it helps to get lucky sometimes," he said, opening his eyes and shaking his head glumly. "But this is gonna be different."

I explained the need to work quickly and quietly before an army of plaintiff lawyers got involved and the whole thing blew up in public. "I know you're a pro, Vince. I'm sure I don't have to remind you that what we're going to do is confidential and very delicate."

This amused him. His entire body shook with winded laughter and he produced a handkerchief and wiped his face and eyes. "A Catholic priest fucking little boys?" he said. "Who's gonna get upset about a thing like that?"

There was an ornate handmade wood cabinet against the wall behind his desk, where he kept a full stock of liquor. Shuffling to his feet, trying to contain his laughter, he opened the cabinet door and chose a bottle of Johnnie Walker Black standing tall and masculine among an impressive collection of gentlemen's amber whiskies.

"Do you know a police detective named Ray Duhon?" I asked him. "He's in charge of the investigation."

He wasn't surprised to hear the man's name. "Ray and me worked a few cases back in the day. Had a drink or two, *di tanto in tanto*. Ray's all right."

"He was with the DA this morning at the chancery, working things out with the black robes and lawyers."

He scooped a handful of ice cubes from the mini-fridge next to the liquor cabinet and dropped them into a tumbler. "Rockin' Roger Finney is a slick prick of the first order," he said. "The brothers in blue have never trusted the man. He'd hang the entire force out to dry if it bought him votes and made him look like a prince on the evening news."

Pouring scotch over the ice, he went on. "Brother Ray and me busted our humps on a gangbanger case for a year, honeymooning a crackhead snitch in the Magnolia projects, keeping his pipe lit for intel. We were one wire away from taking down a bad boy gang leader named Tyrell McGee with a lot of blood on his hands. When the snitch and his ten-year-old brother ended up in a car trunk with their hands tied and a nine-em hole in the back of their heads, Rockin' Roger lost his nerve and shut the sting down. The man's got tiny *coglioni*, Pete. He's better at going after small-time chiselers and singing Vic Damone tunes at high-dollar fundraisers. Which is why we cops had to take care of scum like Tyrell McGee ourselves."

He tasted the scotch and offered to pour me a glass, but I declined.

"Finney's got Ray on the case 'cause he's good at keeping his trap shut," he said. "Ray'll make sure the public don't hear this Father Landry dude was a predator."

"So Duhon's under instructions to look the other way?"

"It's best to stay out of their business, Pete. We've got our own play," he said, gesturing with the tumbler at the box on the floor. "Let's stick to the plan. I could use the bread."

I sat down in a chair next to the box and told him about the black teenager in the rectory, Landry's gold wristwatch, the arrest. I couldn't stop thinking about that young man pounding on the window of the squad car, begging for my help.

"That kid didn't kill Landry," I said. "Can you put me in touch with Duhon? I want to talk to him about this."

"Let it slide, bro'," he advised. "Maybe the kid's dirty, maybe not. I know what Duhon's thinking. Keep it simple. Court-appointed attorney naps through the arraignment and hearing. Slam dunk conviction. The kid goes away, hard time at the Angola farm. Case closed. One more crackhead off the street."

I was disturbed that his conscience would allow him to live comfortably with that cynical scenario. "I understand if you don't want to get involved, Vince," I said. "I'll call Duhon myself."

"What you gonna tell him, Pete? Your story will put you at the crime scene before the cops got there. You gonna tell him you and your uncle tampered with evidence? That you walked off with these videotapes and have no intention of giving them to the police?"

"It wouldn't surprise me if Duhon and the district attorney already know about the tapes," I said, nudging the box with the toe of my shoe. "The Bishop probably told them this morning."

"You sure about that? Because if the Church's sweetheart deal with Finney goes south, you can bet that prick will turn on you and Father Ted and Mother Teresa herself if it covers his own political ass. I can promise you how it's gonna go down. The Bishop will say he didn't know there were videotapes and everybody will believe him. If they need a scapegoat, you and your uncle will be the guys Finney and the Roman Catholic Church will hang a noose around."

Already feeling the abrasive coarseness of that noose, I loosened my tie. I realized I was chewing a fingernail. I didn't want to believe something like that could happen. But the minute I'd walked away from the rectory with that cardboard box, I knew I was in a compromised position.

"This has gotten way too complicated," I admitted aloud. "And to be honest, Vince, I really don't know who to trust right now."

He sipped his Johnnie Walker Black and smiled at me. "You can trust *me*, Pete," he said, "as long as the check clears."

Noise from the café below was drifting up through the floorboards, a dull white drone of voices and clanking plates. I sat forward in the chair, my forearms resting on my knees, trying to think everything through. After a few moments lost in a tangle of bad outcomes, I leaned over and stared into the box of videotapes. It looked like insurmountable work ahead of us.

"Okay, Vince, you're the expert," I said finally, glancing at the VCR and TV set in the corner of his office. "Where the hell do we start?"

EIGHT

THE CIRCUMSTANCES OF NED SCALCO'S SUICIDE were not widely known at the time of his death, only that he'd taken his life in a sleazy French Quarter flophouse notorious for its quick turnaround sex trade. In those days, the Church wouldn't perform burial rites for suicide victims, meaning no Requiem Mass and no interment in consecrated ground. The rationale went something like this: In the final moments of their lives, suicides may have despaired and cursed God. Your body is God's property and only He can decide the moment of your death. Suicide is self-murder and a mortal sin; ergo, the perpetrator is going straight to the eternal flames of hell.

Vince's pastor had declined to conduct the funeral ceremony, and Vince and his devout Italian Catholic family were distraught that young Ned would be laid to rest in a non-Catholic cemetery without a priest's blessing. I called Father Ted to complain about this, and he visited Vince and Martha in person. Two days later, my uncle presided over a full service, with altar boys and smoking incense and ringing Sanctus bells. He performed the rite of committal at St. Louis Cemetery near City Park, a Catholic cemetery with magnificent marble tombs and mausoleums that predated the Civil War.

"It really ticks me off when the Church turns its back on God's most vulnerable children," Ted said afterwards, as we walked together to his car. "Sometimes I want to throttle my brethren for their hard-line callousness. Jesus would not have given up on Ned Scalco."

For his grace and mercy, my uncle received an official reprimand from Vicar-General Karl Fulweiler, although Ted didn't give a damn.

Ned's body had been anointed and buried in sacred ground, and Vince and his family had found consolation.

When we were working on the Martin Landry case, Vince eventually revealed to me the disturbing details of his son's death. He'd cut his wrists with a razorblade and bled out in a bathtub in that flophouse on the dark edge of the Quarter, far from the rowdy promenade of tourists. Ned was sixteen years old. There was cocaine, THC, and alcohol in his system. Vince said that the room had been paid for by an elderly gentleman who registered using an alias. He was described by the desk clerk as well-groomed and cordial, with the persuasive charm of a traveling salesman. Or a clergyman. There were no signs of struggle. The man had apparently checked out immediately after sex and left Ned on his own. The case was still open, in deference to Vince, although he assured me that he was the only person interested in finding the elderly john. He didn't want to hurt the man, he said, but I found that difficult to believe. He told me he wanted to talk to him about his son's mental state during his final hour.

One of the things that got Vince in trouble was his harassment of the flophouse owner. Vince pulled his service pistol on the man, pressed the barrel against his forehead, and threatened to blow his brains out if he didn't close his place down. A few days later, Vince showed up with a gas can and threatened to torch the building. This did not sit well with his superiors on the police force. It was the beginning of the end for Vince's career in law enforcement.

On that foggy gray afternoon in his office, the day after Landry's murder, my old schoolmate and I watched the videotapes labeled *Rectory 1* and *Rectory 2* with a workman-like intensity, jotting notes on lined yellow pads. Vince tried to maintain his professional composure, but he'd miscalculated how viscerally he would react to watching young boys being sexually abused by a priest. I could see that he was becoming more agitated as the videos rolled on in slow and agonizing detail, and I asked him if he wanted to take a break.

"I'm gonna need another drink," he said, running his hands across his loose damp jowls and into that strange black hair that appeared fake but wasn't. When he tried to stand up, he discovered that his legs had gone to sleep. He stomped his feet several times on the old hardwood floor, alternating right and left, dragging the soles of his blue boat shoes as if cleaning them.

"I wish that sick bastard was still alive so I could have the distinct pleasure of cutting his dick off. *Madre di Dio*, I might've crushed his skull with a cinder block myself," he said, hobbling to the liquor cabinet and pouring more scotch over ice. He popped a blood pressure pill into his mouth and raised the glass, saying *Salute, Pietro*. "A couple more of these in me, I might be able to stomach Father Butt Pirate's home movies."

We had established a viable system, pausing tapes to discuss how to classify a boy, his hair color and facial features, his body type. At Vince's suggestion, we gave them nicknames—variations of the Seven Dwarfs. Chubby. Smiley. Red. We weren't frivolous about it. There was no humor in our process.

The *Rectory* tapes were recorded entirely in Landry's bedroom and included nine victims in total, a mix of well-scrubbed Catholic schoolboys and scroungy ghetto kids straight off the streets. He usually kept the two groups separate, and it became obvious why. The ghetto kids were tougher, surly, rude, unimpressed with the title *priest* and its spiritual significance. They laughed whenever they called him *Father Marty*, as if they thought it was a sick joke, this exalted term for a man who was doing what no father should do to his sons. Landry always paid the ghetto boys afterwards. "You can probably use some spending money," he said in one tape. "Here, buy something nice for yourself." Twenty dollars, thirty, whatever he had in his wallet. But he didn't pay the good Catholic boys. They submitted themselves to him for the fondness and special attention he gave them. He was their teacher and priest, after all. Their mentor. They wanted to please him. *Many are called but few are chosen*. They were the chosen ones.

"The thing about this Father Landry creep, he wasn't some pathetic little toad living with his momma," Vince said. "He was out there, man. Livin' large. So fucking full of himself."

There was return trade, the same victims coming back on later occasions, some of them indifferent to the camera by then. I thought about how guilty and shameful they must've felt when they woke trembling in the middle of the night. I thought about their parents, who were going to be infuriated by this betrayal of trust from a man who should've been beyond reproach. And I thought about the boys' exposure to sexually transmitted diseases, especially HIV. Had Landry put them all at risk? Having sex with street hustlers was an invitation to disaster.

At that point in time, the 1980s, HIV and the search for its cure had been widely covered by the media, and we knew that in the US it was infecting the homosexual population first and foremost. In those early years, I wasn't aware of any friends or acquaintances who'd been stricken by that mysterious virus. (Ann's young cousin and others close to us would begin to die soon enough.) But I was as frightened and misguided as everyone else about a deadly disease that might kill you through a mosquito bite.

Near the end of *Rectory 2*, the camera captured a party taking place in Landry's bedroom. The phantom cameraman was making wry comments as he floated about the room, flirting with the boys, coaxing them to strike the poses he desired. I wondered if the party last night was anything like this one, with the phantom recording it all. Although Ted had told me that the camera's tape slot was empty.

"Hold up right there!" Vince said, setting aside his fresh drink. "I know that boy. I've seen him selling his ass on the Fruit Loop."

The Fruit Loop was a drive-around block on the far side of the Quarter, a loop that johns made in their cars, crawling along and eyeing the male hookers loitering on the sidewalks. It was drive-thru sex. Johns selected hookers and then circled the block with heads bobbing in their laps. Vince had cruised the Fruit Loop on many dark nights, searching for Ned.

"His name is Trey," I said, writing the name on my pad. "At least that's what the cameraman called him in another tape."

We froze the image of the longhaired teenager sitting cross-legged on Landry's bedroom floor, smoking a cigarette and drinking straight from a wine bottle, his oily hair falling into his eyes. Vince studied him, lost in memory, and then scribbled a note.

"Any idea who that other sicko is, the one holding the camera?" he asked.

Sometimes Landry fixed the video camera on a tripod when there was no one else in the room except him and a single boy. At other times the camera roamed about, a furtive malevolence crawling out of a dark corner, like a night creature patiently stalking its kill. The man behind the camera spoke infrequently, and when he did, he was terse, sinister, perniciously playful. *He doesn't w-want you anymore, and you've g-got to punish him.*

"I don't recognize the voice," I said. Taking notes, concentrating on identifying the victims, it was easy to forget that someone was actually filming these travesties. "He has a slight stutter. I keep waiting for Landry or one of the boys to say his name."

When we rolled the video again, the greasy-haired boy named Trey looked amused by a wrestling match going on in the center of the room.

"Whoa, and there's the black kid," I said, pointing at the screen. "The one they booked for Landry's murder."

Stripped to his underwear and laughing, the black teenager was wrestling a white boy much younger and half his size. They were scuffling around on the carpet, the blond kid fighting his hardest but no match for the bigger boy who eventually pinned him face-down. The others started cheering and hooting.

"You'd better fight harder, Stevie," said Martin Landry off camera. "You know what happens to the loser."

Vince and I both wrote the name *Stevie* on our notepads.

While the wrestling continued, the camera slowly panned the bedroom. "Pause it right there," I said, and Vince punched the pause button. "Does this thing have a zoom? See that kid sitting on the bed? Can you zoom in on his face?"

Vince examined the selections on his remote control, found the right button, and brought the face into larger view. It was David Hinojosa, one of Roberto's sons and a boy Luke had stayed with overnight.

"You know this kid?" Vince asked.

"I'm afraid I do." An alarm went off in my head. I stood up, my stomach churning. "Vince, I've gotta go home now."

NINE

WHENEVER ANN AND I NEEDED TO DISCUSS A SERIOUS DOMESTIC ISSUE, we shut ourselves into my home office and lowered our voices. It was the small compact room where I'd viewed the first videotape, my personal lair of random icons and practical amenities: a PC clone and telephone, bookcases, a file cabinet with no apparent organizing principle, three of my mother's pastoral paintings, and the boys' artwork from when they were much younger. During those conversations, I always sat in my swivel desk chair while Ann sat on an antique settee she'd reupholstered in blue fabric patterned with tiny pineapples.

"I don't know what to do. I can't tell Roberto about the tapes," I said. "Nobody is supposed to know they exist. Not even you. I'll lose my job, Ann. Remember what that was like?"

She looked stressed from everything that had taken place since early morning. She'd canceled her routine seven-mile run with her running group and had spent the day in rounds of phone calls and the complex logistics of preparing for grief counseling schoolchildren. Her auburn hair was shapeless and pulled back behind her ears, and although it was late afternoon, she was still wearing the long pink pajamas she'd slept in.

"And believe me, if I screw this up, no one will ever hire me again," I said. "PR people value trust and confidence above all other things. Leaking sensitive information is a professional death sentence."

"Roberto is our friend," Ann said. "David and Rico, they're like our own sons. Ah, Jesus, I'm thinking about Stephanie. We've got to find a way to tell him."

"Okay, let's calm down and sort this out," I said. "David was sitting on a bed at a party. That's it. I've looked at most of the tapes and I haven't seen him having sex."

"*Most of the tapes* isn't good enough, Peter. We don't know how many boys Father Landry had sex with but didn't videotape. He had some kind of perverse Mickey Mouse Club going on, and probably every boy in the club, abused or not, has dark knowledge of Landry's behavior. That's going to leave a deep emotional scar on all of them."

When Luke had returned home a couple of hours earlier, bedraggled and exhausted from staying up half the night playing Nintendo games, Ann told him about Father Landry. She said that Luke was shocked and held back tears. Then he went to his bedroom and fell asleep.

"I'm worried about . . ." I began, imagining the worst-case scenario. "What if . . ." I had trouble articulating my anxiety to Ann. "What if David and Rico and Luke were in the rectory last night?"

My question stunned her. "What makes you think that, Peter?"

I hesitated to tell her more than she needed to know. But at that point it was ludicrous to play mind games with my wife and best friend.

"Landry's bedroom looked like a party had been going on. Wineglasses, cigarette butts, maybe even pot. The room was messed up. Things were knocked over and broken. Landry probably fought back." I scratched my unshaven jaw, thinking about what might've transpired. "Somebody dragged his body into the bathroom and dumped him in the tub. I don't know if he was still alive when they weighed him down with a cinder block. It took a lot of physical strength to pull that off. I'm starting to think more than one person was involved."

Her pretty Irish face had lost its natural blush. Seconds passed between us. "Luke came home in borrowed clothes and muddy shoes," she said finally. "He said they got caught out in the rainstorm."

Exactly what I didn't want to hear. "Christ, Ann, maybe they were there."

She rose from the settee, clearly unsettled. "Let's go find out," she said.

I stood up and embraced her, pulling her warm body close. "We've got to keep quiet about the tapes," I whispered. "You know how this works better than I do, Ann. It's like doctor-client privilege. We can't say how we know about David. Not to Luke . . . or Roberto. Not to anyone."

Ann knocked firmly on Luke's bedroom door, and when he didn't answer, she opened the door and went in ahead of me. "Wake up, sweetheart," she said, kneeling beside the bed and giving his shoulder a gentle shake. He was sleeping on his side, breathing through his mouth, the covers pulled to his chest in the chill room. She smoothed her hand through his wavy brown hair, like she did when he was a toddler, and gazed at his handsome face. He was our firstborn, and her tender, wistful smile revealed her unconditional love for him. In that sweet moment, sixteen years had vanished and I was back where we began, her unexpected pregnancy, the sonograms and birthing classes, the months of belly rubbing and all-natural diet and the nesting instinct to prepare the crib and finish decorating his room on the day before he was born.

"Come on, wake up, Luke," she said, shaking his shoulder. She peeled back the covers, found one of his hands, and rubbed it to make him warm. "We've got to talk."

Luke managed to open one eye and say, "What are you doing in my room? I really need to sleep."

He was in that surly phase of teen years when his attitude was inching toward disrespect. Lately he'd begun to pick on his brother, and he'd violated his weekend midnight curfew on several occasions, leading us to ground him for long periods of time. A couple of months earlier, during the Christmas holidays, he and some friends were busted for drinking alcohol at night on the dark playground of a neighborhood elementary school. The school's patrolling security guard was kind enough to call us rather than turn him over to the New Orleans police.

"Sit up, Luke," I said in the sharp-edged tone of male authority. That usually worked. "This is about Father Landry. About what happened last night."

He remained silent and motionless, collecting his thoughts, it seemed, or perhaps calculating what to say. He roused slowly and leaned back against the headboard. "That's such a mindblower," he said in a voice rendered hoarse by lack of sleep. "Do they know who did it yet?"

"They have a suspect," I said. "A street kid who claims he was invited to a party at the rectory. Do you know anything about that? We thought maybe you'd heard some boys talking. Did anyone mention a party at Father Landry's place last night?"

Luke massaged his eyes with the heels of his hands. "Nobody at Benildus hangs with Father Martin anymore," he said. "He's ancient history."

When all of this took place, Luke was a sophomore at my old alma mater, the Catholic high school on St. Charles Avenue. He hadn't had daily contact with Martin Landry since the eighth grade, but the altar boys from Our Lady of Sorrows often stayed in touch with their former religion teacher and sometimes joined the younger boys at the Landry family's fishing camp on the coast.

Ann examined Luke's muddy Adidas kicked off by the bed and the scatter of clothing borrowed from David Hinojosa. "Where are *your* clothes, Luke?" she asked. "I just bought you that nice new pair of jeans."

"We got drenched in the rain. I threw them in the dryer at David and Rico's."

I exchanged glances with Ann. We shared the same disquieting thought. Blood? Had they washed their clothes? I looked at our sleepy-head son, the first glowing light of our hearts, and couldn't imagine that he might be involved in violence.

"Don't you boys have the good sense to stay inside during a thunderstorm?" I said. "What were you doing out there?"

Luke yawned and shrugged. "We walked down to the Prytania to catch a movie. *Dune*," he said. "It started raining so hard you couldn't hear the film. The ceiling was leaking all over the place, so they shut down the movie and gave us our money back. Which was cool, because *Dune* is pretty much a pile of crap. We tried to wait out the rain, but the a-holes at the movie theater wouldn't let us hang around inside. We had to go for it. It was like running through a car wash."

"You should've found a phone and called us," I said. "I would've picked you up. You know that."

He shrugged again, his eyes drooping with fatigue. "It's not that far to their house," he said. "It was an excellent adventure. I outran them both."

Ann was standing next to the bed with her arms folded, her face inscrutable. I didn't know if she believed him. She and I could usually tell when our sons were shading the truth, or if something was bothering them and they needed to get it off their chests. Luke was calm, albeit half asleep, and his explanation sounded plausible to me. He had to know that we could call the movie theater to check on his story about the leaky roof and the film shutting down. I felt relief that there were no obvious contradictions in what he'd said.

"If you hear anything about Father Landry, please tell us," I said, gently squeezing the tendon between his neck and shoulder blade, one of my signature signs of affection since he was a small child. "Anything you hear from your friends, okay? Rumors, whatever. That young man they have in custody—he may have had accomplices. We're trying to sort it all out."

He gave me a wan smile. "Are you officially working on this thing, Dad?" he asked. "You know, communications director, etcetera."

"I bet my answering machine at the chancery has maxed out with calls. It's going to be a busy time at work. You may not see me very much for the next several days."

He slid down beneath the covers and plumped the pillow under his head. "Man, your job sucks," he said, burrowing in for a longer sleep. "I mean, you know—*spin,* isn't that what they call it? Always having to spin something."

"I usually don't have to do that," I said.

Matt suddenly appeared in the doorway, absent his happy-go-lucky smile. "Are y'all talking about Father Landry?" he asked. He had his mother's beautiful face and lovely blue-green eyes, with a constellation of freckles spread across his nose. It was rare to see him in a glum mood.

"Please go away and talk about this somewhere else," Luke said, irritated now, burying his head under the pillow. "Personal space violated. Must have sleep."

His mother assured him we would discuss this again soon and we left his bedroom, closing the door behind us. Downstairs, I took Ann aside in my office while Matt went foraging through the refrigerator.

"His reaction was pretty normal, don't you think?" I said in a low voice. "I didn't pick up any weirdness. I hope to God he's telling us the truth."

"I checked his hands and face," Ann said. "No cuts or bruises or swelling. If he was involved in some kind of struggle, wouldn't there be obvious signs of it?"

I smiled at her. I understood now why she'd taken his hands and tousled his hair. It was a mother's way of expressing love while searching for hurt in the flesh and bones of her child.

"What about David? What are you going to do about him?" she asked.

"I need some time to figure that out."

"Don't take too long, Peter. Hours, not days. Roberto has to know that something may have happened."

"I agree, Ann. But there are so damn many things to consider. Luke is right—I'm spinning a lot of plates in the air right now. I've gotta go to the chancery and check phone messages and take care of some other things. Landry's death may go national. Priests aren't murdered every day in this country."

The way she looked at me, I knew something else was on her mind. She kissed me on the lips and hugged me, resting her head on my chest. "My client called a little while ago," she said. "The one I told you about. He'd heard about Father Landry and he was very upset. He wants to talk with me as soon as possible."

"Oh Ann," I said, separating myself at arm's length to study her face.

"I know," she said, patting my chest and looking away. "You've got your confidences, I've got mine."

TEN

IT WAS NEARLY DARK ON SATURDAY EVENING when I drove to the chancery. That rainstorm the previous night had left in its wake a debris field of downed oak limbs and palmetto fronds floating in streets slow to drain. The streetcar tracks were blocked by fallen branches, and chainsaws were buzzing in the cool gray twilight. Vehicles abandoned on the neutral grounds had still not been claimed by their owners.

As I pulled into my parking space, I thought about what Vince Scalco had said when I was leaving his office: "Go get the priest's file, man. It's gonna tell us all his dirty little secrets. Maybe even some names we can work with."

The Office of Archives, its official title, encompassed what had once been the library and adjoining study hall for Ursuline novices when the building was their convent. The diocesan archives dated back to 1777, originally stored by monks in the Presbytere, next to the cathedral, in the heart of the French Quarter. Most of the early records were written in Spanish or French, the storage drawers now a repository of crumbling certificates for baptisms, first communions, confirmations, marriages, funerals, and interments in a score of Catholic cemeteries scattered across the city and surrounding parishes. The head archivist was Sister Ellen Livaudais, a Dominican nun with light Creole features who was fluent in three European languages and had once taught high school Latin. She employed a staff of diligent young archivists, fresh out of college, who answered queries and mailed photocopies all over the world. She'd recently hired a professional conservator who was renowned for helping to restore the Renaissance archives and artworks of Florence after a devastating flood, and whose latest mission was to preserve *ad aeternam* every yellowing scrap of our diocesan heritage.

I had no idea how long it would take me to read through Martin Landry's file. I'd brought my leather briefcase with half a mind to confiscate the file, in case Vince was right that I would need a bargaining chip in later negotiations. Landry's file would make a splendid companion to the videotapes I was already holding.

It was the weekend, and burglar lights were glowing in strategic positions inside the building. I carried a flashlight to aid me in my stealth, Watergate style, and its beam jittered through the empty corridor ahead of me, leading the way. Security cameras were not yet installed. That would happen a few years later.

There was a crevice of light underneath the sturdy oak door to the archives office, and my first thought was that someone was working late. Possibly Sister Ellen or the conservator. I did not have carte blanche to roam freely through the archives. As a matter of courtesy, and following house rules, I always sought Sister Ellen's approval and guidance for whatever project my staff and I were researching for the diocesan newspaper. But on that excursion, I had already succumbed to the cold hard grip of paranoia and I was determined to avoid disclosing my interest in the Landry file to anyone else.

When I served as director of communications, all senior staff members received heavy bronze keys that gave us access to the front entrance of the chancery and most other office doors, except to the Bishop's suite. The keys were entrusted to us as though they were the Keys to the Kingdom. I trained the flashlight on the lock and used my key, and the deadbolt rang like a pistol shot in the quiet building. I stepped inside the reception area and called out, "Hello, is anybody here?" The silence was eerie and unnerving, as if I'd entered a mausoleum vault. I closed the door behind me and repeated myself in a louder voice: *"Is anyone here? It's Peter Moore in communications. Hello?"*

In those days, the archives were still housed in the original cypress file drawers and bookcases removed from the Presbytere in the 1970s and relocated to these offices. But the new conservator had discovered nests of Formosan termites burrowed deep in the woodwork—little winged vermin infesting the entire French Quarter by then—and over the next year he would replace those elegant old woodcraft masterpieces with sterile metal slide-drawers, bookcases, and filing cabinets that were the very definition of utility over beauty.

A spooky air of secrecy and decay overshadowed that sealed space. The room temperature was cold enough to chill wine and the lighting was minimal, per the conservator's decree to reduce light exposure and heat around all the decomposing paper. The flashlight was my guide as I wandered through the narrow aisles between tall bookcases. The shelves were crowded with deteriorating histories of the Church in *La Nouvelle-Orléans*—family records, pious treatises and memoirs, catechism textbooks, an endless assortment of missals, prayer books, breviaries, and hymnals in various languages. I was familiar with the personnel files, which we commonly referred to as "the morgue." In a recent issue of the *Catholic Spirit*, our diocesan newspaper, I'd used those records to write a profile of a courageous Czech priest who'd escaped the Soviets in the early 1950s and ended up as a pastor in a Bywater parish.

The morgue dominated an entire wall on the far side of the bookshelves, its heavy wood drawers meticulously labeled by some long-dead monastic calligrapher. I slid open the drawer labeled *K - M* and directed the flashlight beam across the file dividers, running the fingers of my free hand through the *L* folders: *Lacoste, Bernard; Lambert, Mary Louise; Lanier, Stanley.* There was no *Landry, Martin* and no slip to indicate that someone had removed the file. I looked again, slower and more carefully this time, one file after another. No *Landry, Martin.* I backtracked through the end of the *K's* and on through the rest of the *L's*, in case it had been misfiled close by.

"I gave it to your uncle," said a voice behind me.

I whirled around, nearly swallowing my tongue, and aimed the light at the hazy figure standing between bookcases. She raised her hand to deflect the glare against her glasses. It was Sister Colleen.

"He took it with him," she said.

I sputtered a few incoherent phrases, rushing to explain why I was there. Nothing I said made a bit of sense.

"I don't know exactly what's going on, Peter," she said, "and I suspect you don't either. The full picture, I mean. There are things happening around here that concern me. The Bishop and Vicar-General are being tightlipped about what happened to Father Landry. I've been shut out. Stonewalled by the boys' club. How about you?"

What could I tell her? I was sworn to secrecy.

"I'm in the weeds, Sister." She and I had always been trusting colleagues and I hated to lie to her. "I don't know what's going on, either."

I'd never seen Sister Colleen in civilian clothes. She was wearing a baggy Notre Dame sweatshirt, male work boots, and male khaki pants that were unflattering to her large thighs. She looked dressed for doing home repairs, painting a bathroom or laying tile. I hadn't realized how *substantial* she was.

"Why are you looking for his file?" Her question sounded more like innocent curiosity than prying.

"The Bishop wants me to write a feature story on Landry for the *Spirit*."

A white lie. A lightly salted fabrication.

She returned to a small carrel where she'd camped out. I could see a notepad and pencil on the desk, a stack of books, and a Diet Coke can that was strictly forbidden in these rooms.

"I read Father Landry's file when he first came here," she said. Her posture was slightly stooped, and when she sat down heavily on the carrel's chair, she wouldn't look at me directly but opened a book and spoke into its pages. "I'd heard through the grapevine that he'd just completed a long stay with the Paracletes in New Mexico."

I knew very little about the Servants of the Paraclete, as they were known, a male religious order whose retreat compound ranged across two thousand acres of Church-owned land in a remote area north of Albuquerque. Their ministry was to care for priests and brothers who were suffering from various addictions and psychological disorders. When I was in the seminary, one of our teachers referred to their retreat as "the place where we send all the drunks and nut cases."

"I wanted to know what kind of damaged goods we were getting," she said. "What was his vice? Alcohol? Pills? Women?" Her eyes shifted away from the book and settled on me. "You probably know by now."

I nodded.

"Dear God," she said, shaking her head in grim acknowledgement. "Children."

It was a rare occasion when Sister Colleen showed emotion. She'd always been the tough, wry, unflappable gatekeeper of the Bishop's private domain. I was surprised by the softness in her voice, the vulnerability.

"Sister, if you knew about Landry," I said, sounding more accusatory than I intended, "why didn't you keep an eye on him?"

My question sent her to a long drink of Diet Coke. For several awkward moments she seemed to be pondering what I had asked. The silence surrounding all those ancient chronicles descended upon us like a black cloak.

"I was told that he was cured," she said with a tinge of sarcasm. "The Paracletes had released him. He was rehabilitated. A new man. His consecration was restored."

I turned off the flashlight and leaned back against the bank of file drawers. We stared at each other, two figures stranded in the pallid safety lights. "Did you discuss your concerns with the Bishop?" I asked her.

"One doesn't discuss such delicate matters with one's superiors," she said. Years of resentment simmered in her tone. "Who am I—a nun, a lowly secretary, a *woman*—to question the wisdom and authority of Church fathers?"

"And so you let it go, Sister?"

She placed a bookmark between the pages in front of her and drank more Diet Coke. "Not entirely, Peter," she said. "I mentioned my concern to Father Landry's new boss. The pastor of the parish he was assigned to." She paused. "Your uncle."

My uncle again. A man I'd trusted and loved and at one time wanted to emulate.

"I like Father McMurray enormously," Sister Colleen said. "Everyone does. I felt comfortable asking him in confidence if he knew why Father Landry had spent time in New Mexico."

"And?"

"He said he knew why."

The coldness of that place was seeping into my body, even with my winter jacket on, and I folded my arms for warmth, contemplating what was troubling me: How much did Ted know, and what was he hiding?

"Peter, when I was in my twenties and thirties, I was a pretty good-looking gal, especially for a nun," she said with a girlish giggle. "To begin with, I was forty pounds lighter than I am now and I had a great head of blonde hair I had to cut short and hide under a wimple. When Vatican Two came along, I was ready to open some windows, as Pope John said we should do. The Church had become musty and oppressive, and I jumped head first into all the changes going around. You know, the English Mass and guitars. Doing away with the traditional habit. And during that exciting time, I allowed myself to fall in love with a young Jesuit priest who was doing social work in the St. Thomas Housing Project. He and I and some others had set up a homework house in one of the units, and we were tutoring project kids who had no quiet place to study at home."

She turned on the little lamp at her carrel, its beautiful green Tiffany glass forming a perfect orb of light over the desk. I saw now that the volume she'd been looking through was a school yearbook. "This is him here," she said, smiling fondly at the photograph. "Father Joseph Dombrowski, Society of Jesus."

I walked over to peer down at the photo of a young priest in the Jesuit High School yearbook for 1964. It was the same year I'd met Ann in college.

"Father Joe was a big shambling guy with a crew cut when I first met him, more like a football player than a Civil War scholar who'd published articles. He taught history at Jesuit High in the mornings and came to the homework house every afternoon. You wouldn't know by looking at him that he was a gentle man, especially with the children we worked with. They adored him. He had that special something all great teachers have. Charisma, patience. Every time I was around him, my knees turned to Jell-O." She laughed, her eyes transfixed on the photo. "And he felt the same way about me. Love at first sight, I suppose. We tutored kids for three or four months together before he found the courage to touch my shoulder and kiss me. I almost *devoured* him. We came very close to having sex on our secret first date in a car borrowed from the Jesuit residence. We didn't have enough money for a motel. The vow of poverty is hell on date night." She laughed again. "I hope this doesn't shock or embarrass you, Peter."

"You've got my full attention, Sister," I said, staring at the image of a large round-faced man wearing a Roman collar and an enigmatic smile. "It's the only happy story I've heard all day."

She removed her glasses and placed a hand on the page, as if caressing his face. "It didn't end well," she said. "I was ready to renounce my vows and marry him, but he wasn't ready to leave the priesthood. So we had to go our separate ways. I stopped tutoring, stopped seeing him, because it was too painful to be together. Too tempting to throw myself into his arms. I cried over that man for a solid year. I suppose I was greatly relieved when he was transferred to Chicago. I've never seen him again or spoken to him. It's been twenty years now, Peter. And I haven't fallen in love again."

I was deeply touched that she would confide in me her most personal story. "That's heartbreaking, Sister. I'm sorry. Truly sorry for both of you."

Celibacy was one of the reasons I'd dropped out of the seminary. At age nineteen, I was far too distracted by young women to forever deny their appeal.

Sister Colleen closed the yearbook and said, "I guess what I'm getting to, Peter, is if priests could marry—if all of us in the religious life could have spouses and raise children together, while still doing God's work— the Church would be much better off. We'd have a healthier family environment. Church mothers as well as Church fathers. Because this is what I've understood for many years, my friend: the Church hierarchy is a good-old-boy network of bachelors and misogynists who are indifferent to families and children. *There*, I've said it. They're obsessed with rules and rubrics and ancient books, and they don't give a damn about two people falling in love. We're being bullied by feudal barons, Peter. Except this bunch of barons wouldn't know what to do with a bawdy wench if one dropped in their laps."

It felt good to laugh. She laughed, too, and wiped the moisture from her eyes.

"Call it instinct, Peter. Call it female intuition, I don't care. If wives and mothers lived in the same rectory with a child molester like Martin Landry," she said, dropping the *Father* as I had begun to do, "the bastard would've been outed long ago. Arrested, sent to jail, whatever. And those children would've been spared the indecency that will scar them for the rest of their lives."

Sister Colleen had made a persuasive argument about what was missing in the Church of Rome. Family values, a family culture. How did it come to pass that for several centuries a group of steadfastly unmarried men had been making decisions for married couples and their children?

I picked up the yearbook the good sister had been looking at and absently leafed through its pages of postage-stamp photographs.

Hundreds of Catholic schoolboys in uniform, their clubs and class activities, their sporting events.

"Do you have any idea when my uncle will return Landry's file?" I asked her.

"He didn't say."

"A day? A week?"

"I have no idea, Peter. He called and asked me to let him in to view the file, then decided to take it with him. I protested—it's against policy for anything to leave this room—but he insisted it was safe in his hands. What was I going to do? Tackle the man?"

"What if he destroys the file, Sister?"

She considered my question while draining the can of Diet Coke. "Then so be it," she said. "I won't cover for him."

I thumbed through more pages, amused by the photos of Mardi Gras floats and parades, the debate team, the homecoming queen and her court from the all-girls Catholic high school nearby. It was no different than my yearbooks from the same time period.

And that's when it struck me. Photos of Catholic schoolboys. Hundreds of them.

"Sister, are there yearbooks from other schools?" I asked her, checking the cover.

She turned and gazed at the rows of bookcases that receded into a distant pool of darkness. "A few years are missing here and there," she said, "but there's supposed to be an entire set for every school in the diocese, going way back."

"Where are they kept?" I asked, following her line of sight. "Where is Our Lady of Sorrows?"

ELEVEN

MY UNCLE HAD MANAGED TO AVOID THE STALKING MEDIA for an entire day, as only a priest could, concealing himself in the secret labyrinths of clerical life like an early Christian avoiding capture in the dark winding tunnels of the catacombs. I had lost track of him myself. But when I arrived at the Church of Our Lady of Sorrows, counting on him to keep his hours for Saturday evening confession, I was dismayed to find the church besieged by TV news vans, scorching set lights, and reporters roaming the grounds, trying to interview winter-clad parishioners hurrying to their cars in the damp weather.

A lone patrolman was sitting behind the wheel of his police cruiser parked in the breezeway between the church and rectory. I got out of my car and approached his vehicle, giving him a friendly wave. He raised a hand, more like a lazy pointed finger than a greeting. I recognized him as one of the cops who'd arrested the black kid named Kwame. The officer rolled down his window. A mournful country tune was playing on the radio, and the burnt-Styrofoam smell of convenience-store coffee wafted from the warm interior.

"Good evening, officer. I'm Peter Moore with the diocese. We met this morning," I said, glancing over at a reporter being videoed next to the yellow crime-scene tape hanging limply across the rectory door. I wondered if my uncle intended to stay there overnight while the reporter and her pals banged on his door at all hours. "I'm looking for Father McMurray. Is he hearing confessions in the church this evening?"

"Another ten minutes and he slams it shut," he said, checking his wristwatch. "My partner is stationed at the front steps, Mr. Moore, making sure these idiots keep their distance."

I walked around to the front of the church. The other patrolman was posted as an armed sentinel under the lights of the alcove, braced for those chill hours in a bulky jacket and watch cap. He'd been alerted by walkie-talkie that I was coming, and he removed a glove to shake my hand. The double doors behind him looked like the fortified gates of a gothic stronghold built to withstand a legion of fallen angels. And reporters from the local networks and Baton Rouge. They had camped on the small plaza, their light stands arranged in a semicircle and pointing expectantly at the stone steps.

"Peter!" It was Sharon Simon, emerging from the cluster of reporters. "Hey, wait a second!"

The officer opened one of the doors for me and I slipped quickly inside the church, avoiding her for the moment. The vestibule was silent and as low-lit and gloomy as a mortuary. The church itself was even darker and smelled like spent sulfur matches and melted candle wax. The pews were empty, and a stooped old lady, the last of the penitents, was making her way slowly up the aisle, wearing what looked like a white cloth doily bobby-pinned to her lank hair. She dipped her fingers in the holy water fount, made the sign of the cross, and frowned at me.

"Why don't you people leave him alone?" she asked in a shaky voice, glancing back in the direction of the confessional, a tall double-curtained closet located in the rear of the church. "Things are hard enough on him already, what happened to Father Landry and such."

"I'm not one of *them*," I said, wetting my fingertips in holy water.

I pulled aside the violet curtain of the confessional booth, knelt down on the cushion, and closed the curtain, enclosing myself in darkness. Father Ted slid open the window, and in the faint light I could see him staring straight ahead behind the crisscross mesh. "Bless me father, for I have sinned," I began, making the sign of the cross. "It has been three weeks since my last confession."

I hesitated, listening to his blessing, unsure of what I was going to say. I took the ritual seriously, that holy sacrament of reconciliation, and I felt morally compromised by everything I'd done. Noting my silence, he said "Go ahead, my son" in a quiet, comforting voice.

"I have lied, Father. I am a witness to mortal sins and felony crimes that have brought shame and suffering and the loss of innocence. I'm unhappy with myself for remaining silent while children of God are living with a horrible betrayal. I'm guilty because of my knowledge and complicity, Father. And so are you."

My uncle sighed deeply, dropped his chin, and sagged in the chair. After a moment of reluctance, he turned his head to look at me through the mesh. "Not in here, Peter," he said.

"What have you done with his file?"

"Let me go have a word with the police officer out front and lock up the church," he said. "Meet me at the side altar of the Sorrowful Mother."

Radiant lighting from the cameras outside had little effect on the cool dark sanctuary of the church. We sat together on the first pew, facing the rows of flickering red votive candles and their coin box. On her perch above the small side altar, a bare marble slab with two tall unlit candles ensconced in gold candlesticks, the grieving Blessed Virgin gazed down upon us with her lips parted in anguish, her hands clasped for mercy, and seven daggers piercing her heart, one for every trauma inflicted on her son. My uncle unlatched a metal briefcase and withdrew Martin Landry's file, dropping it onto the smooth wood bench between us. It was a substantial collection of paper.

"What am I going to find in here, Ted?" I asked, staring at the olive-green cover. "Did you discover anything you didn't already know?"

He scratched his scalp with an annoyed expression, an old and familiar tic that meant he was going to say something that made him ill at ease. He turned to search the empty church behind us, as if some snoop reporter might be hiding behind a pillar.

"Peter, there's something you should know," he said in a near whisper. "I have a homosexual orientation."

I wasn't sure if I had heard him correctly. *Orientation*, did he say?

His face softened into a sad smile, as if a great weight had been lifted but he wasn't certain whether to rejoice at his disclosure or to retreat back into the dark comfort of a long-held secret. "I'm gay," he said, this time louder, less guarded.

Remembering that moment many years later, I'm surprised at how unprepared I was for my uncle's revelation. He was a priest before I was born, and I hadn't thought of him as capable of having a sexual orientation of any kind, straight or gay. It had never crossed my mind. He was a celibate man of the cloth, pure and simple. Something we

Catholics accepted without question. Over the years, Father Ted and I had discussed many things, spiritual and otherwise. A man rising from the dead and ascending into heaven, the Council of Trent, the homerun race between Mantle and Maris, the assassinations of the Kennedys. But not celibacy and the so-called denial of the flesh, not sex. And so his admission caught me off-guard. I'd always considered myself open-minded and progressive, and my views were often unpopular among friends and relatives in the conservative city where I was born and raised. I confess that my uncle's divulgence made me uncomfortable, and when I think back on that moment years ago, I'm disappointed that my response was no response at all, simply an awkward speechlessness.

"It took me a very long time to come to terms with this," he said. "I was already ordained and in my late twenties when I finally acknowledged to myself what I knew in my heart. I thought I was abnormal, with some sort of sexual disorder you might find in a treatise by Freud or Kinsey. I dared not tell anyone, even though I knew there were other priests and seminarians like me. All in the closet, of course. But the world was very different then, Peter. We didn't talk about these things, not even in private. We were at war with the Germans and Japanese, and I was blessing caskets coming home from Europe and the Pacific. In those days, 'four-effer' was the worst thing you could call a man, because it meant he was unfit for duty. Weak, a sissy. When brave all-American men were dying every day overseas, there was absolutely no tolerance for queers and fairies."

What I had always appreciated about Father Ted was that he treated me as an adult. Even when I was twelve years old, he carried on conversations with me as if we were intellectual equals. But this sudden admission had left him more vulnerable than I'd ever seen him. He was visibly embarrassed to be speaking so freely to his nephew, but compelled by some unleashed confidence to continue on.

"I'm telling you this, Peter," he said, "because I want you to know where I'm coming from and why Father Landry's behavior is so difficult for me. I'm gay, all right, but I'm not a pedophile, for Christ sake. When I was a young man, I may have lusted in my heart, but that was the extent of it. I do not tolerate adults—whether straight or gay—who prey on children. And neither did Jesus. But I fear that most people don't understand the difference, Peter. Gay men in stable

long-term adult relationships . . . pedophiles who target little boys . . .
we're all the same in the eyes of the public. That bigotry troubles
me and many gay clerics, and that's why we dread revelations about
priests like Martin Landry. We're all tarred with the same brush."

It was a great deal to take in, especially because it was such a personal account from a cerebral scholar who rarely revealed anything
personal.

"I understand what you're saying, Ted. But are priests and bishops
harboring these sex offenders? Are you making it easy for them to live
under a safe tent?"

He seemed frustrated with me, impatient. Perhaps he thought I
was pointing a finger at him. "We can't just abandon them, Peter," he
said. "They're ordained Servants of God. They've received holy orders
and are expected to lead a consecrated life. We have to help them overcome their horrible proclivities and rehabilitate them."

Proclivities was the word he used. I opened the cover of Martin
Landry's file and tried to read the first page in the dusky candlelight.
All I could decipher was the letterhead from the Servants of the Para-
clete in New Mexico.

"What about due diligence, Ted? Did you bring him into your
parish without knowing his full history?"

A wolf in sheep's clothing had crept into his pasture.

"His Excellency was very persuasive," he said, gazing at the opened
file. "He assured me that Father Landry was incapable of ever straying
again. Martin had agreed to take regular injections of a drug called
Depo-Provera. They call it chemical castration. It kills the libido. He
was supposed to take it for the rest of his life. That was the deal I made
with the Bishop. If Martin vowed to stay on his drug therapy, he was
welcome to be my assistant pastor," he said. "The man deserved a
second chance. We all do."

"So what happened, Ted?"

His eyes betrayed his remorse and confusion. "I don't know, Peter.
Either he stopped taking the injections, or they didn't work anymore."

We stared at each other in silence. I was the one to speak first. I
told him about the videotapes I'd watched with Vince Scalco. Nine
victims recorded, probably more off camera. We hadn't begun to identify their names yet. It was going to be a long and arduous process.

"Christ almighty," he said, exasperated, hunching forward and covering his face with his hands. "This is deplorable. I thought he was doing fine."

He remained that way for several quiet moments in the candle-guttering murkiness surrounding us.

"You want to know the pisser?" he said finally, lifting himself, dropping his hands in his lap. "Martin didn't consider himself gay. Because he wasn't attracted to boys once they reached full puberty. I read it in his file. The thought of grown men having sex with each other was repulsive to him. He believed he was a straight guy with one unfortunate weakness. He told the Paracletes that he admired the ancient Greeks—married men with a boy or two on the side."

Landry's denials and rationalizations were almost laughable, had they not been so reprehensible. "He was a priest, Ted. Whatever happened to the vow of chastity?"

He made that barely audible tsking sound that usually signaled his disapproval. "The vast majority of my fellow priests are celibate, Peter," he said with cold certainty, "and we've been celibate all our lives."

As my uncle and I knelt to pray together before the statue of the Sorrowful Mother with seven daggers in her heart, I thought about the young Sister Colleen and the Jesuit priest and their love for each other. It was at that moment that I began to believe that celibacy was the single most destructive mandate of the Roman Catholic Church.

"Jesus, I'm dying for a cigarette," Father Ted declared after a few minutes of silent prayer. "Let's get out of here."

To avoid the media circus out front, he opened the gate of the communion rail and we crossed through the night shades of the sanctuary, where he would celebrate Mass the next morning to a shocked and grieving flock. I followed him into the sacristy, the dressing room where vestments and sacred vessels were stored, and where priests garbed themselves and gathered with their altar boys before proceeding out to perform the liturgy.

"I hope you're not staying in the rectory tonight," I said, helping my uncle into his overcoat, which he'd left hanging on a coat tree. It reminded me of when I was a nervous young altar boy at six a.m. Mass, assisting him with the chasuble, straightening it on his shoulders.

"They've graciously prepared a room for me at the seminary. I may hide out for a few days, until things die down."

We slipped out the back door of the church and shuffled down the steps into the cold night air. The patrol car was gone, and so was the video crew. Ted paused to fire up a cigarette. We thought we were escaping unnoticed until a flashlight beam flared sharply into his eyes.

"Father McMurray," she said, startling us. "May I have a word with you?"

My intrepid reporter friend stepped out of the darkness.

"Father has had a very long and difficult twenty-four hours, Sharon. Let's do this some other time," I said, taking him by the overcoat sleeve and escorting him toward his car parked behind the rectory. Martin Landry's file was tucked under my arm, and I was trying to conceal the typewritten label from her light.

"There are reports that Father Landry was murdered in his bedroom," she said. "Where were you when it happened?"

"Please, Sharon," I said, urging my uncle to speed up his pace. "Let's talk tomorrow."

"I'm not speaking to *you*, Peter," she said dismissively, the flashlight beam bouncing on the pavement in front of us. "Father, did you see that young suspect—Kwame Williams—in the rectory last night?" She was walking next to Ted now, shoulder to shoulder, bumping him, slowing us down. "Were you able to identify him as the killer?"

Ted stopped abruptly, shook loose from my hand, and dropped his cigarette on the ground, extinguishing the embers with his shoe. "Miz Simon," he said in a soft hush, "I was out of town at a retreat and came home to find Father Landry's body. It was a terrible shock, as you can imagine. The police have asked me not to talk about it in detail. They say it will hinder their investigation. I suggest you speak with them."

Free from both of us, handler and inquisitor, he opened the car door and lodged his tall rigid frame behind the wheel. Sharon bent slightly to question him through the closed glass window, like a penitent in a confessional, but her voice was raised. "Are you satisfied that the police have the right man in custody?"

My uncle cranked the engine, smiled cordially at her, and drove away into the damp moonless night. I marched quickly toward my own car parked across the street, Landry's file under my arm. Sharon trotted after me and tugged at the back of my London Fog.

"Are you running from me, Peter? Stop, damn it."

I reached the old station wagon, turned and braced my back against it, giving her the stone-cold silent treatment. She shined the flashlight on my crossed arms, the file clasped protectively underneath them.

"Have you checked your answering machine lately?" she asked with considerable irritation, the light lingering on my chest. "It's maxed out. Full. Which means a hundred news outlets are trying to get in touch with you. This is a big story, Peter. And if you let some slick major market a-hole from Houston or Atlanta scoop me, I will fucking strangle you. You understand that, right?"

"I haven't said anything to anybody, Sharon. You know who I work for. The world's oldest covert society, with two thousand years of secrets buried in a vault underneath the Vatican. Like you said, they don't tell *me* what's going on."

"I thought it was your job to disseminate information to the media, Peter. So *disseminate*, for crying out loud."

I opened the car door and tossed Landry's file onto the passenger seat as I crawled in. "Go home, Sharon. If this story leaks overnight, it won't be by me," I said. "I gave you my word I'd speak to you first— when the time is right—and I mean that."

But I had a nasty feeling I might not be able to keep my word to anyone in the days and weeks ahead.

"Did you see the body, Peter? Just tell me how he was killed and I won't bother you for, ohh, let's say another eight hours."

"Go home and read a good book, Sharon. Watch mindless TV. Give yourself some down time."

"What have you got there?" she asked, directing the light through the window onto the file lying on the passenger seat. Had she noticed Martin Landry's name on the label?

Watching her in my side mirror, I pulled away as fast as the old wagon could accelerate, splashing rain puddles in every direction as I pressed onward into another restless night.

TWELVE

I HAD BEGUN TO READ MARTIN LANDRY'S FILE in my study when the phone rang. It was Vince Scalco. "I found Trey," he said, sounding drained and in his cups.

"Glory be!" I said, astonished. "How the hell did you do that, Vince?"

Vince was a natural storyteller and a humorous mimic of other people's voices, and over the course of an hour, he related the long, detailed account of what had happened to him in the French Quarter.

Not long after I'd left his office, he had dinner at his favorite table in a café facing Jackson Square, where he could observe the Carnival revelers capering about the central garden while he enjoyed a couple of whisky sours with a basket of redfish beignets and a large bowl of chicken and andouille sausage gumbo. Watching the revelers gave him great pleasure. It took him back to his boyhood enchantment with this city of make-believe, when his father used to haul a tall stepladder to the corner of Napoleon Avenue and St. Charles on parade days so his little son could view those marvelous, magical float pageants from an unobstructed roost.

In New Orleans, Carnival season commenced on the Feast of the Epiphany, the sixth of January, and although Mardi Gras Day was always several weeks away, the Uptown gentry and the art crowd soon began hosting private costume balls. Vince had heard that tonight's merrymakers were destined for the *Scuola Vecchia* masquerade ball underway in an elegant hotel behind the cathedral. They were the usual gaudy lot, he said, dressed for the theme of nobility in Renaissance Italy. Silk capes festooned with sequins and shiny baubles, a spectacle of maroon velvet and full gauzy gowns and frilly sashes, long swords dragging their steel tips across the slate gray flagstones of the square.

At some point, two uniformed cops Vince knew from the force ambled past the café, and the partygoers taunted them at a safe distance. Vince admitted that he was quite content to be nursing his third whisky sour of the evening and not out there on the job with those poor bastards in blue, fielding insults from drunks and stoners who liked to play cat-and-mouse games with the city's patrolmen. He noticed a short middle-aged man escorting the beat cops and speaking into a walkie-talkie, a plainclothes detective in a rumpled overcoat and loosened tie he recognized as Ray Duhon. His old partner noticed him sitting at the café table and gave him a quick smile.

"Say, Vinny, it's that time of year again," Duhon said, walking through the wide-open doors into the café. "The circus is in town."

The detective offered his outstretched hand, saying, "Like the shark said out in the desert, 'Long time, no sea.' What's doing, *paisan?*"

Vince grinned and raised a sauce-dripping beignet to show him that his hands were too messy to shake.

The two patrol officers had followed Duhon into the café. "Better go easy on them fat pills, Scalco," said Buddy Couvillion, a cocky young cop Vince had never liked. "You could stand to lose a few."

"Suck my dick, cooze breath," Vince said with an edgy smile, using the nickname he'd bestowed upon this jerk when he was a rookie.

"This your ride now, Scalco?" asked the other cop, a black man named Rodney Junius who was suppressing a laugh at the Amigo scooter parked at the table like a quiet guest. "What's your top speed on this thing, five miles per?"

Vince was displeased that the cops had interrupted his dinner and people-watching entertainment, and he was doing his best to ignore them. A pig-masked nun clothed in a coarse medieval habit trudged past the café doors, pulling a rope tied to a skinny guy wearing only a loincloth, exhibiting him like a wretched sinner on a leash while a bird-beaked peasant scourged him with a cat o' nine tails.

Duhon sat down at Vince's table with a weary thud. "How's tricks?" he asked. "You making any money in the snoop trade?"

"I should crack the Fortune Five Hundred any day now, Ray."

Vince soon realized that the nun, sinner, and flagellant peasant were leading an austere religious procession, preparing the way for

the main act trailing behind them, what appeared to be a Renaissance pope surrounded by altar boys outfitted in traditional cassocks and surplices. The pope was a jolly man with rouged cheeks,
wearing what Vince described as a jeweled crown shaped like a bee
hive—which must've been a replica of the papal *triregnum*. The lead
altar boy was bearing a tall processional cross, and he was followed
by another altar boy swinging a smoking censer and a third one
holding the bucket that carried a silver aspergillum sprinkler. The
pope was blessing bystanders with copious flings of water.

Vince noticed that the altar boy manning the holy water bucket
was hiding most of his face under a swatch of long hair. "It took me a
sec to *make* that kid," he told me over the phone. He said he dropped
what was left of the redfish beignet onto his plate and stood up from
the table, stepping away from the cops for a better view of the procession. It was definitely Trey.

"I'd love to stay and chat with you geniuses, but my chariot awaits,"
he said to the police officers as he climbed onto his scooter. "I'll give
you a shout, Ray. We need to talk."

The detective shrugged indifferently and raised the walkie-talkie
to his ear, deciphering words spoken through the static. "Whatever
you say, Vince."

The night was raw and damp, light fog haloing the streetlamps on
the square. Vince negotiated the Amigo through pockets of revelers
staggering about in altered states. Some of them laughed at his put-
tering scooter. A knave wearing gold lamé pants and a horse's head
galloped around the vehicle, mocking its slowness. A blonde-tressed
"Borgia-looking babe" shouted *Ride me, fat man!* and tried to mount
him but managed only to spill her fruity red Hurricane drink in his
lap. That bird-beaked peasant lashed him with the cat o' nine tails,
and Vince threatened to shoot him in the face. He wished there was a
siren on the Amigo, or a horn he could beep, or possibly a long deadly
saw blade attached to the front wheel. Progress was measured and
maddening. He considered abandoning that heap of junk and setting
out on foot, but he knew the effort would've left him exhausted and
wheezing in a tourist shop doorway.

He followed the smell of church incense lingering in the sodden air.
He thought he saw the tall processional cross enter Pirate's Alley be-

tween the Cabildo and the cathedral, but squatting on the seat cushion, subjected to that raucous nighttime world at belt level like a dwarf at a Renaissance fair, it was nearly impossible to track the pope's entourage.

He buzzed into the darker shadows of Pirate's Alley and asked one of the strolling couples if they'd seen the pope and his altar boys. "I knelt to kiss his ring and he poked his hard bulge in my face," said a chunky little woman with a walking staff and a bonnet full of huge pink curls—more Little Bo Peep than lady of the court.

"He's supposed to christen *La Scuola Vecchia*," said her companion, a duke of Venetian royalty, pointing toward Orleans Street just ahead.

"I figured that creepy clown pope had to be into teenage boys," Vince said to me. "Why else would a street hustler like Trey go along with the weird dress-up bit?"

He wheeled his scooter through the costumed rabble ambling about near the cast-iron fence of St. Anthony's Garden, a well-tended patch of green behind the cathedral. In the drifting fog he caught a glimpse of the processional cross bobbing toward the Bourbon Orleans hotel a block away. But even at the Amigo's top speed, it took him forever to cross Royal Street and find handicap access to the sidewalk.

The smoldering censer had been abandoned near the hotel entrance, and the pig-masked nun and her two cohorts were huddled over it like hobos warming themselves around a Sterno can on a cold railyard night. The nun had pulled the mask below her chin, revealing her comely young face, and she was sharing a joint with the guy shivering in his loincloth.

"Where the pope at?" Vince asked with a cock of his head.

"Repent, ye gluttonous sinner!" the nun shouted at him, in character, her mouth belching smoke. "Abandon hope, all ye who enter this flesh palace!"

Even on the scooter, the short journey had left his lungs whistling in the humid air. "I'll take that as a 'They're inside,'" he said, retrieving the inhaler from his pocket and huffing asthma medication. When he rolled up to the grand entrance, the hotel doorman raised an eyebrow.

"Apparently my threads—and a big wet red stain on my crotch—did not meet ballroom standards," he told me with a laugh.

The doorman asked to see his invitation. "Police business," Vince said, flashing his old NOPD badge as he motored past him into an opulent lobby stage-designed to resemble Medici Florence. The crowds of chattering royalty were decked out in coned capuchon hats and plumed capitano hats and gleaming tiaras, men dressed as women and women dressed as men. A handful of androgynous, half-naked servants in blackface fanned their masters like Nubian concubines from the Lower Nile.

Vince was on the case now, his heart racing. He knew that if he could corner Trey and talk to him about Martin Landry, sweat him out if necessary, it would save weeks of legwork searching for him all over town.

"Jesus, Vince," I said over the phone, "didn't you figure that kid might be a violent priest killer?"

"I know how to handle killers, Pete," he said. "Ask the late Tyrell McGee."

He rested on the Amigo near the bottom of a broad staircase where jubilant mischief-makers were following the harpsichord music upward toward the infamous old quadroon ballroom, the center of *La Scuola* festivities. They were the lords and ladies of privilege who'd spent wads of money on sumptuous robes, towering wigs, and the hand-held masks they hid behind.

"I was looking around for the clown pope," he said, "and I spied some waiters setting up a long buffet table over in a side lobby."

When he rolled between stately pillars into that smaller lobby, he found two of the altar boys lounging in overstuffed chairs, looking bored and surly, the tall processional standard leaning like a spear against the window drapes behind them.

"Greetings, young catamites," Vince addressed them as he approached on the Amigo. "Where's the rest of your unholy quartet?"

Trey and the pope were missing, but the *triregnum* crown was sitting on the floor next to the boys like "a giant fancy Russian whatta-ya-call-it egg with the bottom sliced off."

"You can blow me for two hundred bucks," said the larger boy with the build of a high school athlete, the one who had carried the cross.

Vince thought about ramming into him with the scooter. "Didn't the good sisters teach you how to speak to your elders, you little *cazzo*?"

The cross bearer took the dripping sprinkler from the holy water bucket and waggled it against his crotch like an erect penis. "It's this long, old man," he said, "which is why I'm not going a dime below one fifty."

Vince wondered if his son had been this brazen and reckless with strangers. It broke his heart to think so. He felt very old and tired and didn't want to play games with these boys. With no recourse other than getting off his Amigo and twisting their ears, he pulled the badge from his jacket.

"Now listen up, Cinderella. I want you to tell me where that boy named Trey is. Otherwise I'm gonna bust you for solicitation and you'll spend a night in O-P-P before momma and daddy know where you are." Orleans Parish Prison, the hardcore local jail. "You got any idea what your bunk pals gonna do to your white candy ass come about three a.m.? When they get done with you, you won't be able to crap for a month without crying like a little girl. Now save yourself some grief and tell me where Trey is."

The men's room was located down a long hallway near the hectic hotel kitchen. A tall bare-chested nobleman wearing nipple rings and a codpiece on the outside of his leather pants opened the door for him, and Vince steered the Amigo into the spacious toilet area. The urinals and stalls were occupied with drunken buffoons struggling to relieve themselves through layers of Renaissance regalia. There was no altar boy at the sinks or the *pissoirs*, and Vince suspected those young jokers had sent him on a wild goose chase. He rolled over to the row of stalls and ducked his head, studying the footwear he could see underneath the doors as he slowly passed by. Riding boots, satin slippers, tasseled loafers. He wasn't sure what he was looking for. He had no clue what Trey might be wearing on his feet.

"There's only one handicap stall," said a masker drying his hands with a paper towel. He was trying to be helpful to a disabled man. "And it sounds like someone's having a good time in there."

They were in the last stall, the large handicap stall, the pope and his altar boy. Vince stopped in front of the door and slid off the Amigo. He could hear what others were snickering about, quick snorts followed by a smacking rhythm, what sounded like cocaine and oral sex. When he pulled on the locked door handle, rattling the latch, the stall went silent, like naughty children holding their breaths in a closet.

"Hotel security," Vince declared in a firm voice. "Open up!"

No response. Not a whisper. He peeped through the sliver of space between the metal doorframes and could see Trey buttoning his long black cassock while the man in papal attire sat ceremoniously on the toilet seat.

"Unlock the door!" Vince demanded. "I need to speak with you. We've had complaints about improprieties." He told me he had trouble articulating the word *improprieties* after three whisky sours, because he'd never spoken that word aloud in his life.

He thought he was in control of the situation until the door flew open and knocked him against the scooter, toppling man and machine onto the grimy tile floor. Trey had burst from the stall and was sprinting toward the exit with the bottom of his robe gathered up in both hands like a woman fording a stream. Struggling to his feet, Vince gazed into the stall and watched the pope rise from his throne, drop a small vial into the commode, and flush with his foot on the lever. A *coke bullet*, they called it on the street, the little plastic container that held cocaine.

"Hey, holy father pervert, you gotta minute?" Vince said, still panting from the spill. "That boy . . ."

The pope wanted nothing to do with this interrogation. He slipped out of the stall and tried to scurry away, but Vince grabbed his silk sleeve and shoved him against the adjoining stall door. "Where you going, padre?" he said. "I need a minute of your time. That boy just now. Where he stays?"

"You don't look like an authorized security guard to me," the pope said, his hands crossed over his chest as if defending himself against a punch to the heart. "Now if you'll please excuse me . . ."

He made another attempt to get away and Vince banged him against the door again and slapped his face, not hard, he said, just enough to focus his attention. The man's cheek was as soft and loose as a bag of sugar. "Look at me," Vince said. "Where can I find Trey?"

Touching his face where the skin had reddened, the pope began to whimper. "Please, someone help me," he cried.

"Stop harassing that poor man!" said the bare-chested prince with the nipple rings. Maskers at the sinks and urinals had taken notice, too.

The pope attempted to flee one final time and Vince snatched the loose papal stole around his neck and yanked him back. "Look, man, I just wanna know how to get in touch with . . ."

In an instant the maskers were on him, clutching his arms, pinning Vince against the wall. "You can't come in here and bully our friends like that!" said a crossdresser wearing a knit snood and lacy face-net.

"Back the fuck off," Vince said, fighting to free himself, "or I'm gonna knee you girls in the pussy."

The tall prince backhanded Vince, stinging his ear, and in retaliation Vince stomped the man's ankle. He fell screaming to the floor, grasping his leg, and that brought several others into the brawl, pummeling Vince as he shielded himself with his arms.

"I got jumped by the fucking Village People," he told me over the phone.

He described how he went down swinging fists and elbows, and when he hit the floor, a half-dozen men piled on him like a rugby scrum. Desperate and bleeding, Vince tried to bite them through the heavy bolts of their beautifully tailored costumes.

"My good-luck fava bean got crushed to powder," he said. "Like I needed *dat*."

Ray Duhon knuckle-rapped the window of the squad car and then opened the door, shoving next to him in the back seat. Vince was handcuffed by a plastic zip-tie, recovering quietly with skinned knuckles and stained knees and a long fingernail scratch across his face. "Hey, *couillon*, you all right?" the detective asked, patting Vince's knee. "Got a call you were in a cat fight with some gay caballeros in the hotel men's room."

Vince stared out the window at the small crowd of *La Scuola* revelers gathering around the two steroidal rent-a-cops who'd zip-tied his wrists and hustled him out of the building. Officers Buddy Couvillion and Rodney Junius were out there, too, enjoying themselves at Vince's expense.

"Some fat creep was doing blow and sucking off a twink in one of the stalls," Vince said, closing his eyes and dropping his head back against the seat. He was crashing from the adrenaline high and the beating he'd taken, disappointed with the outcome of the altercation but mildly satisfied that he'd delivered a respectable flurry of punches against greater numbers. But the fight had made him aware that he was grossly out of shape and far from his best years as a street cop.

"One dude is limping around with a swollen ankle. Another guy has bite marks on his arm. You're lucky nobody's pressing charges,"

Duhon said. "You wanna tell me what's going on here, Vince? Since when does a retired cop think he can bust somebody in a public restroom?"

"I wasn't trying to bust the creep, Ray." Vince opened his eyes and gazed at the scarred ceiling of the cruiser. "I'm working a case. I wanted to talk to somebody and the creep got in my way."

Duhon glanced at Vince's restrained wrists. "This minor you're talking about. You tracking down another runaway?"

Vince sighed, ready for a long night's sleep. "You know how this works, Ray. Client privilege, yackety-yack. I'm not at liberty to discuss."

Duhon scratched at a crusty stain on the knee of his trousers. "This doesn't have anything to do with . . . you know . . ." He hesitated, fishing for words. "With Ned," he said, reluctant to look at Vince. "These runaways, Vince. This snoop work you've been doing. Tell me you're not aching to pull something stupid again, like you did with that flophouse scumbag. Nobody wants to bring you in, man. But you can't go around threatening people and slapping them in the face."

"This ain't about Ned," Vince insisted. But even as he said it, he wasn't so sure. "It's just what I do now, Ray. Supply and demand. You know this fucking town. There's enough bad shit going down to keep the devil working weekends."

They watched a hotel valet roll the Amigo out onto the wet sidewalk. One of the security guards straddled the scooter and pretended to kick-start the motor, working the handle grips as if it was a Harley hog. The partygoers were laughing at his antics and staring at the squad car and the miserable bastard wrist-tied in the back seat.

"You said you wanna talk to me about something. Looks like you've got some time on your hands," Duhon said, nodding at the zip-tie. "So talk."

Vince knew he was trespassing in dangerous terrain. He also knew he might not have this chance again. "That black kid you locked up for killing the priest," he said. "The word on the street is you got the wrong guy."

Duhon reacted with a quick, dismissive scowl. "Who's saying that?"

"The Cat."

The detective groaned. It was a shared cop joke dating back at least twenty years. In those days, when you asked a black informant where he got his intel, the answer was always *the Cat*. The dude. My man. Translation: a reputable but anonymous source. And I'm not giving him up to the cops.

"The Cat should've told you to keep your big dago nose out of police business, Scalco. Why are you interested in that case?"

"A man of the cloth has been murdered, Ray. One of God's holy ordained ministers."

"I'm really touched by your devotion, Vinny. How do you say *embrasse moi tchew* in eye-talian?"

Kiss my ass.

"Be straight with you," Vince said, "I don't give a rat's *culo*, one way or the other. The Cat told me the black kid didn't do it. I thought you should hear that. But I know you'll play it by the numbers, Ray. You always do the right thing," he said with a dark smile, "except maybe that one time."

Vince had helped Ray Duhon beat a confession out of Tyrell McGee, the gang leader who'd pulled the trigger on an informant and his little brother. They dumped Tyrell, half dead, into a weed lot near the Magnolia Housing Project and told the murdered snitch's posse where to find him.

Duhon glanced out the window at the security guard riding the scooter, trying to cut wheelies while the growing crowd watched and applauded. "You're free to go," he said, "but do us both a favor. Stop playing cop. That part of your life is over."

Vince lifted his zip-tied wrists. "You wanna do the honors?"

Duhon looked out the window again at the guard fooling around on the Amigo. "Why don't you give that shit-tard wannabe cop a lesson in restraint management?"

The detective opened the car door and led Vince by the elbow into the sidewalk crowd, his wrists still secured in plastic. Officer Buddy Couvillion said, "Looks like our boy wants to come outside and play. Better let him have his tricycle back."

The onlookers fell into an uneasy silence as the security guard stepped off the Amigo. Released from Duhon's custody, Vince closed in on the buffed-up guard. He was the one who'd strapped that ring around his wrists while he was flat on his back on the restroom floor. When Vince raised his tied hands high over his head, the guard flinched and Vince laughed wickedly, then swung his wrists down into his own gut with quick force, snapping off the plastic lock as if it was a rubber band. He handed the broken plastic to the guard, saying, "Here ya go, *jamoke*. You might need this the next time you bang your sister."

The crowd erupted in laughter. Vince settled himself on the Amigo seat, nodded to Ray Duhon, and drove off toward the handicap ramp, sore and swollen and tired beyond calculation.

"I almost had my mitts on the kid, Pete, but he got away," Vince said, beginning to slur into the phone. He'd had too much to drink. "Now he'll figure out somebody's after him and it'll be hell running that coon dog down."

I told him I was very sorry he'd been roughed up and apologized for involving him in this dirty, painful case. "Do you need anything right now?" I asked him.

"My pride back," he said with a whisky laugh. "But it's too damned late for that."

THIRTEEN

AFTER MY LONG PHONE CONVERSATION WITH VINCE, I brewed a cup of coffee and returned to reading Martin Landry's file, taking notes and listening to the steady tick of moisture dripping from the magnolia tree outside my study window. I could hear the happy noises of Ann and Matt winding down their day—Luke, who knows where?—the television eventually silent, the house soon dark and still. An imperfect picture of domestic bliss, but satisfying enough. How different was the life of a childless, unmarried priest in his grim rectory, shuttered and lonely at that hour, unloved and untouched, promised great reward in the next life for his sacrifices, but not tonight nor in the many nights to come.

At his death, Martin Landry had served as a priest for sixteen years. In that relatively short time, he'd been assigned to five parishes and had taught at four Catholic schools in three states—Louisiana, Texas, and New Mexico—and at a mission in Guatemala for eight months. It was an appalling work record. If he'd been a layperson in the job market, no employer would have hired him with that unstable résumé.

As I read the thick collection of letters and reports, a pattern of predatory behavior emerged. He was very skilled at joining a parish and establishing himself as a popular teacher and charismatic father figure, well regarded for his outgoing personality and entertaining Sunday homilies. He would quickly win over the trust and admiration of his parishioners and their children. But then the troubles began. There were letters to four different bishops from parents, from an alarmed pediatrician in Galveston, Texas, from a child psychologist in Santa Fe, New Mexico—discreet and respectful pleas for the priest to be removed from the parish and school, defrocked, ostracized, ordered to undergo therapy, medicated, whatever it would take—scores of pages of correspondence from loyal Catholics promising not to involve the police or go public if Church authorities would act instantly and rid them of this monster in their midst.

Deeper behind the scenes, there were long sincere exchanges among the bishops, advice from lawyers, mandates for psychological counseling, convincing reports of his recovery and reassignments, then backsliding and more offenses, more boys in new parishes. I found medical evaluations and an article on the effectiveness of Depo-Provera and scheduled treatments by injection. And I read the narrative of his final supervised stay with the Paracletes.

To me, the most striking aspect of these documents was the generosity of so many aggrieved souls, their love and allegiance to the Church and their willingness to forgive. They trusted the hierarchy to take the proper steps. One friend of a victim wrote, "I think T. is a remarkable man because he has not allowed anger to take permanent charge of his heart or his judgment, even though his accusations have been ignored and his cry for help has been disregarded by the archdiocese for many years."

But the bishops and their secretariats and *monsignori*, for the most part, were smug and disbelieving and too often blamed the child victims for *offering the near occasion of sin*. They suspected financial greed as the motive for many of the complaints—scams to elicit substantial cash from the Church in exchange for silence.

"I wonder how God will judge those who try to harm a dedicated priest?" wrote one of the bishops. "It's difficult to be a priest today because so many people whine about everything."

At a parish in Texas, a female housekeeper left a note for the pastor, complaining that Father Landry was providing alcohol to minors in the rectory and on field trips: "I spoke to him about giving beer and wine to young boys," she wrote, "and he told me he saw nothing wrong in what he was doing. Bonding, he called it. And he told me it was none of my business. I am sorry, Father, but it is very disturbing that a priest would be doing this with our children."

The pastor responded that Satan was at work in her accusations and fired the woman.

I read a voluminous exchange between a victim and the bishop's staff at a diocese in southwest Louisiana. From what I could infer, the young man's claim had been handed off to a minor cleric working in the office, and then to another untrained bureaucrat who had conducted a "thorough investigation" that absolved Martin Landry of any wrongdoing. Writing from his college dorm, the young man said, "My innocence and trust were taken away from me at ten years old. I don't think you understand what it feels like when you are losing your faith. The Church and its Servants of God—the ones I have always felt would be there when I desperately needed them—have abandoned me and said they do not believe my story and insist I wasn't harmed at all."

Another city, another diocese, another victim writing to his bishop: "Somewhere deep in your soul, your conscience knows I am telling the truth. I hope you will do something to help Father Landry. Part of my healing will take place when I feel I have given my best effort to make sure he does not have another opportunity to do unto other children what he did to me."

I was stunned by the lack of compassion behind closed doors at the long meeting tables in book-lined *salas regias*. Those in charge spent a great deal of time devising strategies of defense, avoidance, and cover-up, rather than directly addressing the root-cause of the problem, a child molester among them. They showed no sympathy and offered no consolation to the young victims and their families.

One father wrote a concerned letter to an archbishop who refused to meet with him: "The people of this parish love our Church sincerely. Priests are invited into our homes and into our loving arms. We deserve better than the duplicity going on behind our backs. If it wasn't for the many dedicated priests and nuns that I know personally, I would doubt the validity of all I was taught during my many years of Catholic education. All I want is to have a respectful conversation with you, face to face, like a man. Your refusal to see me is making my son's situation far more explosive and damaging than it has to be."

I discovered a lengthy report in which the Church had settled a case by paying off the accusers with cash under the table. It was a troubling revelation, because I had thought our diocese was the first to reduce itself to outright bribery. (I assumed from the outset that we were creating the prototype.) At any rate, the payoff involved Landry's missionary work in Guatemala. A delusional bishop who was aware of Landry's history with boys truly believed that as a southerner, Martin would be less attracted to dark skin. That brilliant plan was cut short when he and two other missionaries were arrested for abusing the same eight-year-old boy over an extended period. The Church paid six figures in hush money to the local police and the boy's mother, who was described in the report as "hysterical and threatening violence and revenge." The three priests were shipped back to the States and transferred to three different areas of the country, their parishes seven hundred miles apart. To my astonishment, in that flurry of letters between bishops and vicars-general, there was no thought given to *laicizing* those priests, a kinder term for defrocking them and sending them out into the real world on their own, where sex offenders were dealt with harshly and without favor by law enforcement and prosecutors.

Threatening violence and revenge, the report stated.

Far more explosive and damaging than it has to be, the boy's father wrote.

I wondered again if Martin Landry's horrendous violations had caught up with him last night in his bedroom at the rectory. Did an irate parent track him down? Did one of his many victims come after him, years later, as a grown man with a terrible secret he could no longer live with? Did someone finally allow anger to take permanent charge of his heart?

I read on, not surprised by a number of letters in his file praising his character, his gift for teaching, his ability to "get where the students are at and knowing how to relate to them." Those cheerful, fawning letters seemed to be part of an organized effort by misguided supporters to defend Landry when his neck was on the chopping block. I found a page of drugstore stationery penned in large looping cursive handwriting from a mother praising him for his friendship and kindness toward her son. She was not a sophisticated writer and the letter contained misspellings and haphazard punctuation, but she was heartbreaking in her love for Donald, the son who'd been committed to a mental hospital. She deeply appreciated Father Landry's visits to anoint him with the Oil of the Sick and offer a priest's blessing and the Holy Eucharist. The letter was signed *Hazel Bertrand*. I stared at her school-girl signature and wanted to cry. She was the mother of my old seminarian friend Donny Bertrand.

It had been twenty years since I'd last seen Donny in the psychiatric hospital across the lake. I had thought about him from time to time, wondering what had become of him and where he'd landed after such a rough early ride. On several occasions I'd considered contacting his parents, who lived on the west bank of the river in the community of Marrero, to see how Donny was doing. Her letter was dated April 1970, and she mentioned that her son had been in and out of various facilities for the past six years. "The doctors see alot of improvement," she wrote, "and we have high hopes he will be well enough to come back home soon and get a job and make something of himself in this life. Father Landry has been very helpful and encouraging."

I thought about the old album and Martin's photograph of Donny lying in a nightgown, smiling blissfully at the camera from his hospital bed, his eyes dancing and content. It appeared that Martin had stayed in touch with him, at least for a time. But why did Donny delight in seeing him again, especially after that sordid incident in the old white dorm? Was it friendship or sacred duty, a priest ministering to the sick? Or was it something darker?

With Ann sleeping beside me, breathing softly against my neck, her body warm and reassuring, I lay awake pondering those questions until the misty gray light of dawn rubbed against the bedroom windows and I heard the newspaper skipping across the wet lawn.

FOURTEEN

AT THAT POINT IN OUR MARRIAGE, Ann and I had settled into a Sunday morning routine that was satisfying and comfortable. We would wake early, while the boys were asleep, enjoy the first cup of coffee in bed and talk about them and our families, our friends, our work. It was our only quiet time together in a life ruled by schedules and responsibilities. Then Ann would dress in her running clothes and Adidas, zip a tube of pepper spray into her pocket, and venture out into the early light, running down to the Tulane campus and Audubon Park for a few quick laps around the golf course. On some mornings she would push herself out past the zoo, slogging up the high grassy banks of the Mississippi River levee and, if the weather was decent, jog on the levee trail for another two miles, watching flat-bottom cargo barges steer southward along the old muddy waters in the sparkling sunshine of a new day.

I would read the newspaper while Ann was gone, always worried about her safety in a city known for its random violence, and at a time before cell phones and GPS tracking. She had long ago stopped accommodating my anxieties, and I had gradually made peace with her running at early hours and often alone. She was in remarkable shape, as tan and taut as a teenager, even after two children, and physical exertion aroused her rather than tired her out. When she returned home, sweating through her sports bra, her skin wet and clammy, her hair matted under a Saints cap, she would shower quickly and we would make love in whispered words and sighs, and then wake the boys for breakfast before Mass.

But on that foggy Sunday morning, with too much on our minds, we drank coffee in silence and Ann chose not to go running. We didn't make love. I was still contemplating what I'd read in Martin Landry's file, and she was mentally preparing herself for meeting the client who'd been abused by a priest.

I left early to pick up Father Ted at Immaculata seminary. The Mother-house, as it was sometimes called, had been constructed in the early decades of the century on the wooded grounds of a former leper hospital, twenty acres of land near the river. The grounds were surrounded by a red brick wall eight feet high. Back in my day, shortly after Pope John XXIII encouraged the Church to open windows and let fresh air in, we iconoclastic seminarians wanted to tear down those walls and let the world in. But our ancient bishop at the time, an archconservative who disdained all changes to Church tradition, including the vernacular Mass, wisely denied permission to take sledge hammers to stone.

The walls were still intact and uninviting. I stopped at the main entrance and pushed the button on the speaker box, identified myself, and waited for the wrought iron gates to rattle open wide enough for the wagon to enter. The campus was tucked back at the end of a live oak lane, and fog from the river drifted in ghostly tendrils across the long green lawn. A menacing figure wrapped in a black overcoat stood waiting on the steps of the seminary's administrative building like an ominous crow eyeing everything from a fencepost. My uncle looked exhausted, dark circles around his eyes, and when he sank into the passenger seat of my car, I noticed that fresh razor nicks had dried into tiny scabs on his neck and chin. I handed him the Sunday morning newspaper, where Sharon's front page story quoted him as saying, "I was out of town at a conference and came home to find Father Landry's body. It was a terrible shock." She also wrote that an anonymous source had speculated it was a ritualistic murder involving a satanic cult, but police investigators and District Attorney Roger Finney had declined to comment about that.

"What nonsense," Ted said, removing his glasses and gazing at the windshield. "The next thing you know, they'll connect his death to the Kennedy assassination."

Clueless in retrospect, we hadn't anticipated that the number of reporters and video crews would double overnight. They'd gotten smarter, covering both entrances to the church. Using the old station wagon like a battering ram, I rolled through their ranks in the breezeway and they reluctantly moved aside to let my uncle get out of the car. He smiled paternally and patted shoulders as he made his way up the steps and into the sacristy, ignoring their volley of questions. They would've followed him inside if I hadn't positioned myself on the top step and advised them in strong language that they could not enter the church and should respect the privacy of the service and its worshippers.

"Why won't Father McMurray talk to us about the murder?" a reporter shouted, video cameras aimed at me like bazookas.

"Tell us about the young man in custody, Mr. Moore!" It was Sharon, dogged and unyielding as always. "Is he a member of this parish?"

"No, he isn't," I said. "Now if you'll excuse me, I'm going in to attend Mass. Please keep a respectful distance, all of you."

In the sacristy, my uncle was garbing for the service in a meditative silence, assisted by two preteen altar boys, their white surplices starched in sharp creases. They looked as timeless as my friend Joey Pevoto and I did in the 1950s, oil-sheened hair parted as straight as a ruler, fervent and scrupulous about their memorized roles in that age-old liturgy. I wondered if these boys would appear in Martin Landry's videos.

"Peter, would you look and see how big the congregation is?" Father Ted requested.

I peeped out the open doorway to the sanctuary. "It's packed. Standing room only," I said, trying to locate Ann and our sons. "It's like Midnight Mass on Christmas Eve."

A low drone of tense anticipation emanated from the pews. They'd come this morning for more than the fulfillment of their Sunday obligation. Father Landry's death had shaken them, a Servant of Christ lost to violence. They needed consolation and assurances, a reckoning for what had happened. If there was a caring God, why did He take those we love and admire? Why did evil sometimes triumph over good?

"Time for bread and roses," my uncle announced to the altar boys with a sweeping hand toward the sanctuary. He was attired in a shiny green chasuble embroidered with a long gold cross. "After you, lads. Let us go to the altar of God."

The two boys paraded out before him, single file, hands folded in prayer, and the congregation rose thunderously to its feet to begin a ritual that dated back two thousand years to a Passover supper in Jerusalem. I remained near the sacristy doorway, following the Mass in its various rubrics, standing and genuflecting and kneeling on the carpet and bowing to beat my chest *through my fault, through my fault, through my most grievous fault.* When Father Ted began his homily, a tempered tribute to his charismatic assistant pastor, I heard the back door open, then a barrage of shrill voices, and I raced to intercept whichever reporter had dared to invade this dressing room I was taught to revere as the holy of holies.

"I thought I made myself perfectly clear," I said in an urgent stage whisper as I rounded a corner with my arms outstretched, palms forward, prepared to shove the intruder back outside.

"Peter?" he said.

The lighting was inadequate in the narrow hallway and I couldn't see him distinctly. He was shorter than I, a smaller man, and offered little resistance when I grabbed the lapels of his suit jacket.

"Peter, it's Eric Gautier. Let go of me."

I released him at once, giving the young attorney a friendly swat on the arm. "Sorry, Eric. I thought you were a reporter," I said.

"The Vicar-General asked me to come. Monsignor Fulweiler," he said, as if I might not remember the man's name. He wagged his head toward the back door. "He thought I could help with the media mob."

"Did you bring a grenade? That would help."

I didn't know whether to be insulted by the Rottweiler's lack of confidence in me or relieved to share this misery with a lawyer.

"I was thinking water cannon," Eric said with a tight smile. "But grenade'll work, too."

He followed me to my spot near the sanctuary door, a few steps out of the bright lights, and we stood shoulder to shoulder in a rigid military formation as my uncle delivered his homily about Father Martin Landry and his hallowed place among the saints and martyrs.

Eric was four years younger than I, a Jesuit boy very fond of himself and his degrees from Georgetown and Virginia. His handsome face was highlighted by a neatly trimmed red mustache and goatee, and his freckled hands betrayed him as a child who'd spent too much time in the Louisiana sun. A gym rat and fitness freak, highly competitive in everything he did, he was known to be as driven and ruthless in a courtroom as he was on a tennis court. He would've been the perfect partner for my jock wife, and I was relieved they'd never met.

"How is Matt?" he asked quietly. "Is he playing indoor soccer?"

"He has a game today," I said without turning my head to look at him. "But with the death and all, we may not go. What about Adrian? I thought we might see you two this season."

"He's taking tennis lessons. Seems to like it more than soccer."

I was too single-minded to waste that moment on small talk.

"I've seen some things on those videotapes you wouldn't believe, Eric. And I've read Martin Landry's personnel file." Eric Gautier was one of the few people I could confide in. "What you and I are supposed to do won't pass for weekend fun with our sons."

He was wearing a winter blue three-piece Brooks Brothers suit with a conventional tie whose stick-pin may as well have been engraved with the words *high-dollar attorney*. It made my suit look like a bargain basement purchase at Dillard's, which it was. His shoes gleamed as if they'd been spit-shined by an old black man in a deluxe hotel lobby, 1953.

"Then I suppose you and I had better learn to hold our noses," he said, "or get used to the stench."

After Father Ted intoned "Go, the Mass is ended" and the congregation made its final resounding response, the altar boys led him back to the sacristy and Eric asked me to dismiss them so he could brief my uncle in private while he disrobed.

"My father asked me to give you a heads up. This afternoon the medical examiner is going to release his findings about Father Landry. Dad doesn't want you to be taken by surprise if the media asks you to comment," Eric told him in a quiet voice, placing Ted's green silk maniple in a shallow drawer next to a colorful array of other maniples. Clearly Eric had once been an altar boy, too.

"The details are horrific, Father. Forgive me for being the bearer of such bad news."

"Go ahead, Eric," Ted said as he removed his chasuble like a pullover sweater.

"Severe trauma to the head from that cinder block. Signs of strangulation, hand marks around his throat. Water in his lungs, which means he wasn't dead when . . ." He was trying to phrase those brutal descriptions as discreetly as possible. "The medical examiner speculates that he was dumped unconscious into the bathtub, then the cinder block was chained around his neck and he was held under while the water filled the tub."

"My God," Ted said, wandering toward a polished wooden chair in the corner of the sacristy. He sat down gracelessly, like a much heavier man, his eyes watery and roaming off to some harrowing place. He was still wearing the long white alb with a gold-fringed stole around his neck, and he slumped forward with his elbows braced on the arms of the chair, overcome by fatigue and emotion. I was concerned that he might be having one of his diabetic spells, which were always unnerving to witness.

"Are you all right, Ted?" I asked him. "Should I get you some orange juice?"

He shook his head.

"Father, I know this is a lot to digest," Eric said, "but as your legal counsel, representing the diocese, it's my duty to caution you about certain things. You can tell reporters you found his body in the bathroom. But no specifics, please. The police have asked us not to mention the tub, the chain, the cinder block, and the party in the bedroom. It's all part of their investigation. And of course it's not in the Church's best interest to say anything about . . ." He exhaled, visibly dismayed. "About the video evidence. That doesn't exist. And if anyone asks about the suspect in custody, you've never laid eyes on him before. Are we clear on that?"

I was appalled by the shameful subterfuge, but held my tongue.

"I wanted to help him recover from his addiction and never do those awful things again," Ted said, "but obviously I failed. I was fooled. Martin was an expert at deceit. He'd slipped back into that secret life and I didn't pick up the signs."

Eric was hanging the chasuble in a closet. "Don't beat yourself up, Father. Men like him are almost never cured," he said. "The recidivism rate is very, very high."

Ted clasped his long fingers together, forming a tight ball, and struck his forehead. "Those boys. Those poor boys at the school," he said, pounding his forehead again. "I won't ever forgive myself for being so damned blind and naïve."

It was unsettling to see my proud uncle so angry with himself.

"Gentlemen, I need a few moments of . . . reflection," he said, unclasping his hands and looking up at us. "Could you give me a little time alone?"

Eric and I waited silently in the altar boys' dressing room, on the other side of the sanctuary, where the cassocks and surplices were hanging in a long neat row. The air was sweet from fresh-cut flowers arranged in vases on a table where the ladies' auxiliary pruned and decorated the church's floral displays. There was a stack of beige metal folding chairs stenciled PROPERTY OF OUR LADY OF SORROWS CATHOLIC CHURCH, and I unfolded one and sat down as Eric paced nervously in the weak rose-colored light from a stained-glass window.

We made no effort at conversation. Father Ted's ruminations had put us both in a dismal mood. But we were paired by the powers that be, for better or worse, and it was going to take hard work to adjust myself to our mutual assignment.

After several minutes of silence, I decided to speak my mind. "Whoever killed Landry," I said, "killed him in a red rage."

"A what?" he said, still pacing, his thoughts elsewhere.

"That's what my brother-in-law calls it. He's got anger issues. He says when he goes ballistic, he actually sees the color red."

He stopped circling the room and looked at me. "I didn't want to say this to Father Ted. He was upset enough," he said. "Detective Duhon thinks there may've been more than one perp. All that trauma to Father Landry's head and throat, dragging the body to the tub, holding him down. It's tough to do, one on one."

"So where does Duhon fit Kwame Williams into that scenario, Eric? When Father Ted and I saw him on the stairs, he was alone."

Eric was suddenly annoyed and impatient. "Maybe he killed Father Landry—with or without others—and then returned later. Because that's what killers do sometimes, Peter. They come back to admire their work," he said. "The lab shows that the kid was positive for alcohol, weed, and crack. He was seriously messed up. Maybe he crashed somewhere in the house, you and Father Ted woke him up, and he decided to go upstairs and check on the body."

It was possible. But my uncle had said he'd searched the house thoroughly.

"If Kwame was lying," I said, "it was an Oscar performance worthy of Sidney Poitier."

He laughed darkly. "You have no idea, man, what a killer is capable of saying or doing. Come with me some time to visit my clients in L-S-P Angola." The Louisiana State Penitentiary, a former cotton plantation with slaves from the African country of Angola. "Psychopaths—even the ones with low IQs—are usually brilliant at the art of deception."

I stood up and joined his pacing. We began orbiting each other among the sweet dying lilies in rose-tinted light.

"Listen, Eric. You and your law firm can burn those videotapes, and the Church can canonize a pedophile, for all I care," I said, bitterness crawling onto my tongue like the taste of ashes. "But I won't let you railroad Kwame Williams into the death penalty. That's not gonna happen, man."

He stopped pacing and glared at me. "What are you proposing, Peter?" he asked with suspicion.

I certainly did not consider it my job to solve the murder. But it was my job to account for every boy who'd been violated and to arrange financial restitution, and Kwame was one of those boys. I took that assignment very seriously.

"I want to talk to Kwame," I said. "Make that happen, Eric. I saw him in one of the videos. He may know who the other boys are. Names, schools, whatever. He can probably tell us how Landry operated, the whole song and dance."

Eric's demeanor had morphed from soccer dad, a casual acquaintance whose son played with mine, to a cold and stoic litigator well versed in courtroom logic.

"Detective Duhon has interviewed this kid extensively," he said. "He agreed to let me know if Kwame divulges any information that might help us with damage control."

"Damage control?" I said. "Is that a euphemism for cover up? Get clearance for me to see Kwame, Eric. You can come with me, if you like."

"The police and DA Finncy aren't going to let us do that. Even a court-appointed lawyer with a lizard brain would drag that into the open and raise too many questions about why the attorney for the diocese and its PR man were allowed to interrogate a murder suspect.

I can guarantee you that lizard brain will depose us under oath or put us on the stand and ask what we discussed with his client."

I hated all those procedures and entanglements, the chess match of legal maneuverings. "It had better not go to trial, Eric." The bitter ashes were still coating my tongue. "It had better not go that far."

"Or *what?*" he said. "What is it you're going to do, Peter? Would you like to discuss your objections with the Vicar-General? He's the one who asked me to become more involved with the public relations aspect of this case. And now I see why."

Through the open doorway we watched Father Ted crossing in front of the altar and stopping to genuflect toward the tabernacle, where the Eucharist was kept in a gold ciborium. He'd changed into his black suit and Roman collar, and his dark overcoat was flapping, unbuttoned.

"Gentlemen," he said, entering the room, "I'm going outside to mingle with my parishioners and see how they're doing. It's never too early for the healing to begin. You're welcome to join me."

Eric was in defensive mode. "The media is out there, Father," he said, alarmed. "They'll make it impossible for you to have a simple conversation with anyone."

My uncle raised an eyebrow and smiled his thin-lipped, confident smile. "I am their pastor. They are my flock. I'm going out there to offer friendship and consolation to anybody who needs it. That's what I do, Eric."

I was very pleased that my old mentor had returned from the barren stretches of melancholia.

"If the reporters become a nuisance," he said, "you two will have to handle them. Are you ready, comrades? Game faces on."

FIFTEEN

ANN RENTED A SMALL OFFICE on the edge of the Garden District in an old two-story house that had been converted into commercial space by a psychiatrist she'd met in her running group. She shared a common waiting room with Richard, what had once been a wealthy Creole family's parlor, modest by modern standards, heavy overstuffed furniture from his great aunt's estate, soft-lit by her antique floor lamps with yellowing parchment shades. Ann admired Richard and talked about him in joyous tones that incited my jealousy. Richard was also an MD who could prescribe medications, and she often turned to him if she thought one of her clients—she called them *clients*, not patients—would achieve better living through chemistry. She took pride in the fact that Richard had never disagreed with one of her prognoses.

Ann had told me that her client Darren—not his real name—was distraught and couldn't wait until Monday to meet with her. They'd agreed on two o'clock that Sunday afternoon, and Ann arrived early to unlock the door and raise windows to air the old place out. It had a persistent odor, despite a professional cleaning crew's weekly efforts, and that clever Richard fellow had conjectured it was the stench of servant girls buried under the house during the slave era.

Ann said that she was upstairs in her office, straightening cushions and clearing her desk of loose notes and file folders, when the chime sounded, signaling that the front door had opened downstairs. "Is that you, Darren?" she shouted. "Come on up!"

She could hear him mounting the stairs in his hiking boots, and soon he was standing in the doorway, an appealing, sandy-haired young man, twenty-six years old, his smile bright and hopeful, but his striking green eyes betraying deeper anguish, a history of regrets and humiliations that had wrecked him. She liked Darren enormously and suspected everyone did. There were times when her maternal instincts almost overwhelmed her, and she wanted to reach out and grab him, as she might one of our sons, and smother his anxieties with a mother's embrace. "Forgive yourself, enjoy love," she wanted to tell him. "Have children, move on." But it wasn't what she'd been trained to do. She knew that platitudes and packaged solutions would've been insulting to a complex soul like Darren. And so she listened. And made practical suggestions that sometimes rang hollow to her. And she prayed for him to find contentment.

She hugged him in her office doorway, an affectionate greeting that usually began their sessions. "Sounds like you need to talk," she said.

"Actually, Ann," he said, his hands resting on her shoulders, "I would like you to meet some friends of mine. They're downstairs in the parlor."

Three young men were standing in the empty circle between a tufted fainting sofa and a collection of austere Victorian armchairs. They were Darren's age, casually dressed in jeans, windbreakers, light jackets. They moved toward her with friendly smiles, shaking her hand one by one and giving their first names. She turned to Darren for an explanation.

"We've all been abused by Catholic priests or brothers," Darren said quietly, glancing at the others.

Ann had been working as a trained therapist for a dozen years, but she'd never treated a group of people with the same devastating secret. When this meeting took place in the 1980s, there were no support groups in our city for sexual victims of the clergy, and I doubt there were such groups anywhere else in the country. This encounter marked the beginning of what would become my wife's vocation in life.

"I convinced these guys that you'd be the best person to hear our stories," Darren began. "We're tired of talking to ourselves."

The others laughed nervously.

Ann invited them to have a seat and locked the front door. "My colleague and our receptionist won't be in today," she said. "We have the house to ourselves."

The only gay man in the group was a few years older than the others. His dark romantic features were turning coarse, like a beautiful but unhappy former child star who was now battling a weight problem. "Lady, I hope you know what you're getting into," Arturo said with a slight Latino accent.

"To be honest," she said, smiling at Darren, "I wasn't prepared for a whole group."

"I'm sorry, Ann," Darren said. "I didn't mean to dump this on you. It's just that . . . we don't know what else to do."

She tried to relax in one of the stiff-backed armchairs, but she told me later that she was as nervous as they were. "I'm listening, gentlemen," she said. "Where would you like to begin?"

Years later, as I was writing this book, I asked Ann if she would talk to me about her initial meeting with the four young men. I promised to use pseudonyms and to disguise the parishes where the abuses occurred. She gave my request serious consideration for several days. She'd stayed in touch with all four of them and decided to contact them individually, explaining my book project and asking them to reach out to me if they wanted to tell their stories. I was surprised that all four of them agreed to interviews. Their memories of that first meeting with Ann were remarkably similar, and they even recalled what certain friends had said, word for word.

They spent the afternoon revealing what had happened to them. There were tears, but also gallows humor and gales of painful laughter and relief. Two of the young men had been abused by the same priest at a parish in New Orleans, another by a pair of teaching brothers from a religious order that operated a handful of elementary schools in southwest Louisiana's Cajun country. Ann listened, her greatest strength, taking it all in, scribbling notes, observing them work their way toward catharsis. She admitted to me that she'd been shocked by the magnitude of the bold and often violent abuses they described, the promises and seductions, the forced sex and physical trauma, the abusers' lack of fear because they were entitled Servants of God who were above being found out or punished.

"I was only eleven years old the first time I was ass raped by one of the Catholic brothers," said a longhaired EMT named Zach who lived and worked in St. Martin Parish. "I bled so bad I had to go home and hide my underwear in a garbage can and stand in the shower for a real long time before the bleeding stopped. But the pain never went away. I still feel it every day."

Ann asked the young men if anyone else, friends or siblings, knew what was happening to them at the time. Why didn't they tell their parents? They all acknowledged that they were too ashamed, too humiliated, too afraid of public disgrace. There was a stigma. They didn't want to be labeled as queers and bullied for the rest of their lives. It was safer to stay silent and go along with whatever was demanded.

"I begged them to leave me alone," Zach said. He'd attended a Catholic school in a small country town. The two pedophile teachers told him if he resisted them, they would force him to perform oral sex on all his male classmates.

"My abuser ran a number on me too, Zach," Darren said. "He told me my mother approved of what was going on, because he was paying her a lot of money for permission to do those things to me."

"That sick fuck," said a burly oil worker nicknamed Strike. He wore a braided rat tail down the back of his denim jacket.

"The sickest part was I hated my mother for it," Darren said. "I didn't realize until I got older that the priest was a lying sack of shit."

"The lord of lies," Strike said.

"All during that time, my poor mother wondered why I wouldn't let her hug or kiss me. One of these days, before she's gone, I'm gonna tell her why I acted that way."

As a mother herself, Ann found Darren's story very upsetting and called for a short break. She went upstairs to her office, where she kept a box of tissues, and dried the tears clinging to her eyelashes. Her own mother had once taught her a trick to prevent her from crying in public, and Ann did that now, imbedding her strong nails into her palms until the pain distracted her from what was really hurting.

When everyone returned to the circle, Ann began by asking, "How did you guys find each other?"

Darren explained that he and Zach had lived in the same dorm at the university in Lafayette, and they became friends. Zach and Strike were cousins, and Strike had known Arturo since grade school.

"Less than six degrees of separation," Zach said with a sly smile.

"Strike, Zach, and me ended up at the same blues bar on Oak Street one night," Darren said, "and after some serious drinking—what we do best—we discovered that we'd all been altar boys. A few drinks later, the bad shit came pouring out."

"I told them I knew another guy—a gay guy," Strike said, "that went through what I went through. So I gave Arturo a shout and he showed up at the next drink fest."

"Straight men have terrible taste in bars," Arturo said. "I've been trying to introduce a little class."

When the joking stopped, Arturo made it clear that his history of abuse was different.

"I was thirteen and I already knew I was gay, although I didn't dare tell anybody. I idolized my priest, and once he started having his way with me, I fell in love with him and blabbered on about being his wife forever." He laughed at his naïveté. "I thought I was his one and only. When I found out he had other boyfriends, including home boy Strike over there"—he pointed an accusing finger and smiled sardonically—"I lost my shit and threw a couple of tantrums in public . . . at school. Father took me aside and threatened to tell my parents I was gay. He said he would kick me out of Catholic school and I would go to hell when I died, etcetera. So I had to accept the fact that I was just another boy toy. And then one day he was gone. Transferred overnight without saying goodbye. I didn't know where he went or why he left. I figured his bad karma had finally caught up with him."

Ann was taking notes furiously now, trying to capture every word. What about the police? she asked. Now that they were adults, had they considered revealing these crimes to law enforcement? If their abusers were still active, it would save other children from harm.

"I gotta be straight with you, ma'am. This stuff happened too long ago," Strike said. "The cops ain't interested in ancient history."

He worked off-shore on oil rigs, two weeks on, two weeks off. He said he liked the isolation. Strike was heterosexual, but he found it difficult to connect with women.

"I'm not ready to turn this into a big deal," he said. "You know, some kind of cause or something. It hits the newspapers, you won't believe how much crap I'll take from the assholes I work with. I'll have to find another way to make a living."

Ann noticed that Darren had gone silent for several minutes and had stopped participating in the discussion. In their sessions together, he'd sometimes turned inward, brooding, becoming unresponsive. She saw that happening now.

"Darren," she said, attempting to engage him, "you've told us that your abuser was fresh out of the seminary and teaching at a parish school here in town before being assigned elsewhere. Do you know where he is now?"

Darren had been staring at his lap and looked up, returning from that black hole into which he'd disappeared. "He's dead," he said.

Ann waited, hoping he would volunteer more information. When he didn't, she asked, "How long ago did he die?"

"Friday night," Darren said with a cold blank expression. "Somebody offed him."

The others exchanged glances. Ann sensed that they'd already discussed this among themselves.

"Do you want to acknowledge his name?" she asked, aware now that everyone in the room knew the man's name. But it was Darren's decision to identify him or not.

Several moments passed. In spite of the open windows, the old parlor felt suffocating and she could smell that faint unvanquished odor, like a defiant stain, seeping through the air they breathed.

"Father Martin Landry," Darren said finally, biting a nail. His bright eyes had darkened. "I can't count how many times I've thought about killing the son of a bitch myself."

Ann found in his expression a hardness that concerned her, something she'd never seen in their private sessions. She couldn't picture the sweet-natured Darren hurting anyone. He was slight of build, a self-described loser at sports and anything physical. The flannel shirts and hiking boots were an affectation. She looked at his bone-white hands, as she had at Luke's, and detected no cuts or bruises or scabbed knuckles, no signs of an altercation.

"We've all been there, bro," said Strike, breaking the collective silence.

Ann looked at Strike's hands, too, the thick hands of a roughneck who worked with heavy drilling equipment. There was dirt under his nails and a long white scar across the back of his left hand, and a bandage on his right index finger. It occurred to her that *We've all been there* could have had a more ominous meaning. Could the four of them have *all been there* in the rectory on Friday night?

She noticed that Zach was sitting on his hands, pumping his knees up and down like a third grader after too much chocolate milk. His eyes were glistening with tears. Arturo leaned over and asked if he was all right, but Zach didn't respond. Seconds passed while everyone focused on their silent and struggling friend. Arturo asked again, "Hey, Zach, you okay?"

Ann stood up and moved toward the shaken young man with her arms outspread. "Zach, come see," she said in a soft but emphatic voice, using the diction a Cajun boy would understand.

He ceased pumping his legs and rose to embrace her, burying himself deep in her bosom. Before she understood what was happening, the others were surrounding them in an affectionate tangle of arms, four young men grieving over the burdens they'd borne too long in secret, their childhoods tarnished, their innocence lost too soon.

SIXTEEN

AT THE SAME TIME THAT ANN WAS MEETING WITH DARREN AND FRIENDS, I was attending Matt's indoor soccer game at a middle school gym near Audubon Park. It was one of those sullen winter days when everyone was glad they weren't kicking a ball around outside in the foggy drizzle. God bless whoever figured out *we don't have to do this outdoors when the weather is bad.* In those days, our indoor matches were played on a basketball court. The goals were stored in the back of a bakery truck driven by a father who owned a pastry business. I was the perfect soccer dad who showed up early to help assemble the goals and stayed to break them down after the final whistle.

Matt wasn't one of our most athletic players, but he was having a great game against tough rivals who liked to shove and bang. That's when I first noticed Stevie. Not because he played dirty, but because he seemed to be the only gentleman on an otherwise malicious, undisciplined team. It took me several moments to place him. And then I realized I'd seen him on a Martin Landry videotape, the blond boy who'd been pinned to the carpet in a wrestling match with the older and bigger Kwame Williams.

Coming across one of Landry's victims in everyday life gave me a visceral chill. *And the Word was made flesh and dwelt among us.* Stevie wasn't just an image on a screen anymore. He was a real ten-year-old boy, flesh and bone, running after the ball as it rolled out of bounds. We parents were sitting in stands elevated on a concrete platform, the old-fashioned kind you had to walk up stairs to access. I looked around to see if I could spot someone who might be Stevie's mother or father. It was a futile exercise, of course, but I felt I had to do something and not just sit there passively with what Ann had called *dark knowledge* in my head. I tuned in to the occasional chatter from parents, hoping to hear someone mention his name. *Nice block, Stevie! Way to go, Stevie!* But the game ended a half-hour later without any telltale sign of a proud parent. Which was just as well. What was I going to do? Introduce myself and tell them they'd be hearing from the Bishop with a check and a waiver to sign.

In the handshaking ceremony after the game, I noticed Matt and Stevie exchanging words and smiling as if they knew each other. I was standing on the sideline with parents from both teams, waiting to take our boys home, when I decided to sidle up next to one of those aggressive dads who talked nonstop to the referees during a game. *Foul, ref! Yellow card!* I broke the ice with "Great game, didn't you think? At this age, they're finally playing like a team."

He was a beefy middle-aged man, friendly enough but disappointed that his son hadn't played better. "Which one is yours?" he asked.

"Number ten."

"He works hard," he said. "I like his hustle."

He told me his son's number and I complimented him, as well.

"That kid Stevie has some really nice moves. Are his parents here?" I asked with faux innocence. "I want to congratulate them on raising a future star."

There was nothing special about Stevie's game, and the man glanced sidelong at me as if I was just another clueless soccer dilettante. He hesitated, then lowered his voice, a confidential aside. "Single mother," he said, making that tippler hand gesture that means *she likes to drink.* "Never comes to the games. Just drops him off and picks him up. Half the time she forgets to do that."

I helped two dads disassemble the goals and lug them to the bakery truck stationed outside the back door of the gym. Matt had stayed within eyesight, our rule, and afterwards we jogged together across the empty basketball court, booting his soccer ball back and forth and talking about the game. All the vehicles except our station wagon were gone from the parking lot in front of the school. A forlorn figure was sitting by himself on the wet school steps, huddled inside a hoodie, his bare knees tucked against his chest. The weather was inhospitable, a fine mist settling over everything, and he should've been waiting for his mother in a dry, safe place.

"Do you know that boy?" I asked Matt.

"That's Stevie Sutton. He goes to O-L-S. He was studying to be an altar boy but he quit."

Altar boy. Martin Landry's entrée.

"He's probably waiting for his mom or dad," I said. "It's too wet out here. Let's invite him to wait in our car."

At first Stevie said no, a knee-jerk reaction to any adult stranger enticing him into a car. He'd been well trained. But Matt said, "It's okay, Stevie, it's me and my dad," and the boy was happy to slide into the backseat with a roof over his head. I cranked the engine and turned on the heater, a soothing tonic for the dampness outside.

"Would you like a ride home?" Sooner or later, I would have to find out where he lived. "We can drop you off."

"No, sir, my mother is coming," Stevie said. "She's usually a little late."

He was courteous and soft spoken, with long feminine eyelashes and a tender, flawless face, still a good four years from acne and the chiseled features of puberty. What was it that creeper had said on the video? "You're too old for him now, T-Trey. Your b-body disgusts him. He likes them younger."

I eavesdropped on the boys in the backseat as they laughed and replayed the game, goal by goal. They talked about their teammates, who they liked and who they didn't. I was waiting for a lull in their conversation so I could collect more information about Stevie. When that moment arrived, I looked at him in the rearview mirror and asked in my cheerful dad voice, "How is your year going at O-L-S, Stevie?"

"It's kinda strict," he said. "I really don't like Sister Antoinette very much. If you forget your homework, she makes you stay after school and clean the blackboard."

Cleaning blackboards, rulers whacked across the knuckles, dodging thrown chalk. Eternal, immutable, the Catholic Church and its teachers. Some things had survived for centuries.

"Did you hear about Father Landry?" I asked.

Stevie didn't respond at first. Then, timidly: "Yes, sir."

"He taught our catechism class," Matt volunteered. "How come you stopped going to altar boys?" he asked Stevie.

Matt had completed his training shortly before the Christmas holidays and had just begun to serve at Mass himself.

"Uh, I dunno," Stevie said. "It was too hard to memorize all that stuff."

A late-model Mazda appeared out of the fog, slowly cruising toward the gym. There was a long rusty scratch across two doors and a dented fender, aging scars from different accidents, judging by the looks of them. She swerved over and hit the brake, her tires scraping the curb, and began honking her horn.

"That's my mom," Stevie said, popping open the door and scurrying out.

"Let me say hello to her," I said, getting out as well. I needed to meet that woman and see who we would be dealing with.

"It's okay," Stevie yelled over his shoulder as he raced toward the car. "I'll tell her who you guys are."

I gave her a friendly wave, forcing a smile as I marched across the wet asphalt to the driver's door. She was nearly an hour late to pick up her son, and I really wanted to scold her for being a bad parent. But I stopped myself from doing that, knowing I might interact with her someday in an official capacity. I stood by her door, waiting for her to roll down the window so we could speak. She was smoking a long filtered cigarette and stared at me through the misted glass, a younger woman, maybe thirty years old, with messy tangles of blonde hair and a puffy face and hard, suspicious eyes that trusted no one, not even a soccer dad who'd just done a favor for her son.

"Hello, Mrs. Sutton, I'm pleased to meet you," I said in a loud voice when it became apparent she wasn't going to lower the window. "My son Matt knows Stevie from Our Lady of Sorrows. We were happy to give him a dry place to wait."

Stevie said something to her and she exhaled smoke, tapping the cigarette into the car's ashtray. Her cup holder contained an empty, fruit-stained plastic daiquiri glass from one of the city's drive-thru daiquiri stands. Without making eye contact again or acknowledging my presence outside her door, she pulled away from the curb and drove off into the fog. She wasn't wearing a seatbelt, and neither was Stevie.

SEVENTEEN

AFTER DINNER THAT EVENING, I retired to my home office, closed the door, and made several phone calls to catch up with what was happening on the various fronts. My executive assistant, Barbara Lavergne, had gone to the chancery that morning to check messages on our low-tech answering machine. She told me we'd been contacted by the major television networks and several big-city newspapers, including the *New York Times* and *Washington Post.* Unbeknownst to me, Monsignor Fulweiler had asked Eric Gautier to visit Barbara at our offices and coach her on how to stonewall the media. The Holy Rottweiler had obviously chosen Eric as the point man of the operation, and I was left with limited access to their elite conclave of strategists.

I phoned Vince Scalco and told him about the chronicle of molestations and reassignments documented in Martin Landry's personnel file, and about the school yearbooks we could examine to identify his victims at OLS.

"Tomorrow night I'll go take a couple of spins around the Fruit Loop," Vince said, "and see if I can run Trey to ground. He'll know what went down the other night in Landry's sex cave."

After hanging up, I sat tapping my fingers on the old 8mm film box I'd brought home from Landry's collection. Where could I find an 8mm movie projector? My parents didn't own one anymore. I tried to remember which of their friends took home movies when I was growing up. All those choppy images flickered through my memory, the abrupt cutaways, the mugging faces and silly silent-movie antics of a more innocent time. My brother had played in a garage band with Philip Owens, and Philip's mother had recorded miles of footage of them banging their electric guitars in her home beauty shop, where they practiced. My teammate Mike Hebert's dad had filmed every down of our junior high football games, and Gladys Stroud had captured me nervously pinning a corsage on her lovely daughter Melanie before a homecoming dance. But I hadn't been in touch with those folks in a couple of decades, and I had no idea how to contact them.

And then I remembered the small audio-visual library at Immaculata seminary, its gallery of black-and-white group photos dating back sixty years, framed and mounted on the walls, and a shelf laden with outdated cameras whose manufacturers no longer made their film stock. Projectors were also stored in that room, including the bulky 16mm reel-to-reel monster that showed the classic movies we seminarians watched every Saturday night, my introduction to De Sica, Fellini, and Bergman.

I phoned Immaculata's residence for retired clergymen, where my uncle was staying, and requested to speak with him. The mumbling old priest who answered the phone did a poor job of denying Ted's whereabouts. "Father, this is his nephew Peter Moore," I said. "I'm the director of communications for the diocese. I work for the Bishop. Could you please ask Father McMurray to call me at home? It's very important."

Ted returned my call within minutes, and I asked him if there was still an audio-visual room with vintage projectors at the seminary. "I believe so," he said, "although I haven't been in that room in years. Brother Alban is in charge of the photo archive, and he's probably the one to ask. Why, what's on your mind, Peter?"

"Do you remember seeing an old eight millimeter home movie in Martin Landry's stash? I need the right kind of projector to see what's on it."

It was late on a cold starlit night when I arrived at Immaculata. I pressed the intercom and gave my name, the wrought iron gates opened mysteriously, and I drove down the lane of dark trees into the heart of the old Romanesque campus. There were only seven seminarians at that time, living in a dormitory built for seventy. The seminaries and convents had been closing down for more than a decade because there weren't enough young Catholics attracted to the religious life. It was a medieval European model, after all, centered around monasticism. Kumbaya and Masses facing the congregation had made little difference. So who was left to carry on the sacred studies and become ordained priests? The Martin Landrys of the world?

Bundled in his black overcoat, Father Ted stood smoking a cigarette near the double doors of the refectory building, where the residents ate their meals. When my headlights glared against his face, he squinted and inhaled a final drag and rubbed out the small glowing tip on the sole of his shoe, casually slipping the butt into his coat pocket.

"I have to smoke in secret nowadays," he said as I got out of the car. "Whenever and wherever I can. The old cranks in this place are always on my case about it. Secondhand smoke and all that. Another good reason to get back to my rectory as soon as I can."

While the number of seminarians was down significantly, the number of retired and infirm priests had tripled since I'd left. They had to build another residence to house the influx of old priests. This was happening all over the world. Anyone doing the math could see that the Church was destined for a very lean future.

The building was dark inside, and Ted used a flashlight to navigate us past the silent dining halls on each side of the corridor, long tables spread with white cloths, their empty chairs like strange little creatures crouching from the light. I wondered if they still maintained the same caste system from my era, the young sems in the big room, the teaching faculty in a smaller room conducive to quiet conversations, retired priests in another, the working brothers shuttled off to a dining room near the kitchen.

My uncle had asked Brother Alban to meet us at the A-V library, which was located on the far side of the building in a warren of closed-off rooms, mostly vacant offices and storage closets. Back in my day, I didn't know what was behind those doors, and there was a tacit rule that you did not open them without permission.

Brother Alban was waiting for us in the only lighted room. The A-V library looked exactly as I'd remembered it, as if gelled in aspic for twenty years. More class photographs were added to the walls, and the junk shelf was still overloaded with outmoded cameras and projector parts. A heavy old Smith Corona manual typewriter sat on one of the reading tables, surrounded by thick reference volumes and small stacks of handwritten note cards. Was someone doing research for a book?

Working brothers like Brother Alban did not study for the sacrament of Holy Orders, usually because they had no aptitude for the priesthood. To put it bluntly, they didn't possess the intellectual gravitas for theology and canon law. The crueler elements of the clergy sometimes referred to them as *male nuns*. Working brothers took the vows of poverty, chastity, and obedience, and they served the religious community through their labor as custodians and groundskeepers, tailors and carpenters and gardeners. They carried clothing to the dry cleaners, drove people to doctor appointments, unloaded truckloads of food and supplies. They maintained the archives and kept track of books borrowed from the main library.

By the time we arrived, Brother Alban had already found the 8mm projector, positioned it on a table, and was assembling a portable viewing screen. My uncle introduced us, and Brother Alban shook my hand with a damp and timid grip. He was a quiet, serious man who didn't say more than hello. I guessed his age at around fifty. Pallid and gaunt, with the graceless carriage of so many clerics I had known, he stood nearly a head taller than I, Lurch-like in his stooped movements.

"Peter, you're in good hands with Brother Alban. So if you don't mind, I'll leave you to it," Ted said, his face sagging from fatigue. I suspected he needed another cigarette before bedtime. "It's been a very long weekend. Let's talk tomorrow."

After he left, I thanked Brother Alban for generously taking time on a Sunday evening to help me. "I hope this old projector still works," I said, removing the small reel from its yellowed box. "When was the last time someone used it?"

He was tightening a knob on the screen stand, and at first I thought he was too preoccupied to hear my question. But he'd heard me clearly. "I c-can't recall," he said after careful deliberation. "N-not for several years."

He had a mild stutter. Or did I imagine that? More alert now, my brain shifted into a higher gear. Had I heard his voice before?

"I'll sh-show you how to remove the reel," he said. "You can turn off the projector and leave it here. I'll p-put everything away in the morning."

He spoke with a distinct Uptown accent, as we locals called it, acquired from the wealthy blue-blood families who'd lived in splendor near St. Charles Avenue for three or four generations.

"This tape belonged to Father Martin Landry," I said. "We found it in his bedroom. A horrible thing, what happened to him, God rest his soul." I made the sign of the cross. "Did you know Father Landry?"

He was as meticulous as a transplant surgeon at looping the old tape through the projector spool. "I t-talked to him once or twice," he said without the slightest trace of emotion, "when he c-came to visit the seminarians."

I could hear that stutter in my head. It had to be him—the phantom cameraman. He seemed harmless enough and slightly feeble, but it suddenly occurred to me that he might have participated in the murder.

"I don't know what's on this film," I said. "Maybe footage of Martin and his family. A portrait of the priest as a young man. It's probably only five or ten minutes long. Would you like to stay and watch it?"

He flipped a switch, the lightbulb glowed, the projector whirred into motion. White leader appeared on the screen, a short segment of hair-thin scratches before the first color image materialized.

"Thank you," he said, still not meeting my eye, "but I will be late for Cuh-Compline." A canonical hour, the last prayers of the night.

"Five minutes, Brother. It's Martin Landry. We may discover something we didn't know about him."

Images flickered on the screen, what appeared to be a family gathering at a picnic table in a wooded park. The magic of Eastman Kodak, 1955. An attractive, dark-haired teenage girl wearing red pedal pushers and a white blouse tied at her waist was waving at the camera as she turned hot dogs on a barrel-shaped grill. Two rowdy little boys raced into the frame, shooting each other with cap pistols and turning to shoot at the camera.

Brother Alban stared at the screen. He seemed mesmerized by the pictures, unable to pull himself away.

"Brother Alban," I said, "we have Landry's entire collection of videotapes."

He looked directly at me for the first time. "I d-don't know what you're t-talking about," he said, his face and high forehead a sudden splotch of red.

I wondered if he'd attended the party on Friday night. My uncle had said there was no tape in the cam, but maybe this man had taken it with him when he left. Maybe Brother Alban had his own collection of tapes.

"You need to speak with your Brother Superior as soon as possible." I said. "Come clean and tell him everything, Alban."

I suspected he was a voyeur, not an active pedophile. He'd hidden behind the camera like a perverse teenager peeping through his sister's keyhole.

"The police are acting like they have the killer behind bars, but they don't," I said. "He's still out there. And he may know that Landry had an accomplice."

He looked dumbstruck, his mouth open but absent of words. He watched the screen, where a handsome boy, maybe thirteen or fourteen years old, was perched at the edge of a picnic bench, talking to his mother. She was a pleasant-looking woman, not yet in middle age, but there was something damaged and convalescent about her. A lack of focus, a blank, unresponsive glaze. When the camera shifted to a different angle, I realized she was sitting a wheelchair.

"He loved his m-mother very much," Brother Alban said, his voice quaking now as he studied the screen.

This unexpected discovery had left me lightheaded. I felt uneasy about my situation and his odd lurking presence. We were alone in a dark building on isolated grounds, and he was no stranger to aberrant behavior. Could he have done those dreadful things to Martin Landry? I wasn't eager to find out how a cornered man would protect himself against exposure, even a man of the cloth. And yet despite my apprehensions, I forged ahead.

"You know things no one else knows, Brother. You can save everyone a lot of suffering by coming forward and identifying the boys Martin Landry abused," I said in a nervous rush of words. "We need to contact their families, and you can help us. The diocese is cleaning up this wretched mess the best way we can."

The Bishop would probably relocate him as soon as possible. Another seminary, another motherhouse, a different state. It was an abhorrent practice, but it had worked too many times for the Church to abandon it.

"Luh-like I said, I d-don't know what you're t-talking about." His stutter was becoming more pronounced. "P-please turn off the lights when you leave."

He turned and walked out of the room.

I wasn't sure what to do next. I noticed an ancient black rotary telephone near the shelf of discarded cameras, and I was surprised to discover a dial tone when I lifted the receiver. I called Vince Scalco's office number, hoping to catch him working late.

"You're never going to believe this," I said in a restrained voice, facing the open door and dark hallway to make certain Brother Alban had gone. "I've found the phantom cameraman."

If he'd been drinking, my phone call sobered him. "This brother," he said, "where is he now?"

"He went to pray in the chapel."

"Don't say nothing yet to his boss. If the black robes get a whiff of what's coming, they'll bury his sorry ass somewhere in Lapland."

"So what should I do?"

Adrenaline was surging through every cell in my body, making me shiver. I was overwhelmed by what I'd uncovered and I felt like running ten miles around a track.

"If this brother is who you think he is, he might skip. Like right away," he said. "You suppose he has a car?"

"I'm sure he can get his hands on one. The seminary has more vehicles than a redneck funeral. Cars, pick-ups, a bus, a tractor, riding lawn mowers."

"Park somewhere outside the gates and see if he goes anywhere."

"You mean a stakeout and tail?" I couldn't believe what he was asking me to do. "I'm not a private eye, Vince. I don't know how to do that."

"It's not rocket science, Pete. You've seen it in the movies. Just find a spot where a driver won't notice you and wait there with the lights and motor off."

"This sounds like a fool's errand. How long will I have to sit out there in the cold?"

"If he leaves the seminary," he said, "find a phone and call me."

I didn't want to play PI, so I dawdled around in that unheated room for a few minutes longer, putting off what Vince was expecting of me.

Eventually I sat down in a chair and watched the rest of the home movie. The dutiful boy sitting with his mother at the picnic table was Martin Landry. The resemblance was obvious. He began to feed her from a paper plate, and the filmer, probably his father, must've asked them to wave. Martin smiled and waved, and his mother attempted to wave as well, but her facial expression did not stray from the listless mask she wore from whatever malady had planted her in the wheelchair. There was a quick cutaway to Martin pushing his mother out of the shady picnic area toward a gothic redstone tower a short distance away, and I finally understood that the family was visiting her on the grounds of some medical facility or sanatorium. I stood up from the chair. I'd seen that tower before. It was at the psychiatric hospital across the lake, where I'd once gone to visit Donny Bertrand.

I parked in front of a row of dark little cottages across the street from Immaculata's brick walls. It wasn't terribly cold or uncomfortable in the wagon, but I much preferred to be lying next to Ann in our cozy bed, enjoying a nightcap and reading a book.

Sitting behind the steering wheel, watching the gates for headlights or any signs of activity, I remembered a cold holiday season when I was in college and had worked as a night watchman for a Knights of Columbus Christmas tree lot. It was my job to guard the trees overnight and make sure none were stolen. My partner was Earl Doucet, a guy who'd once dated Ann, and we camped out in a small freezing trailer in the center of the lot, surrounded by a thick forest of pine trees overtopped with vine-like cords of bare lightbulbs. Earl had supplied a portable turntable, and we listened to the new *Beatles '65* album nonstop, night after night, until I'd memorized all the lyrics. We took turns patrolling the perimeter every twenty minutes, per our instructions, and we carried long tactical flashlights, a walkie-talkie, and a .410 shotgun given to us by the manager of the lot. I'd promised myself I wouldn't fire the shotgun unless I was attacked by a rabid animal.

On patrol one frosty night, around two a.m., Earl encountered three black teenagers dragging a tree away, and he fired a warning shot over their heads, hoping they'd drop the tree and run. When they didn't, he fired another round of bird shot and hit one of them in the back. Hearing the shotgun blasts, I flew out of the trailer with my flashlight and raced through the forest of Christmas trees until I found Earl standing over the teenager, panting vapor and threatening to shoot him again if he tried to get up. I told Earl to back off and point the gun somewhere else, and we almost came to blows. The police and EMS arrived, and the manager showed up to pat Earl on the back. A handful of black neighbors wandered over to investigate the gunshots and were unhappy to see a black teenager handcuffed on the ground. The young man had sustained a pattern of bird shot pellets in his back but wasn't seriously wounded. He was transported away by the EMS team and a police escort. All for trying to steal a twenty-dollar Christmas tree. Earl could've been arrested and sent to jail, but he was a well-mannered white Loyola college boy and nothing happened to him. He returned to work the next night, and we rarely spoke to each other for the rest of the holidays.

I was lost in that reverie, remembering the watchdog nights in the bitter cold trailer and the idiocy of untrained twenty-somethings walking the perimeter with a weapon, when I noticed car lights shining on the seminary gates. Someone was leaving the grounds. The gates reeled inward and a car slowly emerged. For a split second it was captured like a Polaroid snapshot in the blaze of burglar lights mounted on the red brick wall. It was Father Ted's car, that old-lady Buick Skylark. When it turned onto the street, the window glass flashed with light and I could see a man sitting in the passenger seat. He had the stoop-shouldered physique of Brother Alban.

I followed the car as it headed downtown on Magazine Street, its funky little shops and bistros pitch black on a Sunday evening, the sidewalks without casual strollers at that hour in a dicey part of the city. Brother Alban or not, where was my uncle going? It was long past his bedtime.

The Skylark bumped along the rugged cobblestones of the warehouse district and crossed the streetcar tracks on Canal Street, then weaved its way through the small quaint passages of the French Quarter. I kept my distance when the car crawled onto narrow Royal Street and idled past the chain security gates of the antique stores and souvenir shops. A couple of blocks beyond St. Anthony's Garden, the driver surprised me by swerving quickly into a parking space, which forced me to roll on past them rather than squeal the brakes and draw attention. My first failed assignment as a vehicle tracker. I slowed almost to a stop and peered into the rearview mirror, watching two men step out of the Skylark. The driver was my uncle, all right, and his passenger was indeed Brother Alban, both dressed in winter jackets and street clothes. I was troubled by their presence together, my mind scrambling to figure out what that could mean. Dark suspicions gripped me by the neck.

In the mirror I could see them approaching one of the gentrified residences. Ted was carrying a black leather bag like a country doctor making a house call late in the night. I made a U-turn at the next corner and drove back past the residence they'd entered, noting the Vieux Carré green shutters and the house number inlaid in tiles. French doors were open on the second floor balcony, where light spilled across gracefully hanging plants. Someone was up there resting against the wrought iron grillwork and smoking a cigar.

I parked in a loading zone a block away and hurried inside an all-night corner market. At a pay phone in the rear of the store I called Vince, whose office was only five or six blocks away. "You were right," I said. "Brother Alban left the seminary and I followed him here to the Quarter." I asked him to meet me in front of the market as soon as possible. "You're never going to believe who drove him here."

I went outside and leaned against the stucco wall near the market's bright entrance, keeping an eye in both directions, making sure the Skylark didn't drive off. A middle-aged man I'd noticed shopping for frozen dinners stopped to ask, "Do you have the time?" His age-worn gay pickup line was code for *Do you have time for sex?* When I consulted my watch and gave him the actual time, nearly midnight, he seemed disappointed and walked away.

I waited patiently. Fifteen minutes, twenty. I had almost given up when I heard that handicap scooter whining along the dark sidewalk like a golf cart climbing a steep hill. It was hard to imagine how Vince Scalco was able to hunt down runaways in that contraption.

Once the Amigo steered into the market's light, I didn't recognize the driver. It appeared as if Vince's scooter had been hijacked by a homeless man. His hair and beard were an unruly mess, his camo hunting jacket ragged and dirty. A cardboard sign scrawled

HOMELESS VET

PLEASE HELP WITH DONATION

was taped to the scooter's basket, which was heaped with crushed cans and wadded newspapers.

"What's the address?" the driver asked when he stopped the scooter a few feet from me. No greeting, no preamble. "I'll get one of my buddies on the force to track down who owns the place."

Vince was wearing a disguise.

"Jesus, Scalco, I was about to go inside and report a stolen scooter."

"This old dog still got a few tricks," he said, smiling through a huge tangled beard that made him look like Karl Marx on a bender. "Show me where they're at and I'll camp out across the street."

"I don't like what I'm thinking, Vince. The phantom and my uncle together."

"Just show me the place and their car, *compagno*. Then get the hell out of here before Vice rolls up and shakes you down for streetwalking."

EIGHTEEN

THE MONDAY MORNING STAFF MEETING DID NOT GO WELL. To begin with, my briefing was a hodgepodge of basic facts and half-lies about Martin Landry's murder. Barbara began sobbing and repeating, "This is too much. This is all too much." That set off Beth Sanders, the editor of publications, who was less grief-stricken than panicked about covering the upcoming funeral and still meeting her Friday deadline. Father Frank "Podnuh" Norbert, our radio commentator and resident whisky-priest, growled about the lack of security measures for clergymen and the disrespect for authority spawned by Vatican II, and then announced he needed a stiff drink to reduce the pressures of working a four-hour week. He excused himself and took his leave. It was nine a.m.

I was catching up on a slew of phone calls from the media when Barbara knocked lightly on my office door to announce that Vincent Scalco was there to see me. He rode in on his Amigo, saying, "This place spooks the crap out of me. Talk about old school. Where do they keep the thumb screws and the rack?" He gazed around my office, which was much too tidy by his standards. "Keep an eye out for rats, Pete. The Black Plague, you dig?"

He was attired in big-and-mighty jeans and a truly hideous plaid sports jacket that looked like a disco blazer from the 1970s. It was good to see him without a disguise.

I was anxious to hear about the stakeout, and he said, "Our boys were there a couple hours. Father Ted walked out with a black bag like the one that priest carried in the movie where the little chick's head goes spinning around."

"It's where they usually keep holy water and blessing oil for the Last Rites," I said, "and the Eucharist in a pyx." A round vessel that resembled an oversized pocket watch. "Sounds like Ted may've been visiting someone who's very ill."

"*Last Rites* sounds Protestant to me, Brother Pete. I still call it *Extreme Unction*, like the good sisters taught us. It's closer to Latin. We don't want non-Catholics to know what we're up to, now do we?"

He pulled a small notepad from his jacket and started flipping pages.

"After the guys left, there was still a light on upstairs," he said, "so I waited a few ticks and rolled across the street and rang the bell."

He said that a man with a cultured Uptown accent opened the door slightly and spoke through the taut chain latch. It was too dark to get a good look at him. He was annoyed to be called to the door at that late hour, and he scolded Vince for disturbing his household. Vince apologized and said he must've written down the wrong address.

"I'm down on my luck, brother. Flat busted. And I gotta get some medical attention for a bad cough I picked up in Nam," said the hirsute Vince. The cardboard homeless vet sign was visible on the Amigo's basket. "A priest I used to know give me this address and told me to come see him if I ever needed help. Father Martin Landry. So Father Marty don't stay here no more?"

There was a long silence, and then the man said, "You have the wrong address, sir. Father Landry has never lived here. Now will you please go away?"

"So you *do* know Father, right?" Vince said. "How can I get in touch with him? I'm hurting, man, and he told me he'd help me out."

The man threatened to call the police.

"And that was it?" I asked. "He shut the door in your face?"

"Wouldn't you?" Vince studied his notepad. "The property is owned by a man named Perry Blanchard. That name ring a bell?"

"Blanchard coffee?"

"That's him. Heir to the bean fortune. You know, 'a hint of chicory in every drop.' He's a little younger than us. A piano teacher by profession. I checked his sheet and he was popped about fifteen years ago for soliciting a male undercover cop. And before that, two queer rollers put the hurt on him real bad one night in Armstrong Park. His old man the coffee king and his lawyer, Russell Gautier, stepped in and

Perry walked on the solicitation bid. Not even a slap on the wrist," he said, licking a thumb and flipping pages. "Perry left town for awhile. Now he's back and apparently behaving himself."

"Why the Last Rites?"

"Maybe he's got AIDS," Vince said matter-of-factly.

That stark possibility overshadowed every stray thought about gay men in those days.

"Well, there's one person who would know why Father Ted and Brother Alban were there last night," I said, confused by it all. "Let me call Ted."

While Vince sat idly on his scooter, examining framed family photos of Ann and our sons, I phoned the seminary. The old priest who answered the call said Father Ted was out and he didn't know when he would return. I tried Ted's rectory and discovered that his recording still said, "Please leave your message for Pastor Edward McMurray or Assistant Pastor Martin Landry." The recorder was full and accepting no more messages.

Vince was smiling at a photograph of Matt at age seven, standing before a bathroom mirror and laughing at himself because he'd combed his long shampooed hair into a tall pointed updo. Vince set the frame back in place and said, "Those school annuals are in some crypt in this dungeon, correcto?" He called the yearbooks *annuals*, a throwback to the days of yore. "Let's go look for Chubby, Smiley, and Red. Ain't that what they're paying us for?"

I convinced Sister Ellen that I was doing research on an article about Our Lady of Sorrows and that Vince was assisting me with fond recollections of the school he'd attended as a student in the 1950s. He and I set up camp in two carrels in a remote corner of the Archives and spent the next three hours poring through OLS yearbooks. I consulted the notes I'd made on a lined yellow pad when Vince and I were watching the videos in his office, but the process of matching head-shot photos of grinning, well-presented schoolboys with our imprecise mental images and scribbled notes was more difficult than I'd anticipated. We'd counted nine boys being sexually abused by him—three street boys, by their appearances, and six Catholic schoolboys—and that didn't include several others, like David Hinojosa, who appeared in footage where no sex was taking place.

After those hours of intense concentration, with burning eyes and fatigue numbing our brains, Vince and I were cautiously optimistic we could identify four of the six boys from Our Lady of Sorrows. Establishing certainty was another step altogether.

"My head is fried," I declared, standing up and rubbing my sore neck. Ann had been urging me to get bifocals, and after staring at those small black-and-white rectangles for so long, my headache and blurry vision proved she was right.

"What now, Vince?" I asked. "How do we verify?"

He spun the Amigo in a half turn to face me, then looked around the quiet library to make sure no one was watching or listening. "We may have to show the O-L-S nuns a nasty video or two," he said, pulling a silver flask from the inside pocket of his plaid blazer and taking a quick drink. I could smell the Christmas fragrance of brandy. "They'll recognize their students when they see them."

I worked my neck, trying to ease the knotted tension. "We still don't have Trey," I said.

He stole another sip of brandy. "Pete," he said, offering me the flask, "it's time to put on our spy-boy shoes."

NINETEEN

THAT EVENING, I JOINED VINCE in a stakeout of the Fruit Loop. He hunkered down on the Amigo's seat cushion in an unlit *porte cochere* across the street from the small strip of gay bars, and I crouched next to him, cold and nervous and skeptical of his plan. A dry weather front had swept through the city earlier in the day, clearing out the sticky dampness and making way for a starry night in the heart of a New Orleans winter. Traffic was sparse, nothing like the weekends, Vince said, and we spotted only three young male hookers hanging around outside the bars, waiting for the circling chicken hawks to light at the curb and unlock their doors.

"You doing okay, man?" I asked him after a half hour of dead silence.

He was glumly watching the action on the street. His son had turned tricks on the Loop until he was busted by an undercover cop for drinking under age and soliciting sex. It was how Vince and Martha had found their runaway boy the first time.

"Copacetic," he replied with professional brevity. This wasn't the time or place for a conversation.

A shiny new BMW slowed down and angled to the curb. Vince raised his night-vision binoculars, scoping the teenager who scooted out of a rear door. I could see two middle-aged men with nice haircuts, one behind the wheel and the other in the backseat. When the car pulled away, the teenager ambled down the sidewalk toward another streetwalker slouching against a brick wall and smoking a homemade cigarette.

"That's him. That's Trey," Vince said, lowering the binoculars. "The one who just got out of the BMW. Bust a move, Pete, before somebody else picks him up."

Many years later, I'm still not sure why I agreed to help Vince with that stakeout. He'd convinced me that Trey would recognize him from the *Scuola Vecchia* disaster, a fat man riding an Amigo, and there was no other choice.

I reluctantly crossed the street, hands in my pockets, wearing a corduroy sports coat and creased slacks, with polished brown penny loafers, an aging frat boy who sold high-end real estate. That was my cover. But my heart was pounding, my palms were sweating, and I was scared. What if a friend or acquaintance saw me at the Fruit Loop? What if an undercover cop stepped out of a bar and arrested me for soliciting?

"Good evening, gents," I said to the two teenage boys passing a joint between them. They were standing underneath a blinking bar sign, the music so loud it was throbbing a large windowpane. Trey was hiding inside a scruffy hoodie, strings of hair falling over his eyes, making it difficult to tell where he was looking. He seemed smaller in person, less menacing. "Would you care to take a walk with me?" I asked him with a timid smile. Beads of sweat were racing down my back. Even the soles of my feet were damp.

"What you got in mind, mister?" Trey asked, blowing marijuana smoke in my face.

I told him I'd reserved a room around the corner. The same flophouse where Ned Scalco had taken his life. Vince hated that place, but it was conveniently located for what he had in mind.

"Room service is gonna cost you more," Trey said.

"Wanna make it a manwich?" asked the other boy, chuckling.

"A man sandwich," Trey laughed. "Yeah, a manwich."

Heat rushed into my face. What had I gotten myself in to? "I'm an old-fashioned guy. I like it one at a time," I said, mortified to be talking like that to boys Luke's age.

"No cutting, no burning, no choking," Trey said. "We straight on that?"

The lobby of the flophouse had space enough for only two ratty armchairs and a waste basket. It smelled like a nursing home, the odor of disinfectant smothering a multitude of sins. The front desk man, a skeletal junkie whose neck and arms were inked with biblical images and quotations, sat like a zombie bank teller behind a barred window. I slid the cash through a small slot, and without a word he slid back a key.

It was obvious that Trey had been there before. He showed me to the stairs and found room 207, unlocking the door and sauntering inside like it was his own private apartment. It was a cramped, dreary room with a double bed, a toilet and sink, and two rickety straight-back chairs. The wallpaper was peeling in scrolls.

"How you want this to go, mister?" Trey asked, flipping the hood back off his head. "How do you roll?"

He unzipped his jeans and sat on the edge of the bed. There was no spread or blanket, only a stained fitted sheet.

"Wait, hold on," I said, extending my hands in the universal language for *stop*.

Where was Vince? He was supposed to be following us to the room. He was the experienced professional who would ask questions and run the show. I didn't know where to start.

"Can we just talk for a minute?" I asked, buying time.

"This your first hunt for *strange*?" He nodded at my wedding band and laughed through crusty teeth that needed at least three years of braces. "Your wife know what her man likes to do when she's at her Bridge club?"

The door opened, nudging me in the back. A wheezing Vince Scalco stepped into the room and bent over, grabbing his knees. "This fucking place don't have an elevator," he said, gulping air. "Yet another code violation."

Trey stood up and zipped his jeans. "What the fuck, man? You didn't say nothing 'bout a three-way." His eyes darted at me. "Who is this fat fuck? It's gonna cost you . . ."

He stopped mid-sentence and gazed at Vince, who was stooped over and breathing hard. "Hey, I seen you before, asshole," he said. "You're the dude . . ."

Trey knelt quickly on one knee and fetched a hunting knife from a leather sheath concealed under a leg of his jeans. Vince's plan had gone south immediately, and when I saw the gleaming blade, I feared for my life. I was in reasonable shape in those days, six-two and 185 pounds, but I knew how strong and agile Trey was from the videos I'd seen of him wrestling Martin Landry.

"Put down the hillbilly toothpick, son," Vince said, straightening his large body and reaching for something in his hip pocket. "We're not cops. We just want to talk."

"Get the fuck out my way," Trey said, slashing the air with the knife and lunging toward Vince and the door.

Vince had spent many years patrolling the mean streets of New Orleans, and though overweight and out of shape, he still had muscle memory and a handful of nimble moves. I don't think Trey really intended to stab him. He felt trapped and betrayed and wanted to escape. Vince sidestepped another wild jab, locked his huge arm around Trey's knife-wielding arm, and zapped the boy's neck with a sparking stun device that looked like an electric razor from the *Star Wars* future. I'd never seen anything like it. This was several years before the Taser.

Trey dropped the knife and would've collapsed deadweight to the floor if Vince hadn't cradled him on the way down. I picked up the knife and watched the boy twitch on the threadbare carpet, wondering if that zapper had triggered a seizure.

"What the hell did you do to him, Vince?"

"Give me a hand," he said, stooping over the boy. "We don't have much time before he's up on his feet again."

We dragged Trey into one of the chairs. There was a glass at the sink and I washed it out and brought him water. He was rousing slowly and drank from the glass I held to his lips. For a fleeting moment, I remembered bottle-feeding my baby boys.

"Sorry I had to do that, Trey," Vince said, still huffing from the exertion. He was sitting on the other chair in front of Trey, their knees touching. "We just want to axe you a few questions, all right? If you're straight with us, this won't take long."

He rested a forearm on his thigh, the electroshock weapon still in his hand for Trey to see and fear.

"This is about Father Martin Landry, the priest they found in a bathtub with his skull bashed in," Vince said. "You know anything about that?"

Trey wasn't completely alert. There was fright and confusion in his wandering eyes. He looked at me, then at Vince, one man holding a stun gun, the other holding a hunting knife. It was shameful, what Scalco and I were doing, bullying a teenage boy.

"Who *are* you, man? Why you following me?" Trey asked, slurring his words. "How you know my name?"

"We found Father Landry's videotapes, Trey. We know he was sharking young boys. We heard him call you by name," Vince said. "I'll be honest wicha, son, I don't care if you were the one that offed that creep. We're not cops, and that's not why we're here. You're not in trouble with us, okay? What he was doing—a Catholic priest—is disturbing to me on a personal basis—may he burn in hell—but I'm not blaming *you*. He was the bad guy, not you, Trey. Y'understand where I'm coming from?"

Vince had told me that when he was a cop, he had a reputation for being no-nonsense and direct, even violent, in interrogations. But with Trey he'd softened his approach and sounded more like a concerned parent. It was the reason he'd become successful at convincing runaways to return home.

"Let's start with your age. How old are you, Trey?"

Trey fingered the hair out of his eyes and wiped away tears. "Eighteen," he said, sniffing, rubbing his face.

"I'm guessing more like fifteen or sixteen, Trey."

The boy hesitated, shrugging. "Whatever," he said.

"Do you live with your parents?"

The question made Trey uncomfortable. He shifted in the chair, swinging away from Vince's large knees, and for a moment I thought the boy would make another dash for the door.

"It was just my old man and me," he said, finally, "and he doesn't give a fuck if I'm dead or alive. I'm not going back to that shit-hole trailer, if that's what you're planning."

Vince was focused intensely. "Did he ever hurt you?" he asked.

Trey shrugged again. "He took a belt to me whenever he felt like it. When he got real pissed off, he'd hang a leash around my neck and tie it to a post outside the trailer and make me sleep with the dogs. One Christmas he said, 'Here's what Santa brought you, boy,' and piled up some empty beer cans in, like, a Christmas-tree stack. He laughed at me when I started crying, calling me a worthless fucking faggot."

I was horrified. I couldn't imagine someone treating a child like that.

In his line of work, Vince had dealt with every atrocious abuse imaginable, so this came as no surprise. He told me later that every time he encountered a story like Trey's, he asked himself, *Was I like that father?* He didn't make Ned sleep with dogs. But sometimes, when he was angry at his son, he squeezed his arm too hard and left bruises. He slapped Ned's face and roughed him up when he located him after the second runaway. It was the same way he'd treated project thugs in his custody. His wife was furious at him, and Vince blamed his behavior on the stresses of being a cop in a tough town. In his remorse, however, when he looked back on his parenting, he despised himself for yelling at Ned and calling his son the kind of names that Trey's old man called him. Vince acknowledged that he was no different from the alcoholic son of a bitch who'd brutalized Trey and chased him away from home.

"I understand why you ran away, Trey. I really do. I was a bully father to my son and he ran away, too. I've been trying to make it up to him ever since," he said, "even though it's too late now. I've gotta live with who I was and what I did wrong, and most of the time I don't think God will forgive me."

He set the stun gun on the floor and leaned forward in the chair. "How long have you been living on the street, son?" he asked.

Trey rocked back, suspending himself on the chair's rear legs. "When I was nine years old, CPS put me in a foster home in the St. Thomas projects." Child Protective Services. "I was the only white kid in the home, so I got my ass kicked every day. That's where I met Father Marty. He used to come around to a spot where some religious people helped you with your homework and shit. He took me to eat snowballs, and to roll around in those plastic balls at McDonald's. Bought me basketball shoes. He even let me stay at the priest house when that old priest was out of town. Father Marty was the only grown-up man that was ever good to me."

Vince bore down on him with a piercing concentration. "You had sex with him," he said, a declaration not a question.

The boy rode the chair hard to its front legs, a muffled strike against the grungy carpet. "Yeah, so what?" he said. "We rassled around a lot. He sucked my dick and taught me how to suck his. I didn't care. He said he loved me, man. That's all that mattered. He treated me like somebody special."

Vince sat quietly for a moment, letting that information sink in. "What about other boys?" he asked.

156

"There was others, yeah. Kinda made me jealous. But Father Marty always told me I was his favorite," he said with a cautious smile. "Some of them boys was from the school, some off the street, like me. You know that black boy Kwame they busted? I hung with him at St. Thomas. We were tight, man. And the same thing happened to him that happened to me. Father Marty loved on us when we were shorties, but he cut us off when we started growing hair on our nut sacks."

His laughter had a sharp steel edge.

"The police say your friend Kwame killed Father Marty," Vince said.

"That's some harsh shit, man. Kwame ain't gangsta, yo. He wouldn't hurt nobody, 'specially not Father Marty." Trey folded his arms defensively. "He loved that man like I did."

Vince pressed harder. "Kwame was at the priests' house on Friday night, Trey. Witnesses saw him there. When the cops grabbed him, he was wearing Father Marty's gold watch. They figure he did the priest for the watch. Maybe stole some cash, too."

"No way, dude. I seen Father Marty give him that watch at Christmas. Like a love bracelet for a girlfriend," he said. "Who told you Kwame was at the party that night? It ain't so."

"How you know that?"

"'Cause I was at the party. Till Father Marty got that phone call and told us we had to book it on out of there."

"You were at the rectory on the night Father Landry was killed?" Vince asked, glancing at me.

"Fuh sho, man. Me and three other boys. We was having a good time, drinking fine wine and smoking a little weed, when Marty got this call that freaked him out. He said somebody was coming over to see him and we had to fly. Sounded like it might be something serious," he said. "It was raining like a motherfucker, so we had to run for it. I don't know where them other three went. They was tight from the same school and all. Me, I got soaking wet and hid out in that dumpster back beside the carport, where the priests park their rides."

"Did you see who came to the rectory, Trey? The phone caller."

"Tell you the truth, I was mad high from smoking Indonesia and dozed off in that smelly-ass dumpster. At least I had a lid over my head. Didn't wake up till I heard that old priest drive up and park in his space. Figured I better get on out of there before he spotted me. So I hauled ass. It was dark and still raining like a bitch."

"You didn't see anybody else enter the house before the old priest came home?"

"I crashed hard, man. No telling how long. The fucking rats coulda chewed my dick off, I wouldn'ta woke up."

Vince slumped in his chair. He looked like he'd just wrestled with an angel, like Jacob in the Bible, but the strain on his face slowly transformed into a faint triumphant smile. After what Trey had just told us, Vince and I knew more than the police and the black robes, more than anyone but the killer himself.

"Trey, there was sometimes another man who showed up at Father Martin's parties," I said, speaking for the first time. "A man who shot the videos. We've heard his voice. He had a slight stutter. Do you know who he was?"

Trey put his hands behind his head and rocked back again. "Tall old dude we called Al the Creeper," he said. "Some kind of priest or something. Father Marty's buddy from back in the day. Al the Creeper never did the nasty with nobody, just got off on that camera thing. He wasn't there that night, either, if that's what you want to know."

It had to be Brother Alban.

"Could this Al character have been the phone caller?" Vince asked.

"Father Marty wouldn'ta kicked us out if it was Al. It was somebody else, man. Somebody that scared him."

I tossed the knife on the bed and started pacing in a circle, a recent habit I'd picked up from Eric Gautier. It helped me think. "The three boys who were at the party," I said. "Do you know their names?"

Trey turned to watch me. "The parties at Father Marty's crib—I never knew half them kids. And even if I did, I wouldn't dime 'em out, mister."

Something was gnawing at my gut. "The three boys—can you describe them? Were two of them brothers?"

Vince looked puzzled by my questions, my going off script. Trey gazed off at the peeling wallpaper, unwilling to respond. Our conversation had stalled, so I decided to put all my cards on the table.

"My name is Peter Moore, Trey. And this man is Vincent Scalco. We work for the Church."

My approach made Vince uneasy. He was more comfortable relying on the tools of his trade—trickery, ruses, the myriad variations of deceit.

"We're trying to find out the names of the boys Father Landry had sex with," I said. "They haven't committed any crimes, and we prefer to keep the police out of this altogether. But we've got to tell their parents what happened to them. In private, you understand. Without anybody else knowing."

Trey stared at me bewildered, as if he couldn't comprehend why the others might feel shame. Because he didn't.

"Those boys won't want their classmates and the whole world hearing they had sex with a priest," I explained. "Word gets out—goes public in the newspapers and TV—that kind of thing will follow them around for the rest of their lives."

Trey responded with his indifferent shrug. "Like I told you, man, I don't know names," he said. "I didn't go to school with those boys."

"What if we show you photos?" I said. "From school yearbooks. Could you identify which ones you've seen at Father Marty's parties?"

His laugh was too dark and disenchanted for a boy his age.

"Those nice clean-smelling schoolboys, their parents are gonna cry and hug 'em and tell 'em it's all gonna be chill," he said. "They'll send 'em to a head doctor and he'll make sure everybody loves everybody. But what about me, yo? Me and Kwame? Who's gonna watch our backs now that Father Marty is dead and gone?"

I exchanged glances with Vince. We both knew that the boy was right, and there was very little we could do about it.

"This is for you. For your time tonight," I said, removing an envelope from the inside pocket of my sports jacket. It contained $300 in cash, which I'd drawn from an Office of Communications travel expense account I rarely used. "We understand that you were very fond of Father Landry, and he was good to you. But what he was doing wasn't right," I said. "We're not going to abandon you, Trey. The Church will make sure you're compensated for his misconduct."

I handed the envelope to him and he opened it and started counting the money. "You want me to keep my mouth shut," he said. "Is that what this double date is all about?"

"It's about restitution, Trey," I said. "About making amends."

Trey was a fifth-grade dropout. I didn't know if he understood those words, or the Judeo-Christian guilt behind them.

"Can I go now?" he asked like a student in detention at the principal's office.

"How can we get in touch with you again?" I said. "Where do you stay?"

I was worried about him. I didn't want him to become one of the lost ones. The ones who ended up dead in a flophouse, or upstate in prison, or missing, never to be heard from again.

"Are you living on the street, son?" Vince asked. "We'd like to help you find a way out of your situation."

Trey stood up and tucked the envelope inside his waistband at the small of his back. "Father Marty introduced me to a couple of his friends with a nice place," he said, that smile turning even darker. "They let me come and go, like a alley cat."

"Give us an address, Trey. We need to stay in touch," I said, a father pleading with his prodigal son. "I'm trying to keep Kwame from getting sent up to Angola for Father Marty's murder. You know what'll happen to him in there." I gave him my business card. "Right now you and I are the only two people in this whole damned town who believe he's innocent."

He read my card and stuck it in his hip pocket. "The cops won't listen to a street hustler like me," he said. "I ain't chirping at them about any of this. It'd make their dicks hard to throw me in the same cell with my boy Kwame."

He grabbed his knife from the bed and slipped it back into the sheath hidden under his pants leg. "Next time you try to fuck me up with that shocker thing," he said to Vince, eyeing the stun gun lying on the carpet, "I'll be ready for you, fat man."

He moved swiftly to the door and was gone. Like an alley cat.

I sat down in the chair Trey had occupied, facing Vince, and we gaped at each other for several minutes in an exhausted silence. I could smell the droppings left by furry creatures in the corners of the room.

"What did we accomplish here tonight?" I asked him.

"Knowledge, Pete. Leverage. We gained a little leverage."

We'd confirmed what had taken place in the rectory on the night of the murder, at least until the killer or killers arrived. We'd learned there were three other boys who might know more than Trey about the phone caller. It was the identity of those three boys that troubled me the most, because one of them might have been my son.

"I've got to report this conversation to Monsignor Fulweiler and the Bishop," I said. "It's their call on how much to tell Ray Duhon. I'm not sure if he knows about Landry's videotapes yet."

"Ray's a good investigator and you can bet he's already traced the phone calls to the rectory on Friday night. But unless this killer is a complete fucking *chooch*, he didn't call from his momma's house."

I stood up and considered our surroundings. A man was moaning with pleasure in the next room. A faucet was running somewhere, the old pipes rattling. Vince's son had ended his life in this terrible place.

"You're a damned good investigator yourself, Vince," I said. "I don't know how you've managed to do this kind of thing for so many years. It would've chewed a hole in my stomach."

He smiled wearily and made an effort to stand up, too. "Some cops drink to wash away the dirt. Some do street meds to sleep at night. Everybody's got their crutch, Pete. For me, it was *mangia*," he said, making that Italian gesture, a cluster of fingertips to mouth. "Eating is still the only thing that makes me happy."

It was painful to watch him struggle to his feet. His massive legs had lost circulation, and if I hadn't lent him a hand, he might've stayed captive to that chair for the rest of the night. Lifting him was serious labor, but he and I were determined men, and together we managed to raise him upright. He took a few awkward steps, testing his strength and balance, my shoulder lodged underneath one of his arms, walking him like an invalid.

"I need new knees, Pete," he said, wheezing, "but my retired cop benefits won't cover enough of the damage. I might have to blackmail the Bishop into picking up the tab."

He stopped and withdrew an inhaler from his jacket, pumping a dose into his mouth and snorting it down. "Let's get out of this dump," he said, studying the room, "before I try to torch it again."

We were a pathetic sight, two guys who'd broken a sweat holding onto each other, shuffling toward the door like a pair of drunks stumbling out of a bar at closing time.

"What happens now, Vince?" I asked him.

"Go home and kiss Ann and the boys," he said. "Appreciate the good life y'all have made together. And don't stop being that altar boy you still are." He took heaving breaths with every step. "Me, I'm gonna go eat another plate of red beans and rice with hot boudin," he said, "if my scooter ain't been ganked by some fucking crackhead."

TWENTY

THE CALL CAME SHORTLY BEFORE SEVEN THE NEXT MORNING, when I was shaving. Ann brought the portable phone to me and said, "It's Father Ted. He says it's urgent."

"I've been looking for you, Ted," I began. "I left messages."

"I have some very bad news," he said, his words trailing off.

Brother Alban hadn't appeared in the chapel for Matins, the morning prayers, or at breakfast in the refectory. One of the working brothers went to Alban's room and found a note on his writing desk, with instructions to look for him in the old white dorm. They discovered him hanging from a rafter by his belt, the same rafter from which seminarian Brendan McIlhenny had hanged himself thirty years earlier.

"My God," I said, wiping shaving cream from my chin.

"The police and medical examiner are here."

That poor man, I thought. That deeply disturbed man. Had my allegations caused him to reach the tipping point? I was overwhelmed with guilt and could hardly speak. I felt like a bully. The kind of bully who picks on the eccentric, the queer, the other.

"Peter, are you there?"

"I'm here," I managed to say in a quiet, unsteady voice. Ann was waiting just outside the bathroom door, sensing that something was wrong. I knew it would seem rude, but I shut the door so she couldn't hear my end of the conversation.

"I'm almost certain Brother Alban was the cameraman, Ted. The one who shot the videos of Martin Landry with boys."

I heard his exasperated sigh.

"I recognized his voice. And the stutter," I said. "He had access to lots of video equipment."

I still hadn't processed seeing my uncle and Alban together in the French Quarter on Sunday night. There were too many unanswered questions.

"Have the police searched his room? Brother Alban may've kept copies of Landry's tapes," I said, "or he may've had his own personal collection of God-knows-what. You better find the tapes before the police do, Ted. Go search the A-V room, as well. He might've stashed videotapes somewhere in that library."

It wasn't clear to me then, and it isn't clear to me now, many years later, why I was diligently protecting the Church's interests. Why didn't I stop that charade at once and help the police sort out the crimes and culpability?

Call it Catholic allegiance. *Semper fidelis.* Religion had been a blood sport for centuries, and even as schoolchildren, we Catholics had been taught that an attack on the Church was an attack on each one of us. I didn't want to give the smirking haters an excuse for ridiculing the faith I'd practiced all my life. But morally, that made me no different than the clergymen who'd harbored a pedophile priest because he was one of their own.

Ted was still on the line, speaking. "The Vicar-General has requested your presence at a meeting to discuss Brother Alban's death and our official response," he said. "We need to prepare a statement for the Bishop, in case your friend at the newspaper and others come around asking questions. How soon can you meet at the chancery?"

I was being wedged into my shrinking compartment. *Write a press release. Answer phone calls. Leave the heavy lifting to your betters.*

But I was too far down that dark road, with too many misgivings and ethical concessions. I examined my face in the mirror above the sink. The shaving cream had dried into an airy meringue, and it was the first time I'd noticed a small blue branch of broken veins on my cheek, the same branch on my mother's cheek in that exact same place. This ugly business had turned me into an older man overnight.

After long deliberation, I said, "I saw you leave the seminary grounds with Brother Alban on Sunday night. I followed you to the Quarter. What were you doing there with him? I get the feeling you're keeping secrets, Ted, and that bothers me."

I heard someone addressing him in the background.

"No time to discuss that now," he said. "They're asking me to join the community in prayer before they take Brother Alban's body away."

I wiped the shaving cream from my face and emerged from the bathroom to hug Ann and apologize for closing the door. "There was a suicide at Immaculata. A working brother," I said, holding her tight. I'd been waiting for the appropriate moment to tell her about my encounter with Brother Alban in the A-V room. "I suspect he was the one who took videos at Martin Landry's parties."

She stepped back from my embrace. "That's very alarming, Peter." Her eyes grew large and troubled. "Considering what happened to Father Landry," she said, halting in mid-sentence, uncertain. "As you've said . . . they don't have the real murderer." She was struggling to formulate what was on her mind. "Are they certain it was suicide?"

"I don't know, Ann." That question had occurred to me, as well. "My head is spinning."

She took my hand and asked me to pray with her in front of the crucifix on our bedroom wall. It was a beautiful handcrafted crucifix we'd bought on a vacation in Mexico before the boys were born. We knelt in silence, lowering our heads. "Merciful Father," she began, "we beseech You to grant forgiveness and peace to Brother . . ."

"Alban," I said.

"And we pray that You grant peace and healing and closure to every soul who's suffered from these terrible wrongdoings."

I loved my wife for being a generous and forgiving person. But I knew that closure was a long way off. As I knelt in prayer on that melancholy morning, my heart was in turmoil because I still wasn't ready to forgive consecrated men who abused children.

TWENTY-ONE

IN THE MARBLE-PILLARED FOYER OUTSIDE THE BISHOP'S SALA REGIA, Sister Colleen welcomed me with a wisping cup of chicory coffee settled on a beautiful china saucer. "This is a bribe," she said in a soft voice. "What's going on this morning, Peter? Catch me up. Is this about Brother Alban?"

She was still in the dark about the videotapes. Her male superiors were never going to reveal the existence of sexually explicit materials to a woman. It was unthinkable.

"A horrible thing. God rest his soul," I said, sipping coffee the way my uncle did, the saucer held protectively under the cup like a Communion paten.

The intercom buzzed in her office and she rushed in to answer it. I could see her through the doorway, facing the tall arched window behind her desk. She turned quickly and waved me in. "They're asking for you," she said.

Four well-dressed men were waiting at the long oakwood conference table, empty coffee cups in front of them and the remnants of pastry on a silver tray. I expected Father Ted and the Holy Rottweiler, and it didn't surprise me to see Eric Gautier, who'd been bestowed with some special blessing that made him privy to all confidential matters. But I wasn't prepared for a meeting with Detective Ray Duhon.

"Thank you for joining us on short notice, Peter," said the Vicar-General, offering one of the regal high-backed chairs with a commanding sweep of his hand. *Company had come calling*, as my maiden aunts used to say, and the Rottweiler was wearing his best false smile like a wicked stepmother in a dark fairy tale.

"Detective Duhon has been briefing us on the disturbing death of Brother Alban," he said. "He would like to ask you some questions."

It was disconcerting to hear that the police detective had a specific interest in me. I turned to my uncle. He was silent and severe, touching two index fingertips to his lips. Was that a signal for caution?

"Mr. Moore, I spoke to a couple of the brothers at the seminary this morning," Duhon began, consulting the notes he'd made on a small spiral pad, "and one of them reported that this Brother Alban met with you two nights ago."

He was wearing a dull brown sports jacket that was twenty years out of style, and the tie was loose at his neck, the same tie I'd seen him wearing at the rectory crime scene. I suspected he kept that tie in his car and slipped it on when required.

"Why did you go see him?" he asked.

Father Ted shifted his concentration. He and the others were staring at me now, awaiting my response, and I was uncertain how much to disclose.

"I wanted to watch an old eight millimeter home movie, but my family doesn't own that kind of projector anymore. I remembered there was one at the seminary," I said. "Brother Alban is—was—in charge of their audio-visual library, and he set up a projector for me."

I decided not to lie outright, but to shade the truth when necessary.

"That's it?" Duhon asked.

"That's it, Detective."

"Did you know this brother?"

I shook my head. "I'd never met him before Sunday night."

"What kind of mood was he in?" he asked, jotting something on the pad. "Did he seem agitated?"

I shrugged. "He seemed like a very private person. A man of few words."

Duhon snapped open an attaché case resting on the carpet near his shoes and withdrew a plastic baggie. "Can you recall anything he said to you that seemed unusual?" he asked, placing the baggie on the table.

"Let me interrupt for a second," said Eric Gautier, who'd managed to cross his legs and slouch like a bored teenager in one of those rigid high-backed chairs. "This is beginning to sound like a deposition, Detective. We agreed that it would be a friendly chat."

Duhon ignored him. "This is the brother's suicide note, Mr. Moore," he said, studying a piece of paper stored inside the baggie. He began to read the note aloud without removing it from the plastic:

"Dear Lord and Savior, take pity on me. Two nights ago Your messenger appeared. He may be the Angel of Death coming to punish me for what I have done. I watched the little sparrows fall to the ground one by one and believed You didn't count them. Now I know You were counting each one. Please forgive me, for I cannot forgive myself."

The detective slid the baggie across the table. I read the note through the clear plastic, trying to decipher what it meant.

"Any idea what this 'little sparrow' business is about, Mr. Moore?" Duhon asked. "Or the Angel of Death appearing on Sunday night?"

Eric interrupted him. "Peter isn't a mind reader or a psychiatrist, Detective Duhon," he said. He uncrossed his legs and scooted forward, resting his clutched hands on the table. "He can't interpret the words of a disturbed suicide victim any more than you or I can."

I was happy to have Eric on my side for once.

"Did you go to the seminary two nights ago to deliver some kind of message, Mr. Moore?"

"Okay, that's enough, Detective. Your chat has turned into an inquisition," Eric said. "Peter is a very busy man, and he and his small staff have a monumental public relations challenge on their hands, dealing with Father Landry's death. So I suggest we let him go do his job. This suicide is a terrible tragedy, but it has nothing to do with the diocese's director of communications."

Duhon sat back in his chair and tossed his hands nonchalantly. "Okay, fine, if that's the way you want to play it." He was clearly annoyed.

"Detective Duhon, I was there on Sunday evening." My uncle intervened, breaking his silence. "I let Peter into the building and introduced him to Brother Alban. There was nothing unusual about it. Brother Alban set up the projector. I don't recall him saying much at all. He was often hard to read. Phlegmatic, as anyone who knew him will tell you."

Duhon flashed a roguish smile that quickly hardened into a veteran cop's cynicism. "Phlegmatic? I'll have to look that one up, Father."

He laughed and turned to me. "So you're saying no message, no Angel of Death?"

Before I could respond, my uncle said, "I don't think any of us can fully imagine what goes through the mind of someone who wishes to end his life."

The Rottweiler dismissed me from the meeting and asked that I return in half an hour with a draft of the Bishop's statement regarding Brother Alban's death. I was near the bottom of those palatial marble stairs when someone called my name. "Mr. Moore, do you have a minute?" It was Ray Duhon, hurrying down the stairs behind me.

"Tight deadline, Detective," I said. "I have work to do."

"Let's take a walk outside," he said, inserting a cigarette into the corner of his mouth. I remember thinking that cops and priests were the only ones who still smoked in America.

"Do I need to call Eric Gautier down here?" I said. "I have no idea why Brother Alban committed suicide."

He took my arm firmly and hustled me toward the chancery's front entrance. I could have resisted him, I suppose, and made a scene. I looked back over my shoulder to see if there was anyone I could signal for help, but he issued me quickly through the building's front doors and down the outside steps, a seasoned professional with force of will and a hell of a grip. I recalled Vince Scalco's story about Duhon beating a confession out of a gang leader, and I was grateful that we weren't walking alone into an abandoned weed lot.

He let go of my arm to retrieve the pack of cigarettes from his shirt pocket and offered me one. "Cancer?" he said.

I noticed the pistol in a shoulder holster strapped underneath his sports jacket. "No, thanks," I said, "I prefer brain hemorrhage. It's a family tradition."

He lit the wagging cigarette with a tarnished Zippo, then snapped it shut and inhaled a deep satisfying drag, enjoying the nicotine rush in a long moment of breathless ecstasy. He studied the clear morning sky, lost in thought, as if he'd forgotten I was there. The days of dripping fog had gone for now, promising warmer temperatures ahead.

"So here's the deal, Peter. May I call you Peter?"

"Whatever you like."

He started walking again, a slow and aimless saunter toward the fountain. He expected me to keep pace, side by side.

"The district attorney has a gentlemen's agreement with the Bishop," he said, "and I understand the drill. I'm on the Catholic squad, like Rockin' Roger. Like you. And just for the record, the wife and me go to Mass every Sunday and receive the sacraments. So I don't want you holier-than-thou pussy *cocottes* looking down your noses at me."

He told me he'd graduated from Redemptorist High in the Irish Channel, then served in the military stateside between Korea and Vietnam before entering the New Orleans police academy.

"You see where I'm going with this? My picture oughta be on a frickin' holy card. Saint Raymond, good soldier for God and country. The perfect chump for cleaning up messes the Church needs to clean up. And I don't mind that. I really don't. It's what I got signed up for when the priest poured water over my head. I ask only one small favor of my bosses. You know what that favor is?"

"You don't want to be lied to. You want to know the truth."

I'm not sure how I arrived at that observation. It was a lucky guess. He stopped walking and faced me. I saw the surprise in his eyes. He took another long drag of his cigarette and stared at me with a penetrating smile.

"Priests and bishops are a different breed, man. Incense and tassels and all that ancient ceremony," he said. "Their secret cold shit runs forty floors deep. I'm never gonna hear the truth from them. And that hurts my feelings. To them I'm just an obedient little altar boy with a broom and mop."

He glanced back at the imposing chancery building with its stone spires and turrets. A mighty fortress was our God, a bulwark never failing. It exuded power and majesty, an impregnable defense against the Prince of Darkness and his army of demons. But also against mortal men who would attack the sovereignty of the Holy Roman Church.

"That secret cold shit you're talking about, Detective? It's my job to put a cherry on top and call it a fudge sundae."

He blew smoke with a choppy snigger. "My guess is you're on the outside like me, my friend, doing your best to peek in."

We walked to where the parking circle ended, at the edge of the St. Augustine lawn, still soggy from the winter rain, spreading for an acre toward the graceful boulevard where streetcars clanged on iron tracks through a garden scenery. I had never observed a single soul strolling across that green acre in front of us. No dog walkers, no mothers with toddling children, no neighborhood boys playing touch football on the perfect carpet grass. Did they stay away out of respect or fear?

"When I questioned Kwame Williams, he told me he was run off by two men in the rectory on Friday night," Duhon said. "Father Mc-Murray and someone that fits your description. Were you there with your uncle before my men arrived?"

I felt I had to give him something or he wouldn't leave me alone until I did.

"My uncle phoned me in a panic and asked me to come over," I said. "Finding Father Landry's body in the bathtub freaked him out. He didn't feel safe and he wanted company. I was surprised to get there before the police. Maybe the rainstorm slowed your men down."

I was on my own now, in uncharted waters, crafting the story without support from my uncle, the Bishop and Vicar-General, the lawyers.

"A murder and a suicide, and your name comes up in both cases," he said. "And so does your uncle's."

Even I was surprised by the bitterness in my laugh. "Are you serious, Detective? Because if you're trying to sort out the truth, you're heading in the wrong direction."

"Kwame told me Father Landry liked to party, and he heard there was a jam going on at the priest's residence on Friday night." He closed one eye and toked the cigarette. "Funny thing about that. When my men and me got there, Landry's bedroom was clean. No signs of a party. Or a fight. Except for that long blood drag, it looked like the Ladies' Altar Society had showed up to dust and vacuum. You know anything about that?"

The handiwork of Father Ted. I shook my head.

"He also told me this Father Landry dude liked to suck his dick a few years back. Then he felt guilty about it and put money in Kwame's pockets to shut him up. Which is why the priest gave him the wrist-watch. A little Christmas trinket to say thank you, my son. It was sweet while it lasted."

"Do you believe the kid?"

Duhon paused to consider the question. "*Comme ci, comme ça*," he said with a shrug, smoke curling out of his nostrils. "Who knows?

The young blade's a crackhead. Not a reliable source. But you are, Peter Moore. You're the director of communications. You ever heard a rumor that Father Landry had a taste for young boys?"

"Gentlemen!"

We turned to see Eric Gautier crossing the parking circle, heading our way, his overcoat rippling in the morning breeze.

"I hate lawyers," Duhon said.

"Copy that."

We watched Eric zigzag between cars. He didn't look happy.

"Kwame Williams didn't kill anybody on Friday night." I said, lowering my voice and speaking quickly before Eric approached within earshot. "Let the kid go, and I'll tell you everything I know."

I wasn't going to tell him everything, and he probably knew that.

"I turn him loose, the DA will crap his britches. So will my boss, the police superintendent. They think we've got it nailed tight. It'll make them nervous—it'll make the whole damn town nervous—if I tell them a priest killer is still at large."

"The killer *is* still at large, Detective. You and I both know that."

"May I have a word with you, Peter?" Eric said, pinching his breath from the brisk walk. I knew why he wanted to pull me aside. *Don't talk to the police detective unless I'm with you.*

"He's all yours, counselor," Duhon said, flicking his cigarette butt into the wet grass. "No further witnesses."

TWENTY-TWO

SISTER COLLEEN CALLED ME ON THE OFFICE INTERCOM to say the Bishop was ready to read the draft. When I entered his *sala* for the second time that morning, His Excellency was sitting at the head of the conference table flanked by Vicar-General Fulweiler, Eric, and my uncle. Garbed in his everyday amaranth red cassock and skullcap, the Bishop smiled warmly at me and said, "*Salvē, Petrus.*" Greetings, Peter. Speaking Latin was a game he enjoyed playing with young associates who'd studied that dead language in high school and the seminary.

"What have you written for us today?" he asked.

"Well, it's not exactly the Gallic Wars, Your Excellency," I said, placing the two pages, less than five hundred words, in front of him. I passed copies to the others and they all read in silence. Protocol dictated that no one speak until the Bishop spoke first.

It was a very simple statement. The diocese had lost a beloved member of its family. As a working brother dedicated to the religious life, Brother Alban Trosclair had toiled in the vineyard for many years, a humble servant of God and His Church, and we mourned his passing. No mention of cause of death.

"Very good, Peter," the Bishop said, peering at me through those black horn-rimmed glasses that made him look more like an aging football coach than a man of the cloth. "Questions, comments, thoughts?" he asked around the table.

Consummate *yes men*, the others saw that he was pleased with the draft and deferred to his judgment. No dissenting voices, not even the usual appeal for Oxford commas.

The Bishop turned to the Vicar-General: "My understanding is we keep this statement in our hip pocket and use it only if necessary. Is that correct, Monsignor?"

"Yes, Your Excellency. Only if it becomes imperative to comment publicly."

"What about an obituary?" I asked.

"I advise against it," Eric said. "An obit might raise questions. Outside curiosity. It's in the best interest of the diocese to let this unfortunate death slip quietly away."

I wanted to cover all possibilities. "Do we mention his passing in the *Spirit?*"

Every issue of our diocesan newspaper included a section called "Into Thy Hands" that listed the deaths of clergymen, consecrated religious servants, and major donors.

"Same principle," Eric said, shaking his head emphatically. "If we don't splash it, his death will go unnoticed."

I could see that the Bishop wasn't entirely pleased with that position. "Father McMurray?" he said, seeking consensus. "Your thoughts?"

I wanted to ask my uncle the same thing. Father McMurray, what are your thoughts about driving Brother Alban to the French Quarter two nights ago? Have you disclosed the *why* and *what* of that mission to the Bishop and the police?

"A well-written statement, Your Excellency," my uncle said, supporting my quick work. "I think we're good to go."

"Well then," the Bishop said, patting the table with both hands and sliding back his chair. "These are tragic times, my brothers. Let's try to make the best of a very sad day. Are there any other issues?"

In that small pocket of momentary quiet, I raised my hand like a respectful third-grader. "The private investigator and I have examined the videotapes, Your Excellency, and we're reasonably sure we can identify several boys by name."

Scarlet bloomed on the Bishop's cheeks, as if the subject was too delicate or too base for his consideration. He lifted his hands like a surrendering soldier. "Please discuss this among yourselves, gentlemen. I have other business to attend to," he said, rising from his chair and blessing us with three deft strokes of the right hand. "May Our Lord and Savior Jesus Christ bless and comfort you. *Ite cum Deum.*"

Per tradition, we stood as he left the conference table and crossed that deep carpet the color of martyrs' blood, returning to his private chamber down the hidden stairway behind his desk.

As soon as he was gone, the Rottweiler turned on me with teeth bared. "That was *not* the appropriate time to broach such a sensitive matter, Mr. Moore," he said, dressing me down. I was *Mr. Moore* again.

"How about now, Monsignor? Is *now* an appropriate time?" I asked with far too much frustration in my voice. "I need some direction, please. We've got to be certain we've established the correct identities of the boys on those tapes. My colleague Vince Scalco suggests that we show footage to the teachers at Our Lady of Sorrows."

"Good God, absolutely not!" the Vicar-General said. "It would be horribly indecent to expose the good sisters to pornography."

Our exchange had once more stirred the animosity between us. My uncle reached over and placed his hand firmly on my forearm, a gesture meant to calm me down.

Eric offered a practical solution. "Is there any way to capture still frames of the boys—head shots only," he said, "and show them to the teachers?"

My uncle spoke up, reminding us that he gave out report cards every six weeks to the students at OLS, visiting them class by class. He was familiar with many of the boys by face and name. "I'll help you, Peter," he volunteered.

I was surprised by Ted's sudden animation. Ever since the murder he'd been elusive, remote, unforthcoming. He wasn't himself. I couldn't figure out if he was damaged emotionally, like someone injured in a terrible accident, or if his conscience was weighing on him for reasons he wouldn't disclose.

The Rottweiler had begun to chew on me again for one thing or another—the need to expedite the process, the need for discretion, blah blah—but Father Ted interrupted him, a bold maneuver: "Peter, let's begin as soon as possible. I'm ready right now," he said, leaving the peevish Vicar-General to fester in his constant indignation. Or was it his constant indigestion?

After the meeting, I asked my uncle to speak with me in my office. There were too many questions swirling around in my head, and I didn't want to discuss them in front of anyone else.

"It's such a glorious morning," he said. "Can we talk in the garden?"

Even Solomon in all his glory was never arrayed like the meditation garden behind the chancery building, a marvel of colors and cultivated greenery not visible to the public eye and not available to anyone but clergy and employees. It was an inviting space with comfortable benches and walking paths meandering through the crape myrtles, sweet olive, and azalea shrubs. I sometimes ate my sack lunches there, the surroundings as fragrant and soothing as the chancery's public façade was foreboding and grim. I often thought of those grounds as the perfect metaphor for the two sides of Catholicism, the iron and stone ramparts of a fearful hierarchy and the natural beauty of our innocent souls before we were taught shame.

The garden was the creation of a working brother named Brother Benito, who'd escaped the anti-Church persecution of the Mexican Revolution and settled at Immaculata seminary in the 1920s, digging gardens and tending to fruit orchards as his special calling. When I was a seminarian, he looked like Elmer Fudd wandering the grounds in bib overalls and straw hat, stooping to pluck weeds from flowerbeds and leading a slow mule through the persimmon orchard by a rope tether. He often berated the poor animal in Spanish, calling it *perezoso* and *sin valor* as the two of them shuffled along in the dust and pollen haze like aging siblings with an unspoken grudge. Brother Benito didn't wear his dentures when he was working outside, so he always had a toothless, impish smile, as if he'd seen everything and the world was a laughable place, especially flocks of young seminarians wandering around in their unsullied black cassocks. We didn't know why, but he often taunted us in Spanish, treating us like his mule, pointing and slapping his knee and giggling through that sunken mouth. I suspected he thought of us as spoiled apprentices whose faith was untested by fire, who wouldn't have survived running from government troops intent on hunting us down like feral dogs for what we believed.

When he was nearly eighty years old, Brother Benito was asked by the Bishop to plant a garden behind the chancery. By that time the good brother had been studying Louisiana flora for decades and knew which plants and trees adapted well to our southern climate. He handed down his knowledge and traditions to younger brothers, and they'd been carrying on their mentor's legacy since his death, maintaining the garden and expanding it in ways that would've made Brother Benito proud.

We were strolling past a Japanese magnolia tree whose delicate pink flowers were blooming even in that winter season. "What were you and Brother Alban doing in the French Quarter?" I began.

Ted stopped and glared at me with an air of impatience I'd seen many times, but usually not directed at his nephew.

"Brother Alban came to my room and asked me to administer the Last Rites to an old friend staying in the Quarter," he said. "It's no more complicated than that, Peter. The friend had called him and requested a priest."

"I confront Brother Alban about the videotapes and then suddenly, that same night, he has to go to the Quarter to see a friend?"

Ted's expression softened. "Do you remember Donald Bertrand from the seminary? Wasn't he a classmate?" he asked without expecting an answer. "Donald has lived in New York for many years, but he's been diagnosed with melanoma and the cancer has spread to his brain. He's come home to die, Peter. Alban and I went there to comfort him."

It was heartrending news. I remembered the torment Donny had endured at age nineteen, the night terrors and anxieties and electroshock therapy. "Christ," I sighed. "That poor guy's been through enough misery. Last time I saw him, he was heavily sedated in a cuckoo's nest across the lake."

"He just needed the proper medication for manic depression," Ted said. "In those days, the doctors didn't have their hands around the right treatments or effective drugs."

"How do you know so much about Donny?"

He shrugged. "I've stayed in touch with a great many of my students," he said. "They write. They call. Sometimes they drop by to see me."

We were ambling through the Asian orchard, and Ted stopped to smell the bright red blossoms of a Japanese camellia shrub, the rose of winter. It was growing next to a small row of Taiwan cherry trees with dark red bark.

"Donald is in the final stages and doesn't have much energy left," he said. "Why don't you go say hello? I'm sure he'd be delighted to see you."

I couldn't imagine what I would say to Donny Bertrand after all those years. "He's been living in New York?" That seemed strangely incongruent to me.

"When he was confined to the mental hospital in Mandeville, the staff encouraged him to take up a creative hobby. So he started making collages and painting on canvas, and he had a great gift for it. The word got around, and gallery owners from Julia Street started showing up to see his work. Remarkable stuff, Peter. Surreal, whimsical."

He described Donny's style as vintage comic book art meets medieval portrait paintings and Hieronymus Bosch.

"He took plastic medicine bottles and get-well cards and medical trash from his hospital room and glued them on canvases. I can't do justice to how wild and intriguing his artwork is—you'll have to see it for yourself."

Ted believed that making art had proved to be miraculous therapy, giving Donald new life, a sense of hope and purpose. It helped him survive many dark days and nights. He said that when Donald was released from the hospital, he studied art briefly at LSU, then moved to New York City in the early 1970s and threw himself into that turbulent and brutally competitive art world.

"I saw Donald once in New York, when I was on my way to Rome for a sabbatical. He was living in the moment, full of joy and hanging out with a crowd of bohemian artists who appreciated his talent. I was very happy for him. Here was this inarticulate boy from the sticks who hadn't done well in school or the seminary, but he was thriving around all that creative energy. He embraced the culture," Ted said, "and they embraced him. It didn't matter that he was shy and socially awkward. His paintings were popular and sales were strong. For awhile, anyway. But trends and movements come and go in that fickle world."

It was difficult for me to reconcile the hayseed Donny Bertrand I had known with the Donald Bertrand of the New York demimonde.

"I try not to be judgmental, but I must confess that his lifestyle seemed reckless to me. Frankly, I was worried about him," Ted said. "He was very wound up—manic—and he was using street drugs to calm himself down. He even offered me a marijuana cigarette and psychedelic drugs of some sort, but of course I declined. My mind had expanded as much as it was going to expand on caffeine, cigarettes, and Christian Brothers wine."

I remembered those years with great fondness. I'd kept my hair relatively short, but I was anti-Vietnam and loved '60s music and smoked weed a few times in college.

"I was also concerned because he was sleeping with everyone he met. Swinging both ways, something he discovered about himself in the big city. I tried to counsel him—you know, the difference between love and lust, etcetera. I even cautioned him about venereal diseases." He smiled at his misplaced sincerity. "He was polite about my homilies, but he brushed me off."

We walked toward a wooden bench set back in a semicircular stand of tall thick bamboo, the most primitive, untended reaches of the garden.

"I advised Donald to find a loving partner—it didn't matter which gender—and commit himself to that person for as long as possible," my uncle said. "He needed to settle down and have some stability in his life."

Sex outside of marriage? Same sex relationships? Father Edward McMurray always chose goodness and kindness over dogma, which is why everyone loved him.

"Who is this Blanchard guy that Donny is staying with? The coffee heir."

Ted looked surprised that I knew the man's name.

"Perry Blanchard is an old friend who's been kind enough to take care of Donald in his final days," he said. "Perry is an art collector, which is how they know each other. He bought four or five of Donald's earliest paintings and installed some of them in the coffee company's headquarters on Magazine Street. Those sales bankrolled Donald's first year in New York, before his artwork started to sell."

He gestured toward the bench. He seemed a little winded. "Jesus, what I wouldn't give for a cigarette right now."

"It's a garden, Ted."

"I know, I know. I always forget that nature stresses me out."

We sat on the bench surrounded by a jungle of green bamboo stalks that felt like a giant sinister presence lurking over our shoulders. "We've got a hell of a lot on our plates, Peter," he said. "Maybe the Good Lord will provide guidance. Will you pray with me?"

He'd been asking me that question since I was a boy. I had never said no, and I never would.

Sitting next to him, our shoulders touching, I closed my eyes and tried once again to join him in silent prayer. And once again my mind was too troubled to put aside all other thoughts and address the Lord. When I peeked at my uncle, he was relaxing with his arms crossed, eyes closed, lost in contemplation. Or much-needed sleep. I waited as long as I could before disrupting his serenity.

"Why do you think Brother Alban took his life, Ted?"

He remained quiet for an uncomfortable length of time, his breathing almost imperceptible. Without opening his eyes, he said, "The little sparrows, I suppose. In his heart he must've known that God was watching what he and Martin were doing."

We both knew the passage from the Gospel According to Matthew and what Brother Alban had meant in his suicide note: *What is the price of two sparrows—one copper coin? But not a single sparrow shall fall to the ground without your Father knowing it.*

"Did he tell you I was on to him? Did he admit to shooting those videos?"

My uncle rose to his feet and took a few limbering steps on the packed earth path, then turned and stood in front of me as he'd often stood in front of our seminary class, his hand cupping his chin in a variation of *The Thinker*, motionless in outward appearance but a moiling agitation of intellectual energy. In those moments of intense concentration, nothing could still his mind.

"When we got back to Immaculata, he asked me to hear his confession. I was exhausted and suggested we put it off until later in the day, but he insisted," he said. "So we went to the chapel and he requested a traditional confession in the box. I sat on the chair, he knelt with the screen between us, and he cleared his conscience and prayed for forgiveness."

He was bound by the rules of confession, and I didn't press him. He studied me with a grim expression, an embattled soul at war with himself, his high forehead sheened with perspiration even in that cool morning air.

"You'd outed him, Peter, and he thought the police would arrive any minute and drag him away in handcuffs. He was terrified of prison and what would happen to him inside. I tried to convince him that you wouldn't do anything rash—that it was your duty to report this to the Bishop and Vicar-General first—that nothing would happen quickly. I assured him we would hire the best lawyers in the city to give him legal counsel when the time came." He dropped his shoulders and expelled a weary breath. "I don't think he was listening to a word I said."

I could still see the fear in Brother Alban's eyes when I'd said, *We have Landry's entire collection of videotapes.* I shouldn't have been so smug and highhanded with that fragile man.

"How did Alban know Donny Bertrand?" I asked.

My uncle sat down on the bench again, a reluctant surrender to exhaustion and gravity, and slipped his hands into the pockets of his overcoat.

"Brother Alban was in love with Donald. He'd been in love with him ever since he'd first laid eyes on him at Immaculata, many years ago, when Donald was a sem and Alban was a new librarian."

I didn't recall meeting Brother Alban at Immaculata, but it had been twenty years and there were many things I'd forgotten about my short duration there.

"The love wasn't mutual. Donald didn't feel the same way about Alban," Ted said. "But when Donald was in Mandeville, Alban visited him several times, and Donald was grateful for the kindness. They stayed in touch. That's how Alban knew Donald was back in town and asked me to administer the Last Rites."

Brother Alban. Donald Bertrand. Martin Landry. The three of them were inextricably linked. I didn't like the way this scenario was fitting together.

"Alban was facing disgrace and a prison sentence," Ted said, "while the love of his life was dying of cancer. I suppose it was too much to bear."

My uncle and I sat together for several minutes without speaking. The fresh sunshine warmed our faces, and a peaceful breeze whiffled through the garden like a whisper from God's lips. I savored that moment. I knew it wouldn't last.

"How do you suppose Martin and Alban found each other?" I asked. The final piece of the puzzle. "How do two men like that figure out they have the same sick fantasies? How do they *know*?"

Ted reached inside his overcoat. I thought he was fishing for his pack of cigarettes. "I have no idea," he said. "I imagine it started back when they were at Immaculata together, around the same time they both met Donald."

He sounded dispirited, anticipating the worst still to come.

"Did Brother Alban discuss Martin's murder with you, Ted? Did he have any idea who might've been involved?"

"Peter, I've said too much already about what Brother Alban confided in me." He stood up, the better to find whatever he was searching for in his pockets. "Most of it I learned in the confessional."

"I'm thinking about Kwame Williams. His life is on the line," I said. "I've spoken to a teenage boy who was partying with Martin in your rectory last Friday night, and he swears Kwame was *not* at the party."

My uncle stopped his search and gave me a serious look. "I hope you've informed Detective Duhon about this new witness," he said. "Have the police interrogated him?"

Trey had sworn to avoid the police. "The kid lives on the street and he's hard to round up," I said, "but Vince and I are working on it."

He'd finally located what he was trying to find. A small square Kodak box similar to the one that contained Martin Landry's 8mm home movie. "Someone dropped an envelope addressed to me through the mail slot at the rectory," he said, tapping the box against his palm. "No note, just this old reel."

I stared at the box.

"I was hoping Brother Alban showed you how to spool one of these things through that projector in the A-V library," he said.

An old 8mm film delivered to him out of the blue. "Who do you suppose it's from?" he asked, still tapping the box against his palm.

TWENTY-THREE

I CAREFULLY SPOOLED THE SMALL BRITTLE FILMSTRIP through the cogs, as I'd seen Brother Alban do it, and flipped the start switch. To my relief, the wheels didn't snag and shred the celluloid. The usual white leader appeared on screen with squiggling hairs and weird amoebae, and then came the silent faded images of two dark-haired boys about seven and nine years old, possibly brothers, standing shoulder to shoulder in a den or playroom, laughing and elbowing each other and mugging for the camera. Bare-chested kids fresh out of the pool, their wet bathing suits were clinging to their skinny bodies, dripping water, and they were listening to whatever the camera operator was saying to them.

A few jumpy seconds later, the two boys began to dance. They circled each other, spinning and laughing, wiggling their hips, the older boy twirling the shorter one in an awkward jitterbug. The person behind the camera must have said something again, because the older boy's face lit up with surprise and mischief, as if he was being dared, and he took great delight in pulling down his brother's bathing suit. The smaller boy pranced around naked, laughing madly, and they both looked toward the camera, listening to directions, and then the older boy slid down his own bathing suit. Laughing and surrendering to the whims of whomever was holding the camera, they began to touch each other, and then the film began to wash out and white leader scorched the screen and the reel flapped round and round on its worn metal axle.

Father Ted was sitting on the other side of the table in Immaculata's A-V library, staring at the blank screen. We both remained silent and stunned. I was appalled by how the boys' playful innocence was soon manipulated into something so uncomfortable to watch.

"Do you have any idea who they are?" he asked, finally.

In that same room a couple of nights earlier, I'd watched a home movie of boys shooting at each other with cap pistols at a family picnic on the grounds of a mental hospital.

"I'm fairly sure they're Landry boys," I said.

He hesitated, his eyes fixed on the white screen. "I believe the older one is Martin," he said.

"I was thinking the same thing."

"Who do you suppose is operating the camera? The person telling them what to do."

There it was again, a mystery figure behind a camera.

"Someone older, taller. The downward angle," I said. "Maybe a parent. But I can't imagine a mother telling her sons to do that kind of thing."

"It isn't their mother. She'd been institutionalized by the time Martin was this age."

"He had an older sister, right? And two brothers."

"I believe so. Yes."

I'd never spoken to Martin about his family. When I knew him in the seminary, he seemed like someone spawned *sui generis*, an abrasive intellectual too unique and superior to have been born of woman.

"If we showed this film to a psychologist, what would he say about it?" Ted was talking to the screen. Analyzing, processing, more theorem than conversation. "That these were natural impulses? Normal sexual discovery in little boys?" he said. "That all children do this? It's the ordinary course of childhood."

"Sure, if these boys were doing this in their bedroom, just the two of them checking out their bodies and reaching sexual awareness on their own," I said, remembering my childhood and the neighborhood boys playing with one another sexually. "But the camera changes everything, Ted. This is very likely an adult asking them to masturbate each other in front of him."

Normal parents would not have done something like that to their sons.

"Things were different back in those days, Peter. Maybe the filmer thought it would be a great gag to pull on the boys when they got older. You know, let's show this embarrassing video at the bachelor party before the wedding."

"There's a line, Ted, and this crosses it."

If anyone had ever orchestrated my sons in that kind of indecency, I would've taken somebody's head off. I removed the film from the projector and placed it in its box, then disassembled the screen and carried it to the corner of the room where it was kept. When I handed the old 8mm box to my uncle, he said, "So who dropped this in my mail slot, Peter?" He stood up slowly. "What do they want me to know?"

The box and reel were very similar, if not identical, to the one in my possession. Same size and brand, same yellowing cover. Were they both from Martin's secret collection? An unnerving thought. It meant that someone, perhaps the killer, had taken it from Martin's bedroom stash and then returned a few days later to deliver it to my uncle.

"Ted, maybe it's time to turn over all the video evidence to the police," I said, fearing this was some kind of message from the murderer.

"You know we can't do that, Peter. It's not our call to make."

What confounded me about my uncle was that at any given moment he could be the Church's fiercest critic or its most loyal defender. The unity of opposites was a concept he was at peace with.

"Do *not* go back to the rectory by yourself," I said, waiting for the projector to cool down so I could return it to the shelf. "Let me go with you, okay? Or take someone else, preferably a very large cop with a sidearm. We don't know who this film is from or why they want you to have it."

He dropped his chin and exhaled through his nostrils, impatient with unwelcomed advice. "I hear your point and appreciate your concern, Peter. But please don't worry about me," he said, pocketing the box. "Whoever gave me this thing doesn't want to harm me."

"You don't know that, Ted. You really don't know that."

"I'm a priest, Peter," he said, cupping his consecrated hands as if preparing to receive a purifying ablution. "They don't want to hurt me. They want forgiveness."

TWENTY-FOUR

FATHER TED HADN'T SEEN VINCE SCALCO SINCE HIS SON'S FUNERAL.
When Vince opened his office door and greeted us, they hugged like
old friends. "How is Martha?" my uncle asked. "And Paula?" He was
unaware that Vince and Martha had divorced.

"Martha won't talk to me and Paula hates my guts," Vince said.
Their daughter was a senior at St. Mary's Dominican High School on
Walmsley. "There's no family anymore, Father. That went away when
Ned died."

Ted laid his hand on Vince's shoulder. "I'm very sorry, my friend.
Would you like me to speak with them?"

"Maybe sometime down the road, Father. In a few years. When
they stop blaming me for everything that happened."

Vince's office smelled like coagulating grease. What I imagined
as the odor of clogged arteries. It was early afternoon and he'd just
finished a fried shrimp po boy with hush puppies, slaw, and a mound
of bread pudding. He managed a few steps to his desk and retrieved
a martini glass filled with what looked like a vanilla milkshake—an
après manger Brandy Alexander.

"How do you like what I've done with the place?" Vince asked,
gesturing around his office with the glass.

My uncle glanced at the desk buried under paperwork and photographs of missing teenagers, the shelves jammed with file folders,
three shabby chairs arranged in front of the TV. "You *must* give me
the name of your designer," he said with a slightly gay intonation, the
first time I'd ever heard him do that. He intended it as a subversive

joke between him and me, his expression as deadpan as Humphrey Bogart cracking wise.

"So you've come to watch home movies," Vince said, grunting as he stooped to grab a VHS tape from the cardboard box Ted had packed himself on the night of the murder. "We think we've ID'd four subjects," he said, "and there are two other altar boy types we can't nail down. We're hoping you can double-check our homework, Father, and fill in the blanks."

The three of us sat in the Goodwill chairs and Vince worked the remote control, very familiar now with the victims, unsuspecting little boys, eight years old, nine, submitting themselves to their priest-hero's sexual manipulations, trying their best to please him. Vince fast-forwarded through the footage and froze the screen on boys' faces, consulting our collective notes, asking Father Ted if a boy's name was such and such. For his part, my uncle watched with solemn incredulity, seeing enough of the sped-through images to become agitated by the sex acts. He began muttering to himself, occasionally voicing an exasperated *uhh* and closing his eyes, seeing for the first time what Vince and I had already become inured to, the intolerable molestations of a seasoned predator hiding behind the robes of an ordained priest.

"You okay, Father?" Vince asked at one point. "We can do this some other way, if you want."

Ted was hunched forward in the chair, his body tense, two conjoined fingertips pressing his lips like the pointed barrel of a gun. "Keep going. Let's get through this," he said, nearly inaudible.

The incidents on the two *Stella* videotapes took place in confined quarters, a series of naked boys wandering into a tight space as small as a kid's playhouse. Was *Stella* somebody's name?

"Where in Christ Jesus is this place we're looking at?" Ted asked. "It's not the rectory."

Vince and I didn't know.

My uncle was able to verify the names of six boys from the Our Lady of Sorrows parish school. Vince and I had been correct in our search through the yearbooks. When it was over, we all sat back in our chairs and breathed again. We'd come up for air. Going through that torturous process felt like drowning.

"My God, it's worse than I thought," Father Ted said in a hoarse voice. "When you actually see it . . . When you *see* those things . . . and how young and innocent they are."

He placed his hands over his face like Adam and Eve in those paintings of them fleeing the Garden of Eden after the Fall. Vince and I understood that impulse. We'd already gone through the initial phase of shock and disbelief. Like us, Father Ted was learning it was one thing to discuss travesties in a boardroom at a safe remove; it was another thing to watch an eight-year-old child gag and vomit semen and begin to cry.

"Ted, it's time to approach their parents," I said. "We've got six names from O-L-S, and those six will probably lead us to more names. Other boys who were abused. And that won't cover the names in other dioceses. Texas, New Mexico, Cajun country. Guatemala. The victims I read about in Landry's file."

He rubbed his face with his hands in a downward wiping motion. His eyes were teary and red. "We have to heal these boys. And ask for their forgiveness," he said.

His words cast a net of quiet dread over the room.

"Monsignor Fulweiler will be very happy to hear we're ready to make contact with the families and get the settlements underway," I said. I didn't want to admit that I was exhausted by the process and eager to step aside. "So now we hand everything over to the lawyers."

My uncle shook his head slowly, thoughtfully. "We can't leave this to the lawyers, Peter. They're focused on dollars and cents. Contracts and disclaimers. Nondisclosure agreements of silence," he said. "Especially the lawyers from our insurance company. With them it's all about the bottom line. They'll try to settle with these families at the lowest possible price."

"That's why you need to be there, Ted. The parents of these boys should be visited by someone who's caring and above reproach— someone who'll break this awful news to them and listen to their outrage and grief," I said. "Someone like *you* and not some slick bullshitter wearing an expensive three-piece suit who shows up at their door with a briefcase full of forms to sign."

My uncle sighed. "They won't want to see a Roman collar for the rest of their lives," he said, "and I don't blame them. A man of the

Church has abused their most precious gift—their child. They're going to regard priests as the enemy."

Vince rose with great effort and limped over to the liquor cabinet. "He's right, Pete. The parents gonna wanna punch somebody in the face," he said, "and that somebody will be the closest priest. I recommend you stay out of this, Father. How about a drink?"

"A double scotch, if you've got it," he declared without hesitation.

I raised an eyebrow. Ted suffered from diabetes, and for the past fifteen years he hadn't consumed anything stronger than a few sips of altar wine at Mass.

He returned my stare. "Damn it, I've earned a thousand years of indulgences doing this vile business," he said, "so I'm going to indulge myself a little."

"Pete?"

I declined. "I've got to deliver these names to the Rottweiler. If I have a drink, I might bitch slap that Nazi bastard."

Father Ted started laughing and lifted his eyes to the heavens, and Vince joined in. The three of us were laughing so hard that tears flowed down our cheeks. We laughed for a very long time. It was good therapy. Catharsis.

"You know who it has to be," my uncle said, wiping his eyes with a pocket handkerchief and catching his breath long enough to take the first long and generous swallow of scotch.

"Has to be what?" I asked.

He lowered the tumbler and pulled himself together, turning serious. "The peacemaker who breaks the bad news. The one who will listen to their outrage and grief," he said. "It has to be *you*, Peter. For thou art our rock."

TWENTY-FIVE

VICAR-GENERAL FULWEILER LIVED IN FEAR that one of Landry's victims would come forward as an outcry witness now that his abuser was dead. Which is why he hastily assembled *Team Silentio*, as I had begun to think of us, for a meeting late in the day. The usual suspects were gathered around the long table, with the addition of Ken Guidry, the regional representative of a London-based insurance empire that provided coverage for the diocese, and two of his young attorneys. They glad-handed Eric Gautier with the nattering, backslapping familiarity of fraternity brothers at a strip club. I was fairly certain that in Gospel times, they would've aligned themselves with the child-scolding disciples and not with the holy teacher who said, *Let the little children come to me and do not hinder them, for the kingdom of heaven belongs to such as these.*

My biggest concern was that three more laymen had been invited to share a terrible secret we were assiduously trying to hide. I didn't care that these new lawyers were bound to uphold the confidentiality of their client, the Church. They weren't family, they were hired hands, and that's how secrets were leaked.

Fulweiler opened the meeting by disclosing that we'd uncovered the names of six boys from Our Lady of Sorrows who'd been abused by Father Martin Landry, and he speculated that in time, others would be identified. I watched for a reaction from the attorneys who worked for Guidry and the insurance company, and they showed no signs of surprise. They were like palace guards trained to confront every situation with a blank-faced stoicism.

In my report to the Vicar-General two hours earlier, I had informed him that there were three street kids—Trey, Kwame Williams, and another teen—who had been abused by Landry when they were younger but had "timed out" of his target ages of seven to ten, and yet those boys still remained in his party circuit even though they were no longer having sex with him. I had explained to Fulweiler that it was going to be nearly impossible to hunt down those boys and negotiate a legal settlement with them, because they were homeless minors living on the streets, estranged from their families.

"If they're living in a sordid underworld and don't wish to be found," he'd said with a sinister smile, "perhaps we won't have to negotiate with them at all."

Ken Guidry's company was obligated to pay eighty-five percent of all settlements, and the math was not his friend when he outlined the terms of the financial compensation plan. "We're prepared to offer each family a total of four hundred thousand dollars," he said.

I almost fell out of my chair. Nearly a half million dollars to the aggrieved parties. I'm not sure what astonished me most—the staggering amount of money or the fact that the diocese had the financial resources to pay out tens of thousands of dollars. And we all knew that *six* was only the tip of the iceberg.

Guidry was a prematurely gray-haired man with an agreeable face and round, rimless glasses. As he read from his typed notes, he looked like a beleaguered, soft-chinned CEO testifying before a congressional committee, desperate to save himself and his fellow conspirators from insolvency and a minimum-security prison cell.

"The payout is a very attractive package," he said, "but in order to receive it, the parents will have to sign a nondisclosure agreement of confidentiality and swear not to sue the diocese or any individual members of the Church in the future." He paused and added with a tight smile, "*Ad aeternam, amen.*"

For all eternity. The three attorneys at the table laughed delicately.

The total package breakdown was $50,000 to the families up front, a monthly payment until the boys turned eighteen, a lump sum for college expenses, and a final settlement of $50,000 when the boys reached age twenty-five. When Guidry completed the outline, he removed his glasses and placed them on his notes, then gazed around the table for reactions to the proposal. The others seemed satisfied. I may have been the only one left speechless.

"Okay, if there are no questions at this time," he said, "I will read the confidentiality contract my colleagues and I have prepared."

"Excuse me, Mr. Guidry, I needed a moment to collect my thoughts," my uncle said in that whispery voice he used whenever he was struggling to contain himself. "I'm curious, how did you arrive at the figure of four hundred thousand dollars? Did you put a number on sexual violations per child? Or were you relying on industry averages?" He'd been shaken by what he'd seen on the videotapes, and he was seething. "Does the four hundred thousand account for loss of innocence? Father Landry bullied them into keeping his secrets, and they may never trust an adult again. But I didn't hear you address the years of therapy these boys will need in order to heal, Mr. Guidry. And not just the boys themselves, but the counseling their entire families will go through when they find out what he did to their sons."

His hands were folded on the table, his knuckles turning white, his entire body beginning to tremble in anger.

"And so I ask you, sir—will this four hundred thousand dollars compensate the parents for the guilt and blame they'll suffer for not being more vigilant when their child was being abused by a man they thought they could trust?" He stared at Vicar-General Fulweiler, aiming those accusations at the Holy Catholic Church itself. "What price should we pay to win back the good souls who will abandon their faith and leave the Church and curse God for not protecting their children against monsters like Martin Landry?"

Fulweiler furrowed his prominent brow and raised a hand to interrupt him, but my uncle was determined to go on.

"Tell me, Monsignor, is this enough hush money to satisfy the parents when they discover that Father Landry had been committing these crimes for years—against other children, in other parishes? We know that the bishops always shuffled him off to other assignments rather than defrock him and turn him over to the authorities. So how will you and I console these families, Monsignor, when they realize their boys would not have been molested if the Church . . . years ago . . . had done . . . what was right and . . . if . . . if . . ."

Ted's speech had begun to slur and his fingers untwined on the table in front of him as if they were foreign creatures he had no control over. His shoulders slumped and he muttered something unintelligible, and that's when I noticed that his face had lost its color and his lips were dry and sticky when he worked his mouth, trying to swallow. I knew what was happening. I had witnessed this before. My uncle was going into insulin shock.

"I must apologize, gentlemen, for Father McMurray's comments," Fulweiler said with an annoyed wave of the hand. "He has taken us into a maze of speculations that are better suited for another . . . Father?" He realized that something was wrong. "Father Edward?"

I was already on my feet, seizing the lapels of Ted's black suit jacket and bracing him in case he fainted. "Eric, run to Sister Colleen's office and ask her for fruit juice," I said. "She keeps it in her little fridge."

Eric dashed off and returned with an entire carton of orange juice. Sister Colleen was hurrying behind him, concerned, asking, "Should I call nine-one-one?"

"This usually works," I said, holding the carton to Ted's lips while his unsteady hands grasped mine. He drank like a man who'd just spent forty days and forty nights in the desert.

"What happened, Peter?" he asked, a dribble of juice on his narrow chin. "Did I blank out?"

I leaned close and whispered in his ear. "Your diabetes, Ted." He'd downed that tumbler of scotch earlier and I suspected he'd injected insulin without eating anything all afternoon. Of late, he hadn't been careful about monitoring his blood sugar levels.

"Forgive me, everyone," he said, gripping the arms of his chair. "Where were we? I seem to have lost my train of thought."

Fulweiler called for a recess to give Ted time to recuperate, but my uncle stubbornly refused the offer. I tried to reason with him, as well, counseling him to rest for a few moments and clear his head. His pride overruled sound judgment and so we pressed on, Ken Guidry reading the lengthy document that delineated the *terms, conditions, and effects* of the legally binding agreement between the aggrieved family and the diocese in the matter of Father Martin Landry and the One, Holy, Catholic, and Apostolic Church v. the children to whom the kingdom of heaven belonged.

TWENTY-SIX

THE MEETING RAN LONGER THAN I'D EXPECTED, and by the time I arrived at home, Ann and Matt had cleared the table of their dinner dishes and had stored the leftover pot roast in a glass container in the refrigerator.

"Sorry I'm late," I said, pouring myself a glass of wine in the kitchen. I looked into the dining room to make sure the boys weren't listening. "More Landry stuff. Lawyers up the yin yang. The insurance guy went over the agreement to buy off the families."

Ann listened sympathetically but had a more distressing worry on her mind.

"Luke didn't come home after school today, Peter. I'm really concerned about him," she said. "We got a phone message from Brother Amedy"—the assistant principal—"saying Luke was absent from all his classes after lunch."

"Jesus," I said. "Have you checked with the Hinojosa boys?"

"I've called their house, but no one picks up. I've left messages on their machine. I thought about paging Roberto, but that poor guy is always in surgery."

"Should we contact the police?"

"I'm sure Luke is okay. Just pushing the boundaries," she said. "You know how he's been behaving. Sulking, slacking off in his schoolwork. Keeping secrets. It's all a teenage developmental thing. But now this."

"We can ground him again," I said, "although that doesn't seem to make any difference."

"I've caught him in a very serious lie, Peter."

Matt walked into the kitchen wearing his beatific smile, saying, "Hey, Dad," and hugging me. He was such a delightful and affectionate boy. I couldn't imagine him as a surly teenager.

"Sweetie, I'm going to help Dad fix a plate of food," Ann said, "and we'll be in his office having a private conversation."

"Like where the hell is Luke?" he said, half smiling, half serious.

His mother gave him a look that said *no bad language, please.* "I'm sure he'll be home soon," she said, wrapping her arms around both of us in what we'd always called a family hug, even though it didn't qualify as a legitimate family hug without all four of us in the huddle.

We took our usual places in my home office, Ann on the pineapple-print settee while I sat at my desk, sipping wine and eating.

"I called the movie theater and talked to the manager," she began, "and he told me they did *not* shut down the theater on Friday evening and send everybody home. The rain was a little loud, yes, but tolerable, he said. They didn't refund anyone's money."

We stared at each other. Her anguish was palpable. "He lied to us," she said. My darkest suspicions were edging into the light.

"Vince and I talked to a street kid named Trey who admitted to being at the party in Landry's bedroom on Friday night. He said there were three other boys, all friends from the same school. Everyone was drinking and smoking weed."

She lowered her head and uttered a sound I'd never heard her make. It was the sound of a mother's heart being pierced by daggers. "My God, were they at the rectory?" she said.

"If those three boys were Luke and the Hinojosa brothers," I said, "the saving grace is they weren't involved in what happened to Landry. Trey said the priest made them all clear out after he received a phone call. Someone was coming over, and he didn't want the boys to be there."

She raised her eyes to mine. I knew what she was thinking. More was at stake than under-age drinking and marijuana. I'd seen David Hinojosa in a videotape. Had Luke been to those parties in Martin Landry's bedroom? Was our son one of his victims?

"We've got to locate Luke, bring him home, and talk to him," I said. "Let's start with the Hinojosas. I'll drive over to their house."

Roberto and his two sons lived in a beautifully restored Victorian home on Soniat Street, only a short distance from *El Barrio Lempira*, the working-class Honduran neighborhood in the lower Garden

District where the good doctor's immigrant family had first settled in the late 1950s. As I drove toward Soniat on that dismal night, the quiet Uptown streets were slumbering in the deep shadows of tall manicured hedges and dark creaking oaks. When I parked in front of the Hinojosas' iron fence and got out of my car, I could hear the pulsing disco rhythms of "Beat It" at full volume. I let myself through the unlocked gate, followed the brick path to the steps leading up to the gallery, and knocked on the front door. At closer range, the music was deafening. I was surprised that the neighbors weren't banging on the door to complain.

No one answered my second round of knocking, either, so I walked over and peered through a high narrow window into the living room. Luke and the two brothers were laughing and practicing their Michael Jackson moonwalk moves to the booming bass. I could see empty pizza boxes and half-consumed liters of soft drinks. Roberto was obviously not at home.

I tried the handle and discovered that the front door was open. Rico was the first to notice me standing in the receiving parlor, and he tapped Luke on the arm and pointed. My son looked surprised and mortified to see me. He froze, his eyes darting about like a small child deciding whether to run or hide. David rushed over to turn off the music.

"You missed supper," I said to Luke, my voice too loud in the sudden silence. "Your mom has been worried about you. You didn't check in. Among other things."

I could smell the smoky, wood-stain scent of the vintage scotch they'd raided from Roberto's prize collection, which he displayed like artworks on a shelf high above the kitchen cabinets, accessible only by stepladder. As it turned out, the boys had been helping themselves to an inch here and an inch there over time, then refilling those rare and expensive bottles with water. It was the oldest failed trick in the book.

"Put your shoes on, Luke," I said sternly, "and grab your backpack, wherever it is. We're going home."

The brothers went into panic mode and started cleaning up pizza boxes and the plastic cups guilty of scotch. But Luke stood staring at me with a defiant grin, as if daring me to do something more dramatic.

"Where is your father, boys?" I was using my firm paternal voice.

"In surgery, Mr. Moore," Rico said, showing good manners even under the influence of Macallan 1939.

"I'll talk to him about this tomorrow," I said. "Let's go, Luke. *Now.*"

Our son was drunk and stumbled out of the car, falling to his hands and knees to throw up in the grass near the kitchen steps. Ann hurried outside with a wet dish towel and knelt beside him, wiping his face and whispering motherly admonitions. It wasn't the first time we'd seen him in this state, but it was the first time we'd watched him vomit. I went upstairs to tell Matt we would be having a private chat with Luke in my office with the door closed. Fortunately, Matt was too focused on his homework to care.

"Where was he?" he asked without raising his eyes from a math problem he was solving.

"At the Hinojosas'," I said. "Screwing around."

"Why did he ditch school?"

"I don't know, but I intend to find out." I didn't mention that Luke was outside on his knees, throwing up. "Matt, my untroubled boy, do your parents a favor and never skip school, okay?"

"You just wait, Dad," he said with a wry sidelong smile.

Luke sat on the settee, sipping a cup of hot tea his mother had brewed for him. His face was wan and glistening with sweat, his hands trembling, his brown hair greasy and uncombed. He seemed far away, his thoughts elsewhere as he stared down at his unlaced shoes. Ann stood with her arms folded, too agitated to join him on the settee. She scolded him for drinking alcohol and skipping class, and then laid bare the lies he'd told us about the movie theater and his wet clothes. Luke made no effort to refute her accusations or defend himself. He made no effort to communicate at all. He looked sleepy and disoriented, and his silence was meant as resistance, like a prisoner of war refusing to cooperate with the commandant.

"So where were you last Friday night, Luke?" I asked calmly. "The night you *weren't* at the movie theater."

His eyes flashed at me, then gazed into the cup before he took another measured sip.

"I've talked to a kid named Trey," I said. "He told me about the party in Father Landry's bedroom."

I paused, bluffing. It could've been three other boys. I glanced at Ann and she held her ground, arms folded, dispassionate, the perfect chess player.

When Luke didn't respond, I said, "Trey told me that Father Landry received a phone call and then asked the boys to leave. The party was over early. Everyone had to run out into the rainstorm and got soaking wet."

Minutes passed, a solemn wait. Luke took his time finishing the cup of tea. Ann looked impatient and ready to intervene, a therapist confronting her own son.

"It wasn't my idea," he said, breaking his long willful silence.

I hadn't expected him to confess anything. He was well practiced at stonewalling.

"Please tell us about it, Luke," his mother said, her words gentler than her rigid body language.

His voice was hoarse, his speech slow. "What do you know about Father Marty?" he managed to ask without looking at us. "About his trips to the coast and all."

"Why don't you tell us what we should know," Ann said.

He stared into the empty cup, dawdling with it as if it still contained a few dregs he might swallow. "He was into boys," he said. "Mostly younger ones, like Matt's age and even younger. Lots of kids knew about Father's parties and what went on, but nobody talked about it. Keeping it on the down low was part of the deal. Father made you swear on a Bible not to tell anyone. He said if you did, he'd kick your whole family out of the Church and they'd all die and go to hell."

"Did he ever say that to you, Luke?" Ann asked.

He shook his head. "I stayed away from him," he said. "One time when I was an altar boy, he came up behind me in the sacristy and grabbed my butt, and said, 'I want some of this.' I was too young to know what he meant."

That son of a bitch. If I'd known about that incident, I would've broken Martin Landry's nose. I'd thought about punching that arrogant prick several times when we were seminarians, and now I was sorry I hadn't.

"I was glad y'all wouldn't let me go on fishing trips to Vermilion Bay with Father and the other altar boys. I heard stories you wouldn't believe," he said, looking directly at me. "He took me aside one day and asked me why my dad wouldn't allow me to go to the coast, and I didn't know why. He said, 'Your father was in the seminary with me until they kicked him out for being gay. I have some naked pictures of him—with other young guys. Would you like to see them sometime?'"

"He *said* that, Luke?" I was furious.

"I didn't believe him, Dad. I know you're not gay."

As far as I knew, Landry had a single snapshot of me in his photo album, the one in which I was running in my bathrobe from that crazed seminarian who was popping me with a wet towel. By contemporary standards, a PG-13 rating at worst. But that didn't stop a pathological liar like Martin Landry from playing mind games with a young child, trying to manipulate and seduce him.

"For God's sake, son, why didn't you tell us about that?" I asked, feeling the heat of anger trapped inside my shirt collar. "We would've put a stop to it *immediately!*"

He shrugged, setting the empty tea cup on the floor. "I was ten years old, Dad. I didn't want our family to get kicked out of the Church and go to hell."

I groaned and rocked back in my office chair, gazing up at the ceiling, waiting for the cool-headed Ann to take over.

"Luke, if you've been avoiding Father Landry for several years," she said, sitting beside him on the settee, "why did you and the Hinojosa boys go to a party at his place on Friday night? You knew what kind of parties they were."

Without the cup, he didn't know what to do with his shaky hands. "Like I told you, Mom, it wasn't my idea," he said.

"So Rico and David wanted to go?"

He nodded.

"Why?" she asked. Not strident, not demanding. A thoughtful, temperate question.

Luke was reluctant to respond. She waited, giving him more time. Then finally, "Luke, were either Rico or David ever abused by Father Landry?"

Our son struggled with his thoughts until his lips began to quiver. "Both of them," he said.

Ann and I were stunned by the audacity of that man. He obviously believed that his priesthood made him invincible. Was he daring the world to catch him? Was he crying out for punishment?

"According to what Trey told me," I said, "you boys were too old for Landry's appetite. Why, then, did the three of you go to the rectory? Was it for the booze and weed?"

Watching Luke was a painful ordeal. I could read the warring impulses in his eyes.

"Rico wanted to hurt him. He wanted to mess Father Marty up real bad," he said after long deliberation. "You know, kick the crap out of him for everything he'd done. Me and David went along to make sure it didn't get out of hand."

Rico was a tall young athlete, an all-star goalkeeper ranked among the best in the city's teen soccer leagues. He lifted weights in the Benildus gym, and Luke had told me that Rico worked out on the boxing bags with impressive hand speed and endurance. I'd seen him lose his temper when he was younger, and on one occasion his father had to bear-hug him until he calmed down. At age sixteen, Rico Hinojosa had the strength and quickness to beat a grown man unconscious.

"Rico's been talking about it for a long time. He can't get it out of his head, what he let Father Marty do to him when he was younger. And what Father did to David, too. It was like Rico woke up one morning real ashamed of himself and seriously pissed off, and he started planning an ass-kicking. You know, working up the courage. At first I thought he was kidding around. But he wasn't."

That raised a horrifying possibility. "Luke, after you boys left the rectory on Friday night," I said, "could Rico have returned at some point by himself and confronted Father Landry?"

"No, Dad. The three of us hung together the whole night. It was a long way back to their house and we got drenched. I thought we were gonna get struck by lightning," he said. "Rico didn't do anything to Father Marty. It had to be that black kid. The guy they arrested."

"Kwame Williams," I said. "Did you see him at the rectory that night?"

"He wasn't there when we were. But he might've been the caller."

After molesting so many children, in so many parishes, Landry must've known that a time would come when somebody showed up at his doorstep seeking revenge and an unholy reckoning.

"Thank you for being honest with us, Luke," Ann said, circling her arms around him and kissing his cheek, which made Luke wince. He was at that age when he didn't want his mother's affections, at least not in front of others.

"Can I please go to my room and crash?" he asked, staring at his unlaced shoes again. "I don't want to talk about this anymore."

"We'll discuss the alcohol business tomorrow, when our minds are clearer," she said, releasing him from her embrace. "I'm going to pick you up after school."

It had been a very long day for Ann and me. We were lying in bed together, silent, exhausted, decompressing from Luke's emotional revelations and drifting off to sleep with a *Rockford Files* rerun on our little black-and-white television set resting on a chest of drawers. I had treated myself to a second glass of wine.

"This morning a teary sixth-grader named Constance asked me how she could contact the Pope and nominate Father Landry for canonization," she said with a sad smile.

For the past two days, my wife had been grief-counseling at Our Lady of Sorrows, making her way from classroom to classroom, listening to the students' bereavement and responding to their questions.

"I told Constance I would look into it and get back to her. But I'm not going to. I lied to a child."

"Martin Landry was unworthy of all this attention," I mumbled. "And he's made liars of us all."

The phone rang on our night table. "My apology for calling so late, Peter." It was Roberto. "I just got out of surgery and noticed you paged me. Are the boys all right? Is it urgent, or can it wait until tomorrow?"

His syntax was always impeccable, like a high school English teacher's, but traces of an accent still lingered, even though he'd lived in this country since he was twelve years old. His father had been a harvester and his mother a packhouse inspector for the United Fruit Company at one of its banana plantations in Honduras. In the 1950s and 1960s, the fruit company had paid for hundreds of promising young Honduran schoolchildren, like Roberto, to attend boarding schools in the port city of New Orleans, where the company's corporate headquarters was located.

"I went over to your house to pick up Luke," I said, "and the boys had gotten into your scotch. When we came home, Luke started throwing up. He seems okay now, but he's facing serious consequences for skipping school and drinking alcohol."

Facing consequences was the politically correct new term for *punishment*. We were such a civilized and loving generation of parents. We'd read all the popular books on behavior modification.

Roberto cursed in Spanish and said, "My boys are in trouble all the time now. I don't know what I am to do with them, Peter. What do you and Ann suggest?"

"For starters, lock up your scotch."

Ever since his wife had died, he'd called on Ann and me to advise him on parenting. He often phoned Ann at her office and talked things over with her. He'd even considered sending his sons to live with Stephanie's parents in the affluent suburb of Old Metairie.

"Ann and I haven't had a chance to discuss the consequences yet, Roberto." I didn't dare broach the subject of Martin Landry. Not at that hour, under those circumstances. "Are you available tomorrow morning?"

When I hung up, Ann rolled toward me and placed her warm hand over my heart. I was wide awake now and overwhelmed with anxiety.

"How in the world do we tell him that Rico and David were sexually assaulted by their priest?" I asked quietly. "If someone told me this had happened to Luke and Matt, I honestly don't know what I would do. Probably something crazy."

Her breathing was shallow and soft. I wondered if she'd fallen asleep.

"You've got to treat these abused boys like they're your own sons," she said, finally. "Don't just pay them off, Peter. Be the good father you are. Help them begin to recover."

Her advice was starkly simple and true.

"When the time comes, will you go with me to see Roberto? This is the hardest thing I've ever had to do, Ann. I don't know if I can face him alone," I said. "He's been through so much—Stephanie's cancer and raising the boys by himself."

She sat up in bed and cradled my hand in hers. "You don't have to tell him about the videotapes," she said. "It doesn't matter how you know. But don't leave it to the lawyers and Church bureaucrats, sweetheart. He should hear this from you."

I raised up beside her, our backs against the headboard, and watched Rockford cooking breakfast for his father in that trailer home by the ocean. Ann and I stared at the television screen late into the night, until the clock-radio alarm burst into song and I realized that my wife's warm sleeping body was coiled against mine. But I was still sitting up straight, my neck and shoulders stiff and burning, and I had no idea if I'd slept for a single peaceful moment all night long.

TWENTY-SEVEN

IN MID-MORNING, ANN AND I WENT TO VISIT ROBERTO at his home. He greeted us at the door wearing green scrubs and house slippers, beaming his tired handsome smile, a good man still struggling to recover from his wife's death four years earlier. He was elated to see us and kissed Ann on the cheek and hugged her. That joyful exchange destroyed my confidence. I wanted to turn tail and head back to our car. But Roberto seized my hand, nearly crushing it with his amazing grip. He possessed the strongest handshake of any man I'd ever known, and I wondered if that was a trait common to every transplant surgeon.

"Come in, come in," he said, walking ahead of us into the living room.

Nothing had changed since Stephanie's death. Not one painting had been moved, nor the small balsa wood tableau of *calaveras* shooting pool with toothpick cue sticks, the miniature airplanes and cameras made from Mexican beer cans, the papier-mâché Cuban baseball players. She'd been an architect by profession and a collector of Latin American folk art, an interest she shared with her husband. Although her colorful displays may have violated the authenticity of their austere old Victorian shell, it was fun to watch how far she would push the clashing styles. Roberto had once observed at dinner, "No matter where you put us"—meaning Latinos—"we'll mess with your color scheme."

We followed him through the formal dining room and into the kitchen of many windows and exquisite natural light. The aroma of coffee from his French press was rich and tantalizing.

"I'm having *café*. I was in surgery until an hour ago, so I need a little pick-me-up. I hope you'll join me," he said, searching for cups in a nearly empty cabinet. "Hmm, they must be in the dishwasher."

Dirty dishes, smudged glasses, and crusty silverware were scattered near the sink. His sons were even worse than ours when it came to housekeeping. He employed a cleaning lady and a cook, but there was no sign of their tidy work. In the course of twenty-four hours, his boys could wreck a spotless kitchen.

"Here we go," he said, finding three clean cups in the dishwasher. "Are you here to talk about the alcohol? My mistake, guys. But I've grounded Rico and David until they're in grad school. It'll take them thirty years to pay for the Glenfiddich 1937." He glanced up at his beautiful array of scotch bottles on exhibit above the cabinets. "I'll have to put them under lock and key." He turned to Ann and me with deadpan humor. "The scotch, not the boys. Although . . ."

Roberto was a short stout man with thick black hair curling around his ears. His biceps and shoulders were chiseled like a weightlifter's, giving him impressive upper body strength. He worked out in the basement gym at the university hospital where he performed most of his surgeries, and he attended yoga classes twice a week. He'd played soccer when he was growing up in Honduras, and he'd passed on his love of the game to his sons.

While Roberto was a boarding student at the Lower Ninth Ward's Holy Cross School in the late 1950s, political turmoil in Honduras caused his entire family to flee to New Orleans in the first wave of Honduran immigrants. Their sponsor, the United Fruit Company, re-hired many of them as dockworkers and banana warehousemen at the port, including Roberto's father. The Hinojosas were among the early families to settle in the *Barrio Lempira* before moving to the suburb of Kenner several years later.

"Roberto, we're here to talk about something else," Ann said when he filled her cup with strong coffee.

He smiled. "That sounds ominous, Ann. Is there something worse than our boys sneaking around and drinking alcohol?" he asked. "Please don't tell me some Catholic schoolgirl is pregnant. Shall we sit down?"

"That's a good idea," she said.

We sipped our coffee at a table in the breakfast nook, a halved octagon with bright picture windows added onto the house nearly a century after it was built. The small space felt like a greenhouse on the flank of Roberto's lush backyard, only steps away from the koi pond and banana trees and tall elephant ears. Even in winter, his backyard was as verdant as the rainforests of his homeland.

Ann placed her hand on his. "There's no easy way to say this, Roberto," she began with depressing solemnity. "We have reason to believe that Rico and David were sexually molested by Father Martin Landry. We can't be certain until you speak to the boys and get confirmation. But we want you to know that no matter what happens, Peter and I are here for you. We love your boys, and we'll help any way we can."

I will always remember the way his cordial smile disappeared into a rush of facial reactions, one after the other, nearly all at once. Surprise, shock, outrage, hurt. His eyes reddened and I thought he might cry. I thought he might break every dish in the kitchen. Those emotions, his disbelief, are still etched into my memory, haunting me even now, a decade and a half later.

"How do you know this?" He was angry and suspicious, and he withdrew his hand from Ann's. "What about Luke and Matt? Are you saying they were molested, too?"

I looked at Ann for direction, but she was shaken by his sudden fury.

"I don't think so, Roberto," I said. "But we're still peeling back the truth. We can't be sure until we talk to all four of our boys."

"I knew that priest," he said. "I spoke to him on several occasions. My sons went to his fishing camp with other altar boys. I can't believe this is possible. Who told you, Ann?" He stared at me, his voice rising. "Peter, what makes you think such a thing?"

I sat back in my chair, considering what to say and how to keep Luke's name out of it. "We heard it from a reliable source, Roberto," I said, "but not an infallible one."

"This happened a few years ago, when they were younger," Ann said. "It's going to be very difficult for them to confide in you or anyone else about what took place. I have some experience with counseling the victims of sexual abuse, Roberto, and I'm certainly willing to speak with Rico and David, either separate from you or with you present."

"What are the details you've heard, Ann? How long has this been going on? Why my sons and not others?" A torrent of questions any parent would have raised. "I know something about pedophilia. I've read the research. It's rarely just one child or two. Unless the perpetrator is found out and stopped."

"Somebody stopped him," I said.

They both turned to me as if I'd said something inappropriate and in poor taste. But I'd seen his body in the bathwater. Someone had definitely stopped him.

"How *certain* are you, Ann? Peter? Is this just a vicious rumor?"

I couldn't tell him about the videotapes, or that David had appeared in one of them.

"Roberto, I promise you we wouldn't be here if this was a frivolous accusation," Ann said. "The evidence is very strong. You should talk to the boys as soon as possible."

He stood up quickly, banging his knee against the table and splashing our coffee. "I'll go pick them up at school right now," he said, running a hand through his hair. "If you'll excuse me. . . ."

Ann rose to her feet. "Roberto," she said, reaching out to touch his arm.

"No no no *no*," he said, stepping away from her. "No, Ann, please!" He backed against a picture-window. "You've told me a terrible thing and I must find the truth for myself."

I consulted my wristwatch. "Are you sure you want to pull them out of class, Roberto?" I asked. "It'll raise questions with their friends."

He threw up his hands, disconcerted with Ann and me, the messengers who'd borne such unspeakable knowledge. "*Bien*, I'll pick them up at lunch," he said. "Thank you for your offer to help, Ann, but I'll speak to them alone."

The three of us stood facing one another in silence, uncertain of what to do or say. Roberto wouldn't meet our eyes. He'd gone to some distant place that harbored rage and grief.

"The diocese is responsible for these atrocities," I said. "The Church, the Bishop. I'll make sure they do right by you and the boys, Roberto."

I was trying to offer solace, but my words rang hollow. He wasn't concerned with legalities or formal remedies, or the inducement of money.

"This is my fault," he said. "I haven't been there for them since Stephanie passed. Too many surgeries and conferences, not enough time at home. Working day and night was the only way I could cope with losing her. And this is what happened. My boys," he said with a catch in his throat, "my precious boys. God has punished me for neglecting them."

Hunching and knotted, he began to weep, tears streaking down his cheeks. Ann took another step toward him but he shot out his hand to detain her. He didn't want to be touched.

"God didn't do this," she said in a voice so firm and definite he had to take notice. He had to look at her. "He was a bad man, Roberto. A criminal and a deceitful sociopath. We will heal these wounds, I promise you. We'll remove that bastard from all of our lives."

Roberto slid down the window glass until he was sitting on the terra cotta tiles, wiping away the tears with his loose green smock, catching his breath. He was one of the most dignified men I'd ever met, but at that moment his grief was unrestrained. "I miss her so much," he said, laboring to pull himself together.

Ann sat near him on the floor and tucked her legs into a lotus position. I sat close by, the two of us watching him quietly, as if sitting shiva with our old friend, mourning with him and waiting respectfully for his next words, his next step. We were willing to stay at his side and comfort him for as long as it took, even at that most fragile moment when he would gather his sons into his strong and loving arms and ask them if there was something they should tell him about the priest named Father Martin Landry.

TWENTY-EIGHT

WHEN I ARRIVED AT MY OFFICE IN THE CHANCERY AN HOUR LATER, a phone message was waiting for me on the intercom line. It was Sister Colleen directing me to see the Vicar-General as soon as possible. "The younger Mr. Gautier will be joining you, as well," her recording said. "Which reminds me of a joke I once heard, Peter. A lawyer, a doctor, and the Archbishop of Canterbury are sunbathing nude in a rowboat on the Thames. Oops, gotta go. The Bishop's light is flashing. I'll finish the joke later."

I called her back and left a message: "Does this joke involve a mother, a daughter, and newspapers covering the men's private parts?"

Monsignor Fulweiler's office was a short distance from the Bishop's suite on the third floor. I knocked on the door, a barricade hewed out of hard walnut, sturdy enough to resist a pagan army. A voice within said, "Come in, please." Eric Gautier was already seated in front of the Vicar-General's desk, ankles crossed leisurely, oxblood tasseled loafers matching his dark brown suit and burgundy tie. He always appeared stylish and composed, something I could never pull off, especially in the Rottweiler's presence.

Eric stood up and we shook hands like two prizefighters at a weigh-in, eyeing each other warily, and then I sat in the velvet wing-back chair beside him. It was a spacious office with bookcases full of weighty sacerdotal tomes and a round bronze chandelier high overhead that was fashioned as a crown of thorns with candle lighting. Off to the side, near a display of the Vicar-General's framed honors and recognitions, a small conference table supported five chairs and five neatly placed marble coasters, but Fulweiler preferred to address non-clerics from behind his grand desk, the better to remind them who wielded the most ecclesiastical authority in the room.

"Good morning, Mr. Moore. Let's get straight to the point, shall we?" he said in his customary brusque manner. He was reading over the document I'd prepared for him the previous day, the list of abused boys. Eric held a copy, as well. "Your uncle has made a special request to His Excellency that you join Mr. Gautier when he visits the families of these children. His Excellency has agreed," he said, clearly disapproving, "and so it shall be."

I was surprised that Ted had gone over the Vicar-General's head to directly solicit the Bishop, and equally surprised that the Bishop had granted my uncle's wish. Fulweiler looked up from the pages, his bifocals clinging to the tip of his nose like a miserly banker in a Dickens novel. "The two of you are now a team," he said, regarding both of us in turn. "His Excellency is eager to begin contacting families. He expects your work to proceed quickly and with great caution. Am I clear so far, gentlemen?"

I glanced at Eric and he nodded, the ideal team player. For the right price.

I was flattered that Ted thought so highly of me. Did he truly believe I was indispensable to these visits? *It has to be you, Peter.* Or was it more sentiment than substance?

"Monsignor," I said, "I have to be candid with you. I'm really not equipped to handle this sort of thing. I write press releases and brief the media. I'm not a counselor . . . or mediator. You'd do better to hire my wife."

The Vicar-General closed his eyes, removed his bifocals, and rubbed his nose, a bitter old man grappling with his limited patience. We did not like each other, but we were mired in the same holy tar until one of us either died or was indicted.

"Mr. Moore, God knows why His Excellency has so decreed. But what the Bishop hath joined together, let no man put asunder," he said with a baleful smile, spreading his hands as if to grant his blessing on Eric and me in this new marriage made in hell.

Eric studied the document in his lap, the list of boys. I recommended Stevie Sutton as our first official target.

"Why the Sutton boy?" Fulweiler asked, perusing the names.

"I've met him. My son knows him at O-L-S. Stevie's mother is a heavy drinker with responsibility issues," I said. "He's a sweet boy who deserves more love and attention than he's getting."

My only apprehension was that his mother might use the sexual abuse as an excuse to neglect him even more. I didn't know what to expect from her.

"Peter, I hope you understand that our job is to compensate these people on behalf of the diocese," Eric said. "We aren't Child Protective Services. We can't fix their home lives. We state our terms, get the parents' signatures on a nondisclosure agreement, and write the first big check. That's the extent of it. Mother Teresa, we ain't."

"Fine," I said.

"My father and I and Ken Guidry's attorneys have spent a lot of time discussing strategy with the Vicar-General," Eric said, smiling tepidly at the man sitting behind his desk like a stone gargoyle scowling from a cathedral ledge. "We've come up with a battle plan—opening salvo to *coup de grâce*—as to how these appointments with the parents should play out."

No mention of the Bishop attending the strategy sessions. Once again, His Excellency was MIA.

"We didn't anticipate that you would be included, Peter, boots on the ground," he said, "so let me go over a few things that should clarify your role."

"I'm listening," I said.

Our Lady of Sorrows had no work listing for Stevie's mother, so I dialed their home number and she picked up. I introduced myself and asked if we could meet her that afternoon, before her son came home from school. I emphasized that the matter was urgent and private.

"Who did you say you're with?" she asked. I could tell that she'd already started drinking. "Is Stevie sick again? Jesus, that boy's been missing so much school, I don't know what to do with him."

Mother and son lived in the lower half of an old two-story apartment building in the Broadway neighborhood near Tulane. Their street was like many Uptown streets, tastefully renovated homes interspersed with ill-kept eyesores. One look at their building and I knew it was only a matter of time before the neighborhood association pressured the landlord to revamp, tear down, or sell to someone who would.

Sherry Sutton answered the door with a cigarette smoldering between her fingers. She was wearing tight jeans and a sweatshirt, and although her big bottle-blonde hair was teased into high bangs like a heavy metal rock star's, the crimping of her side-drapes was losing its shape. I wondered if she was consciously modeling herself after white-trash pole dancers in Jacksonville, Florida.

"*My*," she said, taking a long uncomfortable gander at the two callers dressed in business suits and ties. "If I knew we were going to the prom, I woulda insisted on a corsage."

The residence reeked of cigarette smoke, and I suspected I would have to send my suit to the dry cleaners afterwards. She showed us into a dining room that appeared to be where they spent most of their time. The table was spread with household bills and drifts of graded homework assignments. One wall was occupied by a cube bookcase that shelved school supplies, cookbooks, plastic binders, and family photographs framed in stands. I noticed a picture of a rough-looking man sitting on a motorcycle with a younger Stevie in his lap. It might've been the boy's father.

"Would you care for something to drink?"

Eric and I declined.

"Have a seat, y'all," she said, indicating the dining table. "I'll push all that crap out of the way."

She returned from the kitchen with an ice-filled tumbler and sat at the head of the table, tapping her cigarette on the metal lip of an old sandbag ashtray. "Like I told you over the phone," she said, "I don't know what's wrong with him. He ain't been sleeping good or eating regular for a long time now. Maybe since last summer. He walks around his room talking to hisself, but I can't get a word out of him. You probably already know his grades have gone to hell. He used to be a straight-A student, but the teacher says he ain't been turning in his homework." She paused to inhale smoke. "I asked his daddy to come by and take Stevie to the movies or something and see if he could figure out what's bothering the boy. He tried, but Stevie gave him the silent treatment, too. The doctor says he can't find nothing wrong with him and recommended a head shrinker. But I don't have the money to spend on that kind of doctor." She squinted at me through the smoke, an unappealing expression. "I don't know, *you* tell *me*. Are the sisters wanting to kick him out of O-L-S? He used to love that school."

"Miz Sutton," I said, "his schoolwork is not why we're here."

"Ma'am, I'm very sorry to inform you that your son, Stevie, has been sexually molested by a priest in our parish," Eric said, leaning toward her as if to better confide this horrible disclosure. "It was Father Martin Landry, the priest who died last week. We've come on behalf of the Bishop to offer the Church's most profound apology. We would like to tell you what we know and what we're doing about this, and answer your questions."

That short speech would become the template for how Eric Gautier began the painful conversations with parents. In theory, it was supposed to be a kind of good cop—bad cop routine. He was the stoic Joe Friday, *just the facts, ma'am*, and my role was to soften the impact and express the Church's heartfelt sympathy. I was to be the caring listener who would share the family's outrage and treat their suffering and distress as our greatest concern.

Sherry Sutton's response was swift and furious. "Are you telling me some fucking priest put his hands on my boy?" She slammed the tumbler down, sloshing drink over her wrist. "Is that what you're saying, mister? 'Cause I'll call up Stevie's daddy, who is one mean son of a bitch, and he'll come over here with his three-fifty-seven Magnum and blow your sorry asses away."

For a foolish moment I thought about offering a consoling hand, as Ann had done with Roberto, but I was fairly certain that Sherry Sutton would grind that cigarette out on my flesh.

"Miz Sutton," I said as calmly as possible, "Mr. Gautier and I both feel the same way you do. We were shocked and mad as hell when we found out about this."

Eric flashed his eyes at me with a disturbed expression that asked, *What are you doing?*

"But the priest is dead now and can't be held accountable for his crimes," I said. "And so we're here to help Stevie and you come to terms with what happened and explain what the diocese is prepared to do."

Her cigarette hand was unsteady as she flicked ash into the tray. "Why didn't they send a priest or a sister?" she asked, her voice quavering. "Don't I deserve some respect? I was baptized in the Church, same as you two, and the good sisters at Our Lady of Prompt Succor over in West-*we*-go taught me my first six grades—catechism and all the rest. I wore a little white dress with a veil to my first holy communion."

Westwego was a working-class neighborhood on the west bank, across the river from the Audubon Zoo.

"So why they treating me and Stevie like chump change? I want to see that other priest—the older one—the pastor at O-L-S." She was trembling now, striving to maintain her composure. "I want him to tell me, face to face, what that goddamned creep did to my boy."

Making these visits without clergy was a calculated risk. As Ted and Vince Scalco had pointed out, some parents would react violently toward a priest.

"I can arrange that," I said. "I know Father McMurray very well and I'm certain he'd be willing to meet with you."

Another nasty glance from Eric. He was concerned about all the moving parts, the contingencies, the deviations from the battle plan. Asking my uncle to counsel a parent? Eric's legal mind refused to make room for the unpredictable, the unrehearsed, the unforeseen.

"Ma'am, the diocese is proposing to offer you and your son four hundred thousand dollars in compensation," he said, rushing in before anything else side-railed the mission. "Our package will include regular payments to you and Stevie, and when the time comes, college tuition and expenses."

"We can't erase what happened," I said, "but we can provide financial security and make sure Stevie has a great life from this day forward."

Eric looked annoyed that I'd interrupted him again. "Miz Sutton, let me outline the agreement I've prepared," he said, his eyes telling me to shut up and let him complete his pitch. His collective *we* and *us* had suddenly morphed into the personal *I* and *me*.

"Did I hear you say four hundred thousand dollars?" She raised a bushy eyebrow and rubbed out her cigarette in the ashtray, nudging the dripping tumbler aside. "Go ahead, mister. Keep talking."

Eric delineated the agreement, step by patient step, taking nothing for granted, breaking down the $400,000 into its various components. "This is a nondisclosure agreement," he explained, "which means you cannot reveal the terms to anyone. Not to your parents and relatives, your friends, the police, the media. No one. Not even Stevie. Are we clear on that, Miz Sutton? If you discuss this with anyone, you've broken the contract and you forfeit all monies. Let me read to you what's required in this settlement."

She rested her elbows on the table, her head bowed slightly, eyes downcast, concentrating on the language. When Eric completed the reading, he asked if she'd understood every point clearly.

Sherry Sutton placed her hands flat on the table, as if examining her nails. "I'm not supposed to tell Stevie's daddy what happened to him?" she asked, her voice steadier now.

"Are you married to Stevie's father?" Eric asked.

She shook her head with an exaggerated insistence. "Divorced that shit heel when Stevie was just a baby."

"Then no, Miz Sutton," he said. "The agreement forbids you to discuss this with your ex-husband."

"Which means shitheel doesn't get any of the money?"

"That's correct. The financial settlement is all yours."

Tears pooled in her eyes. "That motherfucker slapped me around one time too many," she said, "even when I was pregnant."

She needed to cry and she did. Not solely for what a priest had done to her son, I surmised, but also for the whips and scorns that had battered her since she'd picked the wrong man and left her parents' home forever, raising a child on her own, the only existence she'd ever known as a grown woman. I wished Ann had been there to console her. Father Ted, as well. Sherry Sutton didn't know this yet, but it would take more than money to mend what was broken in her life.

Crying into her hands, hiding her face, she was no longer hostile and hard. Something had thawed within her. Eric and I waited in silence for the tears to subside. I caught him checking his wristwatch. And peeking into his day planner. Stevie's mother excused herself to blow her nose in the bathroom. She returned by way of the kitchen, where she rattled fresh ice cubes into her tumbler and filled it with clear alcohol and tonic water and a squeeze of lime.

"After you speak with Stevie about this," Eric said when she returned to the table, "we would like to meet with him, too. With you present, of course. As soon as possible, Miz Sutton. We have to document exactly what happened to him, where it took place, that sort of thing. We'll ask him if he knows other boys who were harmed by Father Landry."

"You're saying this creep priest messed with other boys, too?"

"I can't really answer that," Eric said, pro forma, "but Stevie may be able to help us find that out."

"It's too bad he's dead," she said, lighting another cigarette, blowing smoke, "'cause I'd like to spit in his face."

Eric supplied the gold pen, courtesy of his law firm, and she signed the agreement in triplicate.

"Do you have any questions for us?" I asked in my role as the caring listener.

"Are you gonna write me a check for that first fifty thousand?"

"I'll bring you a cashier's check tomorrow afternoon, personal delivery," Eric said with a lukewarm attempt at a smile. "It's the Church's investment in Stevie's future happiness."

She blinked through the plume of smoke. "I want to see that old pastor, Father what's-his-name," she said to me. "I want him to hear Stevie's confession and forgive him for the sins he committed with that creep."

I was taken aback. "Miz Sutton," I said, "I don't think God blames the child for being sexually molested by an adult. Stevie is just a boy."

"He's old enough to know right from wrong," she said. "He knows better than to act like a queer."

"Miz Sutton, this is a very complex . . ."

Eric intervened. "Why don't you discuss this with Father McMurray when he comes to visit?" he suggested, staring me down. "Mr. Moore and I are not clergymen. Forgiveness is not our area of expertise."

She drank deeply from the sweating tumbler and studied us with the glass to her lips. I sensed that she held us in low regard, as if we were door-to-door insurance salesmen, soulless reps, empty suits.

"I heard they're burying that Father Landry at the cathedral tomorrow," she said. "A big fancy High Mass with priests and nuns coming from all over."

"It's the tradition when a priest dies," I said.

"I hope he's burning in hell," she said, toking the cigarette with narrowed eyes. "That's my tradition."

Eric announced that we were done for the time being and we stood up politely, gathering our notepads and briefcases, shaking her cold wet hand.

"What time you coming tomorrow?" she asked him. "I'll check my dance card to see if I can work you in."

I smiled at her remark, wondering what she did with her time. Ann could certainly help her organize a daily schedule, invest the money wisely, find fulfillment in something that made her happy.

Eric and I were turning to leave when the front door opened and Stevie walked in. I'm not sure why it was so disquieting to see him in person. Perhaps because his dark secret was now exposed to his alcoholic mother, and I knew their conversation would be humiliating for him and overwrought with shame. He would never forget this day for the rest of his life.

He slipped his backpack off his shoulders and dropped it on the floor, a routine I recognized from my own sons. The backpack would lay in that same spot, an object at rest remaining at rest, until acted upon by his mother.

"Hello again, Stevie," I said, extending my hand to shake his. "I'm Matt Moore's dad. You hung out in our car after the soccer game last Sunday."

He ignored my hand and brushed past Eric, moving quickly toward his bedroom.

"Son, can't you say hello to these gentlemen?" Sherry Sutton said without leaving her chair. "Where are your manners?"

I think he suspected why we were there. The moment he'd been dreading for many months had finally arrived. He couldn't face it, and I didn't blame him. I prayed that at the end of this long and excruciating ordeal, Stevie would be able to study and play with his friends again and sleep peacefully through the night.

On the drive back to the chancery, Eric unloaded on me, as I'd expected he would. He complained that I'd interrupted the flow of his presentation. That I'd said inappropriate things, provoking the woman unnecessarily, giving her permission to rant. That I'd made a promise involving Father Ted, which we could not guarantee and should not even consider. That I'd argued with her over an interpretation of *sin* that was far afield and had no relevance to our mission.

He was gripping the steering wheel of his Mercedes as though his freckled hands were around my neck. "In summation," he said in the mock tone of a prosecutor addressing a jury, "you talk too much, Peter. Do us both a favor and control the chatter, okay? Don't borrow trouble, and don't volunteer shit that will lead to trouble. Are we clear on that?"

I recalled what Ann had said to me: "Don't just pay them off, Peter. Be the good father you are. Help them begin to recover."

"If, Eric, my style doesn't work for you, I will happily step down. My wife would've done a far better job with Sherry Sutton than I did."

Eric removed both hands from the wheel in an act of frustration, then gripped it again, as if venting at a reckless driver in the lane ahead. "I don't want you to quit, man. Your heart's in the right place," he said. "Just dial it back a little, okay?"

It was only a ten-minute drive from the Sutton residence to the chancery. Eric parked in the circle by the fountain, saying, "I've got to debrief with—what do they call him? The Rottweiler?"

He laughed.

"That's the *Holy* Rottweiler to you, civilian."

"You're welcome to join me," he said.

"And watch you take batting practice on my deep personality structure? No thank you, Eric."

He shrugged as if to say *Suit yourself* and we parted company.

That evening, a composed Roberto Hinojosa phoned to tell me that a fellow surgeon had replaced him in the operating room so he could continue a very emotional discussion with his sons. After initial denial, and with great reluctance, Rico and David had finally admitted to being abused by Landry over a two-year period, from eight to ten years old, first Rico and later David. Rico felt enormous guilt that he hadn't warned his younger brother about the priest or stepped in to prevent terrible things from happening. He believed that his mother's death was God's retribution for the sex and the safekeeping of Father Marty's secrets.

"Rico is ashamed of himself and very angry," Roberto said. "He feels he's ruined his little brother's life. And he's talking about burning down the rectory. *Literalmente!* I should call the police and get them involved."

"Please don't do that, Roberto," I said. "I wasn't supposed to speak with you about this yet. The diocese has a protocol they're following. But you're such a dear friend, I wanted you to know right away."

"For Christ sake, these are my *sons*, Peter. That evil *pervertido* molested them! I'm not going to wait around until the diocese gets its act together."

"If this goes public, I'll lose my job, Roberto. My livelihood. I won't be able to feed my family. Please hold off another day or two until I get back to you."

"I know several attorneys, Peter, and I have no qualms about suing the Church."

He was a devout Catholic who lit a candle in the hospital chapel before every surgery and asked God to guide his hand.

"I promise you the Church is deeply concerned about this and will be more than generous in its support of Rico and David," I said. "The Bishop is as outraged as you and I."

I had no idea how the Bishop felt about the molestations on a personal level. The only emotion I'd seen him express was awkward avoidance.

"May I speak with Ann?" Roberto had become impatient with my pleading. "I could use her expertise tonight, if she's available. I need professional help to calm Rico down."

"I'll get her, Roberto. But please. *Please* do not contact the police or any lawyers until I have a chance to see you again in person and explain the compensation."

After her long phone conversation with Roberto, Ann and I lay side by side in bed, her smooth round shoulder contoured to mine. "He put Rico on the line and I offered to drive over to their home and visit with him one on one, just the two of us," she said. "We ended up talking about Stephanie. It's hard to hear a macho teenaged boy cry for his mother over the phone. It broke my heart, Peter. I'm going to meet with him tomorrow after school."

I hugged her for a long time, recounting my visit with Stevie's mother and Eric's criticism of my performance. I told her I'd recommended that she replace me as the good cop.

"If you quit the team, Peter, the Vicar-General will get his way," she said. "He'll tell the Bishop it was your idea to quit—and wipe his hands of you. Then it'll be just that lawyer Eric and a briefcase full of signature lines."

She was wearing a soft winter sleeping gown, and I rested my cheek against her warm breast and wrapped my arm around her waist, finding great comfort in the slow steady rhythm of her breathing.

"When you put it like that," I said, drifting off, "it makes me want to stick around and make their lives miserable."

I could feel her smile. "Now *that's* the man I married," she said, stroking my hair.

She told me about her day. She'd spoken to the final OLS class about Landry's death and listened to their questions and concerns. At lunchtime she'd met again with that group of young men who'd been abused by clergymen. "Their stories are very disturbing," she said, her hand caressing my arm. "It's hard for them to close that door and open a new one. No matter what they do—it can be standing in a check-out line at the grocery store—they sometimes think the cashier is giving them a look that says, 'I can tell you were somebody's bitch'—as one of them explained in our session today."

"We got lucky," I mumbled. "It could've been our boys, too."

I must've dozed off. At some point I realized she was talking to me. "What, honey?" I asked, lifting my head.

"Wherever this thing goes, whatever we do," she said, "we can't let it change us, Peter. It's consuming all our time right now, and it'll probably get worse. More boys, more anger and heartache. We have to be strong, okay? For ourselves. For Luke and Matt. For every family hurt by that man. We can't let the ugliness in. We can't allow it to touch us."

"How could it do that, Ann?" I managed to ask through my grogginess and fatigue.

"Being around all that filth might kill our appetite for each other, Peter. Let's not let that happen."

I rolled onto my back, confused and too sleep-deprived to follow what she was saying. "Darling, I'm not sure what . . ." Her warm hand slipped under the covers and into my pajamas, moving slowly, sweetly, but my body wouldn't respond. I'd seen too many haunting images of those boys on tape. They were in my head. She was right. The ugliness had killed my desire. I was only forty years old, in the prime of life, and I didn't know if I would ever feel sexual again.

TWENTY-NINE

AT A QUARTER TO TEN THE NEXT MORNING, the bells of St. Louis Cathedral began to toll, summoning the crowd outside on the plaza to find pews for the Solemn Requiem High Mass honoring the life and ministry of Father Martin Landry. I had arrived two hours earlier at Sister Colleen's request. "I need muscle, Peter," she'd said over the phone, "in case I get into it with those bossy broads in the altar society." She wanted a tall man in a dark blue suit to accompany her as she made the rounds inside the cathedral, inspecting the altar cloths and candles and floral arrangements, checking the sound system, ensuring that everything was spotless and in place for the funeral Mass.

The iconic tri-spired cathedral was the epicenter of our faith in a city once ruled, in turn, by the French and Spanish. It was the third church built on the same site, in what was now Jackson Square, beginning nearly three centuries ago. Colonial dignitaries, city leaders, and a dozen bishops were buried in the stone foundation near the sanctuary. After defeating the British in the Battle of New Orleans, Andrew Jackson hastened to this house of worship to thank God for victory.

When I was in the seminary, our aging church history teacher, Father André Duplantis, took our class on a field trip to the cathedral and walked us through its most notable features. Officially known as the Cathedral-Basilica of St. Louis, King of France, the interior architecture paid homage to its devout patron saint and the only French monarch to be canonized. Louis IX was an avid collector of sacred relics, and in the rear of the church stood a colorful statue of him with sword and a small pillow bearing a piece of the crown of thorns. Several of the stained-glass windows portrayed scenes of his life and good works, and a large mural above the altar depicted the king announcing the Seventh Crusade, which ended badly for him when he was captured by the Egyptians and never reached Jerusalem.

A team of security guards and I had spent the final hour making sure the aggressive camera crews and reporters did not enter the cathedral. I saw Sharon Simon speaking with Detective Ray Duhon near one of the plaza benches, and they both acknowledged me with casual nods.

The tolling bell convened the service, and the pews soon filled with parishioners from Our Lady of Sorrows and other mourners who'd come to pay their respects for a martyred priest. Ann and Matt had saved a seat for me toward the rear of the church. (Luke had adamantly refused to attend the service.) To my chagrin, Matt had outgrown his suit, the sleeves a little too short, the pant cuffs too high, and I felt like a bad father for not checking on that before the morning of a funeral. Seeing me, Ann smiled hello, and despite the somber occasion, and my thoughts in bed the night before, I was attentive to how fetching my wife looked in a waist-cut charcoal-gray jacket over a shape-skimming gray skirt, her mane of auburn hair brushed high and thick, her marvelous face touched lightly with makeup and her lipstick a subtle color that brought out the reddish highlights in her hair. She was such a beautiful woman.

Four rows in front of us, attorneys from Glynn, Gautier & Lesseps occupied nearly an entire bench with attorneys from Ken Guidry's insurance company. Eric was seated next to his father, the patriarch Russell Gautier, who was seated next to the silver-voiced district attorney, Roger Finney. It was a rogue's gallery of high-dollar deceivers. I slung my arm around Matt and hugged him sideways, vowing under my breath that he would never attend law school while I was still alive.

Shortly before the procession began in the vestibule, I heard people stirring at the far end of our pew and turned to see Sharon Simon drawing dark looks from the bench dwellers as she stepped on their polished shoes, stumbling in our direction. I was mortified that she'd tracked where I was seated.

"Come here often?" she said as she wedged into a tight spot next to me. "Hi, Ann. Hi, Ann and Peter's son," she said *sotto voce*.

"Hello, Sharon," Ann whispered. "It's been a long time. I've been reading your articles in the newspaper."

"There's more coming," Sharon said, "but I'm having a hard time communicating with the Bishop's communications director. He won't answer my calls."

I suspected she had a tape recorder spinning quietly in that large leather monstrosity strapped to her side like a postal bag.

Ann leaned across Matt, whispering, "Try bribery. His family could use the money."

At that moment, thank God, the pipe organ crushed the respectful silence with an explosion of sound, the first chord of a grand liturgical composition by Giovanni Palestrina, and the choir in the loft above us roared into song. We all stood as the procession slowly advanced down the central nave, where flags hung from the balconies, the papal crest and the cathedral's coat of arms and national banners that had flown over this city since its founding in the early eighteenth century. Church historian Father Duplantis had referred to them as *Six Flags over Jesus*.

Garbed in white robes with black capelets around their shoulders, a small cluster of seminarians and their cross bearer led the procession, the thurifer swinging his censer, dispensing the sweet purifying smoke of incense. Two of them were trying to keep their tall candles lit until they reached the altar. On their heels marched a young deacon elevating an ornate, gilt-edged Book of Gospels with both hands, so all could witness the word of God.

It was a cheerless parade of symbolic garments. In keeping with the times, funereal black was out, white was in. Death be not proud. Resurrection over mortality, the celebration of life eternal. Representing all the parishes in the southern province of the Church, a long column of priests wore white robes with violet stoles, followed by elderly monsignors cloaked in fuchsia and then the seven bishops of Louisiana in amaranth red with matching birettas, those stiff peaked hats with puff balls on top.

Sharon tilted closer to me and said, "I hear you were in the seminary with Father Landry," raising her voice to find the right volume in competition with the organ and choir. "Did you ever meet his family? His parents are both deceased."

I turned slightly, saying, "Wrong time and place, Sharon. Give it a rest."

"It's never a good time or place with you, Peter."

Ann heard the tail end of what Sharon had said and raised an eyebrow, giving us both an inquisitive sidelong glance.

The pallbearers were priests who'd been ordained with Martin Landry, all attired in simple black cassocks, signifying their humility as servants. I recognized a few of them from the seminary, but I hadn't seen them in years. They had aged with dignity and self-importance. Seymour Fontenot, Timothy Fitzgerald, Fernando Martinez, now using the appellation *Father* in front of their names. They were slow-rolling the casket behind our Bishop, the master of ceremonies and the only bishop wearing a mitre.

The Landry family trailed the casket as if they were invited at the last minute, a necessary afterthought. There was nearly a score of them, two distinct generations, Martin's older aunts and uncles and cousins, dark haired and well turned out. I wondered about the children I'd seen in the home movies, the pretty teenaged sister at the picnic, the younger brothers and their cap pistols. Were they among this group? Two married couples were first in line, closest to the casket, holding hands side by side, controlling their tears. The taller of the two women dabbed her wet eyes with a lacy handkerchief. She may've been the older sister, now in her mid-forties, an attractive woman wearing heels and a long violet dress tucked nicely at her waist, with a tasteful string of pearls around her elegant neck and no head covering of any kind. She walked with her chin held high, grieving but undaunted, projecting authority and grace, the one in charge.

The pallbearers rolled the casket to rest between two rows of tall candles near the altar rail. The Bishop waited for the choir to finish its final verse and then began his blessing as the pallbearers unfurled a white and blue pall and placed it over the chest that enclosed Martin Landry's remains.

"Almighty Father," the Bishop intoned, sprinkling holy water on the pall, "in the waters of baptism, Martin rose with Christ to a new life. May the Son of God share eternal glory with His beloved servant Martin and enfold him in His bosom."

Clothed in a white robe, Father Ted came forward to place a crucifix on the casket. As pastor and Landry's immediate superior, my uncle was granted a position of honor at the Mass.

"Lord, under Your guiding hand, Father Martin fulfilled his sacred office as an exemplary priest and disciple of Jesus, walking in His footsteps," prayed the Bishop. "We implore You to embrace his immortal soul, so he may exult with You in heaven."

Every word the Bishop spoke was a lie, and he knew it. *An exemplary priest walking in His footsteps?* How could the man live with himself? Would he seek forgiveness in confession and be absolved of his lies by reciting a few lame prayers of penance? Was it that easy to clear his conscience?

I had held my tongue for an entire week, doing what I was expected to do, a dancing monkey in the circus of misinformation. But on the morning of Martin Landry's funeral, as I sleepwalked through the rubrics of a Requiem High Mass, I was angered by the hypocrisy of that extravagant charade. I couldn't bear to watch so many decent people, clergy and laity with goodness in their hearts, being duped and betrayed. I thought about walking out, but that would've left Ann and Matt in a state of worry and confusion. And so I remained in place like an obedient altar boy going through the stations, mimicking the right words, following the stage instructions, standing and kneeling and sitting, yet empty of any true feeling that offered closure and peace of mind.

Shutting down was a defense mechanism that allowed me to survive that carnival with my sanity intact. What brought me around was the appearance of a layman mounting the steps to the cathedral's pulpit, a beautiful artwork handcrafted out of dark wood, with a huge clamshell-shaped sounding board looming behind it. As he began to read from the Book of Revelation, I nipped the program from Sharon's hand and searched for the man's name.

"It's his brother," she whispered.

James Landry, the program said. I could see the family resemblance. He was my age, a handsome man who looked comfortable in a business suit and tie, his hair as black as shoe polish. Another lawyer, perhaps, or doctor. Chamber of Commerce, Lion's Club, Knights of Columbus. He read the passage with poise and conviction:

"Then I hear a voice from heaven saying, 'Write this: The dead who die in the Lord henceforth are blessed.'" He handled the microphone like a veteran public speaker. "'Yes,' says the Spirit, 'Let them rest from their labors, for their deeds will follow them.'"

Their deeds will follow them. Was James Landry the younger brother in the home movie? The naked boy prancing around with an erection?

Two Landry grandchildren, a boy and girl, walked down the main aisle carrying the wine cruets and a large white host resting on a gold paten, presenting them to the Bishop and Father Ted waiting at the altar rail. The Bishop circled the altar with the puffing censer, then raised the host and chalice in short succession, consecrating them as the body and blood of Jesus Christ. Transubstantiation, my old *bête noire*. And that's when the commotion began. A young man rushed from a pew behind the congregation of priests, shouting something I couldn't hear, and splashed Landry's casket with a vial full of what turned out to be human blood. There was a collective gasp throughout the assembly, an antiphon of fear in an era of untrustworthy blood.

"The blood of innocents!" were the first words I understood. *"You sick monster! You spilled the blood of innocents!"*

Several middle-aged priests hurried from their seats, trying to prevent the young man from doing more harm, and in the wrestling match they knocked over two of the tall burning candles stationed next to the casket.

"Jesus, he's one of mine," Ann said, rising from her knees and scrambling over a handful of parishioners to reach the aisle.

The young intruder had allies. Partners in crime. Three of them had appeared out of nowhere and were shoving priests aside, freeing their friend from grasping hands.

"Stay here!" I said to Matt, stumbling after Ann and falling in step with the security guards who were racing down the aisle toward the scuffle.

That was my introduction to Ann's client Darren and the other victims she'd begun to counsel. The four of them blew past Ann and then past me, retreating toward the cathedral doors, and when the security guards tried to apprehend them, fists flew and the young men quickly slipped away and kept running. I saw Detective Duhon step out of the shadows in the vestibule and raise his badge high in the air, but he made the wise choice to stand aside and let them flee into the sunlight.

Ann and I and the security guards found ourselves outside on the plaza, surrounded by camera crews filming the young disruptors as they disappeared down the lane of sketch artists and street musicians in front of the Pontalba Building.

"Desecrating a casket. That's not something you see every day." Ray Duhon strode up behind us with a walkie-talkie in hand. "Anybody know who they are?"

The guards shook their heads, mumbling, "No, sir. Never seen 'em before, sir."

"Ma'am, I heard you say something to those guys." Duhon was addressing Ann. "Do you know them? Is that why you left your seat?"

Ever the protective mother, Ann had felt obligated to rescue her boys.

"This is my wife, Detective," I said, bent over with my hands on my knees, sucking air.

"Pleased to meet you, Mrs. Moore," he said with what looked like an awkward bow but was really a glimpse at her unshod feet. "What can you tell me about them?"

Ann's tight skirt was unsuitable for running, but she'd kicked off her heels and had done the best she could.

"Detective, I can't answer that question," she said.

"Can't or won't, Mrs. Moore?"

He had an unhealthy interest in her panty-hosed feet. Ann told me later that she thought his fascination bordered on the abnormal.

"I'm a licensed therapist," she said. "To say anything at this point would be a breach of ethics."

"Ahh, so you're *treating* one of those fine gentlemen?" he said. "Makes sense. Dude's gotta be pretty messed up to do something like that in church."

He turned and studied me. "You agree with that, Mr. Moore?"

"A rare moment of consensus, Detective." I stood up straight, still catching my breath. "What he did was messed up."

The walkie-talkie sounded like somebody coughing up a fishbone. Duhon turned his back to answer the call. "Check the parking lot by the levee. Both sides of the old brewery. And Café du Monde," he said. "These frickin' *bibittes* might be hiding under cover of beignets."

"I have to go find my shoes," Ann said to me, "and make sure Matt's okay."

At the cathedral doors, she nearly bumped into Sharon Simon, who was hurrying out with Ann's heels. They hugged each other, and Ann held onto Sharon's arm for support as she slipped on her shoes and returned inside.

"Holy shit," Sharon said, approaching me. "What was that all about?"

"You know as much as I do, Sharon."

"I sincerely doubt that," she said. "Any idea who that one guy is and why he'd do something like that?"

"Not the slightest."

"Your wife almost got trampled," she said. "What was she doing?"

"Ann's a mediator. With a big heart. I'm sure she was trying to help."

Detective Duhon was still barking orders into the walkie-talkie. Annoyed by the TV cameras, he waved them away and turned to address me in a loud voice: "Where is your wife? I need to ask her some questions."

"Trust me, you'll be beating your head against a wall," I said. "Let's take a walk, Detective. Away from these cameras. There are some things you need to know."

He consulted his watch. "I'll give you five minutes, pal. I'm juggling a lot of balls right now, and it's starting to feel like they're the balls in my nut sack."

We walked past the old Presbytere museum toward the corner of St. Ann Street and Chartres, leaving behind Sharon Simon and the news media and security guards and the long black hearse waiting near the cathedral doors to convey Martin Landry's casket to the cemetery. Duhon was on high alert with his walkie-talkie, monitoring the police search for the disruptors, calling backup officers to the scene.

"What's on your mind?" he asked with considerable irritation, and for a moment I thought he was addressing someone on the other end of the squawk box. "You still playing the violin for your boy Kwame Williams?"

"I've made contact with four boys who were partying with Landry in his rectory bedroom on the night he was murdered," I said, "and they all say the same thing. Kwame wasn't there. Somebody phoned Landry and said he was coming over, and the priest shooed the boys away. It wasn't Kwame on the line. The boys were sure about that. So who called the rectory last Friday night, Detective? I assume you've looked at the phone records. Where did the call come from?"

228

I was surprised that Duhon would tell me anything. "A pay phone outside a K and B drugstore on St. Charles. No video monitor," he said.

"You know it wasn't Kwame Williams, Detective. Why are you still holding that kid? Because the DA wants it that way? Because it makes the Bishop happy? You're better than that, Ray."

Duhon was incensed. "Do not call me *Ray*. We're not asshole buddies, okay?" he said. "You do not have permission to call me Ray."

"I know you're not willing to put your badge on the line until you've got an airtight reason to let Kwame walk. So I'm going to introduce you to a teenage street hustler named Trey and let him tell you what happened last Friday night in the rectory. He was there."

I wasn't inclined to volunteer Luke or Roberto's sons to tell Duhon the story, unless there was no other choice.

"Trey got kicked out of the rectory with the others," I said. "It was raining buckets, so he jumped into a dumpster to get dry—the one near the priests' carport. He may've seen who showed up at the door."

Trey told us he didn't see anybody, of course, and maybe he didn't, maybe he did. I had faith in Detective Duhon's persuasive skills as an interrogator. And this is where I may have sold my soul to the devil. I knew that in time, under pressure, Trey would tell Duhon about the videotapes, and I wouldn't have to.

"What makes you think the DA and me are gonna believe a street hustler?"

I remembered Trey saying the same thing.

"Because you're a good cop," I said, "and you know the truth when you hear it."

He managed to extract a cigarette from his coat pocket and light it with his Zippo in one hand and the walkie-talkie in the other. He took two long ponderous drags without looking at me or speaking. We were standing in front of a sidewalk café that was usually overrun with tourists sitting at outdoor tables under the old wooden eave. But it was wintertime and its glass doors were closed and steamy, the patrons inside with their cappuccinos and quiche. I thought I recognized someone eating breakfast behind the large square window, watching us.

"This Trey kid," he said with the cigarette wagging between his lips. "If he was there, I wanna talk to him. Can you make that happen?"

It wasn't going to be easy. "He's on the street. It may take me a couple of days to find him."

His walkie-talkie hawked static, a cop on the other end. It sounded like they may've located the suspects. I wondered if I should tell Ann.

"Your five minutes are up," he said. "Bring that kid in. And one more thing. Kwame told me this Father Landry creep liked to videotape his dirty shit. You heard anything about that?"

Was he testing me, or was he truly in the dark? I didn't know how much Vicar-General Fulweiler had revealed to him and the DA.

"He said sometimes there was another old maggot working the camera," Duhon said. "The kind of maggot that likes to watch but not touch."

"I'm on the outside looking in, Detective. Just like you said. The black robes don't trust me any more than they trust you. That hasn't changed."

"If you fucking people keep lying to me," he said, "I might forget how Catholic I am."

Duhon wasn't finished with his cigarette, but he dropped it on the slate flagstones and mashed it underfoot, kicking it away with the edge of his shoe.

"When you bring the kid in," he said, giving me a cold hard stare, "bring the videotapes too. I don't give a crap who's sitting on them. Even if it's His Holiness, the Polak Pope hisself. Track down those goddamned videotapes and bring them to me. You got that, hoss?"

He turned back toward the cathedral, striding with grave urgency, issuing commands into the walkie-talkie. I watched him approach the camera crews, dodging Sharon and the other reporters as they tried to stick microphones in his face. He warded them off with a dismissive hand, passing through their numbers without shedding a thread of information, making himself unapproachable, intensely focused on his duty to protect and defend, and no doubt as troubled as I was about serving two masters.

THIRTY

VINCE SCALCO WAS EATING either a late breakfast or early lunch, possibly both, at a table next to the dewy café window facing Jackson Square. He was wearing his signature brown leather jacket with a loose wool scarf around his thick neck, and when I slid back a chair to sit down, he caught a waitress's attention, saying, "Hey, dawl, give this gentleman whatever suits him and bring me another Brandy Alexander, *per favore.*"

I kept an eye on the cathedral. I didn't want to lose track of my wife and son when the pallbearers transported the casket to the waiting hearse and the crowd poured out into the square.

"What was with all that skuh-dat-duh-dat?" he asked with a mouth full of grits. "Them young cats running out the church. They forget their proper *ecclesiae suae sanctae?*"

"One of those cats threw skuh-dat-duh-dat on the casket. It looked like blood."

"Jeezum, Pete, I'm sorry I missed the act," he said. "Any idea who this joker is?"

I leaned toward him and lowered my voice. "My guess is he's one of Martin Landry's victims, now in his twenties. The Church had better put a lid on this thing before it blows wide open."

I told him about the meeting with Stevie's mother and that Eric was taking her the down payment that afternoon.

"While y'all handing out checks," he said, "how 'bout cutting one for yours truly? I gotta make groceries too, brother. And with you and the Gautier lad starting to hold hands, it sounds like my time ain't long on the squad."

"You're not done yet, Vince. You saw me talking to Ray Duhon?"

"Brother Ray didn't look too happy wicha. He can get mighty *coup de fiyo*," he said, washing down food with that sweet milky drink, "when somebody tries to yank his tail feathers."

The waitress brought my coffee and another Brandy Alexander for Vince.

"Duhon knows about the videotapes," I said, "and he wants them. He wants Trey, too. If we can deliver Trey and the boy tells him about the party, maybe Duhon will let Kwame go and start looking for the real killer."

"That's one too many *maybes*, baby," he said. "You give all that up, you got squat for leverage, Pete. Besides, those tapes ain't really ours to give. We're babysitting them for the padres that put coins in our pockets."

I saw crowd movement in front of the cathedral, and I wiped the cold wet condensation from the café window. The black-robed pall-bearers were wheeling the casket down a ramp toward the funeral director and his team of solemn young men dressed in dark suits, waiting at the back of the opened hearse.

"There's my cue," I said, taking a quick gulp of coffee. "I'll make sure you get a check today, Vince. Paid in full for your services. But you've got to help me find Trey. I can't do that without you."

He smiled warmly and wiped his mouth with a napkin, then used it to daub the glaze of sweat on his forehead. "I got your back, man, as long as the check don't bounce," he said. "And with the Vatican bank and the nine choirs of angels as collateral, I figure cha dooky doo, cuz."

I walked Ann and Matt to the station wagon parked a couple of blocks away in a commercial garage attached to the Royal Orleans hotel. Ann seemed distracted, concerned, possibly embarrassed for kicking off her heels and running down the aisle in the middle of a Requiem Mass. I assumed she was turning over in her mind the response she would give to those errant young clients who'd disrupted the service. It would take considerable patience and skill to register her disapproval while remaining sympathetic to their outrage. But if anyone could walk that line, Ann could.

Before getting into the car, Matt asked, "Dad, why did that guy do that?" He was definitely his mother's freckled-faced son, with her startling blue-green eyes and inquisitive nature.

"I'm not sure, buddy," I said. "He's probably very angry about something."

Was he angry enough to bludgeon Martin Landry with a cinder block and drag him to the bathtub? Did he have a little help from his friends?

I returned to the cathedral to see if Sister Colleen needed my aid with those hidebound women of the altar society, but she'd joined the Bishop and Monsignor Fulweiler in the limousine cortege on its short journey to the Garden District and Lafayette Cemetery, where Martin Landry would be buried in the family crypt next to his parents. When I arrived at the square, the faithful had dispersed, for the most part, and the cameras had disappeared, too, except for one lone team interviewing a PTA mother I knew from Our Lady of Sorrows. No sign of Ray Duhon or Sharon Simon.

I didn't know what to do with myself. I was expected at the cemetery, but that wasn't going to happen. I should've gone back to the chancery to assist my staff with the phone calls that continued to light up our circuits, but my heart wasn't in it. After a chaotic, unsettling week, my energy had been depleted and I was too racked with doubt to play the chipper PR flack for the diocese.

One of the few things I had liked about being a seminarian was the long rambling walks around Immaculata's verdant grounds during silent meditation periods. In those days we wore black cassocks routinely, even in the deadening summer heat, and I enjoyed the peaceful solitude of strolling under the giant live oaks, more than three hundred years old, with their rich earthy smells and gray beards of Spanish moss. The Father Director gave us many options. We could pray, contemplate the sacred mysteries, say the rosary to ourselves, or even read inspirational books on his approval list. Anything that strengthened the inner spirit and brought us closer to the life of Christ.

I'm not sure how much serious meditation I actually accomplished. I was contented to have a few moments apart from the constant weight of community and hardy male fellowship. So I would wander along the grassy banks of a small lake with an island of tangled swamp foliage at its center, passing through shady groves near the persimmon orchard and the grotto shrine to the Holy Mother, drifting aimlessly in a dreamy daze of self-absorption, fantasizing about my high school virgin girlfriend Melanie and hearing popular radio songs in my head, scraps of this and that. At eighteen years old, my mind was fogged by frivolous diversions, impure thoughts, and visions of heroism in football and war. I was preparing myself to die for my faith, like St. Sebastian and Padre Miguel Pro, if God so desired.

Before I realized it, I was walking down Royal Street, away from the cathedral and Jackson Square, in that same dreamy, meditative state of long ago. A German-speaking couple was taking photos of the quaint lampposts and wrought-iron balconies decorated with flags and year-round ferns. Other tourists were window-shopping at the usual schlocky art galleries and souvenir stores. There was a sameness to the salmon-colored buildings, the green shutters and carriage doors, and I wondered if I'd lived in this city too long, disenchanted now by its gaudy exhibitionism and exotic allure. Sometimes I wished I'd escaped as a younger man, fifteen or twenty years earlier, like Donny Bertrand, whose talent had blossomed in New York. What might I have discovered about myself in a thriving metropolis? What hidden gifts would I have unwrapped?

I suppose I knew where I was going, after all. To find that pristine white door with the house number inlaid in tiles, the one through which my uncle had carried his black leather bag to administer the Last Rites. I recognized the place ahead, and as I drew closer, I peered up at the balcony where I'd noticed someone leaning on the iron-laced railing and smoking a cigar. Today the balcony was absent any human presence, only a tidy arrangement of outdoor furniture and those ubiquitous French Quarter ferns.

Standing before the door, I could hear someone playing piano inside. When I rang the doorbell, the music stopped abruptly, and in a short while, footsteps creaked down a stairway and approached. "May I help you?" said the voice behind the peephole. When he saw I was wearing a respectable suit and tie, he must've decided I wasn't a salesman or homeless veteran, because he cracked open the door.

"Hello, my name is Peter Moore," I said with my most polished smile. "I work for the Catholic diocese of New Orleans. I understand that an old friend of mine, Donald Bertrand, is residing here. Donald and I were in the seminary together. Are you Perry Blanchard?"

He declined to identify himself. "Is Donald expecting you?"

"I haven't talked to him in ages. I was at a funeral Mass in the neighborhood and thought I'd drop by and say hello."

"Father Landry?" he asked.

"I'm the communications director for the diocese," I said, hoping that would impress him. "I helped make arrangements for Father Landry's service."

Perry was in his late thirties, the scion of a prominent family that had been roasting beans and selling packaged coffee for nearly a century. He was a portly fellow with a soft round face and neatly combed hair balding on top, where I imagined a fluffy wave had once crested in his younger days. He was wearing a powder-blue Izod shirt and penny loafers without socks, an aging frat boy still pining for the Greek life. On first impression, I couldn't envision him as the heir apparent CEO of the family business. Vince had told me that Perry was a piano instructor, and that made more sense.

"Tell me your name again, please." When I did, he said, "I'll see if Donald is taking callers today," and closed the door in my face.

Taking callers? Had I wandered onto the set of a Tennessee Williams play?

He left me standing outside for quite a long time. I considered the possibility that he wasn't going to return and decided to give him five minutes more and then leave. But the door soon unlocked and he said with a charming smile, "Welcome, Peter. Please come in. Donald is elated you're here."

The main living area was on the second floor, a large open loft with smoky gray light ghosting through the balcony doors. I hadn't seen Donald in twenty years and didn't recognize the emaciated figure parked in a wheelchair. I walked toward him with a fond smile, extending my hand with the trepidation I'd always felt when touching a terminally ill person, secretly worried that his disease might be contagious, even though I knew better. But what if it wasn't melanoma? What if it was HIV that had turned into AIDS? Everyone was asking themselves that question then and scrubbing their hands afterwards. There was so much tainted blood in the world.

"Peter!" Donald said with a cadaverous grin, his teeth protuberant and stained yellow within a skull that had seemingly shrunk around them. "It's great to see you, man. You look exactly the same. In fact, you look even younger. What happened to those Coke-bottle specs you used to wear?"

"An amazing new thing called contact lenses," I said with a grin.

"Have you noticed how trim *I* am?" he asked, patting the loose pajama shirt bunched around his vanishing waistline. He worked his dry lips, his speech slow and faintly slurred, a patient on multiple medications. "Wanna know my secret for keeping the pounds off?"

I tried to laugh at the gallows' humor, but I was genuinely shocked by his gaunt appearance and made every effort to conceal my reaction. His arms and legs were like a Holocaust victim's, his skin was waxy pale and spotted with a rash, and his once sandy hair was a lank gray patch that had somehow survived chemotherapy.

Perry returned from a bedroom wearing a teal green windbreaker. "I'm off to the market, y'all," he said with a grocery list in hand. "That'll give you two time to catch up. Peter, would you care for an apéritif before I go?" he asked. "Mother would chastise me for failing to offer."

I passed. It wasn't quite noon, but every hour was happy hour in New Orleans.

"Donald, dear heart, don't worry about your meds. I'll be back in time to play nurse."

Perry shook my hand and we exchanged friendly good-byes. "I hear you're Father Ted's nephew," he said. "That man is a living saint. Please kiss his ring for me. Or is that just for bishops?"

After he left, Donald said, "I have nothing but good memories of you, Peter. I wondered how you been getting along. In Mandeville they kept me drugged up on Thorazine and other nasty stuff . . . and I slept most of the time. One day I noticed you signed the visitors' register, but I couldn't remember seeing you. Thanks for being a friend, man," he said, tapping a fist against his heart. "I haven't forgotten your kindness."

My uncle had told him I was married, and Donald asked about Ann and our sons. I asked about his family, as well, and he said his father had died of a massive stroke on his shrimp boat a few years earlier, and his mother was still living in the same house in Marrero, helping to raise grandchildren and devoutly attending Masses on Sundays and novenas every Wednesday evening, lighting candles and praying for his recovery.

"I hear you're working for the diocese now," he said. "Didn't you get enough of the Church when we were at Immaculata?"

I smiled. "It pays the bills. But I don't know how much longer I'll last. My problem is, I don't seem to have a special calling in life. Like the priesthood. Like making art," I said, gazing around at the colorful menagerie of contemporary artworks populating Perry's walls. Track lights shone on them as if this space was his own personal art gallery. "I admire you for finding your true vocation—what you were meant to do with your life."

"It was fun while it lasted," he said with a rictus smile. "But nothing that sweet ever lasts long enough."

He noticed I was staring at one painting in particular. "That was the very first piece I ever finished," he said. "Art class one-oh-one in the nut house. Go have a closer look and tell me what you think."

It was a large rectangular canvas, the kind of mixed-media collage that Ted had told me about. Darkly comic little angels and demons were floating around a sleeping figure as if they were vying for his soul. It was a busy canvas, frantic swaths of thickly layered paint and found objects from his hospital room glued to the surface—empty pill containers, latex gloves, a tissue box, an enema bottle, a white sock, get-well cards from friends and family. But what had really trapped my attention was the central image, an enlarged photograph of the slumbering artist himself, one I'd seen before.

"This print of you sleeping," I said, studying it with my back to him. "I found a photo exactly like it in an old album Martin Landry kept in his bedroom at the rectory." I turned around and looked at him. "Did Martin take this photo?"

He struggled to respond, as if words were buried too deep for immediate retrieval. His thought process had become impaired by the tissue damage to his brain, and he was making a concerted effort to formulate a sentence. "Not Martin," he said. "His brother."

"James?" I said. "I just saw James read a passage at the Requiem Mass."

"No, the other one. Chris. He took the picture," Donald said in a halting manner. "I got to know Chris when Martin and him . . . came to visit their mother on Sundays. She was shipped to Mandeville when they were kids. Schizophrenia, I was told."

"Martin's album has several photos of you sleeping. I figured he took them."

Donald blinked, hesitated, blinked again, as if fighting the urge to drift off. "I never liked Martin. Remember that bullshit move he pulled on me . . . in the old white dorm? You were the only person I told . . . besides the Father Director."

"I remember. Martin was an arrogant jerk."

I wanted to tell him about Martin's transgressions with children, but I held my tongue.

"When Martin came to Mandeville to see his mother . . . he'd drop by my room and say hello . . . that was about it. But Chris was a really sweet guy. He'd sit and talk with me while Martin was down the hall . . . holding his mother's hand." He laughed at a distant memory. "Chris smuggled in candy bars and *Mad* magazines . . . things I liked. He took those pictures with a Pentax . . . Spotmatic, I think it was called. A boss new camera at the time. He musta given prints to Martin . . . who was a shutterbug, too. It ran in the family. Their old man . . . took a lot of eight-millimeter home movies . . . when the Landry kids were growing up."

"There were two of those home movies in a box in Martin's bedroom." The second one was deposited through the rectory's mail slot, of course, but this was a simpler explanation. "One of them is very disturbing."

I realized I was baiting him. I suspected there were things Donald could tell me about Martin Landry.

"How much do you know about their . . . home situation, Peter?" he asked. His blinks were becoming longer and sleepier. "I'm gonna tell you something that will shock you. And maybe it'll explain Martin's behavior . . . that day . . . in the old white dorm."

He scratched at the rash on his arms. "Chris came to New York a few times and we hung out together," he said. "He got really drunk one night . . . and told me about his daddy's favorite hobby."

In Perry Blanchard's French Quarter loft that day, many years ago now, Donald Bertrand confirmed what I'd already witnessed, but it was worse than I imagined. Their father often filmed two of his sons, Martin and Chris, in the nude and talked them into playing with each other sexually. Chris had revealed to Donald that Mr. Landry, owner

of a very successful construction company in town, kept a large collection of those 8mm home movies locked away in a vault somewhere
and watched them from time to time with his poker buddies.

"When Chris turned ten or eleven years old . . . their old man
stopped filming them. Chris didn't know why. His daddy . . . just
didn't want to do it anymore. Maybe his conscience was bothering
him. Who knows?" Donald said. "But the abuse didn't stop. . . . Not
for Chris."

Martin pressured Chris into having sex with him until Chris
reached puberty, and then Martin called an end to it. It was that same
pattern Trey had told us about.

"The changes really screwed Chris up," Donald said. "He was
ashamed of the sex . . . and at the same time really hurt . . . because
his big brother had dumped him . . . like an ugly girlfriend. Martin
wouldn't even talk to him. He accused Chris of being a boy whore
seducer . . . an evil influence sent from Satan . . . and he didn't want
to have anything to do with Chris anymore."

Donald believed this was the reason for Chris's long downward
spiral into depression, drug abuse, and depravity. Always a straight-A
student, Chris began to struggle in school and was suspended numer-
ous times, and at age fifteen he was busted for possession of marijuana
and cocaine. He was sent to the juvenile detention facility in Bridge
City, where he was raped by inmates, and when he returned home
after two years, he dropped out of high school and started wandering
around the country, homeless and eating out of dumpsters and strung
out on drugs.

"He showed up on my doorstep in the Village," Donald said,
"looking almost as bad as I do now. I called his brother James . . . and
he flew up to New York and brought Chris back to New Orleans . . .
and put him in a rehab program. James also persuaded their father . . .
to hire Chris at the family construction business . . . and he settled
down for awhile."

Donald told me that Chris married a young teacher and they had a
child, but then bad things began to happen again. FBI Agents showed
up at the construction company and arrested him for buying child pornography magazines and 8mm films of underage sex in Southeast Asia
(long before the Internet). He was eventually sentenced to five years in a
federal prison in Fort Worth, Texas. His wife divorced him, and he lost

all visitation rights with his son. For the rest of his life, Chris Landry would have to register as a sex offender wherever he lived.

"Where is he now?" I asked.

"I wish I knew. I lost track of him after he was released from prison. . . . That's gotta be five or six years ago. I talked to James . . . around Christmastime. He doesn't know where Chris is, either."

Donald was fighting valiantly to keep his eyes open, but fading nonetheless. I wondered if he knew that Martin Landry had become a prolific pedophile. I wondered too if Chris was aware of his brother's secret life. After hearing about their father's movies and the long absence of a protective mother, I was beginning to piece together Martin's heinous path.

"Peter, it's important to understand that Chris didn't have sex with children," Donald said, conjuring up all his strength to continue speaking. "He would never do something like that. . . . Never. That sick obsession was all in his head. Coiled up inside him. A fantasy . . . a mind game. Child porn was how he stayed in touch with . . . with memories of the father and brother he loved . . . even though they'd abandoned him."

Tears were running down Donald's haggard cheeks. He was deeply concerned about his old friend and desperate to help him.

"He paid the price . . . hard time in Texas," he said, "but Chris isn't a predator, Peter. I want you to understand that. He never hurt anybody but himself. I wish I could reach out to him . . . and let him know he still has a friend."

I'd never seen a grown man cry himself to sleep. But that's what Donald did. One moment he was blinking and wiping away the tears, apologizing for his emotions, and the next moment his chin dropped and he was blissfully asleep in the wheelchair—in a place of peace far from the night terrors and Mandeville and the canvases he'd splattered with the wreckage from his dark struggles. Despite his ravaged face in repose, it was possible to see vestiges of the unblemished young man who appeared tranquil and sublime in those old black-and-white photographs. And with just a pinch of imagination, I could picture a host of small bright angels floating around his head, claiming victory in the happy realms of light.

THIRTY-ONE

AFTER RETURNING MATT TO SCHOOL FOR THE AFTERNOON, Ann went to her office to check the answering machine for messages from Darren, suspecting he would be in touch. She heard a car door open as she was standing on the wraparound porch, sorting through her keys for the one to unlock the front door. "Mrs. Moore," a voice said. She turned to find Detective Ray Duhon approaching from the sidewalk, still dressed in the suit he'd worn to the Requiem Mass. He'd parked across the street in an unmarked car.

"Can we talk?" he asked, walking up the steps toward her.

That evening, when she disclosed the incident with Duhon, she told me she decided not to invite him in, but to keep him visible on the porch in case Darren rode up on his bicycle.

"You're wasting your time, Detective," she told him. "Please don't make me call my lawyer."

They were face to face, and if Duhon expected my wife to back down, he was sorely mistaken.

"The district attorney was at the Mass this morning and he called my boss, the superintendent, irate at what went down," he said, staring at the running shoes she'd changed into, "and my boss called me to say he wanted to nail the blood splasher with criminal mischief and criminal damage to property. He could get six months in jail and a thousand-dollar fine." His eyes reverted to Ann's face. "We're not playing slap and tickle here, Mrs. Moore. That jackass is in serious trouble."

"I understand that, Detective. And I agree it was a horrible thing to do. I don't condone that kind of behavior."

"I'm not asking you to tell me anything he's discussed in confidence," he said. "All I want is his name."

She knew she was on shaky legal ground. Protected client privilege had its limits.

"I'll ask him to contact you. That's the best I can do," she said. "But I'll also advise him to hire a lawyer. He obviously needs one."

She described Duhon's smile as chilling. "So many lawyers," he'd said to her, "so little regard for the law."

He looked around the porch as if inspecting its paintwork, then stepped over to the large window, cupped his hands around his eyes, and peered into the parlor with its fainting sofa and Victorian armchairs.

"You know, I keep asking myself, 'Why would some young dude throw blood on a priest's coffin?' And the only conclusion I can come to is this priest musta done something really terrible to make the dude react that way."

He continued to gaze through the window, as though he might find his suspect sitting on a divan.

"If you're waiting for me to comment," Ann said, "we'll be here a very long time."

He stood back from the glass, straightened his tie in the reflection, and walked toward her with that same icy smile. "You and your husband think you've got this whole thing sewed up tight, don't you, Mrs. Moore? He's sitting on hard evidence and you're hugging the guy that mighta killed a priest. Now aren't you two the power couple of the month?"

Ann had had enough. "The newspaper says you've already caught the killer, Detective. So why do you keep peeping through windows and second-guessing yourself?"

His smile disappeared. He glanced at her shoes again, then into her eyes with an alarming intensity. "I'll give you forty-eight hours to tell me his name, Mrs. Moore, and if you don't cooperate," he said, "I'm gonna get DA Finney's blessing to charge you with obstruction of justice."

She envisioned herself in jail, paying a bondsman, hiring an attorney. Money we didn't have. She hadn't planned on becoming a martyr to her profession.

After Duhon left, Ann went upstairs to her office and listened to a phone message from a contrite Darren: "I'm sorry, Ann. I just couldn't let a child molester get away clean in front of all those true believers. I collected blood from the guys. It was a team effort."

Messages blitzed our recorders all afternoon. When I returned home and checked my machine, Barbara Lavergne was on tape begging me to return to the office and help answer calls, which were pouring in since the incident at the cathedral. "What the devil happened at the funeral Mass?" she asked, disappointed that she'd been stranded at the chancery, unable to attend. "Reporters are asking about *blood*!"

There were three urgent messages from an exasperated Sharon, demanding that I speak with her about the splasher. Demanding a comment from the Bishop. "After the rites at the cemetery, he hightailed it into a limo like a Beatle escaping teenyboppers," she said. "And where the hell were *you*? I've got some serious questions about that scene at Mass, Peter. Call me, damn it!"

I tried Sister Colleen's office number, and to my surprise, I found her sitting at her desk. "He's hiding out at the seminary," she said. "And ya have to be wearing a Roman collar to get through the gate. Boys only, I regret to say."

I knew that the seminary had planned to host a luncheon for the clerics attending the Requiem Mass, more than a hundred of them, but now it sounded as if they'd all retreated into a medieval fortress and pulled up the drawbridge.

"If peasants approach the walls," I asked, "will the defenders of the faith be using boiling oil and crossbows?"

She cackled with delight. "I'm not sure when His Excellency will be returning to the chancery. He might be boarding a plane for Bora Bora," she said. "Isaiah is downstairs at the main door, directing traffic and keeping the media outside. It's starting to feel like a feeding frenzy. What was going through that young man's head when he splattered blood on a casket?"

It was the lead story on the evening news on all three local channels. Reporters were standing next to the chancery fountain with the dark front entrance framed in the background like the lone remaining arch in a gothic ruin.

"Despite our repeated efforts, the diocese has not responded to our phone calls."

"The Bishop has not been available for comment."

"It's unclear where the Bishop is at this hour."

The phone rang shortly before midnight. I was still awake, nursing a glass of pinot noir in my home office, staring at the random phrases I'd pecked onto the blank screen of my word processor. *Compassion and forgiveness for that troubled young soul,* etc. I was struggling to compose a statement for the Bishop in the unlikely event he deigned to call on his director of communications for assistance.

"You weren't going to return my calls, were you, Peter?"

"I don't have anything to say, Sharon. I'm not sure where the Bishop is, either."

"Why *blood?*" she asked. "What did that signify?"

"Why don't you track down that young fool and ask *him?*"

She ignored my deflection. "The cops have sent a bloodstain to the lab to see if it's infected with the AIDS virus," she said.

It didn't surprise me. I assumed that was now standard procedure.

"He had accomplices." She was on a fishing expedition. "Does Ann know who they are?"

"Anarchists," I said. "Protestants. Free thinkers. Pantheists, Dadaists, Red Brigades." I sipped the dark wine, hoping to numb my brain. "Ann doesn't know, Sharon, and she's asleep."

"Please tell her I need to speak with her before my deadline."

"Will do," I said.

Her shriek felt like an icepick through my eardrum. "*You're impossible!*" she shouted.

"As soon as I hear from His Excellency, I'll let you know what he says. Good night, Sharon."

I hung up and unplugged the phone. The Bishop wasn't going to call me tonight, or perhaps ever again. I finished the glass of wine and deleted what I'd typed onto the screen. I knew full well he'd call Eric Gautier instead.

THIRTY-TWO

SISTER COLLEEN RELEASED THE FUNDS for Vince's handsome pay-check, and for the next two evenings he ventured into the French Quar-ter fat and sassy, buzzing through the dark backstreets on his Amigo, maintaining a low-key, under-the-radar surveillance. On Friday night, he stopped at a pay phone in the Sho-Bar on Bourbon Street and called me to admit that finding Trey was proving to be a frustrating task. The kid was too streetwise to work the Fruit Loop anytime soon, not after that takedown in the flophouse. Trey knew we'd be looking for him again, sooner or later, pressuring him to speak with Ray Duhon and help win Kwame's freedom.

Despite the French Quarter's quaint charm and bustling night life, there was a skeevy underworld of drifters, project strays, and con art-ists who fed on the good will and the slumming, laidback posturing of tourists far away from home, drinking hard and careless in the City That Care Forgot. *Laissez les bons temps rouler!* Vince was familiar with the scams and schemes and most of the players by name. As he made his frequent rounds in the Quarter, searching for the runaways he'd been paid to track down, he sometimes acted as an ombudsman between the gullible sightseers and the hustlers who plied their trades at separating fools from their money.

Bourbon Street, naughty and boisterous, was the dark heart of all wickedness, a pulsing foot traffic of drunk college kids and wide-eyed vacationers, the easiest marks. Vince usually avoided Bourbon, primarily because runaways avoided its crowds and the possibility of being recognized by their math teacher or an aunt in town from Bay St. Louis. That night, as he was crossing Bourbon to look for

Trey at a known hangout farther back on Conti Street, he spotted trouble brewing between a stylish young white couple and a stoned black street musician named Stalebread Stanley, who was trying to take their baby out of its cloth carrier strapped to the father's chest.

"I bring chirren good luck," he was telling the couple, unsteady on his feet. "You let ol' Stalebread hold your baby and kiss him on the head and he'll grow up to be the next Louis Armstrong."

"Please, sir, back off and give us some space," the father was saying, removing Stalebread's nicotine-yellow fingers from the baby's tiny arm.

"Yo, Stalebread!" Vince said in a strong, commanding voice. "We need to talk," he said, crooking his finger back and forth, summoning the man.

The baby had started to cry.

"Aww, come on, chief, I'm just trying to be friendly like. Welcoming these good folk to Nawlins, is all."

"Don't make me get up off this ride," Vince said.

Stalebread Stanley dragged his trombone over to where Vince was sitting on the Amigo. A crowd had gathered quickly, sensing drama.

"Stop fucking with people's babies, Stalebread," Vince scolded him. "What's the matter with you? Get your sorry ass on out of here and go play that 'bone somewhere down the street before I beat you over the head with it."

"Chief, you cold, man. *Cold*, ya heard me? And rude. This is some rude judgment, man."

Stalebread trailed off toward Royal Street and the crowd applauded, dispersing as quickly as it had formed. Vince wheeled over to the relieved couple, who thanked him copiously for intervening.

"Bourbon Street ain't no place for a baby, y'all," he told them in the kindest way possible. He hadn't allowed Paula and Ned to visit the Quarter without adult supervision. "Too crowded, too crazy. Stalebread Stanley being exhibit A. Y'all go find a legit babysitter at your hotel and come back by yourselves. Make it a date night. You'll enjoy it better."

Ombudsman on call. Ambassador at large. The couple thanked him again and the wife hugged him. Everyone always thanked and hugged him and praised him to their friends when they returned home. *We met this New Orleans character riding one of those grocery store scooters* . . . Everyone loved him except the occasional out-of-step junkie hustler too blown and stupid to understand why Vince was kicking his ass back to whatever roach haven he'd crawled out of. A layer of polish was required in the tourist locales, and if a street artist lacked grace and humor, he was run out of the Quarter with a greasy shoe print on the seat of his pants and a warning to never show his face again.

Vince puttered up Conti Street at three miles per hour, the clot of tourists dissolving into smaller numbers block by block. Locals knew that the closer you approached Rampart Street, the shank end of the Quarter, the darker and less safe you were. On the other side of Rampart lay the ornate old mausoleums of St. Louis Cemetery, where voodoo priestess Marie Laveau was buried, and the area called Back o' Town, home of once-rowdy Basin Street and the notorious red-light district of Storyville, which was demolished in the 1930s to make way for the Iberville Housing Project. Nowadays, if you were courting trouble, you crossed Rampart Street and trekked into the projects to find all the trouble your reckless heart desired.

Across the street from the touristy wax museum, a narrow, open-air parking lot was wedged into a block of green-shuttered buildings in disrepair. At night, the lot's sliding gate was rarely locked, and the unlit space was sometimes used as a drug shooting gallery with quick street sex. On two occasions, Vince had found runaways in that grim place, being mounted on their hands and knees between parked cars.

He was nearly to the gate when he heard someone begging *Oh please, please, I'm sorry, don't hurt me* and the sound of rough fists pounding solid bone. Vince clicked on the flashlight he carried in his scooter basket and traced a teenage boy running out of the lot at full stride, flying past him, and he realized too late that the hood-wearing runner was Trey. Vince spun his Amigo 180 and watched Trey stop a short distance away, breathing hard. He'd recognized the scooter.

"Hey, I know you—you fat fuck!" Trey shouted at him, walking in a circle while catching his breath. "Next time I see you on the street like this, I'm gonna pull you off that fat-mobile and cut your tiny nuts off!"

Before Vince could respond, the boy had raced off toward the bright lights of Bourbon Street. As Vince explained to me later, Trey had lured a smartly dressed college student into that parking lot with the promise of sex, but instead had beaten him up and stolen his expensive watch and wallet full of cash and credit cards. When the college kid staggered out of the dark lot and stood trembling on the sidewalk, disoriented and struggling to find his bearings, Vince shined the flashlight beam on him and the young man shielded his bloodied face.

"You awright, son?" Vince asked, rolling slowly toward him.

"Please turn that light off," the young man said. He was wearing an Italian sports jacket, *Miami Vice*-style, and his pastel shirt had been torn open. Vince inspected him from head to toe with the flashlight and saw that the knees of his chinos were ripped and his exposed kneecaps were scraped raw and bleeding.

"Take some advice from an old hound dog that's been snooping around the *Vieux Carré* for many moons," he said, guiding the Amigo within handshaking distance of the young man. "Go back to your dorm and fall in love with a nice gay kid from one of those good families with money. The ones that can afford Tulane."

If he could've turned back the corroded hands of time and done it all over again, it was the advice he would've given to Ned.

"Stay off these streets, son. There's nothing but bad juju out here. And getting baited and bashed is not the *worst* thing that'll happen to you. You're gonna end up with something in your blood and die a miserable death. Don't take that risk. Your parents love you and don't wanna lose you. It'll break them, and they'll walk under a dark cloud for the rest of their lives. I know what I'm talking about, *passerotto mio.*"

My little sparrow. It was what Vince's grandfather had called him, and what Vince had called Ned when he was in short pants.

The young man bent over stiffly and spit a mouthful of blood, then stumbled past Vince in silence, holding himself like a survivor emerging from the wreckage of a head-on collision. He was moving slowly and inexorably back toward Bourbon Street. Vince figured that Trey had smiled at him outside a bar and asked what time it was, so he could check out the expensive wristwatch, and then invited the young man to slip away from his frat brothers and smoke a joint with him in a private place where they could be alone together.

"You wanna file a police report?" Vince asked, turning his scooter to watch him wander away in pain. "You might get lucky and get your credit cards back."

"No, nooo, please let it go," the young man moaned.

248

It occurred to Vince that this beating was the perfect solution to nabbing Trey—an arrest warrant for assault and theft. That would make him negotiate. That is, if Vince's old buddies on the Quarter patrol could ever find and cuff the elusive alley cat.

He followed the young man, a slow steady piloting of the Amigo. "You're not thinking straight, son," he said to his back. "You want your pals to see you with a bloody face? They're gonna ask a lot of questions. You can't walk around like that in public. Let me get you a cab back to your crib."

When the young man didn't respond, Vince raised his voice. "I know a dozen cabbies that owe me a solid. *Let me call you a cab.*"

The young man turned awkwardly, almost losing his balance. He was pinching his nose to stop the bleeding. "Why the fuck are you doing this?" he asked, choking on blood. He was holding his side and breathing raggedly, and Vince was worried that a broken rib may have punctured his lung.

"I had a son," Vince said, and that was as much as he could manage. He was overcome with sudden grief. He felt as if someone had punched *him* in the heart. He knew that this confused and humiliated young man didn't understand how damaged his life was, no more than Ned did when he was living with secrets and lies. But in that moment, on that dark night, Vince tried to put those painful memories behind him. He was too concerned about *this* young man to dwell on a past he could not resurrect.

"Forget the cab," he said, standing up from the Amigo and testing the steadiness of his unfaithful legs. "I have a van and I'm taking you to the ER."

THIRTY-THREE

I COULDN'T SLEEP THAT FRIDAY NIGHT, knowing that Ray Duhon had
threatened Ann with arrest. Early the next morning, I began tracking
down the one person who could prevent that from happening. I phoned
Sister Colleen at her community home, where she lived in walking distance of the chancery with Sister Ellen the Archivist and two female
social workers. Gone were the days when nuns lived in convents.

"Can it wait, Peter? The Bishop's playing tennis at the club in Old
Metairie," she said. "Saturday mornings are the only time he gets any
exercise. And you know how much the news people have been hound-
ing him since the Requiem Mass."

The country club had luxurious indoor courts, seven percent humidity year round and heated or cooled to accommodate the four New
Orleans seasons—early summer, summer, late summer, and Carnival.

"Is there any way to reach him? Will the club page him for me?"

"Is this another Father Landry emergency? What's going on, Peter?
Maybe I can help."

I didn't want to involve her in the conflict between Ann and Detective Duhon.

"I promise I'll wait for him to finish his match," I said.

Unpredictable as usual, the weather had turned wintry and wet
again, another raw foggy morning in February, inching toward fifty
degrees. The boys were asleep upstairs in their bedrooms, and after
a restless night, Ann had decided that the best remedy for frayed
nerves was to go running at daybreak with her intrepid friends. I was
nearly out of the house with a travel mug of coffee in hand, intent
on buttonholing the Bishop at the country club, when the phone
rang. I hesitated, then decided I'd better answer it.

"Peter, he broke into the rectory." My uncle didn't sound as panicked as he did the night of the murder. "Please come over. Our friend left a note this time and a VHS tape."

"Jesus, Ted, call the police!" I said. "Are you inside the rectory? I warned you not to go there alone."

"Bring a camera so we can watch this thing."

"Ted, will you please call nine-one-one and then get the hell out of that damned place! Wait for me outside. I'll be there in ten minutes."

He didn't heed my advice, of course. When I arrived, there were no police cars and no sign of him in the breezeway, or on the small front lawn, or back near the carports. He opened the side door of the rectory without urgency or alarm, as if we had a date for tea and a cordial game of Scrabble.

"Good," he said, taking the Camcorder out of my hands and tucking it under his arm like a football. I followed him through the living room toward that small cramped study where he spent many laborious hours hunched over his desk, chain-smoking, paying bills and completing the reams of paperwork necessary to manage a large, flourishing parish.

"He ransacked my file cabinets. I have no idea what he was looking for or what he took."

The intruder had jerked open the file drawers and scattered hundreds of documents on the carpet. Correspondence, spreadsheets, invoices and bills, handwritten notes, architectural drawings.

"He left this on my desk."

Ted handed me a VHS cassette. Scotch-taped to it was a message typed in all caps:

HE SWORE HE WAS CURED
BUT HE COULDNT RESTRAIN HIMSELF
IT WAS HIS NATURE
HE WAS HARMING MORE INNOCENTS
AND WOULD CONTINUE
FOREVER AND EVER
I HAD TO STOP HIM

A shiver that felt as cold as liquid oxygen raced up my spine and froze the muscles of my neck and shoulders. "Christ, it's the killer, Ted," I said, glancing back into the gray shadows of the drape-drawn living room, expecting to see him coming at us with a cinder block raised over his head like Moses with the tablets.

"He trashed Father Martin's bedroom, as well," my uncle said. "It wasn't vandalism, Peter. He was definitely searching for something."

We went upstairs to the room where Martin Landry had been beaten and dragged. The mess was even worse than what I'd witnessed the week before. The mattress was overturned, shoes and clothing were flung from the closet, the dresser drawers were pulled out and underwear and t-shirts were dumped all around. The small writing desk had been plundered.

"Ted, are you going to straighten everything up again, like last time, and pretend nothing happened?" I asked him. "Or will you please call Ray Duhon and get him over here as soon as possible. He has to read that note. It should convince him, once and for all, that they don't have the killer in custody."

My uncle wandered into the middle of the bedroom and surveyed the disorder. "Do you suppose it's that disturbed young man who threw blood on the casket?"

"It isn't him."

He turned to me with an admonishing frown. "How can you always be so certain about these things, Peter?"

"Because I'm pretty sure I know who killed Martin Landry. And my guess is he came back here to hunt for incriminating films he thought Martin may've stashed in his room. Old home movies. The kind he dropped in your mail slot. He wanted you to see what he'd gone through as a boy."

I told him everything that Donald Bertrand had said about Martin Landry's younger brother. Their father's 8mm home movies, the jail time for kiddie porn, the homeless wandering, the failed marriage and the child he was forbidden to see.

"Merciful Jesus," Ted said, exhaling a deep mournful breath. "That poor lost soul. What they did to him was shameful." His eyes darted at me. "I knew Father Martin was fighting demons, Peter, but I didn't realize how far back his sickness went and what a hold it had on him."

"If you're right about this guy seeking forgiveness from a priest, he'll want to see you in person, Ted. And that's a scary thought. You'll probably hear from him again."

He closed his eyes and lifted his chin to the heavens, praying aloud, part sincere supplication, part performance for my benefit. "Given the circumstances, Heavenly Father, I would rather not sip from this bitter cup," he prayed, like the Man from Galilee hedging his bets in the Garden of Gethsemane. "Yet not my will but Thine be done."

Back in his study downstairs, I slipped the cassette into my JVC Camcorder and we hovered over it, watching the images play on the small glass preview panel. I should've anticipated what was on the tape, but it caught me completely off guard to see my son Luke and the Hinojosa brothers sitting cross-legged on the floor of Martin Landry's bedroom, passing a joint and sharing a bottle of wine. Martin was holding forth, beguiling and magnetic and red-faced from drink and weed, but the audio was too low and indistinct to hear exactly what he was saying. Trey was the fourth teenager in the circle. No sign of Kwame Williams anywhere in the room.

"Ted, there was no cassette in Martin's camera when you checked it that night," I said, "because the killer took it with him when he left. This is that cassette."

He looked up from the panel and stepped backwards. "My God, do you think it will show the murder?"

Our foreheads nearly touching, we continued to view the cassette, patiently reserving our thoughts and reactions until the end. I kept an eye on Roberto's son Rico, because I knew he was there to confront the priest and possibly attack him physically. Rico did appear agitated and disengaged from the conversation, head down, deep within himself, breathing hard and staring at the carpet. He seemed to be gathering courage, ready to explode at any moment, when the phone rang on Martin's desk and he stood up to answer it. He spoke to the caller with his back to the boys, to the camera, and once more I couldn't make out what he was saying. It wasn't a long exchange, two minutes, and when Martin hung up and turned around, he looked ashen and distraught. He'd lost all his mirth. He told the boys they had to leave and apologized for the party's breakup. When they were slow to stir, he clapped loudly several times and began to shoo them with quick hand motions, as if they were a sluggish and dimwitted herd of barn animals.

"That was probably his brother on the phone," I said quietly.

We watched Martin walk toward the camera and switch it off. The preview panel went dark. End of tape.

Ted sat on the chair behind his desk and lit a cigarette with a jittery hand. I leaned against the pine-paneled wall, troubled by the smoking and drinking I'd seen on the tape but enormously relieved that Luke and the Hinojosa boys had done nothing violent. With the cigarette forked between two fingers, Ted tapped a thumbnail against his teeth, perplexed and thinking. "What now?" he asked.

"Call Duhon right away. Report the break-in. Give him the note and the videotape," I said.

"I should speak with Monsignor Fulweiler first."

"Fine, whatever. I know you've got your own obligations, Ted. But Duhon needs to read that note."

"Are you leaving?" he asked.

I told him that Duhon had threatened to arrest Ann. "I have to find the Bishop this morning and ask him to intercede on her behalf," I said. "For professional reasons, Ann can't talk about the young guy who slung the blood, but I suspect he was one of Martin's victims when he was a boy. Why else would he do something so radical at a priest's funeral Mass?"

My uncle carefully weighed what I was telling him. "If the young man was abused by Father Landry, you and Eric should speak with him soon and . . . and . . ."

"Buy his silence?" I said. "Offer him four hundred thousand dollars to go away?"

Ted crushed his half-smoked cigarette in an ashtray and peered up at me with a dour expression. For a moment I thought he was angry about my remark.

"I'm very sorry I dragged you into this, Peter," he said, as upset and contrite as I'd ever seen him. "I'm sorry for everything. For giving you the box of those awful tapes and asking you to trust me. For involving you in a cover-up you don't believe in."

His neck and sharp cheekbones were blotched with strawberry patches like a rash, a telltale sign of his distress.

"And look at what the diocese is doing," he said. "Withholding information from our parish families. Hiding things from the police.

Bribing our way out. And why? To spare the Church from public embarrassment and lawsuits? Is this what Jesus would've done?" He pressed the heels of his hands against his eyes. "God, what a farrago of hypocrisy and deceit. I feel like I'm standing in brimstone, and I've talked you into standing beside me."

He rose from his desk chair and walked over to where I was leaning against the wall.

"Will you please forgive me, Peter? I've always loved you like a son. You were such a good kid growing up. A very smart kid. Mature beyond your years. And now I've done the worst thing I've ever done in my life. I've compromised your goodness."

I grappled him in a bear hug. It was the only way I could express my affection. I knew he might resist. He was definitely not a hand-holder. He hated sentimentality and had always avoided feely-touchy sappiness in its myriad modern forms. He still believed in old-fashioned *manliness*. But I was a little taller, a little heavier, a little stronger. I gave him no choice. I hugged him the way I hugged my sons, with strength and reassurance and unconditional love.

"Apology accepted," I said.

My uncle and I had accumulated a library full of shared history. I could remember him coming to our home for Sunday dinners after High Mass when I was a child. I could remember the books he gave me to read and the serious discussions we'd had about every subject under the sun. And so I hugged him harder than I'd ever hugged him, and instead of resisting me, he returned the affection.

"I'm going now," I said, releasing myself from his grip. "Please get Detective Duhon over here to look at this break-in and the note."

The strawberry patches had spread across his face. "I'll speak to him about Ann," he said, patting me on the arm. "Maybe I can convince him to leave her out of this altogether."

THIRTY-FOUR

IT WAS THE OLDEST AND MOST EXCLUSIVE COUNTRY CLUB in New Orleans, dating back to the First World War, known primarily for its sprawling green acres of golf course. For such an opulent and storied institution, the entrance was an inconspicuous little driveway, difficult to find, no doubt by design, its guardhouse as small and cute as a child's playhouse with a terracotta tile roof. I pulled up to the sliding window where a gimlet-eyed old coot wearing a dark blue uniform said "May I help you, sir?" in a voice burned raw by a half century of bourbon and nicotine. His snow-white hair and bushy white mustache made him look more like an alcoholic southern novelist than a gatekeeper.

"His Excellency, the Bishop, is here playing tennis. I'm his communications director," I said, handing him my driver's license and a photo ID card that identified my position at the chancery. "We've got an emergency on our hands, and I have to speak with him right away."

While he studied my cards and made a phone call, I noticed an armed security guard watching me from a canopied golf cart parked near the tall brick privacy wall. His hands were buried in the pockets of a heavy parka, and he looked bored and cold.

"Did the colored kid finally confess?" asked the old coot with a jaded grin as he handed back my cards.

"I'm sorry, sir, I'm not at liberty to discuss the matter."

I had always wanted to deliver that line to someone in high places.

The security guard followed my car in his golf cart. He'd obviously profiled me as a heedless speed demon bent on driving faster than fifteen miles per hour. I'd been a guest at the club on three or four occasions—fundraisers for the diocese and a debutante ball for the daughter of one of Ann's clients—so I knew my way around the grounds, its alley of moss-draped live oaks popular for wedding photographs, its wandering peacocks and turtle ponds afloat with lily pads.

The damp gray morning explained the lack of traffic. There was no one at the first tee and not a soul out on the foggy fairways. I parked underneath the colossal oak tree that arched as gracefully as a bell-shaped hoop skirt in front of a columned mansion straight out of *Gone with the Wind.* Gone, too, were the dapper black valets and old Negro waiters wearing white gloves and tailcoats, serving Sazeracs and mint juleps on silver trays. Eighty years late, the twentieth century had finally arrived in the heart of Old Dixie. The club had even painted its lawn jockeys an acceptable shade of white.

Once inside the mansion's chandeliered entrance parlor, I showed my credentials to the blonde Junior Leaguer seated behind the welcome desk. The guard had already phoned her. She asked me to sign my name on a large visitors' ledger, then said "Let me walk you back to the courts" with a subzero smile and a hint of suspicion disguised as professional courtesy. Did she suppose I would try to steal their Newcomb pottery?

She donned a blazer with the club's coat of arms embroidered on the pocket and escorted me down a grand hallway lined with portraits of its long-dead founders, whiskered cotton barons and oil men. We passed by the cavernous ballroom and a smaller banquet hall and ventured out-of-doors through a trellised patio too unpleasantly cold for the brunch crowd. When we entered the indoor tennis facility, my escort pointed out the Bishop playing doubles on the far court. I assured her I would wait in the viewing area for the game to end before pulling him aside. She smiled briskly, saying, "A pleasure to meet you, Mr. Moore. I should get back to the welcome parlor. Please sign out when you leave."

I almost didn't recognize the Bishop in tennis whites and headband. He was a large man with an unflattering paunch and flabby thighs, his skin untouched by the sun. He lumbered after the ball, sweat circles on his t-shirt, front and back. His partner was DA Rockin' Roger Finney, who was the same age but in much better shape, tall and lean, with muscular calves and a powerful stroke, doing most of the work on their side of the net.

The Bishop's opponents were attorneys Russell and Eric Gautier, *père et fils,* who moved fluidly in tandem as if they'd been tennis partners for decades, which was probably the case. I'd learned the hard way that Eric was a formidable player, and I could see that our one-and-only match had not been a fluke. Thirty years younger than the others, he was the fastest and most skillful player on the court and the primary reason the Gautiers were ahead in sets.

What a cozy foursome they made.

A handful of club members were scattered about in the tiered viewing stands, watching matches and waiting their turns. The temperature and humidity control was a marvel, and I unzipped my jacket, found a soft cushioned seat, and relaxed. A young waiter came by for my order. At that early hour, he recommended a Bloody Mary or a screwdriver.

Eric was the first to notice me. He was bouncing the ball with his racquet, a rhythm ritual before serving, and he stopped abruptly, distracted by my presence. "Moore!" he yelled, clearly irritated, as if I'd showed up that morning solely to disrupt his game. "What the hell are you doing here?"

"Waiting for a tequila sunrise," I said. "Would you like me to order you one?"

The others turned to see who Eric was addressing. Finney didn't know me, and the elder Gautier had probably forgotten who I was. The Bishop gripped his racquet with both hands and used it to bless me lightheartedly with the sign of the cross, as though the oval racquet was a gold monstrance. "I wish I could proclaim *Veni, Vidi, Vici,* Peter," he said, winded, his face glowing, "but the Gautier legionaries are clobbering us worse than Caesar clobbered the Gauls."

Nursing a tequila sunrise, I waited another half hour until the match ended, victory in straight sets for Team Gautier. Giddy from the liquor on an empty stomach, I left my comfortable seat feeling bold and a little reckless and walked onto the court in street shoes to speak with the Bishop. "Your Excellency," I said, "may I have a word with you in private?"

He was stooping over a gym bag, wiping his flushed face with a towel. "Of course, Peter," he said. "What brings you here this morning? Is that reporter friend of yours still trying to interview me and win a Pulitzer?"

Before I could respond, Eric appeared at my side like an unpopular cousin at a family reunion. "Is there something I can help you with,

Peter?" he asked, clutching both ends of the towel draped around his neck. As I'd expected, he and the Bishop had collaborated on the official statement to the media regarding the blood-splasher, leaving me out of the process. *We have no idea why. We are struggling to understand. We are willing to meet with the young man to discuss whatever grievances he may have. We call for understanding and forgiveness,* etc.

"This is a personal matter, Eric," I said. "Your intervention is not required."

He frowned at me as if I was the one being rude and intrusive, then turned to the Bishop. "Would you like me to take care of this, Your Excellency?"

I had had enough of his condescension and was beginning to lose my temper. The tequila didn't help. "Take care of what, Eric?" I said. "You have no idea what I want to speak with him about. Why don't you go hit the showers, amigo?"

To ease the tension, the Bishop wrapped a long damp arm around my shoulders like a teammate offering consolation after a stunning defeat. I could smell his body sweat. "Give us a moment," he said to Eric.

Eric shot me a hostile look and said, "Certainly, Your Excellency," before retreating toward his father and Roger Finney, who were observing our exchange from the sidelines.

Gym bag in hand, the Bishop walked me off the court to a bar area with table service, where several club members were having breakfast. "*Comedamus,*" he said. *Let us eat.* "I'm dying of thirst and could use a little sustenance."

A little sustenance included coffee, juice, and a full breakfast of eggs, bacon, pancakes, hash browns, buttered grits, and fruit. I ordered another tequila sunrise.

When he wasn't under fire and burdened by the responsibilities of his office, the Bishop was an affable man with a brilliant mind and a charming sense of humor. He'd earned two doctoral degrees, one in theology from Notre Dame and one in nineteenth century European history from Fordham. Occasionally, after we'd completed the draft of a speech together, he'd slouch back in one of those tall unyielding chairs at the conference table and chat about a book he'd just read or a football game he'd watched on television. We were never going to be friends, but he seemed to enjoy my company.

"Something is bothering you this morning, Peter," he said, chewing, sipping coffee. "What is it you want to discuss?"

The Landry ordeal had not affected his appetite.

"Your Excellency, I tell you this as someone who admires you and thinks you've always been an honorable man," I said after a long quaff of tequila and orange juice. "You cannot play the plausible deniability card. It's not going to work long-term. Certainly not morally, and probably not as a legal strategy. As your communications director, I advise you to ignore what Rome and the Vicar-General and the lawyers are counseling you to do." The alcohol had loosened my tongue. "You've got to stand up before your flock and the people of New Orleans and tell them the unvarnished truth about Martin Landry." I paused, lowering my voice. "You've got to tell the world he was a pedophile who abused children here and in other postings. And to ask for forgiveness and announce publicly that the Church will make restitution to the victims and their families. As the father of two boys, that's what I would want to hear from you if this had happened to them."

I could see by the wounded expression on his face that he was not prepared to take that step. Not at that time, and possibly never. "This thing is so troubling and complicated," he said, pouring syrup over his buttered pancakes in the same precise way he poured wine into a chalice. "I keep praying for God's guidance. But frankly, I'm not getting much of a return signal." He looked up from the pancakes and offered a worn smile. "Let me know if you hear anything from Him, will you?"

"Innocent lives are at stake, Your Excellency. That kid Kwame Williams didn't murder anyone. And now Detective Duhon wants to throw my wife in jail, too."

That raised an eyebrow. He put down his fork. "Why on earth?" he asked.

I explained Ann's dilemma. And speculated that the blood-splasher may have been molested as a child by Martin Landry.

"Would you please ask your tennis partner to call off his dog?" I said, nodding at the district attorney, who was advancing toward a table nearby. He was accompanied by the Gautiers, the three of them freshly showered and dressed in sporty weekend wear, track jackets and sweatpants that looked ridiculous on the two older gentlemen. Finney had blow-dried his short silver hair into a dandy fluff.

"I don't want Duhon to harass Ann anymore," I said. "She's a wonderful mother to our sons and a more devout Catholic than I am. She'll help that young man find peace. And when the time comes to provide mental health counseling for Landry's victims and their families, there's not a better family guidance counselor than Ann in this entire city."

"God bless her," the Bishop said, wiping his lips on a white napkin monogrammed with the country club's coat of arms. "I will advise the district attorney to show great sensitivity when investigating that incident at the Requiem Mass."

I found no solace in his tepid response. When it came to my wife and sons, I did not waver, negotiate, or compromise.

"I'm afraid you'll have to do more than that, Your Excellency. You'll have to give me your word they'll leave my wife alone."

The Bishop was taken aback by the force of my insistence. He wasn't used to receiving demands, even polite ones. "I'm not an officer of the law or the courts, Peter," he said. "I can't wave a magic wand and make things happen the way I want."

"I have the videotapes, Your Excellency. No one else knows where they are," I said. "I'd rather not get ugly about this. But I will if I have to. Please tell the district attorney to call off his dog. He's trying to drag my wife into this sordid mess, and I'm not going to let that happen."

I downed the last of the tequila sunrise and stood up to leave.

"I'm not very happy with your attitude, Peter," the Bishop said, sounding more hurt than angry. "Monsignor Fulweiler may be right about you, after all. Perhaps you don't have the character and fortitude to help us do God's work."

I laughed harshly. "Your Excellency, does God's work include covering up sexual abuse committed against His innocent children?"

He pushed aside his half-eaten breakfast and stared at the table-cloth, unwilling to respond or meet my eye. I didn't care what he was thinking. I walked over to introduce myself to the district attorney.

"Mr. Finney, my name is Peter Moore," I said, although Eric had no doubt briefed him on who I was. Finney shook my hand, something he was well practiced at. "I've asked His Excellency to speak with you about Detective Ray Duhon and that disruption during Father Landry's funeral Mass. It involves my wife. She's the woman who kicked off her heels and ran down the aisle to stop those young men."

His polished smile vanished. It wasn't what he was expecting to encounter on a serene Saturday morning at the club. He glanced at the Gautiers, but they remained silent.

"Gentlemen, I enjoyed your game," I said. "We'll talk again soon. Have an excellent day."

As I was leaving, I glanced back over my shoulder and saw the unhappy Bishop making his way to their table, coffee cup in hand, with the guarded demeanor of a monarch who was coming to warn his generals that the barbarians were approaching the gates.

THIRTY-FIVE

WHEN THE PHONE RANG THAT EVENING, the caller didn't identify himself but I knew from his unmistakable accent that it was the Holy Rottweiler. I was surprised to hear from the chancery so soon. After all, it took the Vatican decades to apologize for Nazi appeasement and centuries to admit that the Inquisition was a tad excessive.

"His Excellency has asked me to relieve you of your duties as Eric Gautier's partner during the settlement negotiations," he said, only a skosh less abrasive than it would've sounded in German. "He feels that you and Mr. Gautier do not have the proper chemistry together. And he added that you yourself will probably consider this to be good news."

"Very good news indeed," I said.

"His Excellency has also asked me to speak with your wife about teaming with young Mr. Gautier on these negotiations. We are aware of her outstanding reputation as a family counselor. Our sources tell us she is exceptionally good at what she does."

"So you've been checking up on my wife, Monsignor?"

"Due diligence," he responded in his usual humorless manner. "Father McMurray, among others, speaks very highly of her."

"Does this mean that Detective Duhon won't be arresting her?"

"His Excellency has asked me to apologize to your wife for the misunderstanding. The authorities will not be questioning her about that nonsense at the cathedral."

The Bishop had taken me seriously. He'd understood my message loud and clear.

"I suggest that Mrs. Moore and I meet in person at the chancery tomorrow afternoon to discuss her role and see if we can come to terms," he said. "As you well know, His Excellency feels we must move ahead posthaste with the process."

"Monsignor, in this country—in this century—women speak for themselves and negotiate their own agreements." I wondered if he'd ever touched a woman's bare skin, other than his mother's as a child. "Would you like to talk to her? She's in the kitchen baking cookies with our son."

It sounded like a contrived June Lockhart scene out of the 1950s, but it was true. I could smell the baked dough and melting chocolate.

Ann took the call on our bedroom extension, and after fifteen minutes or so, I went upstairs to see if she was still talking to that wretched man. She was sitting on the edge of the bed with a perplexed look, lost in a labyrinth of serious thought.

"Did you make a date with a dashing foreigner?" I asked. "I've seen his stylish outfits. The buttons match the beanie."

She didn't smile at my remark. "I agreed to meet him and Eric Gautier tomorrow afternoon at the chancery," she said. "I'll see what they have to say. I don't think I want to get involved in this horrible charade."

I sat down next to her. "They don't deserve you, Ann, but they need you. You'll do an infinitely better job than I did with Stevie's mother," I said. "Eric is a numbers guy. Letter of the law. Wham bam, sign this, initial that. He has the soul of a carp."

She closed her eyes and rested her head on my shoulder, becoming quiet and motionless, reflecting on what to do.

"As you've said, honey, it all comes down to the boys and their families. Roberto, Rico, David—and a whole lot of others," I said. "They're going to need consolation from a caring person. But other than Father Ted, there isn't anybody on Team Silentio with a warm pulse. Certainly not Eric," I said. "You'll be able to reach those kids, Ann. You'll comfort their moms and dads and listen patiently to their anger. If you don't do this, God knows who they'll choose."

Ann fell asleep early and woke early, going for a long run with her group before Mass. We skipped our Sunday morning routine for the second week in a row. Neither of us was in the mood. She had her reasons, I had mine. I wondered if this was how the slow erosion of physical affection began, the things that marriage counselors and women's magazines warned you about. Too stressed for intimacy. Not carving out special time for each other. Neglecting love's delicate friction.

That Sunday afternoon, while Ann was at the chancery, Matt and I watched TV together on the couch, eating the cookies they'd baked and giggling at the absurd antics of a pro wrestling match, one of our shared weaknesses. The phone rang. It was my uncle. I assumed he was calling to report what the police had said about yesterday's break-in.

"Our friend called me," he said. "I don't know how he tracked me down at the seminary, but he called and I spoke to him."

At first I didn't understand who he was talking about.

"He wants to meet me in person, Peter. Just as you said he would. He wants me to hear his confession."

"Holy Christ," I said, suddenly realizing who had called him. "Let me take this in my office."

I asked Matt to hang up the phone when he heard me pick up the line in the other room. "Call the police, Ted," I said, closing the office door so my son wouldn't hear the panic in my voice. "This isn't something to mess around with."

"I'm going to meet him tomorrow," my uncle said. "It takes a little more than two hours to get there by car. Peter, will you drive? I've got cataracts and I'm not seeing the road as well as I should. We can take my car."

"Ted, I'm not driving you to meet a priest killer. Are you out of your mind? Hang up and call Ray Duhon." I was pacing from one end of the room to the other, as far as the phone cord would stretch. Adrenaline was coursing through my body and I was beginning to hyperventilate, my voice rising to a high and fragile pitch. "If you don't call him, Ted, I will."

"I'll pick you up at your house at eight in the morning. With coffee and pastries from CC's."

"This is insane, Ted. Where the hell are you meeting him?"

"Eight sharp, Peter. No cops."

THIRTY-SIX

WITH FATHER TED BUCKLED IN THE PASSENGER SEAT, drinking coffee nonstop yet unusually quiet, I drove his Skylark down through the fields and farmland alongside old Highway 90, heading southwest out of New Orleans past the small roadside communities of Paradis and Les Allemands, crossing high above Bayou Gauche and its ramshackle fishing village, traveling deeper into a world of trailer homes, pickup trucks, flimsy prefab warehouses, and scrap metal junkyards. Merging onto the highway in a steady flow were the heavy rigs of the oil and gas drillers, the boat trailers of fishermen and trappers, game and gator hunters, roughnecks and rednecks, their livelihoods precariously coexisting and sometimes turning to violence.

It was another February day in South Louisiana, the brooding sky the color of tarnished nickel. The only birds I'd seen all morning were red-shouldered hawks sheltering in high evergreen branches beside the elevated highway. We motored through the thick swamp foliage near Raceland and the flat open rice fields outside Houma, and in time we spanned the bridge over the Atchafalaya River at the port of Morgan City, a stone's throw north of the bayous and wetlands. Ted requested a pit stop, and just before Franklin I followed an exit to a gas station and convenience store located in the middle of what appeared to be a thousand acres of dead crop rows flooded by recent rains. He went inside the store to find a men's room, and when he returned, I watched him hunch over outside the passenger door and light a cigarette in the winter chill. He began to stamp his feet, restoring warmth and circulation. I got out of the car and walked around to stand beside him, marveling at what smokers will do to satisfy their craving.

"Give me a hit of that," I said, reaching for the cigarette. He hesitated, with a questioning look, then shrugged and surrendered the cancer stick.

I took a long drag and coughed most of it into the damp air. "We don't have to do this, Ted," I said, reading doubt and apprehension in his eyes. "We can call Duhon and the sheriff of Saint Mary Parish and let them work out an arrest. This guy is dangerous."

"He didn't sound dangerous to me," my uncle said, retrieving the cigarette and flicking ash with a practiced finger. He was wearing a black suit jacket over a dark gray sweater, the rim of Roman collar visible at his neckline. "He sounded like a broken soul who wants to speak with someone he trusts."

He told me he'd met Christopher, as he called him, a couple of times when he was a teenager visiting his brother Martin at the seminary during family weekends. Ted had even spoken to Chris about becoming a priest. "But I haven't seen him in twenty years," he said. "I don't think I could pick him out of a police lineup."

"Let's hope you won't have to," I said, stamping my feet too, my toes beginning to feel like brittle ice. "Are you ready for this, Ted? I mean really ready? Because I don't mind admitting I'm scared as hell."

He rubbed out the cigarette on the wet sole of his shoe and slipped the butt into his jacket pocket, a distasteful habit that reminded me of hoboes during the Great Depression.

"How is your blood sugar level?" I motioned toward the convenience store. "Should we get you a bottle of orange juice? You know, just in case."

He exhaled through his nose, a faint whistling sound and a familiar sign of his exasperation. "I'm fine, Peter. Stop worrying about me. Let's be on our way." He was shivering, underdressed. "It's cold out here. Cold as a Presbyterian's heart," he said with a straight face.

The road southward to Cypremort Point was a pitted old two lane with a shallow wall of greenery on both sides, windbreaks protecting the sugar cane and rice fields from storms and internal combustion engines. It was a rural farm-to-market road, its fence lines swallowed by marsh trees and wild bushes. Small shabby houses appeared here and there, the homesteads of cane cutters and crawfish trappers who worked for the land owners. These lowlands were only ten or fifteen feet above sea level, with fetid canals crisscrossing the terrain. The word *cypremort* meant "dead cypress" in French, and the early explorers of this stubby, misshapen peninsula on Vermilion Bay, an inlet off the Gulf of Mexico, must have chanced upon a bog of age-old rotted stumps somewhere in the vicinity.

The Point itself had a small unpretentious marina of older fishing boats and yachts, plus three or four blocks of fishing camps with private piers jutting out into the bay. My uncle had been to the Landry camp years before, for a weekend celebration when Martin and his classmates were ordained, and he remembered where the place was. "Up there a little farther," he said as we rolled slowly past camp after camp.

A "fishing camp," Louisiana-style, could be anything from a one-room shack on stilts deep in the bayous to a splendorous three-story home on prime waterfront. It was a "camp" if you didn't live there year-round.

"There's one thing I neglected to mention," Ted said when I parked on the shell lot facing the Landry place. "He told me to come alone."

I planted my forehead on the steering wheel. "Mother of God," I whispered. "Are you trying to get me killed, Ted? He beat his brother to death with a cinder block, dragged him into a bathtub, and wrapped a chain around his neck."

"I'll explain that I'm half blind and couldn't drive here by myself."

"Has it occurred to you that he's lured you down here to his remote family camp to do you harm?" My eyes were closed and my forehead was resting against the hard wheel. "What if he thinks you were in on the molestations?"

"He knows I wasn't."

"How do you know that, Ted?"

"Because he would've killed me already."

Cold comfort. "Jesus," I said. "Do you want me to stay here in the car until I hear you screaming?"

"Lift up thine eyes and show courage, Peter," he said, opening his door. "Come on. I'll introduce you. I don't want him to think I'm hiding something. God knows, there's been too much of that already."

He removed his black leather bag from the backseat—the one he'd carried to give the Last Rites to Donald Bertrand—and waited for me to lift up mine eyes and get out of the car.

The Landry camp was a modest one-story structure whose cheerful red paint had weathered poorly in the relentless sun and wind and salt spray off the bay. The backend was supported on pier beams driven into the shoreline sand, and the house was boardwalked on three sides by bare wood decking with spaces between the slats for rain drainage and fish cleaning. The left side became a narrow pier that extended a hundred feet to where a cabin cruiser was docked on lapping water.

"Are you sure this is the right place, Ted? It looks vacant."

The camp's windows were dark in the sullen midmorning light, and there was no sign of movement within. I turned a full circle, taking the measure of our surroundings. The Skylark was the only vehicle parked on the Landry's shell lot. If Chris Landry was waiting for my uncle inside, he hadn't arrived by car or truck.

Ted knocked on the front door, and when no one responded, he tried the handle and discovered that the door was unlocked. He took a couple of steps inside the house and said in a loud, insistent voice, *"Christopher, are you here?"*

Dead quiet.

"Christopher, it's Father Ted McMurray!"

He walked slowly into the eerie stillness of the living room with the black bag in hand.

"Ted, this is Louisiana," I said from the doorway. "If we're trespassing in the wrong camp, they'll shoot us."

He wandered deeper into the grainy gloom and disappeared around a corner. "Ted," I said, hoping he would return to where I could see him. He didn't answer. I waited for several heartbeats and repeated my call, louder this time. *"Ted!"* Again, no answer. I paused, delaying my next move longer than I should have, and finally decided, against my better judgment, to enter the place.

The camp house was cold and smelled closed-up and moldy, unoccupied. White drop cloths covered armchairs and two sofas. Storm shutters darkened the windows, letting in only cracks of daylight. I had the impression that no one had been there in months. It was wintertime, after all, and only the macho diehards visited their fishing camps at this time of year. Which made it the perfect hideaway for a murderer.

To the right I could see a sleeping room with bunkbeds and bare mattresses. It must've been where the altar boys slept on their weekends with Party Marty. A bicycle without a chain was leaning against one of the bunks.

The living room's knotty-pine walls were adorned with the seaside detritus of an earlier time—a glazed marlin stuffed and mounted, a decorative white anchor, a spoked captain's wheel, a ring life-preserver bearing the words *RMS Titanic*. In various framed photographs, family members were proudly holding up their prize catches from the bay, hefty red fish and speckled trout. I wondered if the talented Chris Landry had taken some of those photographs.

"Ted, where the hell are you?" I said in a cautious voice, following his path around a corner and into the dining room.

My uncle was examining a photo on the wall. "Martin and his father," he said. A grinning man and a teenaged boy were standing beside their captured five-foot spinner shark hanging by its tail from a pulley hook. "We've got the right camp. I remember this room. The wine was flowing freely."

The long dinner table and its many chairs were also shrouded by white drop cloths. I checked out a couple of knickknack shelves with collections of sand dollars and polished seashells, conch and whelk, clam and scallop, a woman's graceful touch. I wondered if Martin's mother had played some part in the camp's décor before she was committed to the hospital in Mandeville.

The house gave witness to their Catholic faith. A different style of crucifix was fixed above every door, and they'd placed commemorative dinner plates of Pope John XXIII and President John F. Kennedy on the wall side-by-side, a staple of every Catholic family I'd known when I was growing up.

The odor of day-old fried seafood was emanating from the kitchen, and I turned on the light to find a counter top littered with shrimp tails, soggy fries, a half-dozen beer bottles, and stained paper bags from a place called Vermilion Crab Shack. Roaches were crawling around in a spill of red cocktail sauce. Someone was staying here, all right.

"Did you see this?" Ted asked.

He'd set his black bag on the floor and was looking at a vintage hi-fi console, one of those old radio and turntable combinations, crouched underneath the dining room window. What had caught his eye was an 8mm projector sitting on top of the console.

"My father was very fond of that old projector. I wish I could say the same."

The speaker was standing partly obscured in a dark doorway that led to some other part of the house. He was gripping a long-poled fishing gaff with a nasty-looking hook near the point.

"He used to invite his poker buddies out here, and after they were all good and liquored up, he'd show them his favorite home movies," he said. "Sometimes he'd make me watch with those disgusting men. They laughed and laughed at the tapes of my brother and me. Little boys playing nasty."

Chris Landry was my age, around forty, but he appeared much older and harder in the shadowy light. He'd served time at a juvenile facility and a federal prison, and he'd lived homeless on the skids for months at a time. There was something edgy and damaged about him, a piercing toughness in his eyes and the intimidating carriage of a man who knew how to use that fishing gaff. He was wearing jeans and toe-scuffed Doc Martens and a bulky green turtleneck sweater underneath an unbuttoned Navy pea coat. Long black hair curled below his wool knit cap. He looked like a weathered sailor returning home to a world he didn't belong to anymore.

"Father, I asked you to come alone," he said, his cold dead eyes measuring me.

"Christopher, this is my nephew Peter Moore," my uncle said, walking toward him with a disarming smile and both hands cupped, as if he was beginning the *lavabo* handwashing at Mass. "I couldn't have come without my trusty driver. These days, I see the world through milk-colored glass, I'm sorry to say. I'm having cataract surgery in a few weeks."

Chris clearly wasn't prepared for my uncle's embrace. He extended the gaff away from his body in one hand like a spear, and they held each longer than either man had anticipated. I thought about the parable of the prodigal son. *While he was still a long way off, his father saw him and was filled with compassion for him, and he ran to his son, threw his arms around him and kissed him.*

Chris struck me as someone longing for human contact, but wary of whom to trust or where to turn. He said, "Great to see you again, Father," clapping Ted on the back. "Thank you for coming such a long way." He looked at me and nodded at the projector. "I despise that God damned machine. Bring it with you. I've got the perfect spot for it."

He led us down a tight, unlit hallway checkered with more family photographs, which probably hadn't budged a centimeter since the day they were first hung. In that close space, I worried about the deadly steel hook so near my face. We passed a stinking bathroom and another bunk room and quickly reached the master bedroom at the far end of the house. Its glass jalousie windows were opened to the salt air and dreary winter light. As soon as I stepped inside the room, I recognized it as the backdrop in some of Martin's videos. The ocean-blue chenille bedspread, the wide fish net fanned out as a wall decoration, dried starfish and seahorses snagged in the netting like fresh catch. The bank of jalousies crossed the entire room, with a view of the Landry pier and other piers and a jumble of docked boats and the bay beyond. A picturesque seascape, but also a haunting crime scene where the Reverend Father Martin Landry had filmed his abuses of young boys.

"I was nearly done when I heard y'all come in the house," Chris said, pointing to a wheelbarrow parked next to an old-fashioned black safe squatting inside a closet. The safe looked heavy enough to sink through the floor into the shallow water splashing against the pier beams below. The safe's door was open, and Chris had been emptying the contents into the wheelbarrow. Dozens of small yellow 8mm boxes that contained Landry home movies, each one with a brief description and a date handwritten in ink.

"I don't have the patience to go through them one by one and pick out the ones that say 'Marty and Chris,' so I'm gonna deep-six them all. Nobody will miss them. My brother and sister haven't watched these things in decades. And now that Martin's gone, I'm the only sib who knows the safe's combination." He turned to Ted. "Father, did you bring the tapes I left for you in the rectory?"

My uncle opened the black bag and withdrew the VHS cassette and the 8mm film we'd viewed together. Young Martin and Chris mugging for the camera. My son and the Hinojosa brothers on the night of the murder. Ted tossed them both into the wheelbarrow.

Chris took the projector from me and dropped it into the wheelbarrow, as well. "I'm gonna dump this load of crap into the deep blue sea," he said. "I don't want to think about any of this for the rest of my life."

I gazed out a window at the cabin cruiser docked at the end of the pier and realized how Chris had arrived and how he would leave. My mind had wandered for a moment, visualizing again how he'd brutalized Martin on that final night, and suddenly Chris was standing in front of me, uncomfortably close, peering into my eyes. That's when I noticed the scratch marks on his cheek. Fingernails had raked his skin, and the scratches were infected and scabbing. It explained why Chris hadn't shaved in several days. He was growing a beard to hide what his brother had done, fighting for his life.

"Tell me, nephew," Chris said in a mocking tone, glancing at my uncle as though they were conspirators in secret collusion. "How much do you know?"

I couldn't imagine what Ted wanted me to say. I considered playing dumb. But after a brief and awkward silence, I decided it didn't matter. This man wasn't going to harm the nephew and driver of the priest who'd come to hear his confession.

"Father Ted called me that night," I said. "I got there before the police. I saw your brother in the tub. I didn't like him very much, Chris, but I won't ever forget what you did to him."

To my surprise, he quit his intense staring and dropped his eyes. I had shamed him, which was a thoughtless thing to do. He began flexing his hands, balling them into tight fists then opening them, fist and open, fist and open, like a bareknuckle fighter loosening up for a brawl. I noticed scabs on his knuckles and a large bruise on the back of one hand. Ted walked over to stand close beside me, and I was grateful he was there.

"You have no idea what I went through as a child," Chris said, speaking to the floor, still gripping and releasing his fists. "Losing my mother, the only one who ever loved me. Then the dirty games for the camera. The bullying and humiliations. Calling me a little queer, blaming *me*. And then one day my dad decided to end it, saying *no more*, we were too old now. But playing nasty was the only way I could get their attention. I hated myself for wanting to satisfy them. I still hate myself, and that's never going away."

His shoulders began to quake. I couldn't tell if it was rage or grief.

"I had to stop him. All those little boys. The manipulations, just like he manipulated me. I couldn't just sit around and let him get away with it again. I told him it had to stop, but he didn't care what I thought." He raised his wet eyes and looked at me. "I have a son. I knew what I'd do to somebody who did those things to my boy. Do you have children?"

"Two sons. Sixteen and ten."

"Then you know what I'm talking about, man. 'Whosoever shall offend one of these little ones that believe in me, it is better that a millstone were hanged around his neck and he were cast into the sea.'"

A good Catholic boy. He knew the Scriptures.

"He told me he was cured. He'd seen some shrinks out in New Mexico. They gave him medications, chemicals. And I know he stopped for awhile," Chris said. "But then I caught him doing it again, raping boys right here in this room, making videos of it to watch later."

His entire body was shaking now, and his face had gone blank and colorless. "Men like him can't be cured," he said in a quivering voice. "They always find a way back into the game. Somebody had to stop him."

I thought he was going to collapse. Ted took his arm and guided him to a reading chair in the corner of the room. "Peter, would you give us some time alone, please?" my uncle asked.

I waited outside on the pier, turning up my coat collar and resting my forearms on the old wood railing, watching fat white seagulls hover and screech overhead, scavenging for food scraps left on the boardwalks. They were dipping and searching, no doubt disappointed by those barren winter piers washed clean by cold rains.

A half hour passed. My conscience was telling me to find a phone, call the local sheriff's department, and report the whereabouts of a murderer. And yet I felt very conflicted about Chris Landry. Everything he'd said about Martin drew my sympathy. But that didn't justify spilling his brother's blood and wearing the mark of Cain. I worried, too, that if I called the authorities, Ted would never forgive me for betraying a tortured soul seeking the forgiveness of a priest.

Another half hour passed. I needed to make sure my uncle was all right, so I walked back to the house and peeked through one of the open jalousies. Chris had removed his knit cap and was sitting in that same corner chair, and Ted had dragged an ottoman next to him. He was wearing the purple stole that priests drape around their necks in the confessional. Chris appeared to be in agony, his face a study in torment, and Ted was listening patiently, as he always did, a most remarkable man whose wisdom and compassion had the power to heal.

To kill more time, I wandered back down the creaking boardwalk to the cabin cruiser anchored at the end of the pier. When I read the name painted on the side of the vessel, the hair stood up on the back of my neck. *Stella Maris*. The word printed on two of Landry's video-tapes—*Stella*—was not someone's name, but Latin for *star*. Only an old-school Catholic family would name their boat the *Stella Maris*—after the Virgin Mary, Star of the Sea. I found myself staring at another crime scene.

I'd never been on board such a deluxe craft. It was a double decker with a flat canopy topside, shading the pilot's wheel and passenger seats and a fighting chair to wrestle in big fish like that marlin mounted on the living room wall. I knew that Clarence Landry's construction company was one of the busiest in New Orleans, and this expensive toy was proof of how prosperous he'd become from building concrete stadiums and overpasses.

When I stepped onto the boat, the first thing I noticed was a jet ski sunning on the aft deck like a large sleek sea creature hauled aboard in exotic waters. Stationed next to it were three olive-green metal Jerry cans, vintage World War II, and I could smell the gasoline that had leaked down their sides. Was it fuel for the jet ski? I looked back toward the camp to make sure no one had spied me snooping around, then decided to explore the boat belowdecks.

It was nearly dark down there, a shadow world of unfamiliar shapes, and I searched for a switch and finally turned on the lights. I imagined it had once been a beautiful cabin in its early days, the walls and flooring and cabinetwork made of cherrywood with a now-fading satin finish. The layout was a marvel of form and function. Each piece—compact kitchenette appliances, dining table, cushioned benches—fit together like an intricate puzzle concocted in the brain of a blond-bearded Scandinavian designer obsessed with tight, efficient spaces. But the furnishings were showing signs of wear, and it was obvious that a sloppy housekeeper, no doubt Chris, had been nesting down here recently, leaving fast-food trash and beer bottles all over the table and counters, and a stack of crusted cooking pots on the stove's small burners. The place smelled like a Popeye's dumpster.

More family photos were framed on the walls, more pictures of children displaying their trophy catches. I inspected one that featured a black-robed Martin and his parents, possibly at his ordination. His mother was seated in a wheelchair between her husband and son, a sad-eyed woman with Mamie Eisenhower hair and that same impassive stare I'd seen in the picnic video. Martin was smiling jubilantly, a dark-haired, handsome young priest, newly consecrated and proud of himself. He was showing off the engraved watch that was a gift from his parents, the watch he'd given to Kwame Williams. Martin's father the construction boss looked a little like Huey Long, the same broad, coarse facial features and comma-shaped lock of hair falling roguishly onto his forehead. There was a perceptible arrogance rooted in Clarence Landry's jaunty grin. He exuded the confidence of a self-made man, cocksure, a commanding presence, the captain of his ship. I could easily picture him bullying his wife and children, his employees, coercing his sons into playing sex games with each other while he filmed them, and showing those images to his friends. The *paterfamilias* himself was where the sickness had begun. And though I was taught not to speak ill of the dead, I felt he belonged in some horrific, blazing corner of hell with all the other child pornographers.

I made my way toward the bow, where a small master bedroom was flanked by two even smaller bedrooms. Fastened above the main door was one of those silver Chi-Rho Christian symbols entwined with a withered palm leaf from a Palm Sunday Mass long before. These were the close quarters I'd seen on the videotapes. Not much headroom, really, with a bed where Martin Landry had committed more of his grievous crimes. The sliding door was halfway open, and there was a black wetsuit laid out on the mattress the way my grandfather used to arrange his only suit before dressing for weddings and funerals.

Wetsuit. Jet ski. Gasoline. I was beginning to put things together.

Back up top, crossing the deck to deboard the *Stella Maris*, I saw Chris Landry pushing the wheelbarrow full of home movies down the pier toward the cabin cruiser. My uncle was walking by his side, speaking to him in a confidential voice, and the three of us met at a pier post a few feet from where the boat's dock lines were secured to a row of metal cleats.

"Find what you were looking for?" Chris asked with a sarcastic smirk.

"Unfortunately," I said. "Where are you headed?"

He smiled darkly and pointed out to sea. I noticed the VHS cassette in the pile. Martin Landry's last night on earth. I was glad Chris was taking it with him.

"Thanks for bringing your uncle," he said, extending his hand to shake. It was a rugged hand, calloused and bruised, the knuckles split and swollen. Not the hand of a priest or banker, the vocations his brothers had chosen. He winced slightly as I gave him a firm grip. A bone may've been broken when he'd used that hand to beat his brother down. Even there at the end, when our business was over and it was clear I would never see him again, he studied me with a chilling stare. A male thing, I supposed. He wanted me to know that he could've taken me in a fight, if it came down to brute force and bloodshed, and that I should keep my mouth shut about what I'd seen and heard on that dismal February morning in Cypremort Point.

Ted embraced him strongly, like a loving father bidding farewell to his drifter son, who had appreciated the bountiful feast but had decided to return to that far country and the reckless life. When they released each other, an emotional Chris pushed the wheelbarrow onto the aft deck and asked us to free the dock lines. He waved forlornly at my uncle, and at me as well, and then climbed a ladder to man the pilot's wheel on the upper deck. The engine soon roared to life, and Ted and I stood at the end of the pier, watching the *Stella Maris* veer slowly away from the seashore of camps and their slips and sailing rigs, setting its course southwest into Vermilion Bay.

After a long silence, my uncle said, "I asked him to turn himself in." We were standing shoulder to shoulder, tracking the boat as it lurched away through choppy gray waters toward a fog bank in the distance. "But he'll never do that. He said he'd take his own life before going back to prison."

A bitter wind was gusting into our faces, watering our eyes. It was a foul day, and only one other vessel was visible out there.

"How much can you tell me?" I asked.

I was mindful of the confessional privilege.

"You know the most important details, Peter. The rest was unloading a lifetime of pain."

For several moments we didn't talk or move, impervious to the cold.

"Any idea where he's going?"

"He mentioned Mexico," Ted said.

We watched the cabin cruiser shrink smaller and smaller, until it disappeared into the fog.

"He loves his son and misses him terribly," Ted said. "The boy's a teenager now. Christopher asked me to go visit him and his mother. He said he still loves her. He wanted me to tell her that."

I don't remember how long we stood there, as if frozen in a spell, staring out at the bay waters and that wall of fog miles away.

"An innocent young man is still in jail," I said, my face stinging from the cold wind. "When we get back to New Orleans, I'm going to see Detective Duhon. You okay with that?"

My uncle was gathering his thoughts, considering how to express his feelings, when we saw a burst of light in the fog, a ball of fire burning through the gray mist. The sound reached us a few seconds later, like a sonic boom rumbling across the saturated air.

"Mother of mercy," Ted said, striding to the far side of the pier and returning halfway, gazing dumbstruck at the bleak horizon. "Dear God, Peter, do you think that's him?"

The fireball had risen quickly and disintegrated and left in its wake a plume of black smoke and a steady flame floating on the water, what was left of the *Stella Maris*. My uncle fell to his knees, made the sign of the cross, and folded his hands. "Please pray with me, Peter," he implored, his voice thin and shaken.

I walked over and laid a consoling hand on his shoulder, peering out at the burning wreckage in the distant haze. "He's gonna be all right, Ted," I said, making sense of the jet ski, the wetsuit, the cans of gasoline.

I understood Chris Landry's volatile anger and his hatred and resentment, but I couldn't accept that disappearing was the solution to what he'd done in the rectory on that horrible night. He was still accountable for that. And someday, Mexico or not, he would have to face a final reckoning.

THIRTY-SEVEN

FATHER TED DIDN'T SHARE MY CONVICTION that Chris Landry had set fire to that wheelbarrow full of 8mm home movies, torched the cabin cruiser, and sped away on the jet ski. "We've got to call somebody," my uncle insisted. "The sheriff, the Coast Guard. Somebody. That poor boy might be floating around out there in a life vest."

He was understandably distraught by what had taken place at the Landry camp, and he remained quiet and reflective on the drive back to New Orleans. Midway through the swampy woods near Gibson, he spoke for the first time in an hour. "When he asked to see me, he requested that I hear his confession but also perform an exorcism," he said. "As it turned out, it wasn't for him but for that bedroom where those videos were shot. He thought he could see demons lurking in the corners and dark spaces."

"You don't believe in demons, Ted. I remember our long discussion after that movie came out."

"I believe in schizophrenia," he said, "and a host of other mental illnesses. But yes, I have trouble believing that little demons sit on your shoulder and whisper in your ear."

"So what did you do?"

"I flung holy water around the room and rubbed holy oil on the doors and windows," he said, mimicking a blessing with his thumb. "I recited some Latin mumbo jumbo from the *Rituale Romanum*. It was a pretty good performance, if I do say so. It seemed to satisfy him."

When we neared the city, he said he wanted to move back into his rectory. "It feels like I've been away too long," he said. "My parishioners need me, and so do the kids at O-L-S."

I helped him collect his things at the seminary and drove him to his residence. He drew back all the curtains and opened the windows. The morning fog had burned off, and it had turned into a pleasant sunny day with temperatures in the mid-sixties.

"Are you going to contact Detective Duhon?" he asked.

"As soon as I get home."

"I trust you to do the right thing, Peter. I don't think I know what that is anymore."

At home I called Ray Duhon at his office in the Homicide Division and left a message on his answering machine, asking to speak with him right away. "Detective, I have new information about the Martin Landry murder," I said, "and why you should release Kwame Williams immediately."

In a short while, Ann came home dressed in her only power suit, a bright-red outfit with wide shoulder pads and an oversized blazer. It was a terrible era for fashion.

"I need wine. Multiple glasses," she said, pecking me on the lips before removing her blazer and heading into the kitchen. "I spent most of the afternoon with Roberto and Eric Gautier. What a company man *he* is. Everything by the book."

It was after five, happy hour all over town, and we poured wine and took our glasses and the bottle to my office and shut the door. The boys were up in their rooms, doing homework or pretending to, and we didn't know how much time we had before they rumbled downstairs, grazing for food.

Ann disclosed that Roberto struggled to contain his anger, but in the end he agreed to the $400,000 payout per child and the terms of the settlement—under one condition. "He wants an audience with the Bishop," she said. "Eric assured him he'd speak with His Excellency and try to make that happen."

"I hope the Bishop doesn't understand obscene words in Spanish," I said. "Did it help that you were there?"

"Maybe. Roberto focused his wrath on Eric," she said, sipping wine and smiling. "God, please forgive me, but I enjoyed that more than I should have."

I sat down next to her on the pineapple settee, looped my arm around her shoulders, and told her what had happened at Cypremort Point. When I reached the part about the explosion in the fog, she was horrified and wriggled away from me. "Are you sure he wasn't hurt?" she asked, nervously filling her glass. "Did you report it to the Coast Guard?"

"I called the sheriff's office from a pay phone at the Vermilion Crab Shack but didn't leave my name."

"Good Lord, Peter. You and Father Ted are in this way too deep."

She walked out of the room, exasperated with me, and went to make supper.

I waited another hour, and when Duhon didn't return my call, I phoned Vince Scalco at his office and asked if I could visit him. "Sho, Pete, slide on by," he said with a jolly laugh. I could tell it was happy hour for him, too. "Everything down this way is tee na nay."

When I knocked on the door stenciled VINCENT SCALCO INVESTI-GATIONS, he was sitting behind his large messy desk, knocking back a glass of wine with the mound of red beans and rice he was eating out of a carry-out container. It was Monday, after all, and beans-and-rice was a New Orleans tradition harkening back to when Mondays were washdays and the domestics would simmer the red beans and rice while they were busy scrubbing laundry.

"Hey pocky way," he said, a Mardi Gras Indian greeting. "You had your beans today?"

"Gonna pass," I said. "But I'll take whatever you've got in the liquor cabinet. Something stronger than that girly Alexander you're always drinking."

I nursed Jack Daniel's Black on ice and told him what had taken place in the Landry fishing camp. He stopped cutting a link of sausage and stared at me across the desk, saying, "You fuckin' wit' me, Pete? He blew his boat up?"

"He's probably halfway to Mexico by now. Or wherever."

I looked over at the shelf where he was storing the cardboard box of VHS cassettes and other smut my uncle had collected from Martin Landry's bedroom. "Our work is done here, Vince," I said. "We were asked to study the tapes and identify the victims. Mission accomplished. We should return that box to the black robes and get it out of our hair. I don't want to be responsible for it anymore."

He set aside his fork and knife and washed down a mouthful of sausage and beans with wine. "We keep two tapes," he said, the wheels churning in his brain, calculating every move. "Two of the really bad ones. One for you and one for me. We stash them someplace nice and safe, Pete, like a bank deposit box, and we hang onto them until the groundhog shakes our hands." Until we were six-feet under. "Ya nevuh know when you might need to play that card. It's your ace in the hole, *capisce?*" he said. "The Church, the DA—they play hardball, man. They might try to make you their *cagna*. That tape is gonna save your bacon someday."

"Why do *you* want to keep one?"

I already knew the answer.

"It's my four-oh-one kay," he said with a cunning smile.

I leaned back in my chair and drank the whisky down to the rocks and watched Vince finish his meal with another glass of wine. We were both consumed in thought, enjoying the unencumbered moment.

"Today is Ned's birthday," he said, softening his voice and looking away. "He woulda turned nineteen years old today. I took some flowers to his grave. And guess who was there, kneeling beside his marker? Martha, saying a rosary."

He said they hadn't seen or spoken to each other in nearly a year. She'd put on weight, too. They made small talk, he said, gazing at the dates on Ned's headstone, their words laden with grief. He asked about their daughter, Paula, and Martha said she'd been inducted into the National Honor Society at Dominican High. She was dating a boy she'd met at a party.

"Give me his name and I'll run a background check on him."

Martha disapproved with a forbearing look.

"I'm kidding, girl," he said. "Have you forgotten what a wise ass I am?"

He asked if she was seeing anyone, and she said, "Who would want to go out with a dumpy old gal like me?"

They talked about their son. How much they missed him. They both cried, and Martha let Vince hold her in his arms for the first time since their divorce. He invited her to have lunch with him at a lakeside seafood café in Bucktown, near the West End Marina.

"Come join me," he said. "It's never a good idea to let a fat man eat fried food all by hisself."

She was reluctant, uncertain. He asked for her forgiveness. He told her he would go to his own grave devoured by remorse for every malicious thing he'd said or done to Ned.

"Vince, you need *his* forgiveness more than you need mine," she said, staring at the plot of ground where their son was buried. "And it's a little too late for that."

He told her he would wait for her in a corner booth at R & O's café. "That's where I'll be, Martha. Where we used to take our boy and his pals when they were little. It's his birthday—let's share a meal. That corner booth we always sat in with Ned," he said. "I'll wait for you till midnight if I have to."

It was late in the afternoon when he arrived at R & O's. The place wasn't busy, and he claimed that corner booth and ate a fried oyster po boy with three Brandy Alexanders. He sat there for two hours, wishing and hoping and thinking and praying, as the old song went. But she never came.

"Damn, Vince, I'm sorry, man," I said when he'd finished the story. "I'm gonna need another drink."

I walked back to the liquor cabinet behind his desk and splashed more Jack Daniel's over ice. The phone rang. "Vincent Scalco," he said into the receiver, then, "It's your wife, Pete."

I'd given Ann his number, in case Duhon called.

"He said he'll be working late in his office at police headquarters on South Broad," she said, "the Homicide Division. Show your ID at the front desk. He'll let them know you're coming."

"Wish me luck," I said.

"Tell him everything, Peter. Everything."

I gulped down the whisky and fetched my coat.

"You want me to tag along?" Vince asked, hoisting himself up from his chair with an expression of concern. "Ray and me go back a long way."

I gave his offer serious consideration. "I really appreciate that, Vince, but I've got to do this myself. You'll be my one phone call if Duhon decides to jail me."

Vince found his asthma inhaler under a heap of papers on the desk and pumped a dose into the back of his throat. After a moment with his eyes closed, he slid along the desk, leaning into it for support, making his way toward me with a padded envelope. "Like I told you, man, I'm never gonna forget that tear rolling down your cheek at Ned's funeral," he said.

He squeezed my shoulder and patted my face like an elderly Italian don.

"Here, carry this in your pocket," he said, handing me a dried fava bean. "*Buona fortuna*, my friend."

I left his office and set forth into the cold starless night, clutching the padded envelope with the VHS cassette Vince had stuffed inside it, wondering what was going to happen when I told Detective Duhon what I knew about the death of Father Martin Landry. I was obligated to confer with my superiors at the chancery first, and forbidden to discuss anything with homicide investigators, but that would mean Duhon would never hear the truth and Kwame Williams would face execution or rot in prison for the rest of his life. By seeing Duhon on my own, I would probably lose my job. And possibly face criminal charges for withholding evidence from a police investigation. I didn't care anymore. It was the price I had to pay for bearing witness to all I'd seen and heard in those troubling days of Carnival season many years ago.

2001

ITE, MISSA EST

"IF I'M ELECTED," THE BISHOP SAYS, "I will become the spokesman for the entire congregation of American bishops. I haven't decided whether to keep my name in play. My confreres tell me the job is mine if I want it. I have the overwhelming majority of votes. There's even talk that Rome is considering me for the College of Cardinals."

They are standing together at the stone balustrade on the Bishop's terrace, gazing out across the wooded neighborhood toward the river.

"Your Excellency, did you ask me here because you want to know if my book will harm your reputation?"

The Bishop nods slowly, pensively. "Yes, Peter, that is precisely what I need to know," he says with a rueful smile. "My fate seems to rest in your hands." His sigh is deep and weary. "And so I'm asking you with all due respect. Should I let them elect me or not?"

Peter remembers with painful clarity what transpired in those dark days surrounding Martin Landry's murder. Writing the book has kept his memory fresh. What astonishes him now, more than anything, is that the scandal has never leaked to the public. No victim has come forward as an outcry witness, not a hint of disgrace in nearly twenty years. The settlement payouts were all made in full and on time, and the families and their sons have honored the obligation of silence. Peter hasn't followed every single case, but he's aware that his friend Dr. Roberto Hinojosa created trust funds for his boys and sent them both to ivy league colleges and medical school for David, who followed his father into transplant surgery while Rico became a high school soccer coach in Atlanta.

After Ann was hired to visit offended families with Eric Gautier, fourteen in all, she urged the Bishop to establish a commission composed of clerics and laypersons, men and women, to investigate allegations of child sexual abuse by members of the clergy and other teachers at Catholic schools in the diocese. The Bishop took her advice, and in the intervening years, as scandals erupted around the country and exposés appeared in the media, the Diocese of New Orleans was lauded as a model of vigilance and virtue. The Bishop and Team Silentio had escaped unscathed. But that was going to change.

As he stands next to His Excellency in the warm spring breeze, contemplating how to respond, Peter remembers the many people whose lives were forever marked by the murder and its aftermath. Donald Bertrand was the first to die, a month after Peter had visited him, and Peter still regrets that he hadn't gone to see him again. In accordance with Donald's will, his ashes were spread along the levee in Marrero, a place he'd wandered as a boy with a fishing pole. To make Donald's mother happy, Father Ted presided over a Requiem Mass at Immaculate Conception Church on the west bank, where Donald had served as an altar boy. Peter sat in the pew next to a grieving Perry Blanchard, who had held Donald's hand in his final hour.

Ann accompanied Darren when he turned himself in to the district attorney a few days after the incident. She was very direct with Rockin' Roger Finney in his corner office in the cold gray industrial bunker off Tulane Avenue. No arrest, no fine, no jail time. "Darren would prefer not to go public with why he did what he did. It wouldn't be good for Father Landry's reputation, and it wouldn't be good for the Church," she said. "I've discussed this with the Bishop and he agrees."

Finney's scampish, lounge-singer smile lacked its usual brio, as if he'd lost big to the house at a blackjack table. "I spoke with His Excellency last night myself," he said with a shrug, "and I left it up to him." Finney offered Darren a year of probation and forty hours of community service, which the young man accepted graciously. The episode at the cathedral never appeared on his permanent record.

Five years later, the Holy Rottweiler was relieved of his duties as Vicar-General due to dementia, and he was sent home to Germany to live out his days in a retirement home for clergymen. Shortly after that, Peter's good friend Sister Colleen suffered a stroke, retired as the Bishop's aide and office manager, and moved into a nursing facility for nuns run by the Sisters of the Holy Family in New Orleans East. Peter visited her on several occasions, and one day, while he pushed her wheelchair through a patio rose garden, she said, "Guess who came to see me?"

"A lawyer, a doctor, and the Archbishop of Canterbury?"

She rolled her eyes at him and then spoke slowly and deliberately, a consequence of the stroke. "My old crush, Father Dombrowski. He's back in New Orleans after all these years."

Reality sometimes eluded her, so he couldn't be certain if she'd imagined a visit from the Jesuit priest or if he'd actually appeared in the flesh.

"My goodness, how did it go?" he asked.

"He brought me flowers," she said, beaming. "We talked about what we'd been doing for the last hundred years. He taught history at a Catholic high school in Chicago."

"Did you make out with him?"

She turned her stiff body in the wheelchair and slapped Peter's hand. "Tell you the truth, he's a little too old for me now," she said, laughing. "The old flame has burned out, Peter. I was happy he came to see me and kissed my cheek. That was enough. But I couldn't help wondering what would've happened if we'd gotten married and left the religious life."

"You wouldn't have met me, Sister. What a tragedy that would've been."

She smiled wistfully. "I might've had a child or three," she said. "I would've named the oldest boy *Peter* and called him Rocky."

"You know, Sister, I wish the Church was run by women like you and my wife, Ann."

Her face glowed and she patted the hand she'd just slapped. "I read your article on women in the priesthood," she said, referring to one of his publications. "It tickled me pink."

After Cypremort Point, Father Ted had renewed his dedication as pastor of Our Lady of Sorrows, ministering to his parishioners, paying off church debts, constructing new classrooms at the school. A young Vietnamese American priest named Father Danh Vo was assigned as the new assistant pastor, and although Father Vo lacked Martin Landry's charisma and his rapport with the OLS students, he was faithful to the consecrated life and his behavior was beyond reproach.

In time, Father Ted grew restless and resigned as pastor to become the Catholic chaplain at the Orleans Parish Prison. "I'm tired of dealing with the three Ws—whiny wealthy white people," he explained to Peter, "and I need a more fulfilling challenge." He was nearly eighty years old.

Father Ted thrived at teaching prisoners how to read and write, the majority of them African Americans. He conducted Bible studies, celebrated Mass, and heard confessions. Peter had never seen him so elated about his ministry. It was clearly the work he'd been called to do in those waning years of his life.

But diabetes took its toll on him, and when he was eighty-two years old, half of his right foot was amputated because of gangrene. While recovering from surgery and undergoing wound therapy, he lived with the Moores in Luke's old bedroom. Peter and Ann cared for him and attended sessions on dressing his amputation. Peter was delighted that Matt and Ted had become good friends during that time, a second generation of Moores exposed to the same intellectual curiosity and spiritual struggle. The family would always look back at Father Ted's residence with them as a very special moment in their lives.

On his death bed a couple of years later, debilitated by diabetes for the final time, Father Ted opened his eyes and gestured for Peter to come to his side. His voice was weak and his strength was depleted, but he was determined to leave his nephew with parting words. "Peter, I want you to know that I'm proud to be gay," he said, straining to be heard. "I've always lived a celibate life, never once straying from my vow. That's important to remember. Especially if you're going to write about Father Martin someday. Please explain to your readers the difference between him and me. Please promise me that."

Peter promised.

"Always respect gay people. You never know when a son or a brother might be gay—and conflicted about coming out—because he doesn't know how to tell his parents," Father Ted said. "Love him, Peter. Never turn your back on one of God's children. Love him as much as he loves you."

Although Peter didn't understand it at the time, his uncle was telling him that their son Luke was gay and would one day bring home his partner to meet the father and mother he loved very much.

A week after Father Ted's Solemn Requiem High Mass at St. Louis Cathedral, Peter received an anonymous sympathy card in the mail, postmarked from Oaxaca, Mexico. Underneath the Hallmark message in Spanish was a brief handwritten note, unsigned: *I'm very sorry for your loss, nephew. He was a good man.* It was the only time he would ever hear from Chris Landry. When Peter called the Homicide Division and asked if Detective Ray Duhon was still an active police investigator, he was told that Duhon had retired and moved to Key Largo, Florida, with his wife. No phone number available. So Peter let it go.

"Your Excellency, I brought you something," Peter says. "It's in my briefcase. Let me get it."

He returns indoors to the armchair where he'd left his briefcase and retrieves a VHS cassette tape. "I want you to have this," Peter says, handing the cassette to the Bishop, who has remained by the balustrade in the sharp sunlight. "It's something you should've looked at after Martin Landry's death, when you were trying so hard to keep your robe clean from the mud that the rest of us were wallowing in."

Peter remembers the night he went to see Detective Ray Duhon with a cassette like this one in a padded envelope. Duhon was sitting at his desk in a roomy corner office, studying a case file with his sleeves rolled and his shoes propped on the desk, locked ankle to ankle. Peter removed the cassette and tossed it onto the desk in front of him. "I borrowed this from the Landry stash," he said. "There's more, believe me. You want them all, you'll have to negotiate with the Bishop and the Vicar-General. I'm washing my hands of this whole rotten business."

Duhon picked up the cassette and read the label. *Cypremort 2,* Vince's random selection.

"I know who killed Martin Landry and why," Peter said.

Before he could finish telling Duhon the final details about the gasoline and jet ski, the detective said "*Jesus H fucking Christ*" and swiveled in his chair, rising quickly and rummaging through several loose pages in a box designated *To Do.* "This came in about an hour ago," he said, skimming through a bulletin from the US Coast Guard. "The burning vessel was registered to a Clarence Landry with a New

Orleans address."

"Chris and Martin's father. He's deceased. It was the family cabin cruiser."

Duhon paraphrased as he browsed the text. "No bodies found on board or stranded in the water. . . . Investigators suspect arson for the insurance," he said. "Eyewitnesses on a fishing vessel in the vicinity reported seeing a man on a jet ski heading toward Intracoastal City."

An industrial port on the west side of Vermilion Bay, mostly a dry docks for shrimp boats and offshore drilling companies.

"That's probably where he parked his getaway truck," Peter said.

Duhon dropped the bulletin on his desk and stared at the cassette tape. He rubbed his face hard, as if his flesh was as molten as the *Stella Maris*, then kicked his roller-wheel chair halfway across the office. "I fucking *hate* to be jerked around!" he barked.

Peter knew the remark wasn't aimed at him, but at the DA and the Church fathers. He waited for Duhon to calm down, but the detective grabbed a folder full of handwritten notes and other papers and threw them in the air. The pages fluttered all around him like giant leaves. It was the Martin Landry file.

"Ray, do the right thing and let Kwame Williams go," Peter said. "He didn't kill Martin Landry."

Three days later, when Kwame Williams walked out of the juvenile detention center a free man, Peter and Vince Scalco were waiting for him at the front gate. No one else was there for him, not a parent or relative, not even his friend Trey. Peter introduced himself, and Kwame remembered him from that night at the rectory.

"How come you didn't tell them people—them priests and cops—I didn't do this thing, man?"

"Chill, tee nig," Vince said from his scooter seat. "This guy's the only reason they let you walk, son."

Peter handed Kwame an envelope that contained $300 in cash from the office travel account, the same amount he'd given to Trey. He knew there was a strong possibility that the young man would spend the money on drugs or other vices, but he was hoping he'd also buy food and necessities.

"Who I gotta suck off?" Kwame asked, looking suspiciously at the bills in the envelope.

"It ain't like that, home boy," Vince said.

"My business card with my phone number is in the envelope," Peter said to the young man. "Stay in touch with me, Kwame. If you need something, call."

Peter believed that Trey and Kwame deserved the $400,000 payouts that the other boys would receive, but he knew that wouldn't happen. There were no responsible parents or guardians, no bank accounts in which to deposit funds, no financial advisers to oversee their spending. As far as Monsignor Fulweiler was concerned, street hustlers didn't merit college tuition and trust funds. Kwame and Trey were destined for the gristmill of the penal system, and maybe hard time in LSP Angola, and do-gooders like Peter Moore were powerless to do anything about it.

After they dropped Kwame off in the St. Thomas Housing Project, the closest option he had to a real home, Peter asked Vince to keep an eye on Trey and Kwame in the French Quarter. Vince added them to his growing list of runaways. For the rest of his life, he would continue his search for missing children, making daily rounds from Decatur to Rampart Street, but he never saw Trey and Kwame again, not even at the Fruit Loop, and he never found Leah Bordelon and a hundred other teenagers who'd lost their way.

Vince and Peter stayed in touch, meeting for lunches and happy hours. The Moores invited him to their dinner table on several occasions, especially holidays. Vince was a lonely man, defeated by an unquenchable grief, incapable of relationships with women, filling the void inside him with brutal hours on the streets, growing heavier day by day, relying entirely on his Amigo to convey him everywhere. Eleven years after the Landry case, Vince was found on the floor of his office, dead from congestive heart failure at age fifty-two. Peter felt the loss deeply. He'd kept that fava bean on his desk in his home office, next to a menagerie of mementos he'd collected over the years. At Vince's funeral, he hugged Martha and Paula and offered his condolences, and the saddest part of all was that Paula hadn't seen her father in years.

The Bishop examines the VHS tape in his hands, as if it's a daunting book he's required to read. Vince had stored it in a safe deposit box

293

at the Whitney Bank on St. Charles Avenue, and after his old friend's death, Peter received a phone call from a probate attorney saying that Vince had bequeathed the key to him. The videotape was the only thing inside the box, no other papers or savings bonds or personal notes. For Peter, no explanation was necessary.

"This book you've written," the Bishop says. "Do you include your uncle in the story? Father McMurray was homosexual, you know. Over the years he had three or four 'particular friendships,' as we used to call them. Fellow priests and seminarians he favored. Do you talk about his sexual orientation in your book, Peter? If he was alive, he would not be pleased. He was very private about such things."

The Bishop is skillful at inserting the spear point in a soft spot between paternal protection and a mean-spirited dig.

"I'm aware that Father Ted was gay, Your Excellency. He told me himself, many years ago. His friendships were friendships. He was a very likable man."

Peter believes what his uncle had told him. A lifetime of celibacy.

The Bishop leaves the balustrade and walks toward the pair of tangerine trees imported from Rome. He carries the videocassette at his side like a breviary and stops to examine the fruit weighting down the branches. It's the spring season of abundance, and ripe tangerines have dropped all around the slender trunks.

"These damned worms," he says, plucking a tangerine, studying the soggy, ruined skin.

Writing the book had been good therapy. It had helped Peter come to terms with his own guilt at concealing the truth. And it had helped him find a small measure of forgiveness for the Bishop and others. Now he feels only sorrow and melancholy from so many deaths and the scar tissue of growing older without grand ideas to believe in anymore. The sessions with his shrink and the antidepressants had not worked. Peter doesn't pray anymore, he doesn't attend Mass, he doesn't confess his sins. If someone asks if he is a practicing Catholic, he tells them his life sentence has been commuted and he's on *papist parole*, an agnostic who still wishes for a just and merciful God but who sees no evidence of Him anywhere. Certainly not in a world torn apart by war and terror, nor in a cosmos of unfathomable violence and chaos, black holes and dark matter and dark energy and billions of exploding stars and the haunting, frightful shapes of nebulae too vast and far away to comprehend. The micro, the macro, nothing offers him hope or consolation. Only friendship and love, and they can be fickle and fleeting.

When Peter returned Martin Landry's box of horrors to the Vicar-General and declared that his work was done and he didn't want the responsibility of keeping the videotapes any longer, the Holy Rottweiler removed him from Team Silentio and from his role as public spokesman for the diocese. Peter was exiled to his office on the ground floor, and his job description was reduced to overseeing publication of the diocesan newspaper and answering mundane phone calls about donations to the Church, where to find Catholic marriage counseling, what to do about abortion clinics, why abstinence from meat was not required on Fridays in Lent.

For four long months, Peter endured the slights and humiliations of losing his executive title and a mounting lack of respect from his staff. His uncle tried unsuccessfully to persuade the Vicar-General to restore some of Peter's duties. When he submitted his resignation to Monsignor Fulweiler in late June of that year, the Rottweiler quickly rounded up the heavy guns for an official exit interview. The Bishop was not present, per usual, and Father Ted had not been invited. Peter sat at the long conference table with Fulweiler, Eric Gautier and his father, and insurance man Ken Guidry, listening to their passive-aggressive demands that he maintain absolute silence in the Landry matter. With a genial smile, Russell Gautier slid the pages of a legally binding nondisclosure agreement in front of Peter, asking him to sign and accept the mandate of secrecy for the rest of his life in exchange for a severance package of $200,000, payable immediately. Peter was stunned by the magnitude of the offer, knowing that it would help his family enormously and provide him with generous time to find new employment. But after a few moments of reflection with his eyes downcast, feeling the sting of their distrust and the Rottweiler's tiresome contempt, he stood up from the table and said, "I need more time to think about this and discuss it with my wife." He enjoyed the nervous murmur he heard behind him as he left the room. He went downstairs to his office and cleared his desk and shelves. What could they do to him if he didn't sign the agreement? Bring down the hellfire of excommunication? That thought produced a smile. He knew he was holding all the cards, and it wasn't wise to hurry him or call his bluff.

In the end, he didn't sign their agreement. Not then, not ever. He didn't accept their $200,000 hush money. He had too much dirt on his hands, and accepting the money would've made him feel even dirtier.

Two hundred thousand dollars. He didn't dare tell Ann about the offer he'd turned down, because for the next year, they were in financial straits once again, when Peter couldn't find a job. The most unlikely person came to his rescue. Sharon Simon left the newspaper world to become director of public affairs at their old alma mater, Loyola University, and much to his surprise, she hired Peter as a deputy director. "I need someone who can speak Jesuit and keep secrets," she said, and they were happy to be on the same side for a change.

"Your Excellency, do you remember the Watergate hearings?" Peter asks the Bishop.

"I watched them religiously," the Bishop says without irony, dropping the worm-eaten tangerine onto the garden grass and wiping his hands with a clean white handkerchief he pulls from his pocket.

"Then you may remember Senator Sam Ervin quoting Shakespeare to one of Nixon's yes men," Peter says. "The quote was from Cardinal Wolsey in *Henry the Eighth*. The cardinal says, 'Had I but served my God with half the zeal I served my king, He would not, in mine age, have left me naked to mine enemies.'"

Worry lines crease the Bishop's brow.

"Your Excellency, you should've listened to God and your own conscience rather than to the Vatican and the papal nuncio in DC."

The Bishop understands what Peter is telling him. The book. "Peter, are you mine enemy?" he asks with a tinge of indignation.

"I'm not your enemy, Your Excellency. I'm a reluctant witness. I saw the sexual atrocities on all those tapes. To this day, I am still shaken by them," Peter says. "Father Landry's crimes have been covered up for far too long, and it's time for you to stop pretending you didn't know anything. You need to watch that tape, sir, and take a good hard look at what one of your priests was doing to innocent little boys while you and other bishops were hiding and protecting him."

The Bishop's entire body sags. He looks old and besieged by his mistakes. "Peter, I know the judgment I must face one day before my

Maker," he says, "and my penance will not be quick or kind."

Peter is astounded by his admission, by his acceptance of guilt. "Your Excellency," he says, "you already know the answer to the question you invited me here to discuss."

The French doors open with a jarring rattle, and both of them are drawn to the woman who is stepping out onto the terrace in low heels. It is his assistant, Margaret Dunn. "Your Excellency, we have a situation," she says, clearly alarmed, her eyes darting at Peter. "May I have a word with you?"

"Go ahead, Margaret," the Bishop says. "Mr. Moore is an old colleague."

Even so, she hesitates. "Isaiah buzzed me. There's a very upset man trying to see you. An angry father. I paged Juan for backup assistance." The chancery has added a second security guard. "I may have to call the police."

"Dear God," the Bishop says, rushing toward her and the French doors. "Does he have a weapon?"

"Isaiah didn't mention one."

This moment is a revelation. Peter realizes what is coming. The floodgates of righteousness will soon burst and engulf every cubit of this ancient leaking ark.

"Your Excellency, I hope you still have that escape chute in your little cell," Peter says, primarily for his own amusement. "*Tempus fugit, pater.* Judgment Day may be arriving sooner than you think."

With no formal farewell to his guest, the Bishop hurries into the *sala regia* and retreats in his tennis shoes to the stairway behind his desk, disappearing into the private quarters below. Margaret Dunn is on threat-level alert and asks Peter if he would like to wait in her office until the *situation* is resolved.

"I'll go see if I can help Isaiah," he says.

Despite her anxiety and caution, he leaves the office, briefcase by his side, and walks quickly out into the corridor. Near the security desk, Isaiah and another uniformed guard have backed the unexpected visitor against a marble wall and are warning they will Taser and handcuff him if he doesn't cooperate.

"I just want to speak with him face to face and get a straight answer about what he's gonna do about the creep priest that did that to my child!"

Peter squints up at the angelic blue scrollwork on the arched ceiling, looking for the bullet hole Isaiah had told him about. The shouting escalates, loud threats are exchanged, but he's confident that Isaiah and the other guard have everything under control. On his way to the stairwell, he takes a final look at the angry father and sees in his flushed face and thrashing arms the outrage of a thousand parents enraged by what has happened to their children by Men of God.

Outside near the burbling fountain, Peter calls Ann on his cell phone and asks if the boys have arrived yet. It's Jazz Fest weekend, and their sons are bringing their partners and children home to stay in their old bedrooms during the music festival. Peter and Ann haven't met Sonia yet, Matt's vegan girlfriend who lives in the same co-op in Austin, but they know and love Brian, Luke's partner for several years now, a professor at Rice University where Luke also teaches. Luke and Brian have adopted two biracial toddlers, brother and sister.

"They won't be here until later, honey," Ann says. "Don't worry, the house is spotless and the sheets are clean. We'll put the little ones in Luke's room or ours, whichever they want." The children adore their grandparents.

They do this every year, a family tradition. They gather for Jazz Fest on the last weekend of April, the boys in their old bedrooms, partners by their sides. All they know about Sonia is her last name is Garcia and she's a budding filmmaker. Brian is a Jewish Republican-turned-Democrat by George W. Bush's policies. This is what family looks like to Ann and Peter now.

"Why don't you pick up an extra bottle of pinot noir on the way home?" Ann suggests.

In spite of her declaration that the Landry case should not affect their relationship, it had sent her and Peter in opposite directions. Ann became more devoted to the Church, more committed to saving the institution from itself. She began to dedicate long hours to counseling victims and their families, six days a week, and as the revelations increased in the 1990s, her reputation spread and troubled parents contacted her from as far away as Lake Charles and Mobile, Alabama.

"I'm in a rare mood to break my vow of chastity before everyone gets here," Ann says. It's a joke between them, this vow of chastity. Her code word for menopause. "Besides, we haven't celebrated your book enough, Peter. Bring wine and there's a good chance you'll have your way with me, you agnostic brute."

Peter has been reading the galleys at a snail's pace every morning, as if they're precious scrolls discovered in a cave. He spent four years writing the manuscript while holding down his day job at Loyola. The book is both confession and catharsis. The process has dredged up buried memories and suppressed emotions. He admits his own personal failures and moral timidity.

A half-dozen times a day, he doubts his writing talent and wonders if publication is the right thing to do. Old wounds will reopen, influential people will face the harsh light of exposure. Forceful voices will denounce him, attorneys will almost certainly depose him, he might lose his job too many years before retirement. He has already been attacked for his articles on the Vatican's finances, the movement for women in the priesthood, and liberation theology in Latin America. He's an unpopular writer in many Church enclaves.

But those vexations aren't important to him right now. This is the most beautiful day of the year. Their sons are on their way home with loved ones. He and Ann will share the pinot noir, kissing each other and accepting their differences after thirty-five years of marriage, waiting with contented smiles for the voices of children to fill the house again. Waiting for the music to begin.

AUTHOR'S NOTE

This story is set in a New Orleans of my imagination, which resembles the real New Orleans and yet doesn't. I have separated my narrative from the real New Orleans intentionally, inventing a seminary and chancery and other details of a fictional Diocese of New Orleans, which does not exist.

ACKNOWLEDGMENTS

MANY YEARS AGO, I READ THE GROUNDBREAKING BOOK *Lead Us Not Into Temptation: Catholic Priests and the Sexual Abuse of Children* by New Orleans writer and filmmaker Jason Berry. His work both shocked and inspired me to learn more about that subject. In subsequent books, articles, interviews, and a documentary film, Mr. Berry has established himself as a major authority on the proliferation of sexual abuse by Catholic clergy. I met Jason when I lived in New Orleans, and I have had the good fortune of speaking and corresponding with him over the years. He is as generous to fellow writers as he is scrupulous and dedicated to the pursuit of truth. I admire him greatly for his courage and determination, and I thank him personally for his wise counsel.

I also thank my friends Patrick Slattery and David Heard for patiently reading my first draft and offering invaluable feedback and advice. Both have been involved in counseling and supporting victims of sexual abuse by clergymen, and this book is stronger and more accurate because of their knowledge and caring guidance.

Novelist Jim Magnuson has read first drafts of my fiction since the 1980s, and his friendship and exceptional insights have proved indispensable to any success my work has achieved. Likewise, authors Jan Reid and Jim Kunetka were outstanding readers of this book— and earlier books—providing essential criticism and fellowship as I muddled my way to the final word. And careful readings by Annette Carlozzi and Peter O'Carroll have saved me from several blunders. I am indebted to these good friends for their wisdom and perception.

My son, Danny, discussed this book with me in its earliest stages, made crucial suggestions, and urged me to keep writing when I was uncertain if these pages were worthy of print. He is always my guiding star.

Being published by TCU Press has been one of my happiest experiences as a writer. I am deeply grateful to director Dan Williams and his staff for their dedication to excellence, their artistry and careful attention to detail, and their friendship and personal support. I cannot thank them all enough for their incredible teamwork: editor Kathy Walton for her keen eye and magic touch; Rebecca Allen for bravely marketing this difficult book and always saying yes to my quirky suggestions; Molly Spain for her adeptness in both editing and publicity; and Melinda Esco for pulling the many pieces together and producing a beautiful book.

And finally, I thank my old buddies Armand Gonsoulin, David Heard, Dave Murrin, and Peter O'Carroll for the friendship we have shared for more than fifty years. They understand the struggles of faith in a modern world, and they have always stood tall for what is right and just, and not for what has been pontificated or decreed. I respect and cherish them as my band of brothers cut from the same cloth.